PUPPY LOVE 3: REAWAKENING

PUPPY LOVE 3: REAWAKENING

JEFF ERNO

fannypress
Seattle, WA

Published by Fanny Press
PO Box 95462
Seattle, WA 98145

Cover Design: Sabrina Sun

Cover Illustration: Paul Richmond (PaulRichmondStudio.Com)

Contact: info@fannypress.com

Copyright © 2010 by Jeff Erno

ISBN: 978-1-60381-482-9 (Paper)

ISBN: 978-1-60381-483-6 (Cloth)

ISBN: 978-1-60381-484-3 (ePub)

1

My two favorite places in the whole world are both in the presence of my Master. I love the security and warmth that I feel cradled in his arms, particularly when I'm lying with my head on his shoulder and my arm draped across his chest. I love the sound of his breathing, the feel of his beating heart. I love the smell of him. When he shifts his body, even slightly, I respond, moving with him to accommodate his comfort. His arm always remains around me, though, and I sense that he craves my dependence upon him as much or more than I crave his protection.

My other favorite place is sitting between my Master's legs. Of course every sub yearns to kneel and serve their Master, but I'm not now referring to service, sexual or otherwise. I do not necessarily even mean kneeling. As my Master sits watching television or using the computer, being beneath him with the strength of his powerful legs around me makes me feel safer than I ever have before. It is at these times that I most feel as if I genuinely am his pup, resting contentedly at my Master's feet.

It wasn't until Matt and I began living together that I ever realized I felt this way. I'd never actually imagined that I would willingly choose to physically place myself in submissive positions such as these, yet even when it was just he and I alone together, I'd find myself curled up at his feet. I could have easily elected to sit on the sofa beside him or in any one of the empty seats around us, but I instead chose to rest beneath him, between his legs.

The fact that I nearly lost him made his physical presence all the more significant to me. One might think that my clinginess would become annoying to him or perhaps even disturbing on some level, yet to me he never expressed such sentiments. Actually his responses were quite the opposite. As I rested contentedly there beneath him, he'd reach down affectionately from time to time to gently stroke my hair or to graze his thumb across my cheek. When I lovingly looked up at him, he'd simply smile and sometimes would squeeze his legs together ever-so-slightly to remind me that I was where I belonged.

Sometimes I would sit there and read; other times I'd watch television with him. I would even nap there in that position if I was really relaxed. Of course there were also moments when my Master simply could not resist taking advantage of the convenience of having me so close at hand, and he'd present me with the honor of servicing him.

Those first few weeks that he and I began living together at Alex and Drew's apartment were both beautiful and disconcerting. Our need to be with each other physically was paramount, and this opportunity to do so never was wasted. On the other hand, we both had concerns about our future. We did not so much fear that our relationship would dissolve or necessarily even suffer, but we worried about how we would find our way independently as a couple. At least I worried about this, I should say.

Of course Matt insisted that he pay rent for both himself and me. He immediately handed Alex a check to cover the first three months. Matt told Alex that since there were four of us he would also pay for half of the rent and utilities. I begged Matt to allow me to hand my own paycheck over to him to help with these expenses, but he very curtly refused my offer. "Keep your money, pup," he said. "Put it in the bank, and show me your statement every month. I don't want you wasting your money on a bunch of junk, and I'll make sure you don't, but I'm also not gonna have my pup supporting me."

The first couple of weeks in the apartment were a time for me to focus on my school work and preparation for finals. Although we had already thrown Alex his graduation party, we also were preparing for the actual ceremony. I quickly realized that it was probably a good thing that Matt had sprung the surprise party on both Drew and Alex the way he did, for in observing Drew I knew that, had he been aware of it beforehand, he may have given himself a nervous breakdown.

It was so cute to see how obsessed Drew was in anticipation of his Master's upcoming day of recognition. He broke out his special credit card, the one he used only for emergencies and really important occasions, and informed me that we were going on a shopping trip.

"Oh my god! I love shopping sprees ..." I gushed.

Drew leaned in to whisper in my ear. We were in the hallway and our Masters were only feet away in the living room watching television. "I wanna get Alex a nice suit and a new pair of shoes." In spite of myself I clapped my hands excitedly. "Shh!" he scolded me and gave me a stern look. My face instantly became stone serious as he tucked the card neatly and secretively into his pants' pocket.

"What will I tell Matt?" I whispered.

"Just tell him we're going shopping. We can get him something special, too."

"Oh my god ... yes!" I quickly agreed. "But I gotta use my own money, Drew. If you pay for it, it won't be from me."

"He'll never know, hon," Drew suggested.

"Yes he will," I said. "You know I don't lie to him. I can't."

Drew nodded. "Yeah, what am I thinkin? Hey I could loan you the money, though."

I shook my head. "He'd just pay you for it immediately as soon as he found out. It's okay, Drew, I have some money saved. Plus Matt has lots of expensive suits already. I just need to get him something special is all. It doesn't even have to be expensive."

Suddenly Drew's eyes grew wide as he looked above my head. I quickly turned to see Matt standing behind me. "What doesn't have to be expensive?" he asked.

"Um ... oh nothing, Sir. Um ... Drew was talking to me about Alex's graduation."

"Oh that's right," he said. "And my pup wants to get Alex a present?"

"Yes, Sir," I quickly agreed. I wasn't exactly lying because I did indeed plan to get him a gift.

"Well, yeah you're right. It doesn't have to be real expensive, but we don't want to be cheapskates either. Why don't you get him something just from you, and I'll get him something from both of us."

"Wasn't the party your gift, Sir?" asked Drew.

Matt shook his head. "Nah, was just a surprise. Was kinda fun, too, other than the ... incident."

I glanced into the living room to see that Alex was still engrossed in his television program. "I wonder what I should get him, Sir."

"I'm sure you'll come up with something nice." Matt then reached for his wallet.

"I wanna pay for it myself, Sir!" I said, a little too loudly, because Alex looked over in our direction at the sound of my raised voice. "Please Sir," I said in a whisper, "with my own money."

Matt paused, as if thinking about it. "Okay," he said finally, "since it *is* your gift, you probably should pay for it yourself. Just be sensible."

"Oh I will, Sir. I promise." I glanced over at Drew excitedly. "When are we going?"

"In a little bit, Petey," he said. "I wanna get the bedroom cleaned up first."

"I can help if you want," I offered.

"Sure."

Matt then leaned in and kissed me on the forehead. "Okay, let me know when you're leavin, pup. I'll cover for Drew with Alex." We then scurried off to clean the bedroom.

Cleaning Drew and Alex's bedroom consisted of making the bed and picking up a couple articles of clothing for the laundry, but Drew was almost as much of a neat freak as was I. Afterwards Drew lay on the bed face-down and I sat next to him, Indian-style, on the mattress. He was resting his chin in his palms and staring blankly ahead.

"What are you thinkin bout?" I asked.

"Alex ... I'm thinkin bout how proud I'm gonna be of him when he steps up there to get his diploma in front of everyone. He's worked so hard for this."

"Well I'm glad that he's still gonna get paid for that software program he made for Matt."

"Yeah, but I wish Matt was the one managing that gym. What his dad did to him really sucks."

"I know," I agreed, "but Matt's already had a few interviews. I'm sure it won't be long before he gets a job. Yesterday he interviewed at Bally's."

"Really? Why didn't you tell me? That's great. When will he know if he gets the job?"

I shrugged. "Not sure, but he said the interview went well."

"Come lie next to me," Drew patted the mattress beside him. "and snuggle with me for a little bit."

"I thought we were goin shoppin," I whined.

"In a minute. Just lie here, okay?"

I sighed, feigning irritation. "Oh okay, but just for a minute." I then flopped down beside him and he quickly wrapped his arms around me, pulling me into himself. He dug his fingertips into my side and began mercilessly tickling me as he held me in place against him. "Stop it!" I screamed and then burst into giddy laughter. "Drew!"

As quickly as the torture started, it abruptly ended, and he laughed into my ear. "I love how ticklish you are, Petey," he said.

"You're mean!" I accused him, a broad smile still covering my face. "One of these days I'm gonna pay you back, too."

"I'm just glad your ribs are better," he said. He was holding me tightly against his torso.

"Me too," I agreed. "Drew, you always smell so good."

"You smell like melons," he said. "Did you use melon-scented shampoo?"

"No, I smell like a melon cuz I'm a fruit." I laughed.

He laughed and wrapped his leg around me, continuing to squeeze me, but very gently. "Oh Petey," he said, "you're so adorable. It's no wonder Matt calls you his pup." I was touched by his affection and snuggled back against his body. Then I noticed something that I never had before. Was Drew getting aroused? I could feel him against my back.

"You think we should get goin?" I offered.

This time he was the one who sighed. "Yeah, we probably should." Slowly he unwrapped his leg from my body and released his grip on me, but before I was completely free of him, I felt his lips on my cheek. "I love you, Petey," he said.

"I love you too," I whispered back to him, and then quickly I shot out of his arms and grabbed a pillow from the head of the bed. Instantly I swung around and thwacked him right in the head with it. "That's for tickling me!" I screamed.

"You shit!" Drew retorted, a bit dazed by my blow. Quickly he jumped up and grabbed a different pillow. I was already screaming again by the time he had it fully in his grip.

"No! Stop it!" I yelled. Then bam! He landed a solid blow right to the side of my head and I toppled over instantly, laughing all the while. "You ass!" I screamed, trying to sound angry but betraying myself with my own laughter.

Drew was then on top of me, pounding me over and over with the pillow, all the while I continued to laugh as I tried covering my head with my small hands. "I give up!" I was yelling, "Stop, please stop!"

And then almost instantly and without warning he was off of me and the pelting ceased. I looked up and saw Drew being hurled across the room. "God damn! He said stop it!" It of course was Matt, coming to my rescue. As I looked up to see him fully, I realized he had his fist clenched and was about to punch Drew.

"Wait!" I cried. "Sir, please wait! It's okay. We were just playin. Honest, he wasn't hurtin me!"

Drew had landed on his butt on the floor and was staring up at Matt in stunned silence, his mouth agape. "I'm sorry!" he whimpered.

"Don't hit him, Sir. Please!" I jumped up and rushed over to Drew. "Sir, we were just having a pillow fight. It was just for fun."

I saw Matt start to relax, and I breathed a sigh of relief. "I thought you were crying," he said. I shook my head vigorously.

"No Sir, only laughing ... or maybe I was cryin ... but it was from laughing so hard."

Matt then got a very strange expression on his face. I think he felt kind of silly actually. Was it embarrassment?

"Sir, I swear I'd never hurt Petey. Honest!" said Drew.

Matt shook his head. "I don't know what's wrong with me ..." and he turned quickly and walked out of the room. I looked over at Drew with a puzzled expression. He returned the look, and it seemed to me that he was both bewildered and concerned.

"It's okay, Petey. He's just so stressed out right now. Plus, after what Ryan did, I think he's a little over-protective."

I didn't know exactly how to respond. "Yeah, I guess so."

I had been so confident that everything was okay with Matt. I knew that he was indeed under tremendous stress. Not only did he have the remainder of the semester to finish at school, but he also had to seriously focus upon landing a job soon. In spite of these potential stressors, though, I'd truly believed everything was fine between him and me. In fact, in my view, things had never been better.

But it did make sense that after all we'd been through over the course of the past few weeks Matt would be extremely cautious when it came to my safety. He'd seen me get my nose broken, my ribs fractured, and even witnessed the collapsing of one of my lungs. Worst of all, he knew I had been raped. I thought about that time, just outside this building, when Matt had taken me into the alley to do a scene with me and I had freaked. This was not long after Devin and his friend had attacked me, and I had a horrible flashback of the incident as Matt became aggressive with me. So I did understand how it was possible to project fears into a situation where they really didn't belong. Matt obviously was beginning to do this with me. When he heard me screaming, it triggered a protective response within him, and he reacted instantly.

On the one hand this had the potential for being quite troublesome. Certainly it was neither practical nor necessary for

Matt to protect me every second of the day. Were he to continue in this manner, I would never have the freedom to even fully experience life. Yet on the other hand, it was an indication to me of the depth of his love. I knew that in the strictest of terms I was his property. He had laid claim to me and I had submitted to him. He and I both regarded him as being far more than a partner or boyfriend. He was indeed my owner, and an owner of any property realized that it was his responsibility to take care of it. In that sense, my heart swelled at the notion of him rushing to my aid so readily.

As I knelt there on the floor staring into Drew's cherubic face, I was certain that he understood all of this. My sweet Drew was wise far beyond his years. He had been my mentor and my dearest friend. Other than Matt, Drew was the single human soul on this planet that I loved the most. Although I was younger than he, in some ways it seemed as if we were twins—twin souls. Nobody understood me the way Drew did. Nobody knew exactly the right thing to say to me like Drew. Nobody could calm me and reassure me the way he could, and nobody made me feel so perfectly thrilled to be the Petey-pup that I was as did Drew.

"I'm sorry, Drew," I said to him in a hushed tone. "He didn't mean it, I swear."

"I know," he smiled, "don't worry Petey. Like I said, he was just protecting his pup. He was doin exactly what a good Master should do ..."

And just as he spoke this last sentence his eyes grew really wide and his whole body stiffened. He stared directly behind me at the bedroom doorway. Quickly I turned to see what had shaken him and there stood both Matt and Alex. Each was armed with huge sofa cushions, and they both were grinning down at us evilly.

"AAAAAAAAHHHHHHHH!" I screamed, and bolted quickly toward the bed, trying frantically to snag one of the pillows that we'd left laying there. Before I made it two steps, Alex intervened and thwacked me mercilessly right in the face with his big soft pillow. I was hurled backwards and landed right on my butt similar to the position in which Matt had thrown Drew moments before.

Drew was already up and had his hands on a big feather pillow. Matt rushed up to him and began pelting him repeatedly with the huge cushion in his hand. Drew was laughing and flailing his arms frantically, trying desperately to retaliate against the big, soft-yet-forceful pummeling that he was receiving.

We all were laughing hysterically as Alex dove down to the ground in a kneeling position beside me and continued his violent, cushy assault. "Stop!" I was screaming. "Matt, please help me!" I was yelling and kicking my feet, trying to roll away from the blows but unable to do so because of the rapidity of their succession. Matt seemed to ignore me, focusing instead upon nailing Drew. Although I couldn't see my best friend, I sensed that his predicament was similar to mine. I heard him screaming for mercy as well.

When I finally was able to roll away from Alex and slide up into a kneeling position, I think that it was due only to the fact that Alex was nearly beside himself with laughter. He practically choked on the gales that erupted from deep inside him. This allowed me an opportunity, perhaps my one-and-only, and I seized upon it. I grabbed my pillow from the floor beside me and charged him, thwacking him as hard as I possibly could right alongside the head.

He rolled over on his side, hitting the floor, all the while continuing to laugh hysterically. I then jumped up on top of him, straddling him in a manner similar to what Ryan had done to me, and just wailed on him with my big feather pillow. After only three good blows I felt the impact of another fluffy boulder against my back, and I was hurled off of him. It was Matt, and he had come to the rescue of his hysterical friend. Now Matt was on me, pelting me just as he'd done seconds before to Drew, but Drew was now behind Matt, pounding the back of his head with his own giant pillow.

At that point it all turned to pandemonium. We all were flailing our arms frantically, swinging our pillows carelessly and violently into one another. I must have gotten blindsided by every single one of their pillows at some point or another. We all were laughing and screaming and running back-and-forth. Then at some point, Drew's pillow must have gotten snagged upon something, for I heard it rip. It's rending sounded almost like a zipper being opened, and then instantly we were in a sea of feathers. The white billowy particles rained down upon us as we all continued to laugh and swing our pillows at one another. I was dancing around, holding my hands in the air, feeling almost as if I'd been transported into a magical world of feathers.

I'm not sure how it stopped. Perhaps it was just that we were all exhausted, but as the adrenaline and high-intensity emotion began to fade a bit, I found myself in the arms of the man I loved. Matt was embracing me, pulling me securely against himself. I looked up at him, his hair covered in feathers, and pressed my soft lips against his own.

Yes, I knew it was gonna be okay. Everything was gonna be just fine. He was protective of me for sure, but not so much so that he was not afraid to still have some fun.

******

Drew and I were still laughing about the pillow fight hours later as we trudged through the mall. We had already completed most of our shopping, and Drew had not been a bit stingy when it came to outfitting his Master in an Italian suit. My mouth dropped when I watched Drew sign his name to the credit card receipt. "Oh my God, Drew," I whispered. "I've never spent that much money on anything in my life!"

He smiled as he turned to face me. "Isn't it hot?" he whispered back. "I love spending money on my Master."

I looked down at the floor, a bit saddened. "Matt won't even let me get him gifts. He says a Master isn't really a true Master if he allows himself to be supported by his pup."

"Well that's a good point, Petey. I do understand what he's sayin, but Matt's probably gonna eventually figure out that if he allows you to give him a gift, he will actually be the one giving to you. I mean you *need* to express your love for him, and what better way to do that than with an occasional little token of affection?"

"Yeah," I sighed, "but he says I can show my affection without spending money."

"Okay, I agree with that. Don't you?" I nodded. "So maybe there's a way you can get him a gift that doesn't cost any money."

"I already obey him and do anything he says. I cook for him, clean for him, wash his clothes, and even shine his shoes. I'm not sure what else to do. Maybe I could bake him a cake or something ..."

"Maybe, or maybe you could do something entirely different for him."

"Like what?" I asked.

"Well, I was thinkin about this, and I just might have an idea."

"Okay, tell me! What?"

"You know those guys who were passing out flyers down at the mall entrance? Those coupon things?"

"Yeah, those coupons for family portraits?"

"Right. Well I know the guy who owns that store. He took one of my classes a couple semesters ago."

"So?" I said. "I don't understand."

"Well don't you think it'd be cool to get a family picture of you and Matt?"

"Oh my God! Yes! And maybe we could get Petey our dog in the picture too! But wait, that would cost money. He'd never let me do it."

"No, you wouldn't have to spend a penny. I'm sure I could get Blake to let you work for it. You could pass out those flyers for a few hours."

"Drew, I don't think I could do that! I'm not good at talking to strangers like that." I felt an overwhelming sense of dread wash over me.

"Hon, how would it be any different than what you do at work? Don't you have to talk to strangers there?"

"But that's different. They come into the store to buy stuff, and I just wait on them. I ring up their sales on the register."

"And you talk to them when you do it, don't ya?"

I nodded. "Yeah, but I don't know. Plus if I do get the portrait and have to bring Matt down here for the picture, it won't be a surprise anymore."

Drew got a sly grin on his face. "Hey, why don't you get a picture of just you? That'd be the perfect gift for Matt!"

"He already has a ton of pics of me," I said.

"Not wearin your collar and holdin Petey, your dog ..."

I thought about it for a minute. "Don't you think that's a little bit ... I don't know ... like kind of snobbish on my part? It just seems conceited to give someone a picture of yourself."

"Not if that someone is your Master and you're his pup."

"Well, maybe ... but ya know, I haven't even got Alex's gift yet, and that's what we're here for. Besides, even if I did decide that I wanted to do it, how would I get Petey pup? He's over at Matt's mom's, and she's not gonna let me have him. Matt said he's really attached to her now."

"I guess you'd just have to go talk to her," Drew said, raising his eyebrows.

"I've never even met her!"

"All I'm sayin is that if you wanna do something really nice for your Master and show him just how much you love him, it's probably gonna have to be something that involves a payment of some kind. Nothing of value is free, ya know."

"Drew, you know I'd pay anything to please Matt. Anything!"

"Well, doin something that you're not comfortable doing, to me that's a real sacrifice. That's more valuable than just spending money."

I thought about what he was saying. Drew was right. It would be real easy for me to just go pick out a gift for Matt and pay for it. I knew that Matt didn't want that though. He'd already specifically told me not to spend money on him, but if I were to do something really special for him that obviously came from my heart, that would be far more meaningful to him. And if that gift happened to be something that required me to step outside my comfort zone and do something I really didn't like, well then it would be all the more meaningful.

"Okay, let's go talk to him!" I said, "and maybe I'll find a gift for Alex along the way."

"Cool," he said, "but I wanna put these things out in the car first. It's too much to carry around. Plus I need a smoke."

I sighed as I looked over at my best friend. "Drew, you know those things are gonna kill ya! I hate that you smoke."

"Shut up, puppy boy!" he said, swatting me playfully on the butt. "Respect your elders!"

I giggled as I picked up one of the bags and headed for the door. "Wait'll Matt finds out you hit me again! You're in big trouble." He picked up the remainder of the items and headed after me.

"Wait'll he finds out you were checkin out that hot sales clerk who just waited on us!"

"Shut up, Drew!" I whispered, my face turning instantly red as I looked over to the salesclerk who was now eying me curiously. I rushed out the door without looking back.

****

My heart was racing about ninety miles per minute as Drew drove me over to Matt's parents' house. We had already talked to Drew's friend and former student Blake at the portrait studio, and he was very accommodating. That Blake proved to be far different than I'd have ever imagined him to be. He was by far one of the most hyper guys I'd ever met. He talked so fast that I could barely understand him. He was a super-skinny guy, almost to the point of being anorexic, and he had bright red hair, which he had cut real short and crested in the front. He looked sort of like a cartoon character. He was one of those guys that almost made you laugh just from looking at him, and he seemed to always be smiling, even when he was serious.

We had a deal worked out where I would pass out flyers for the next three Saturdays for three hours each day. He said that he normally paid eight bucks an hour, so when you did the math that would be $72 worth of labor. The portrait package that he was giving me normally sold for $99 but was being offered with the coupon for $75. The way it worked out, it was pretty much an even trade. I offered to pay him the three bucks difference, but he just laughed and tousled my hair affectionately. Drew laughed as well when he did this, and I of course shot my friend a disapproving look.

I had indeed found Alex the perfect graduation gift, which was tucked safely in the trunk amidst the multitude of presents that Drew had bought for his Master. I knew now that there was just one thing that still needed to be done. I had to convince Matt's mom to let me borrow Petey for a couple of hours for the photo shoot. If she agreed, I would be getting the picture taken on Friday morning. I'd be lucky, though, if she didn't simply slam the door in my face. I had begged Drew to go with me to talk to her, simply to lend moral support, and being the best friend that he is, of course he agreed.

When he pulled his car up in front of the house, for a brief moment I began to doubt the significance of the visit. All of a sudden it seemed like a very stupid idea. "Drew, I changed my mind," I said. "I can't do it!"

"What are you talking 'bout, Petey?" he asked. "Of course you can do it. We're here now, and there's no backin out now. C'mon!" He opened his door and stepped out without waiting for my response. Reluctantly I followed, crawling out of the car nervously.

Drew walked over to my side of the car and placed his hand on my shoulder. "What's the worst that can happen?" he asked.

"She'll say no and slam the door in my face!" I retorted.

"Exactly, and would that be so bad really? So what if she does? Then we'll just come up with some other plan. We'll get you a stuffed dog that looks exactly like Petey Pup to hold in the picture."

"Yeah!" I agreed. "Let's just do that anyway."

Drew looked at me sternly. "C'mon!" he said. "You've gotta at least try."

Fearfully I then made my way up the walkway to the front door. I remembered how nervous I'd been the very first time I'd come here to meet Matt. I was so scared that I almost went away without even speaking to him. I was so thankful now that I hadn't done so. But it was not Matt who was on the other side of the door this time. It was his parents, and they obviously didn't think much of me. What would they say when they saw me for the first time? What would they do?

I took a deep breath as I approached the door and rang the bell. I got a sudden urge to make a run for it, but stood my ground as I heard movement on the other side of the door. I glanced over at Drew nervously, as he stood there looking quite serious. I wondered for a second if she would think we were Mormons or some sort of door-to-door salesmen. The door then opened and a rather young-looking middle-aged woman stood before us. I knew instantly from her eyes that she had to be Matt's mom.

"Yes?" she said sweetly. "Can I help you?"

"Um ... Mrs. Porter?" I gulped.

She nodded and smiled sincerely. "Yes, that's me."

"Um ... I know you don't know me. I'm a friend of your son's, of Matt's. I'm Petey. Petey Drinkell, and this is my friend Drew."

Her face got instantly serious and it seemed that her posture stiffened ever-so-slightly. She took in a breath and then again smiled, a little less sincerely it seemed. "Well hello," she said, "It's nice to finally meet you." She extended her hand to shake mine, and I quickly obliged her. "Won't you please come in?" she offered. She then turned and led us into the entryway of her home.

I glanced over to Drew while Mrs. Porter had her back to us. I'm sure my gaze was one of wide-eyed bewilderment, for I hadn't expected this level of cordiality. We followed our host quietly into the dining room where she politely asked us to have a seat. "Can I get you boys something to drink?" she offered.

"Oh, no thank you, Mrs. Porter, but that's very kind of you," I answered. Drew politely refused as well. Just as I pulled out a chair to sit down, I heard a very familiar sound and quickly turned to see my all-but forgotten dear friend Petey Pup, wagging his tail and rushing over to greet me.

"Petey!" I cried, as I instantly lowered myself to his level, scooping him into my arms. He was wagging his tail furiously and licking my face. "Oh yes! Him's a good boy! Did you miss me, Petey Pup? Did ya miss me? I missed you … yes I did! Awww!"

Mrs. Porter and Drew were both laughing as they watched our exchange of affection. "Wow, he really likes you," Mrs. Porter said. "I take it you've met before."

I looked up at her and nodded. "Yes, ma'am, Matt got Petey about the same time we met. He named him after me."

"I kinda wondered about that," she smiled. "He said he was naming the dog after the one on Li'l Rascals."

I smiled warmly. "Yeah, that too."

After greeting my canine friend for a few more seconds I assumed a seat at the table. Drew and I were sitting across from each other and Mrs. Porter was on the end of the table, seated between us. Petey Pup was lying at my feet.

"Well, may I ask what the nature of this visit is? What is it that has afforded me the pleasure of your company?" It sounded so formal the way she stated it, almost like something out of an old movie.

"Mrs. Porter, I'm actually here because of Petey Pup. I know how attached to him you are, and I understand that completely …"

"And you want me to give him to you and Matt?" she asked. Her eyes seemed moist, almost as if she might cry.

Immediately I shook my head. "Oh no, ma'am, not at all. I'd never ask that. I just want to get my picture taken with him. I want to do it for Matt, as a surprise."

She looked at me quizzically for a moment and then responded. "Well that's sort of sweet. How *is* Matt?"

Quickly I looked down at the table in front of me. It was almost accusatory the way that she'd delivered that last question. It was as if she were implying I'd stolen her son from her. She had to ask me, a virtual stranger, about the wellbeing of her only son.

"Matt's doing great," I said. "He is looking for a job right now, and he's almost done with the semester at the college. He had a couple interviews this week."

"I want to ask you something," she said, now in a very unpretentious tone. She had suddenly dropped the fake yet pleasant lilt from her voice. "If my son hurt you the way that he was accused of doing, then why are you with him still?"

"Mrs. Porter," I said, forcing myself to stare her directly in the eye, "Matt has never hurt me and he never will. I'm positive of that. I told the police that from the very beginning. I'm with Matt because ... well, because I love him."

And now tears did fill her eyes. "And he loves you?" she asked.

I nodded. "Yes," I whispered, "yes he does."

She pushed her chair back and turned to grab a tissue from a buffet table behind her. "Excuse me," she said graciously and dabbed her eyes daintily, "I just honestly don't understand all this. Matt was always so ... well, um ... always so *normal*. I had no idea that he might ever be ..."

"Gay?" I offered.

"Aren't parents supposed to sense that sort of thing about their kids? Aren't they supposed to know them well enough to at least have some clue?"

"I know it's hard, Mrs. Porter. I'm so sorry ..." I looked quickly to Drew, not knowing what else to say.

"Mrs. Porter," he said, speaking softly and most compassionately. "I know I probably seem like an intruder here, but I've known both Petey and Matt for a long time now. May I please say something?"

She nodded. "Of course."

"Gay people are often portrayed a certain way on television shows and in movies, and most people think of us all as being that way. The truth of the matter, though, is that gay people are just as different from one another as are straight people. Some of us are really shy and quiet and soft-spoken like Petey. Others are athletic and masculine and extroverted like Matt. Those clues that you mentioned are really just stereotypes, and a lot of times they're not true."

"Well I see what you're saying," she said, "but I realize that all *gay* people are not the same. That really isn't the issue. It's that it seems like I should have known somehow. I should have known my own son better than I did."

"I don't think Matt really knew himself. It wasn't until he fell in love with Petey that he realized he might not be straight. I mean he always had girlfriends, didn't he?"

"Yes, yes he did, so what was it that changed him?"

"Mrs. Porter," I spoke again, "I don't know all of the answers about why Matt kept his sexual orientation hidden from you, but I do know that he loves you very much. Not having you in his life has been devastating to him. I think that for many years he didn't really want to be labeled as 'gay' or 'bisexual' or anything like that. He just wanted to be his own person. He didn't really have everything figured out yet, and the last thing he ever wanted to do was to hurt you."

"Honey," she said, "I know Matt doesn't want to hurt us. I don't want to hurt him either." She was again crying openly. "It's his father. He just doesn't understand. He's hurting so badly himself, but he only knows how to express his pain with anger. He feels as if Matt has betrayed him in some way."

"Matt idolizes him," I said. "Matt loves his dad so much, I swear. He was so proud when his dad gave him the gym to run. Now I'm afraid he feels like he's failed in some way." I was tearing up myself, and Mrs. Porter slid me the box of tissues.

"We have to figure out a way to get Matt and his dad together, so they can talk," offered Drew.

Mrs. Porter shook her head. "You don't understand the way Paul is," she said. "He's a very stubborn man, and when he makes a decision about something, there's nothing I can say to get him to change his mind."

"I know exactly what you mean, Mrs. Porter," I nodded. "Matt's the same way, and it's like you said, he's the decision-maker, but ya know what? I've figured out already that sometimes I can make suggestions to him, so long as I do it really subtly. If I plant an idea in his head and get him to think about it, sometimes he will change his mind on his own." I was remembering the way I had earlier convinced him to allow me to pay for Alex's gift with my own money.

Drew spoke again. "If you could just get him to think about the fact that Matt is the exact same person he always knew and loved as his son, maybe Mr. Porter would realize that Matt has not suddenly become a bad person just because he's gay."

She sighed as she looked first at Drew and then returned her gaze to me. "I know Paul doesn't want to lose Matt. I know he doesn't want to disown him. He'd always planned to hand over the business to Matt when the time was right ..."

"He might feel sort of embarrassed," I suggested. "It's probably not easy for a man like Mr. Porter to admit that his son is gay. Maybe he's worried about what other people will think of him."

She was nodding her head ever-so-slightly as I spoke. "That's exactly it," she said, "he's worried about what other people are gonna think."

"And I bet he's not usually the type of man who gives a damn what anyone else thinks," Drew stated.

"He doesn't, which is why it's so hard to believe that he would be willing to lose his only son just because of what other people think ..."

"Mrs. Porter, with all due respect, you need to remind him of that. Tell him you can't believe he would allow the opinions of other people to cost him a relationship with Matt." I leaned forward and placed my hand on top of hers. "Please—"

"Well I think you two should work together," Drew smiled, his gaze moving back and forth between Mrs. Porter and me. "Petey, you should work on Matt, and Mrs. Porter, you should work on your husband. I mean you both have the same goal, don't you?"

"Ma'am," I said, "has your husband forbidden you from contacting Matt?"

She shook her head. "He doesn't forbid me from doing anything, but he knows I've always supported him in his decisions, and I don't know what he'd do if he thought I was defying him."

"But Matt is your son too," Drew said. "Maybe you could just talk to Matt ... tell him how you feel."

She was crying openly now, shaking her head. "I'm sorry, but I'm afraid you don't understand. I can't go against my husband. I just can't."

"Mrs. Porter, we do understand," I assured her calmly. "We really do. I would never do anything to go against Matt either. Maybe you can't contact Matt, but you can keep in touch with me, can't you?"

"Yes," she forced a smile through her tears.

"Okay, well let's do that. Let's try to do this together, not out of defiance, but because we love them. We both know that Matt and his dad really love each other; we just gotta remind them of that."

She then got up and walked across the room to retrieve her purse. "Let me take down your phone number," she said.

When we left, we had agreed to return later to pick up Petey Pup. I told her it would be Friday morning, the day I had scheduled the photo shoot. In the meantime we were both going to try to talk to the men in our lives and hopefully put some sense in their heads.

As we were leaving the house, Mrs. Porter grabbed hold of me and hugged me. "You're just the sweetest boy," she said. "I can see why Matt likes you so much."

"Thank you, ma'am," I said, "that means a lot to me."

2

When Drew and I got home, we discovered that Matt and Alex were gone, so it was not difficult to sneak Drew's purchases into the apartment. He planned to give Alex his gifts right away, but he wanted to have them all laid out for his Master so that he walked in and was surprised. We busied ourselves in Drew's bedroom, neatly arranging the purchases on the bed.

"Alex is gonna look so handsome in this suit," I observed.

"He's gonna look hot!" Drew corrected me.

I smiled at him. "So Friday is the big day. Alex finally graduates. Aren't you excited?"

"Oh Petey, I've been so anxious for this day. I always thought that it sort of bothered Alex that I had a degree and he didn't. I mean I know it really doesn't matter. He's so smart; he's so much better than me at so many things ..."

"But you worried he'd feel that you were in some way superior to him?"

"Well, I don't know. If Alex wasn't the kinda guy who had a lot of self-confidence then he wouldn't really be a Master, so I don't think it's really so much about how he feels. It's about how I feel."

"You think you're superior to him, then?"

"Oh god no! I should spank you for even saying that!" We both laughed. "I just worry that maybe in the back of his mind he will feel he can't control me completely. He might think that because I know more about certain things than he does that I won't really regard him as superior ... even though I totally do."

"But Drew ..." I turned to him as I fluffed the pillows, arranging them neatly on the bed, "you just admitted that Alex is smarter than you about so many things. Look what a genius he is about computers."

"And money. I totally suck at handling money. When we first got together we kept our incomes separate, but finally I asked him to just take over all of it. He was a poor college kid at the time, but look at him now. With his Web-design business he makes almost as much as I do sometimes."

I sat down on the edge of the bed, careful not to disturb the array of gifts spread out beside me. "You always say I'm the one who worries too much, but I think you're just as bad as me. It's so obvious that Alex is your Master; anyone can see he's superior, so why do you let yourself get so worried?"

Drew sighed and sat down beside me. He slid his arm around my shoulder. "Petey, I just think it's the sub in me. If we didn't constantly strive to be the best we can be for our Masters, then what kind of subs would we be? My job is to please him, and I just get worked up sometimes, worrying about if I'm good enough."

"Sounds more like you're worried that you're too good. You need to stop that." I raised my eyebrows as I leaned back slightly in order to look him in the eye. "You already said Alex has a ton of self confidence, so stop thinking he's gonna feel you're too good for him. Actually I think—" I didn't know how to finish my sentence.

"You think that it's not very submissive of me to think like that." He finished for me.

"Being good at what you do does not change who you are as a sub! I want to be a writer, Drew. What if I wrote a hundred bestsellers and made a million dollars? Would that suddenly make me superior to Matt? I'll always be his pup, no matter what, and he wants me to succeed. Alex wants you to succeed, too!"

"Petey, I love you so much." He squeezed me tight and kissed me softly on the lips. "Since when did you get so smart that you started giving me advice?" There were tears in his eyes.

"Stop it," I said, "or you're gonna make me cry too! Let's go get dinner ready. They should be back from the gym within the hour." I stood up and gently brushed a lock of Drew's hair from his forehead. "And I love you too ... with all my heart."

When Matt and Alex walked in, I was putting dinner on the table: lemon chicken, steamed rice, dinner salad, and raspberry cheesecake for dessert. "Smells good," Matt said as he walked up behind me. He wrapped his arm around my waist and nestled his chin into the crook of my neck.

"That tickles, Sir," I complained. "I think you need to shave."

"You think that tickles," he whispered into my ear, "wait'll ya feel these whiskers on your other body parts."

I giggled. "Sir, dinner's ready. You hungry?" I turned around to face him and he wrapped his arms around my torso.

"I'm hungry for my pup," he growled.

I looked out to the living room where Drew was sitting. "Do you wanna skip dinner, Sir? I can always warm it up later ..."

Matt laughed. "Nah, actually I really am hungry. I'll still be hungry for my pup later, though." He gently kissed me on the lips, then pulled away from me slightly.

"Sir, you could never be as hungry for me as I am for you." He leaned in again, this time kissing more passionately, sliding his tongue rather forcefully past my teeth. I moaned just a little as he pressed against me. I felt myself becoming aroused.

"We better eat," he said as he suddenly released me.

I smiled at him, allowing my gaze to linger upon his face just a few seconds longer. "Dinner's ready," I announced to Alex and Drew, though not looking away from my Master.

As the four of us sat down together, Matt and Alex began loading up their plates while Drew and I patiently waited for them to take all they wanted. When the serving platter finally made its way to me, there was just one piece of chicken left. Gingerly I picked up my knife and fork and began slicing it in half.

"Eat the whole thing," Matt stated. "It's just a little piece."

I made a face at him momentarily but then quickly sobered my expression. "Yes, Sir," I said, and scooped the remaining piece of meat onto my plate.

"Got some good news today," Matt said, just before shoveling a forkful of rice into his mouth. "Got a call back from Bally's."

"You did, Sir?" I asked excitedly. "Oh Sir! That's so cool."

"Well, I'm not sure yet. I mean, they didn't officially offer me a job, but I gotta go in tomorrow for another interview."

"That's a really good sign, Sir," Drew offered. "Means you're on their short list."

"Sir, what's the job? Trainer?"

"Manager," he said, shoveling more food into his mouth.

"God, that'll piss yer dad off if he finds out you got that job," Alex said.

Matt laughed. "I know." I glanced over at Drew, exchanging a look of concern with him. "He hates them cause they're his biggest competitor."

"Be a lot different working for a big company like that, though, than for your dad," Alex reminded him.

"True, but it's chill. I'm totally cool with working for them. They run a good program."

"Sir, I'm so happy for you," I said. "I mean ... if you get it. I'm happy you got a callback ..."

He smiled at me and reached over to grab my wrist. "Thanks, pup. God is this chicken good."

"Petey, I can't believe what a good cook you are," Drew chimed in. "How did you learn to make all the stuff that you do?"

"Ancient Chinese secret," I laughed.

The others laughed. "Speaking of Chinese, you should invite your friend Jason over for dinner some night," Drew suggested.

"How do you know he's Chinese?" I asked. "All I know is that he's Asian."

"Whatever ..." Matt said, "but it'd be cool to have him over, don't ya think?"

"Yes, Sir," I responded, "if you want."

"I do," he said. "I like him." I raised my eyebrows just slightly as I stared back at my Master. I was fighting just a tiny pang of insecurity. "Is that jealousy I see?" Matt asked. "You know how I feel about *that*."

I squirmed a little in my seat, quickly looking down at my plate. "No Sir," I said quietly. "I'm sorry."

There was an awkward silence that then lingered for a few seconds, and then Matt spoke again. "I have only one pup. That's all I want ... you know that, right?"

I looked up at him, feeling my eyes suddenly becoming moist. "Yes, Sir," I smiled as I looked at him.

"Oh my god!" Alex suddenly blurted out. "Do you two need to get a fucking room?"

Drew started laughing. "They've already got one, Sir, but I think in a couple seconds they're gonna just use this table ..."

Matt smiled across the table at his best friend and then suddenly got serious. "Just want my pup to know he's my only pup. I'll say that anywhere. Don't need a private room to speak my mind."

"Joking ..." Alex said.

"I know," Matt responded. I felt his hand slide under the table and rest upon my knee. I reached down and slipped my own hand next to his and he pulled it into his own.

"How did you have time to make that cheesecake?" Drew asked, suddenly changing the subject.

"I made it yesterday," I said.

"Oh my god, it looks good," Drew sighed.

"Well, after dessert Alex and Drew are going out," Matt said to me. I found it a bit odd that he suddenly was talking about them in third-person, as if they were not even there. "So you need to do cleanup without Drew's help. Understand?"

I nodded. "Yes, Sir," I said. I usually cleaned up after dinner anyways. Sometimes Drew was there to help, but it didn't really matter to me one way or the other.

"Then we need to talk. I need to have a serious conversation with you ... about something important."

Instantly a wave of panic washed over me. Was I about to be punished? Had Matt found out about my visit with his mom? Maybe she had called him and he was pissed. Maybe he knew about my secret plan to get him a special gift. Maybe he was really upset about the pillow fight. Within the matter of seconds I was imagining all kinds of crazy possibilities, none of them making much sense.

"Yes, Sir," I repeated, "um, is everything all right?"

He looked over at me, chewing another bite of chicken, and nodded. "Sure pup, I just wanna talk to you privately." Then he winked at me.

I audibly sighed and smiled back at him. "Sure, Sir ... of course." I then glanced over at Drew and saw him shrug his shoulders slightly, as if to say he had no idea.

After I served dessert, Alex told Drew to get his shoes on, and they rather abruptly left. I began clearing the dishes from the table and headed toward the kitchen with a plate in each hand. As I set them down on the countertop near the dishwasher, I turned and nearly ran right into my Master. Matt was standing there, directly behind me, carrying two plates. "Here," he said, "I'll help ya."

I looked up at him, confused. Matt had never once helped me with any domestic chore. Something wasn't right. "Thanks," I said, a strain of trepidation in my voice.

Matt laughed. "What's wrong?" he asked, "You think I'm too much of a snob to help with the dishes?"

I shook my head and smiled at him. "Well, um ... no Sir. No, it's just ... well, you have me. Why should you need to do dishes? It's my job, isn't it?"

"Your job is to do whatever I tell you," he corrected me.

"Yes, Sir." I looked down at his feet.

"Down," he said, and instantly I dropped to my knees. I suddenly was at eye-level with his crotch, and he was sporting a rather sizeable bulge in his Umbros. I craned my neck to stare up at him, awaiting his orders.

He reached out and gently grabbed my head with both of his hands, all the while maintaining eye contact with me. "Pup," he whispered, in the most soothingly gentle voice. "Pup, I love you."

"I love you too, Master," I whimpered.

"I still want to talk to you," he reminded me, "but it'll have to wait. I need you to take care of something for me first ..."

I smiled up at him mischievously. "What's that, Sir?" I grinned.

"Did you get enough dessert?" he asked teasingly.

I shook my head. "No Sir."

He quickly removed his hands from the sides of my face and pulled down the waistband of his shorts. My gaze locked onto the most delicious dessert I'd ever seen. "Do you want it?" he asked.

"Oh Sir ..." I sighed. "Yes, Sir!"

Matt was so aroused that his cock was hard as steel. It jutted out in front of him like a javelin. Slowly he stepped back from me, moving toward the counter. I remained in my fixed position on my knees, continuing to hungrily eye his throbbing prick. Quickly he stepped out of his shorts and tossed them aside, and then he reached beside him and pulled the remaining cheesecake to the edge of the counter. He slid his finger across the top, scooping up a big glob of bright red raspberry topping. I looked up at him with anticipation.

"You need some more dessert, pup?" he asked.

"Yes, Sir! Oh please ..."

There still was about two feet of distance between us. He quickly moved his finger over to his cock and smeared the syrupy liquid onto his rigid pole. Slowly he slid it back and forth across the top, and then worked his way down around the sides. He reached over again and scooped up a little more topping, then used it to liberally coat the underside of his shaft. "Come on boy," he said, "come get your dessert."

Instantly I slid over toward him, positioning myself between his legs, my lips barely brushing against his testicles. Reverently I kissed them, then teasingly darted out my tongue to lap up a droplet of the red syrup. I then began to lick, very slowly at first. I ran my tongue very gently across his nut sac, back and forth, cleaning off the tasty sweet topping. I licked my way upwards, licking it as I would an ice cream cone. Slowly and deliberately I savored every little drop. I heard him moan just a little as my tongue found its way to his most sensitive spot.

I knew all about pleasing my Master orally. I knew exactly what to do to make him moan. I knew what he liked and didn't like. I had the feeling of his cock memorized by my mouth. I knew ever little ridge, every little indentation. I knew where to apply pressure, where to stroke, where to suck, where to nibble. I knew every detail of his cock.

But for the moment, I knew it was not my job to devour him. He'd instructed me first to have my dessert. I knew he was rewarding me, offering me a treat. As I continued to lick my way around his shaft and onto his bulbous, bright-red cock head, I felt my own arousal throbbing in my pants. I resisted the urge to reach down and grope myself.

"You like that dessert, pup?" he asked.

"Mmm," I responded and nodded quickly.

"Say it," he said, a little more sternly.

"I like it Sir!" I shouted. "I like it a lot!"

"How much do you like it? Do you love it?"

"Oh god, Sir! Oh yes ... I love your hard cock!"

"Take it, boy!" he commanded. "Eat your fuckin dessert!" He then reached down, grabbed my head with both hands and rammed his cock fiercely into my hungry mouth. Mercilessly he stabbed it into the depths of my throat, but I did not even flinch. I hardly ever gagged any more, regardless of how brutally he throat-fucked me.

"Take it!" he repeated, and began to pump himself in and out of my hole. I wrapped my lips tightly around the girth of his prick and concentrated on maintaining a tight suction as he began to piston himself in and out. He knew exactly how to fuck my mouth. He knew all too well the silky pleasure of my warm pie hole, and he proceeded to use it expertly.

As he fucked my face this way, he held my head firmly in place. He was not really allowing me to do any work at all other than to maintain suction and avoid scraping him with my teeth. At this point, it really was no longer even a challenge for me. I could have knelt there in that position for two hours without even flinching. He was my Master, and he'd trained me to serve him well.

Matt was not interested in prolonging the ordeal, however. I knew by the intensity of his fuck that he was on a mission to bust a nut. He was soon gonna drain his load, and I had little doubt of where he'd deposit it. When I heard him begin to moan a little louder, I knew the climax was near. Then without warning he thrust himself deeply into me, forcing my head all the way down on his shaft. My nose rammed against his pubes as I felt the trigger of his cumload throb against my tongue. And then there it was—that all-too-familiar sensation. The pump. His cum was firing up his shaft, and I felt every throb against my tongue. Then he erupted!

Like a volcano it blasted deep into my throat, and eagerly I gulped. The tightness of my constricting throat walls very effectively milked out every drop of his load. Blast after blast of his seed fired into me and went straight down in my gullet. I, too, was now moaning.

Suddenly I shuddered, feeling a shiver wash over me as I felt my Master's firm grip continue to hold me in place. I was also cumming! I was releasing my load right into my pants, though I hadn't even so much as touched myself.

As he finally loosened his grip and began to slide out of me, a wave of fear washed over me. I knew I had failed! I knew I was never allowed to cum. Never without his permission. "Oh Sir," I cried, "I'm so sorry!"

Matt stepped back and looked down at me. I was now holding my hands in front of my lap. "Did you touch yourself?" he asked authoritatively.

I shook my head. "Sir, it was an accident!"

"You came ... without touching yourself?" he asked.

"I didn't mean to, Sir!"

I felt the urge to drop to the ground and kiss his feet. I was prepared to beg him for mercy, but instead I looked up at him, tears now forming in my eyes. And then I saw him smile.

"You fucking came ... without even touching yourself!" he repeated.

I nodded, "Yes, Sir." I looked up at him, wide-eyed, and continued to monitor his expression. He was now grinning broadly.

"Fuckin hot!" he said. I smiled back up at him.

"Really, Sir?" I asked. "I'm not in trouble?"

Matt then reached down and slid his hands beneath my armpits, smoothly and quickly pulling me up off my knees. He pushed me against the counter and then hefted me up, plopping my butt on the counter top. As he did so, I bumped the cheesecake with my rear end, and before I knew it, it sailed off the ledge, splattering all over the floor.

Matt didn't seem to notice, and quickly forced his lips against mine, locking them in a passionate kiss. His tongue rammed into my mouth, and I responded by pressing my syrup-coated lips against his. I wrapped my legs around his waist as he firmly held my head in both hands and Frenched me.

For the next five minutes, Matt continued to ravage me with ceaseless, passionate kisses. I expected him to begin disrobing me, perhaps with the intention of fucking me right there on the kitchen counter. He didn't, though. Instead he just kissed me. Over and over. As he did so, I thought momentarily that I might just cum again. Finally, though, his kisses became gentler. Then at last he pulled away. "I love you pup," he said again. "I really, really do."

It was there in that post-coital moment that the significance of his repeated declarations hit me. Sure Matt had told me numerous times before that he loved me, but today for some reason it seemed he could not say it enough. I knew what all he'd been through in the previous weeks. I knew he had honestly felt that our relationship was over. I knew he had resigned himself to the fact that he must release me in order to keep me safe. He'd nearly lost me, and I'd nearly lost him. And now ...

Now he was doing everything in his power to cling to me. For all these months, every since I first met him, I had considered myself to be the one clinging to him. I was the needy one. Was it really possible that Matt also needed me?

Could a Master really need his sub?

"I love you too, Sir," I said, "I really, really do."

Matt and I did finish clearing the dinner table, and although he really wasn't all that much help when it came to cleaning up, I recognized the significance of his gesture. Had I been a little bolder, I would have gently shooed him from my kitchen, because honestly he was just in the way. Finally he did announce that he was going to take a shower, and I cleaned up the splattered cheesecake from the floor while he was in the bathroom. I even had enough time to change out of my cum-soaked pants before he was done, and I then went and waited for him in the living room.

It really concerned me that he'd made such a point to tell me he needed to talk to me. Previously whenever Matt wanted to talk to me about something, he just did so. Why would he feel the need to inform me ahead of time? It made me worry that the matter was really serious. Maybe it was something to do with Ryan and his incarceration.

When Matt finally entered the living room to join me, my heart raced just a little, partially because I was still obsessing over the possibilities of our impending conversation and partially because my Master was wearing only a towel. For a few seconds, I had the urge to roll over on my back and beg him to just fuck me senseless. Instead, though, I waited for him to speak.

He sat down on the sofa beside me and pulled me over next to him, wrapping his arm around me. I wondered if I should move to the floor. It was truly where I was most comfortable, resting between his legs. Matt, however, offered no indication that he wanted me to move. He just held me for a few minutes.

"Petey," he began. His use of my first name did not go unnoticed. "I'm sorry about how I acted earlier today—when you were playing with Drew in the bedroom."

"Sir—"

"Shhh ... let me finish." I wrapped my arm around his torso and placed my head against his chest. "Pup," he started again, "I know Drew would never hurt you. I shouldn't have grabbed him like I did and thrown him across the room. I really could have hurt him."

"Sir, he understands. He's not mad or anything!"

"I know. Not sayin he was. Drew's a good sub; he'd never be mad at me for protecting my pup. Thing is, though, my pup didn't need my protection. Not then anyway."

"You always protect me, Sir. It's your job."

"You're right. It's my job to protect you, but I haven't always done it really well. And I think the fact that I fucked up so bad at protecting you from Ryan is what has kind of made me over-protective now. I really just wanna keep you safe. You just got out of the hospital a few weeks ago, and when I saw Drew wailing on you, it kinda scared me. Pissed me off too ..."

"Thank you, Sir. Thank you for protecting me the way you do."

"Well ..." Matt sighed. He paused for a moment before continuing. "Well, I was talkin to Alex today about the whole situation. Only you and me know what happened here that day— the day of your birthday party."

"When Alex served you," I said.

"Right. Alex subbed for me, and you know it's our secret. I don't want Drew ever finding out about that."

I shook my head. "No Sir."

"Well in spite of the fact that Alex is sub to me, he is someone I really trust when it comes to giving me advice. He's a good Master, at least in my opinion. He's not perfect ... he fucked up that one time with you, but overall he's chill."

"Yes, Sir," I agreed.

"Look at me," Matt said, and I pulled away from him a bit, sitting up so I could see his face. I wondered for a second if I should kneel, but Matt made no indication that I should do so. "Alex asked me a question today, and it got me thinking. See, we were down at the bookstore—the adult bookstore—lookin at some kink stuff. I decided to pick some things up for us. Some stuff I think is gonna be real interesting. Real hot."

"Really, Sir?" I asked excitedly.

Matt smiled for a second and nodded. "Yeah," he said and then again got serious. "Anyway, Alex asked me about what we used for a safe word."

"What's that?" I said.

"Well, it's sort of a special word that you can say if you need me to stop doing something that scares you."

"But why?" I asked. "You never scare me ..."

"Pup, I know I've scared you. I know I've scared you more than once." He was staring intently into my eyes. "Right?"

"Maybe ... but Sir ... whenever I've been scared, you stop. Remember that time out in the alley? Remember how you stopped right away when you saw I was afraid? And I felt so bad afterwards, cause I knew I should have trusted you!"

"And if you'd had a safe word, that wouldn't have happened. There's no reason for you to feel bad about being scared. I do want you to trust me, but that's something we have to build together. You trust me a hell of a lot more now then you did back then, right?"

"Yes, Sir," I nodded.

"Pup, I want us to do more things ... things you might never have thought of before. They can be real hot so long as we do them the right way, but the only way we can do em is if I know you trust me—"

"But Sir, I *do* trust you!" I interrupted him.

"Quiet," he said calmly. "Not one more word. Understand?" I nodded and continued to stare at him wide-eyed. "You're gettin too excited, pup. I need you to just listen to me for a minute. Then you can talk. Okay?" Again I nodded wordlessly.

"All right. Well, having a safe word does not mean that you don't trust your Master. All it is, is an additional safety measure. It is not something you will ever use frivolously. If you're tired or bored or irritated, that is not a reason to use a safe word. Sometimes you're gonna have to do things you might not understand or you might not particularly like. Those also are not reasons to use a safe word. The safe word is not ever to be used as a means of getting out of your responsibilities. It is never to be used as a way to end a scene just because you don't like it.

"Honestly I don't think you'll have to use our safe word very often. In fact, you may never have to use it. Hopefully you won't. But if you do feel you need to use it, you should never think that I'd be disappointed. You should never feel that it means you don't trust me.

"A safe word is something you use when you feel afraid or when you feel you can't go on with what we are doing any longer. If you are in more pain than you can endure, you can use the safe word. If you are terrified like you were that night in the alley, you can use the safe word. If you know that I'm hurting you but I'm unaware of it, you can use the safe word.

"Do you understand?" I nodded. "You can speak now, pup."

"Sir," I said, suddenly hearing my voice crack, "I don't want to have a safe word! I just want to trust you!"

Again Matt wrapped his arm around me. "Pup, listen to me. If you do trust me, you have to trust that I'm doing this for a good reason. Almost every Master and sub have a safe word. Alex and Drew have one."

"They do?"

Matt nodded. "Yep, yeah they do ..."

"Can I talk to Drew about it?"

"Absolutely," Matt said, "I want ya to. By giving you a safe word, I'm not telling you that I think you don't trust me. I know how much you trust me. I'm also not telling you that I'm unworthy of your trust. I'm your Master. I deserve your trust! The reason I want you to have a safe word is so you can trust me even more."

"So I can trust you to stop when you're scaring me?"

"Yep. Exactly. If I'm truly scaring you, I want to stop. My goal is never to frighten my pup. My goal is to strengthen you. My goal is to protect you. My goal is to have really, really hot scenes with you ... like a few minutes ago."

"Mine too!" I sidled up even closer to him.

"Think of it as a stop sign. It is your stop sign. It is your one-and-only means of stopping a scene. And it is only for when you are honestly scared or in too much pain."

"But Sir ... why pain? You've never hurt me that way ..."

"What about when we first made love. When I first fucked you ... wasn't that painful?"

"Yeah, but only a little."

"But if it had been a lot painful ... too painful for you to stand, how would I have known?"

"Sir, you kept asking me. You made sure it was not too painful. You would have never hurt me."

"But if it had been too painful for you, and you had a safe word, you could have stopped it."

"Well, I'm glad I didn't have one!"

"Maybe that's not the best example. I may be doin some scenes with you, pup, where you will have to endure some pain for me. Don't worry, it will be hot—for both of us. But since it's gonna involve pain, you have to be able to tell me if it's too much."

At this point he really was starting to scare me. "Sir ... I don't understand."

"Well I need you to trust me on this. We're gonna try some new stuff. It may involve some pain, but you have to trust me ..."

"Yes, Sir," I said.

"Do you have any questions?"

"Sir, so if you're spanking me and it hurts me too bad, I can use a safe word and you have to stop?"

He laughed. "If I'm spanking you as part of a scene, yes. If I'm spanking you as a punishment and you try usin the safe word, you're getting yer ass blistered even harder. Got it?"

"Yes, Sir," I smiled at him sheepishly.

"Anything else? Any other questions?"

"Yes, Sir. What's the safe word?"

"Davenport."

3

I hate driving, which is why it's so perfect that Matt always drives when we go somewhere. But early the next morning he had me use his car to run his suit down to the dry cleaners. He and Alex had gone to the gym together before Matt's class. I had to drop off the suit, stop at the mall, go to the cake decorating supply store, and then meet Kathie for lunch. After lunch I had to pick Matt's suit up from the cleaners and then take his car back to him. I'd already been nearly frantic that morning, busy with my tasks around the apartment. I had gotten up early and shined Matt's dress shoes, ironed his shirt, and given him some great head before he even rolled out of bed.

"Be careful with my car, pup," he warned me, "and don't be late. My class gets out at 2 and my interview is at 3:30."

"Yes, Sir ... or I mean no, Sir ... or um ... I'll be careful and I won't be late!"

"Gimme a kiss." As he leaned in to kiss me, I inhaled his scent. He hadn't yet showered and would do so at the gym, so the smell of his cologne from the night before still lingered. I buried my nose into his neck before he released me, nuzzling him affectionately. I felt him wrap his arms around me and grip my butt cheeks with both hands, gently squeezing.

"Come on!" Alex hollered. "We're gonna be late." He was standing behind us by the front door. Matt ignored him and gave me another passionate kiss.

"Love ya," he said, and then slowly released me and turned to Alex. "Jus chill, dude," he said. "We're not gonna be late. Jus goin to the fuckin gym."

Alex rolled his eyes and laughed. The two headed out the door together as I went through my mental checklist to make sure I had everything. Matt's display of affection was a bit of a distraction, though not unwelcomed, stirring an unexpected arousal in me. If I hadn't been so busy, I swear I would've rushed into the bathroom to beat off right then.

After our conversation the night before, he'd made love to me right there on the living room sofa. Then he'd carried me to the bedroom where we cuddled until I fell asleep in his arms. He was spooning me the next morning when I woke up, which was when I'd felt his morning hard-on pressing against me. I forced myself out of bed, nonetheless, and performed my chores, then went back to the bedroom and sucked him off before my shower. I knew it was his favorite way to wake up.

I was glad to be done with my classes for the semester, and wished I had more days like today where I could focus solely upon serving my Master in a domestic capacity. Apparently Matt liked it as well, for when I'd suggested that I ask my boss for more hours at the bookstore, he discouraged it. "Don't need to work more hours. Ya need to just focus on serving your Master."

"But Sir," I'd reasoned with him, "the money I make could go toward paying our bills ..."

"Are you trying to argue with me?" he scolded.

"No, Sir." And that was that. I sincerely hoped that Matt's interview went well and that he got the job. He'd be done with his classes this week as well, and I knew that without a job, he'd be getting antsy. He wasn't the type to just sit around and play video games, not to mention the fact that we were going to need the income.

When I got to the dry cleaners, I had to circle the block three times until I found a parking space. By this time I was a nervous wreck. I also hated the fact that I had to parallel park; I'd never been real good at it, and in most instances when I had to park like this I would just look for two empty spaces adjacent each other and pull straight in. Unfortunately this time I was not afforded that option.

As I left the dry cleaners I began thinking about our conversation from the previous night. Although I completely understood Matt's reasoning for implementing a safe word, I worried that he might fear I did not really trust him fully. It made sense to me that he could possibly have doubts. After all, he had virtually claimed responsibility for the fact that I'd been raped. It was logical to assume that if he felt responsible for this horrible act, then he would not expect me to completely trust him to keep me safe. This was so disturbing to me, because it was the exact opposite of how I really felt.

There was no one in the world I trusted more than my Master. And as far as the rape was concerned, I did not blame Matt in the least. The intense rage and ferocious protectiveness that he demonstrated that day he confronted Ryan for the first time told me just how far he would go to keep me safe. The way he'd so quickly rushed into the bedroom when Drew and I were play-fighting was an obvious indication that as long as he was around, no one was going to hurt his pup.

On the other hand, I did understand why Matt would want us to have a safe word. If it were true what he'd said about most Masters and subs having such a safety precaution, then I probably should just accept it as a standard, which was a normal part of our lifestyle. It just seemed odd to me, though, that Matt made such a point of discussing it last night but then did not even bother to do any of the sexual activities to which he'd alluded.

He had stated that he'd purchased some items for us to use in our sex play, yet instead we just had our plain ol' vanilla sex. This is what Drew would have called it, anyway. He'd taught me that plain old fashioned, non-kinky sex was considered to be "vanilla." And truthfully, as far as I was concerned it was just as hot as any sort of kink I could have imagined. Matt had been so romantic with me the night before. His lovemaking was very passionate, yet at the same time he was gentle. He had even done to me as he'd threatened—

he'd rubbed the stubble on his chin against my most private parts. I almost thought he was gonna even suck me a little like he'd done once before.

Perhaps it was just that Matt was going to wait until a specific time to introduce this new kink. Maybe he was saving it for a special occasion. Maybe he wanted to keep me wondering, build up a bit of anticipation. What concerned me, though, was that I was starting to wonder if he might have some reservations about even trying anything that might possibly frighten me. Although this would have been very noble of him, for sure, it seemed so out of character.

Matt was my Master, and in the past he had always done whatever he pleased when it came to sex. If he got something in his head that he thought might be hot, we did it. He was not one to hesitate when it came to pleasing himself, and this was exactly the way I wanted it. I depended upon the fact that my Master would use me for his pleasure. I literally craved serving him, and nothing pleased me more than pleasing him. If this dynamic had somehow changed, I feared what it might possibly mean to us as a couple.

At the mall, I had to pick out a new tie to go with Matt's suit. I wanted him to look perfect for his interview. Also, this gave me an excuse to stop at the portrait studio to see Blake. When I got to the men's department at Macy's, though, I realized that sending me by myself to pick out a tie for Matt might not have been the wisest decision he'd ever made. I was beside myself within a matter of minutes. I just couldn't make up my mind which one to get, and the sales clerk was not much help. She had no idea what to suggest, actually, for she hadn't seen the suit. After about ten minutes of indecision, I sensed that she was beginning to get a tad annoyed with me, understandably so. I finally selected the very first tie that I'd picked up when I first got there.

Checking my watch as I left Macy's, I realized I only had a half hour before it was time to meet my sister for lunch, and the drive itself would take me at least fifteen. I could skip going to the portrait studio and head directly to the cake decorating store, which thankfully was on the way. Then I'd just call Kathie and tell her I was running a couple minutes late. I reached in my pocket to retrieve my phone, deciding to just go ahead and call her now. As I fumbled for my phone, I discovered that the only thing in my pocket was Matt's car keys. Fuck! I must've left my phone at home. I immediately stopped and looked around, wondering if there was a payphone anywhere in the mall.

I had an idea. I'd go to the portrait studio after all and ask Blake to use the phone. His store, though, was in the opposite direction, so I swiftly turned around to change course. When I did so, however, I slammed right into a man who had been briskly walking behind me.

"Watch where the fuck yer goin!" he barked. Nervously I stepped back and accidently dropped the bag I was carrying. It was Matt's tie. The bag slid across the floor, and before I could even began to react, what appeared to be a stampede of excited teenagers rushed by, trampling the bag under their feet.

"Stop!" I tried to yell, but they didn't even hear me. "I'm sorry, Sir." I said to the man I'd bumped into, but he was already gone. Frantically I rushed over to retrieve the mangled Macy's bag. Damn! The tie was ruined. A huge size-eleven boot print was smeared across the front of the tie, which had completely slid out of the bag.

I was so frustrated that I was nearly in tears. I just stood there holding the new tie in my hands as a throng of people barged right on past me, seeming not to even notice my existence. I felt myself beginning to panic, and I knew if I didn't force myself to remain calm I'd be literally trembling. What was I gonna do? I had to go back and get another tie. I couldn't pick up Matt without one!

What should I do first? Where should I go? Fuck! Macy's or portrait studio? I took a deep breath and tried to calm myself, stepping back toward the side of the thoroughfare, out of the way of the oncoming foot traffic. "Calm down ..." I told myself. I looked down again at the pathetic piece of wrinkled fabric that used to be a neck tie, and I saw that already my hands were shaking.

I'll just go ask Blake to use the phone, and I'll call and cancel lunch with Kathie. Then I'll have plenty of time to go get Matt a new tie, go to the cake store, and pick up the suit from the dry cleaners. Now where exactly was Blake's shop located? I thought it was in the next wing, adjacent to the one where I was currently standing.

I was starting to feel confused. I remembered that Drew and I had passed through the food court on our way to the studio. That would be easy to find. It should be, anyway. Straight ahead ... no, it was the other way. Wait! Which entrance had I come in? Was this the same door that Drew and I had used yesterday? I couldn't remember. There must be one of those kiosks close by that had a mall map. They were everywhere ... usually. I looked around. Shit!

As I was standing there, now in a state of nearly-paralyzing fear, I saw a familiar face. About fifty feet from me Eric was walking, and he was headed directly toward me. I almost cried, I was so relieved. Just as I was about to take a step in his direction, though, he stopped. As he did so, he turned to look at the person who was walking on the other side of him. At first I hadn't noticed that he was not alone because his companion was walking slightly behind him. Then I saw who it was.

Ryan!

Ryan was there with Eric, only feet away from me! He was supposed to be in jail. He was supposed to be locked up right now. Oh my god! A wave of terrifying panic washed over me, and suddenly I felt weak in the knees. I had to get out of there! I had to get back home. Back to Matt. Back to safety!

I dropped the bag and spun around, briskly walking in the opposite direction of Eric and Ryan. My pace quickened rapidly, and soon I was running. I had no idea where I was or where I was going. I just had to get the fuck out of there. By the time I saw an entrance door, I was in tears. I'd been bumping into people, trying to weave my way through the unrelenting stream of shoppers on the thoroughfare. I could barely breathe, and I knew that soon I was gonna start to hyperventilate. Oh my god! I needed air.

I rushed through the exit doors into the parking lot, now sobbing. I needed Matt! I needed my Master!

As I stood there, panicked and confused, I allowed myself to drop down to the ground, sidling up next to the embankment behind me. It was a stone ledge that was part of the landscaping. I sat there, pulling my knees up to my chest, rocking back and forth and trying to calm my breathing. I had to think. Where had I parked? Where was the portrait studio? What time did Matt get out of class? Where was my phone? What should I do ...?

I don't know how long I sat there, for eventually I buried my face in my hands and just wept. How could everything have suddenly gone so wrong? I then was abruptly jolted back to my senses when I felt someone touch my shoulder. Instantly I opened my eyes and pulled away. I looked up and saw Blake standing there.

"Hey, are you all right?" he said, leaning over me.

I looked up at him and shook my head, but I couldn't even speak.

"What's wrong, little guy?" he asked.

I tried to open my mouth to respond. Nothing came out. I just sat there, continuing to tremble.

He crouched down beside me. "Come on. It's okay ... Wanna go inside? Want me to call someone? Are you sick?"

I shook my head. "No ..." I finally managed. "No, I'm not sick. I ... um ... I don't know where—"

"Are you lost?"

"I can't find my car. I don't know where I parked ..."

"Well come inside." He held out his hand to me. "You shouldn't be driving right now anyway. Are you with someone?"

I shook my head.

"What about your friend? Is Professor Tompkins with you?" It seemed odd to hear him refer to Drew by his last name. I shook my head.

"I'm sorry!" I finally blurted out. "I ... uh ... oh ... um, I'm not sure—"

"Hey, calm down. It's all right. Can you stand up? Here, let me help you." Blake reached around me and slid his hand under my arm. "Let me help you up. Get you inside."

"I didn't know ..." I was gasping for breath in between sobs. "I didn't know where I was, how to find—"

"You forgot where you parked, did ya?" he laughed. "It's okay. That happens to everyone."

"No ... I mean yes ..."

"Let's go back to the store. I'll get you something to drink. You can sit down and relax. If you want, I'll call someone for ya. All right?"

I nodded as I wiped my eyes, finally getting back on my feet. "I have to get a tie ... for Matt."

He looked at me puzzled. "A tie?"

"A necktie, Sir. For him to wear with his suit."

"Ahh, oh I see. Well you've come to the right place then, haven't ya?"

"You don't understand!" I again gasped for breath, struggling not to burst into tears once more. "I already got him one ... from Macy's. It's ruined."

"What happened to it?" he asked as he gently coaxed me toward the door.

"I dropped it, and some kids walked all over it. They trampled it!"

"Aww, I'm sorry to hear that, but don't be upset. It's not like it's the end of the world. We can get you another tie. Want me to go with you?"

I stopped in my tracks, suddenly again feeling a wave of terror wash over me. I'd almost completely forgotten about the real reason why I was upset. I hadn't even mentioned to Blake that I'd just come face to face with my rapist. I shook my head. "No! No, I can't go in there!" I screamed. I pulled my arm away from him and backed away. "I've gotta go!" I yelled as I turned and ran out into the parking lot.

"Wait!" he screamed. "Petey, please wait!" He was racing behind me, trying to catch up.

All I could think of was that I had to get away from that mall. I had to get away from Ryan. Where'd I park? Where'd I fuckin park? Finally I saw the car. It was two aisles over. I remembered ... it was right by the lamppost. I hurried even faster, running at breakneck speed. I fumbled in my pocket for the keys, depressing the remote to unlock the door. Then at last I was there, my hand on the door latch. I looked down to open it and instantly froze.

Oh my god! It couldn't be!

I stepped back from the door, staring at Matt's car in disbelief. A horrendous scratch had been keyed into the driver's side of the car, and it ran from the front fender all the way down to the back bumper. "No!" I screamed, covering my mouth in a gesture of shock and horror. "Oh my god! Matt's car!"

Not knowing what else to do, I opened the car door anyway and slid inside. Slamming the door, I shoved the key into the ignition and fired it up. As I was peeling out of the parking space, I saw Blake in the rearview mirror. I couldn't stop, though. I couldn't let him take me back into that mall.

What was I going to do? I didn't have Matt's tie. I'd let his car get ruined, and I now was late for my lunch appointment with Kathie. I still had to get the supplies from the cake store and pick up Matt's suit, but what about his tie? What about Ryan? Why was he out of jail?

My hands were still shaking as I tried to concentrate on the road in front of me. Maybe I could just call Kathie from the dry cleaners. Maybe she would go with me to a different store to get Matt a tie and we could just skip lunch. Maybe she would drive me over to the cake store. But what was I gonna do about the car? Matt was going to kill me!

I was trying to think rationally, but everything was just so damned confusing. Just wait a minute! He won't be mad at me. I know he won't. He'll know it wasn't my fault. How could I be responsible for someone vandalizing his car? I wasn't even there. I was in the mall.

It was my fault I'd dropped the tie, there was no denying that, but if I got a replacement, he might not even care. I just had to get back to the dry cleaners and get everything back on track. Matt surely must have auto insurance that would pay for the repair of his car.

I was starting to calm down finally. Although I was still trembling, at least I was not in a complete state of panic. Everything would probably have been all right if I hadn't seen Ryan. I couldn't believe he was out of jail. I couldn't believe he had been right there, just a few feet from me.

Then I remembered the last time I'd seen him. It was at the apartment when the police had arrested him. I'd had to face him that day too, and I hadn't been afraid. Matt had been there, though. Matt had tried to rip him limb from limb. Ryan had been the one who was panicked and sobbing that day. Why was I letting myself be frightened by him now? He couldn't hurt me anymore. He couldn't touch me.

I was starting to feel better, and for a few seconds I debated turning around and going back to the mall to get another tie. I couldn't do it though; I wouldn't have time. I needed to call Kathie as soon as possible.

At last I was back at the dry cleaners. Actually everything would turn out okay just as long as I got to Matt by the time his class was out at two o'clock. I had to be there and have the suit with me. He might not be happy about the tie situation, but he actually had plenty of decent ties already. Why did he need a brand new one just for this interview?

Okay that was the solution. I'd call Kathie and cancel lunch. Then I'd skip buying the new tie and would probably still have enough time to stop at the cake store before picking up Matt. It looked like my luck might be changing. Things just might turn out okay after all. There even was an empty parking place right in front of the door! Yes!

I pulled in and got out of the car. Taking a deep breath, I stepped up on the curb and headed for the entrance. Crap! I'd left my dry cleaning ticket on the front seat of the car. I turned back around and unlocked the door, reaching in to snatch up the ticket. Good, it was right there where I'd left it. I grabbed it and looked down at the receipt. I nearly passed out when I read the words on that page.

The box labeled, "RUSH: FOUR HOUR SERVICE" was empty. Instead the standard 24-hour service had been selected. This can't be happening! How could I have been so stupid not to tell them I needed the emergency service? I turned and raced toward the door of the shop. Oh please, God, give me a miracle!

As I hurriedly explained my dilemma to the clerk at the counter, she looked at me sympathetically and attempted to rectify the error. "Sir, this happens all the time. It's not a problem, we can upgrade your order to a rush and have the suit ready to be picked up by four o'clock."

I looked at her exasperatedly. "But ma'am, you don't understand! The interview is at 3:30, and I have to have the suit by two. No! I have to have it by 1:30!"

She shook her head and smiled at me. "I'm sorry, but it's already twelve o'clock now."

"Isn't there anything you can do? Can I get the suit back from you now?"

"But we haven't even touched it. It hasn't been laundered."

I was trying to decide what to do. Matt had other suits, but he'd specifically picked out this one. Would he even know that it hadn't actually been dry-cleaned? I mean it was practically in perfect condition when I brought it in. The dry cleaning was more-or-less a formality.

"Do you have a phone I can use?" I asked. "Please!"

"Of course, Mr. Porter. Let me get our portable phone for you. One moment."

I didn't bother to correct her about my name. I paced back and forth in front of the counter for the next few moments until she returned with the phone. I took it from her and thanked her, immediately dialing Kathie's number.

"The number you have dialed is no longer in service." I listened to the recording in stunned disbelief. Crap! I was calling the apartment, and she had apparently already had the phone shut off. She was in the process of moving in with Carter. Plus she wouldn't have been home anyway, because she was probably already at the restaurant waiting for me.

I had to call her cell number. The only problem was that I didn't have that number memorized. She'd gotten a new phone a few weeks prior, and I'd merely programmed it into my phone. I did not know the number yet by memory.

Who could I call? What was I gonna do? Suddenly I felt as if I was on the verge of another panic attack. I reached into my pants pocket and retrieved my wallet. It would do me no good to try calling Drew; he was at the college teaching a class. Matt was in class also, and God-only-knew where Alex was at. My friend Jason would be no help.

As I opened my wallet I saw the tiny piece of folded paper containing the number I had acquired the day before. I hesitated for a moment and then unfolded it. I nervously dialed the number.

"Hello, Mrs. Porter? This is Petey, and I need your help!" I was now crying.

It was two o'clock when I pulled into the parking lot at the college. I sighed with relief as I saw my Master walking out of the Commons Building, right on schedule. I easily slid into a parking place in front of the entrance, which seemed to have been reserved just for me. As I put the car in park and opened the door to get out, Matt approached me. I smiled up at him nervously.

"How was class, Sir?" I asked him.

He shrugged. "Ahh, same ol' same ol' … and how was my pup's day so far?"

I laughed nervously, trying to sound as casual as possible. "Same ol', Sir—just like you said."

He leaned in and kissed me. "You taste like cinnamon," he observed.

"You taste like my Master," I whispered.

He wrapped his arms around me, right there in public, and kissed me again. "I missed you, pup," he whispered in my ear.

When he released me, he looked down at the door of the car. "What happened here?" he asked.

My eyes widened as I looked back at him. "What do you mean, Sir?"

"There's a little smudge or something," he said, and rubbed his thumb gently against a mark he'd noticed just above the door handle. "Oh it's nothing," he said. "I thought my pup damaged my car," he laughed.

"Sir, we gotta get goin," I said. "You only have about an hour to get ready ..." then I lowered my voice to a whisper, "and I need to suck you off before you go!"

"You do, huh?" he laughed.

"Yes, Sir ... for luck!"

He smiled at me evilly. "Oh is that why you do it?"

"Among other reasons," I smiled back at him. I turned and ran around to the passenger side of the car.

"Did you get all your errands done?" he asked.

"More or less, Sir," I said as I slid into the seat beside him. "Kathie cancelled on me, so I didn't have lunch with her."

"She still pissed about everything?"

I shrugged. "I'm not sure, Sir. She didn't sound mad though. You know she's moving right now, and she's just really busy."

"Yeah, don't worry about it. She'll come around. I know how much she loves you."

"I know, Sir," I said.

As Matt briskly backed the car out of the parking space I smiled to myself, remembering all that had occurred during the previous two hours. It had taken Mrs. Porter exactly ten minutes from the time I'd called her to arrive at the dry cleaners. Ten minutes later, two specialists from the auto body repair shop arrived at our location. Mrs. Porter just happened to know the owner of the dry cleaners, and she called in a personal favor. When she walked through the door he came out to greet her and assure her that the suit would be ready in an hour. She and I then went outside to speak to the auto body repair technicians. They had some sort of silicone spray that they said would completely cover the scratch and restore the car to its original finish. They said it would take about an hour and they would do it right there in the parking lot.

Mrs. Porter then drove me down to an exclusive men's shop in the downtown district—much nicer than Macy's—and helped me pick out a new tie for Matt. On the way, we stopped at the restaurant where Kathie was supposed to meet me. I ran in and explained my situation to her, apologizing profusely. She wasn't thrilled, but she understood. "So are you officially cancelling lunch with me, then?" I asked.

"Petey, you're the one who's cancelling."

"Kathie, please! Just say it ..."

She stared at me for a moment and then a look of recognition crossed her face. She smiled. "Yes, as a matter of fact," she said. "I'm very busy today and I need to cancel lunch." I smiled at her, knowing that now I would not have to lie to my Master.

"Thanks a million, Kathie! I love you." I quickly kissed her on the cheek and ran back out to the car where Mrs. Porter was waiting for me. We then headed over to the cake decorating store and got my supplies before it was time to return to the dry cleaners.

"Do you like the tie?" I said to Matt as I reached behind me to retrieve it from the backseat.

"Wow, did you pick that out yourself?" he asked.

"More or less," I said. "I made the final decision."

"And you did a good job, too. I do like it. I like it a lot. Good pup."

"Thank you, Sir," I said, beaming as I looked over at him.

We made it home in plenty of time for Matt to get his lucky blowjob and then get ready for the interview. I got lucky myself that day, too, because when he returned from the interview at five o'clock, he fucked me senseless!

4

Matt and I were in bed together later that night. I'd made him a special meal to celebrate his successful job interview. He had been offered a position, although it was merely to be a manager-in-training. From what he'd said, it sounded as if the company had high hopes for him, but before he'd be given a store (or in this case, a gym) of his own, he must first complete their eight-week training regimen. They were giving him two weeks to finish up with school, and then he would start his new job the first week of June.

All three of us were so happy for Matt—Alex, Drew, and I—and Matt seemed as if a huge weight had been lifted from his shoulders. I had planned to tell him about seeing Ryan at the mall earlier that day. I wanted to wait until after Matt was done with the interview, though, because I did not want to distract him. I feared that if he had any idea how upset I had been, he might not want to leave me alone and would end up missing his chance at a good job.

Then when Matt did finally come home, we were all too excited about his great news for me to even think about spoiling the mood. I also feared that if I told him about seeing Ryan, he would press me for details and I'd then end up saying way too much. I couldn't tell him yet that I had been talking to his mom, but I also couldn't lie to him.

Then while we were lying together in bed, I decided that at the very least I did have to tell him I'd seen Ryan. My Master had to know the truth about Ryan being out of jail, and I knew if I didn't tell him about how much seeing Ryan had upset me, then I would truly be withholding vital information from my Master. It was his job to protect me, and if I didn't make him aware of my fears, how could he do so?

"Sir," I whispered as I lay in bed next to him, my head resting on his shoulder. "I have to tell you something."

"What is it pup?" he said, suddenly sensing the urgency and trepidation in my voice. "What's wrong?"

"Something happened today, Sir, and I have to tell you about it."

"What is it?" he asked, shifting his position in order to pull slightly away from me. He looked over at my face. It was dark in the room, but my eyes had already adjusted to darkness and I could see his silhouette.

I decided to just blurt it out. "I saw Ryan today," I said.

"What?" he said. "Are you sure it was him?"

I nodded. "Yes, Sir. He was with Eric."

"Are you okay?" he asked. And it was with this one single question that I was suddenly overwhelmed with emotion. I'm sure Matt interpreted my tears as an indication that I indeed was not okay, but the truth was that I was just so moved by his response.

I would have expected Matt's initial response to be about Ryan. Why was he out of jail already? What were the circumstances of our encounter with each other? What was said? What did Eric do? But no—Matt did not at first ask any of those questions. He simply asked about *me*.

"Yes, Sir," I whispered, "I'm okay."

"Are you sure?" He pulled me back against his chest. "Did he say anything to you? Did he threaten you?"

"I'm not even sure if he saw me, Sir," I said. "As soon as I saw the two of them, I ran away. I ran, and I lost your tie. I had to go somewhere else—to another store—and get a different one."

"Aww, pup, fuck the tie!" he kissed me on the side of my head. "You should have called me right away."

"You were in class, Sir," I said, "and plus I forgot to take my phone with me."

"Fuck the class too," he said. "I knew I shouldn't have let you do all those errands and shit today by yourself. I fucking knew it!" He was getting pissed.

"Sir!" I cried, "please don't be mad."

"Pup, I'm not mad at you ... for god's sake. I'm mad at *me*."

"That's even worse!" I whined. "Why should you blame yourself? It's not your fault Ryan's out of jail, and I did fine. When I saw him, I just took off. It was not a big ..." I couldn't finish my sentence.

"It wasn't a big deal?" he asked. "Why do I sense you're lying to me?"

My tears were now flowing in earnest. "Well," I whimpered, "cause it really sort of was a big deal. But still ... it's not your fault!"

"Petey, tell me what happened," he urged me. "Tell me why it was a big deal."

I took a deep breath and wiped my eyes with my one free hand. My other hand was beneath me, under the covers. "I just kind of panicked, I guess. I sort of freaked out."

"It scared you, seeing him again for the first time?"

"Yes, Sir," I confessed.

"And then what did you do?"

"I just ran! I ran away as fast as I could."

"Good, pup. Good for you. If ever you don't feel safe in a situation, get the fuck outta there."

"I did, Sir. That's exactly what I did. I ran outside and got away from them. Then I left. I was too upset to go back to Macy's to get another tie."

"You should have just forgot about the fuckin tie, pup. You should have just come right to the college and gotten me."

"Well I'm glad I didn't, Sir. I'm glad I was able to handle it. I knew I still had to pick up your suit at the dry cleaners. I still had to get the stuff for Alex's cake."

"We could have done all of that together later. I have a ton of suits I could've worn."

"But that one was my favorite," I whispered. "That's the one you wore that day at Alex's party. The day we made love at the gym …"

He smiled at me. "You sayin I wouldn't have looked hot in one of my other suits? And why do I need to look hot for a job interview anyway?"

"Sir, you know what I mean!" I said. "Yes, of course you'd be hot-looking no matter what you wore. I just wanted you to look your best. Plus I wanted to please you. I wanted you to be proud of me for getting all my errands done."

"Pup, I'm already proud of you. Do you think a stupid suit or a goddamned tie would make me stop being proud of *my* pup?"

"Well, it all worked out, Sir," I said. "I got the suit and the tie and the cake stuff … and everything was fine."

"But are you fine?" he asked. "I'm not sure you are."

"Yes, Sir, I promise. I'm fine, really I am."

"I'm calling that detective in the morning. I need to make sure they still have a restraining order in place. I don't want that bastard going anywhere near you, and I wanna know why we were not fucking notified when he was released from jail."

"Eric probably posted his bail," I suggested.

"Then Detective Murray should have fuckin called us!"

"Do they even do that, Sir? I mean why would they?"

"Because you're the victim here, pup. They've gotta let you know so you can be prepared to report it if Ryan violates the conditions of his bail. Did he say *any*thing to you, pup? I'm positive that if he talked to you at all he'd be in violation, and I could have his ass locked back up!"

"He didn't Sir. He didn't say one word, and I'm not even sure that he saw me."

"I'm callin right now. I don't fuckin care what time it is!" Actually it happened to be 11:15 pm.

"Please Sir, don't call him now! Please! It's so late; we can call in the morning."

"I don't fuckin care. I'll get that motherfucker outta bed. How is it that he could *not* let us know about this? This is total fuckin bullshit!"

"Please Matt!" I cried, "please don't be so mad!" I hadn't even realized I'd just addressed him by his first name, but in so doing I think I startled him. Instantly he grabbed hold of me and pulled me back against his chest.

"Shh," he said. "It's okay, you're right. I'll call him in the morning, and I'm not mad. I'm not mad at you at all."

"I'm sorry, Sir!"

"Shh," he said again, even more soothingly. "Don't be sorry. You did everything right today. Everything."

"I guess I should have come to you ..."

"Well, it's okay. I'm just sayin you could have come to me when you were scared. It didn't matter whether I was in class or not. You could have come. But it's okay you didn't. You were strong, and I'm proud of you."

If only Matt knew the whole truth! I really hadn't been all that strong, and had it not been for Matt's mother, I probably would have had a complete meltdown. Plus there was the whole issue of the vandalism to Matt's car. Someone had done that deliberately, and I feared that it possibly was Eric and Ryan. I knew for sure that they were both at the mall, and other than them, who would want to key Matt's car?

If I told Matt about the car, though, then I'd have to explain about the visit I'd had with his mom. I'd have to tell him about meeting Blake and about the surprise gift I'd planned for him. Worst of all, I'd have to tell him I had freaked out. Then he'd be worried about me again. He'd be upset and realize just how weak and pathetic I really was. I couldn't tell him, not yet.

I curled up next to him, pressing my body as firmly against him as possible. I wanted him inside me. I wanted him around me. I needed to feel his strength. I reached down to feel his hard-on beneath the sheets. "Will you sleep inside me, Sir?" I whispered, "Please."

He then slid sideways on the bed and gently kissed me. "You want me to make love to you now, pup?" he asked.

"I just want to feel you inside me," I explained.

"Come here," he said, and I turned around to slide myself against his body. He wrapped both his arms around me and held me close against his strong chest. After a couple minutes he reached down beneath the covers and guided himself gently into me. I fell asleep feeling his fullness inside me and the warmth of his breath against my neck.

Matt was at school taking one of his finals. It was his very last day of class, and I was completely finished with my classes as well. Drew and Alex were both gone, and I had the apartment to myself. I was standing alone in my kitchen, wearing nothing but an apron that had a big wet spot right about waist-level. I smiled to myself as I thought about the events of the morning.

When I got up that morning I knew it was going to be a big day. I had to finish Alex's graduation cake and then go down to the mall to get my picture taken with Petey pup. I'd arranged to ride my bike over to Mrs. Porter's house, and then we'd go to the mall together.

Later that evening we were all going to the graduation, and then we had a small reception planned at home afterwards. It would not be like the surprise party that Matt had thrown for Alex. We were simply having a few of Alex's family members and friends come by for cake and champagne.

Earlier that week, when I was at the cake supply store, I had dropped off a photograph of Alex. They could then take that picture and enlarge it, then mechanically airbrush its exact replica onto a frosting sheet. Mrs. Porter assured me it would be no problem for her to run me by the cake shop to pick up the frosting sheet. That would be the final touch that I'd add to the cake. I merely had to lay out the frosting sheet and add some piping around the border of the picture.

Drew was like a maniac during this time. For the previous two days he had been stressing like there was no tomorrow. He was so persnickety about everything that he wanted to make sure each little detail was just right. I think he must have gone through about three times as many cigarettes as he normally would have during that time period.

Many times I tried offering reassurances to Drew that it was all going to be just fine and that stressing over it all did not really do much good. Of course, my attempts were futile. Just like me, it was in Drew's nature to worry about things. Usually he had his Master to calm him and shoulder the burden of responsibility, but in this case, the event was in his Master's honor so Drew sort of felt that the burden of responsibility then fell upon him.

"Drew, why are you so worried about everything?" I asked him that morning before he headed out to work. "You know we already had a party for Alex. This is just a small gathering. You should relax and just focus on pleasing your Master."

"But I *am* focusing on him! That's why it's so stressful. I want to make sure it's perfect for him!"

"Alex knows your heart, Drew. Even if it didn't end up being exactly perfect, he knows the effort that you've put into making it special."

"Thanks Petey, but if you really wanna be helpful, just promise me you won't fuck up the cake."

I scowled at him and placed my hands on each of my hips. "Drew, because I love you so much I'm gonna forgive you for that."

Drew placed his hand over his mouth, as if he suddenly wished he could take back what he just said. "Oh Petey, I'm so sorry. I know you won't fuck up the cake."

"Come here," I said and held out my arms. "Gimme a hug. I know you don't mean to be an asshole."

He stared at me for a couple seconds, astonished, then stepped over to hug me. As we embraced each other we both laughed.

That exchange occurred just prior to Drew leaving the apartment that morning. Alex was the next to enter the kitchen. "Hey Petey, what ya doin?"

"I'm makin your cake, Sir," I smiled up at him.

"Oh cool, let me see."

I pointed to the front door. "Get out!" I demanded. "Get out of my kitchen ... Sir ... please."

He started laughing. "Ohhh, you're scary when you get so bossy. Matt better watch out."

"You can't see it yet, Sir. It'll spoil the surprise. Please!"

He shook his head and then reached over to ruffle my already mussed-up hair. "Ah, okay then. Hey I gotta ask ya somethin though, real quick."

"Yes, Sir," I said, remaining steadfast in my stance at the end of the kitchen in order to prevent his entry.

"Have you noticed anything weird about Drew lately?"

I laughed. "Yeah ... or I mean yes Sir. He's about to have a stroke."

"What do ya mean?" Alex asked. "What's wrong with him?"

"Well, please don't tell him I told you, Sir. I mean of course it is your decision, but I just don't want him getting upset with me."

"No, I won't tell him, Petey. Go ahead."

"Thank you, Sir. It's just that Drew has been very obsessed with your graduation."

"Really?" he said. "What's there to obsess about?"

"Your gift, your clothes, the reception afterward, your cake, your cap 'n gown ... everything really. He just wants it all to be perfect."

"Well that's just crazy," he said, shaking his head. "Why would he think all that shit is his responsibility?"

"No disrespect, Sir, but you do realize how much he loves you, right?"

"Of course."

"And since you're his Master, he feels it's his job to make this day perfect for you."

"His job is to be responsible for what I assign to him, nothing more," Alex stated authoritatively.

"But since you didn't assign him anything in particular, Sir, he's kinda taken on the responsibility for everything."

Alex cocked his head as he looked down at me, as if thinking over what I'd said. "Ya know, I think you're right, Petey pup. I think I kinda left him hangin. He needed some direction from me, but I just let him worry about everything all on his own. I guess maybe I didn't really think of it all as being such a big deal."

"Drew is so lucky to have you, Sir. It'll all be over after tonight, then things will get back to normal."

"Well thanks for doin the cake. I'm sure it'll be awesome."

"Thank you, Sir. I just hope you like it."

"I'm sure I will. Hey I gotta get goin though. See ya tonight."

About twenty minutes after Alex took off, Matt stumbled to the kitchen wearing only a pair of boxers.

"You slept in, Sir," I said as I stepped over to kiss him. He still had about an hour and a half before he had to be to class for his final.

"That's cause my pup never came and woke me up like he knows I like," Matt said before kissing me.

"That's cause your pup was in the kitchen making a graduation cake, Sir. And also cause your pup wanted you to be fully awake when he sucked your big fat cock."

"Mmmm," Matt said. "So I guess you better get your ass back in the bedroom ... now."

"Yes Sir," I smiled up at him and then instantly sobered my expression. "Should I leave the apron on, Sir?"

He just pointed down the hallway, not answering. I left the apron on and headed for the bedroom, my Master following immediately behind me.

An hour later I was finally alone in the apartment. I was standing in the kitchen again, wearing only my apron. I smiled to myself as I remembered what had just happened between Matt and me in the bedroom.

Of course it had begun as the typical wake-up blowjob that I gave my Master every morning, but at some point Matt got it in his head that he wanted me wearing nothing except my apron.

Of course I had to strip down completely, and then put back on only the apron, which rather amusingly tented in the front from my own arousal. He laughed as my face reddened. "You're my little housewife," he teased me. "I ought to make you hold a spatula in one hand and a scrub brush in the other while you kneel and blow me."

"Yes, Sir," I answered meekly.

"Go on!" he said, "Do it! Go get a spatula from the kitchen and a scrub brush. Now!"

Hurriedly I raced back out to the kitchen, rummaging frantically in the utensil drawer until I located the big stainless steel spatula. It was my favorite one to use for pancakes, wide and flexible with an extra-long handle. I then reached into the cup beside the sink and retrieved the dish-cleaning brush. It was what I used to scrub cups and glasses when I had just a few and didn't want to run the dishwasher. Hands full, I quickly turned and raced back to the bedroom where Matt was comfortably reclining in the desk chair.

His cock jutted out in front of him, still slick from my saliva. Just seeing it there throbbing in front of me made my mouth start to water again. Matt laughed as he watched me stand there practically drooling over his pure masculinity. "You want more of this, bitch?" he said.

"Yes, Sir!" I cried. "Oh god, yes!" My voice was raspy, like a growl, which seemed to make Matt throb all the harder.

"That's what you are, aren't ya?" he asked rhetorically. "You're my little housewife bitch!"

I nodded to him, uncertain if he expected an answer. "Speak up, boy!"

"Yes, Sir!" I shouted, my voice cracking from my own excitement.

"Say it! Say what you are!"

"I'm your bitch, Sir! I'm your housewife bitch!"

"Yes you are ... and my cocksuckin bitch too, aren't ya?"

"Yes, Sir!"

"Down!" he ordered, pointing to the floor. Immediately I dropped, though it was rather awkward to do with my hands full.

This, too, seemed to amuse him. "Now crawl over here and finish your job, bitch."

Quickly I slid closer to him, crawling on my knees. Then, holding my hands out to the side and resting my wrists against his thighs, I bowed my head and took his cock once again in my mouth. "Oh yeah," he moaned. "Suck it!" I began to bob frantically on my Master's cock.

"That's it, boy. Take it all the way in. Suck it! Suck my cock, bitch!"

I was so turned on, wanting more than anything to just drop the utensils and grope myself as I sucked my Master, but of course I knew better than that. It didn't take long, though, until Matt was ready to drain himself, and he did it right down my throat. He was holding my head in place like he always did when he climaxed.

Afterwards I looked up and smiled at him, only to learn the scene was not yet over.

"What you smilin at bitch?" he sneered at me. "You proud of what you are?"

I wiped the smile from my face and continued to maintain eye contact with him, nodding my head confidently. "Yes, Sir!" I shouted, and then he broke into a wide grin.

"Fuck yeah!" he exclaimed. "You better be! Now get up off your knees and onto my lap ... now! And gimme that spatula." He quickly snatched it from my hand.

Instantly and obediently I leapt up from my kneeling position and bent myself over his lap, face down. My ass was upraised and fully exposed to him. Without hesitation, he then swatted my bare behind. *Thwack! Thwack! Thwack!* His blows were not terribly forceful, but I flinched none the less.

"I'm gonna redden your little faggy ass, and then I'm gonna fuck it like a pussy!" he announced. "You want that, boy?"

"Yes, Sir! Thank you, Sir!" I cried.

"You better thank me. You like my discipline, don't ya? You need it! You need to have your ass paddled!"

"Yes, Sir!" I replied.

"Beg for it, then. Beg me to redden your cute little ass!"

"Please, Sir, redden my ass like I deserve!"

Then in rapid succession he proceeded to deliver a series of swats to my butt. Each of them did sting, but he was obviously not using the full force of his strength. When he was done, he dropped the spatula and gently rubbed my cheeks. "Oh yeah," he said, "they're fire-engine read, and hot! You ready for your Master to fuck your hot little ass, boy?"

"Yes, Sir! Please Sir, fuck my ass!"

"Your hot little ass!" he corrected me.

"Please fuck my hot little ass, Sir!"

He then pulled me up and quickly stood himself, steering me toward the bed. "Bend over!" he commanded. I immediately assumed the position, keeping my ass pressed high in the air behind me. Within seconds I felt his lubed finger probing my hole, and then without warning he thrust his cock into me.

"Ahhh!" I moaned, and he instantly pulled back.

"Are you all right, pup?" he asked, and I sensed he was about to end the scene.

"Yes, Sir!" I screamed. "Please don't stop!"

"Are you sure?" *Damn it!* I cursed myself. I just about ruined the whole scene by crying out.

"Yes, Sir! I'm sorry, Sir!"

Matt hesitated for just a moment and then slid back into me, more slowly this time. "Oh yeah," he moaned. "I love that tight ass. I love that tight boypussy!"

I cried out again; this time it was more like a moan of pleasure.

"I'm gonna fuck your hot little red ass now, boy! You want it?"

"Yes, Sir!" I screamed, my voice practically a whine.

And then he proceeded to fuck me, gradually increasing the speed. As his throbbing cock rammed deep into me I felt the constant stabbing of his movement massaging my prostate, and I feared I soon would cum.

"Oh Sir! Oh god!" I cried.

"You gonna cum, boy? You gonna cum for your Master?"

"Oh Sir! Can I cum for you please?"

"Do it, boy! Cum for me now! Shoot it! Now!"

As he continued to grind forcefully into my tight hole, I felt my body begin to tremble and I knew I could hold back no longer. "Ah, ah, ahhhh!" The orgasm washed over me and I involuntarily slumped forward as the cum fired from my raging hard-on. Matt remained within me, and I felt his body pressing against my back, surrounding me. He wrapped his arms around me and enveloped me as he himself began to convulse. Then he cried out as he released his own load deep inside me.

Within seconds he had flipped me over onto my back and was passionately kissing me. "I love you, pup! Oh fucking god, that was hot!"

I wrapped my arms around his neck and kissed him, driving my tongue into his open mouth.

And now here I was standing in the kitchen, a big wet spot on the front of my apron. I waited for Matt to finish showering, not wanting to get dressed just yet because I too had to shower when he was done. He came and kissed me goodbye, praising me for a super hot scene, and then left me alone to complete my cake decorating. As I replayed the events of the morning and my interaction with each of my three housemates, I realized just how much I loved my family.

Matt may have been merely acting out a scene when he'd called me his little housewife, but honestly, I could think of nothing more I wanted to be than exactly that!

5

Mrs. Porter was smiling broadly when she opened the door to let me in, and of course, there stood Petey the pup beside her, wagging his tail excitedly. "Oh Petey, come on in!" she greeted me. "I've been looking forward to seeing you!"

"Thank you so much for helping me the other day, Mrs. Porter."

"Will you please just call me Diane?" she asked. "It really makes me feel old being called Mrs. Porter all of the time."

"Oh, I'm sorry Mrs.—or I mean Diane. But you are Matt's mom, after all ..."

"Are you afraid he'd frown on you addressing me by my first name?" She motioned for me to come inside as we were talking.

"I doubt it, ma'am, if he knew you'd told me to do it, but simply out of respect, I'd probably always call you Mrs. Porter while he was around."

"Fair enough," she said. "You look really nice, by the way."

"Thank you, ma'am." I smiled at her. I was wearing one of the new outfits that Matt had bought me a few weeks previously. In my pocket, I had my collar, and as I looked down at Petey the pup I noticed that ours matched. If Diane was going to be present during the photo shoot, I wondered what she'd think of me wearing a dog collar. I guessed we would find out soon enough.

"You know, I really hate getting my picture taken," I confessed to her. "This whole idea actually was Drew's."

"Well I think it's a really sweet idea, and I just know Matt's gonna love it. Did he find out about the damage to his car?"

I shook my head. "No ma'am, I didn't tell him. It sort of feels like I'm lying to him, and I'm afraid that whoever did it to him is going to try to do something else. So I really kinda feel I need to let him know."

"Why don't you just tell him then, honey? I'm sure he'll realize it wasn't your fault."

"Oh, I know, Mrs.—um, Diane. I know he won't be mad at me. Well he might be a little bit mad at me now for not telling him right away, but he won't blame me for the vandalism. It's just that if I do tell him, then I will have to explain how I got the car repaired. He will know I've been talking to you."

"And you think he will be upset about you talking to me?"

"Maybe it's not my place to interfere in his relationships with his family."

"Well, as far as I'm concerned, you are a part of his family. And if you're really worried about him finding out that you talked to me, then how do you ever plan to give him the picture? He'll know you talked to me because Petey's in the picture with you."

I sighed and looked at her dejectedly. "Yes, I know you're right, and I've been thinking about all that. I have to find a way to get Matt to patch things up with his dad before I give him the picture."

"Did Matt get the job he was applying for?" she asked.

"Yes! He got the job and starts the week after next. He's very excited."

"Well I'm really glad to hear that! And it may just provide me the leverage I need with my husband."

"Really?" I asked. "What do you mean?"

"I might be able to use this to talk some sense into him. If he finds out that Matt has moved on and taken a job with his competitor, it may motivate him to bury the hatchet."

"Or it could just make him really angry!"

"Paul doesn't want to disown Matt, and he certainly doesn't want to let the company business fall into someone else's hands. He wants to hand it down to Matt; he's just being stubborn."

"And you think when he learns that Matt is going to be running another business similar to his own, that he may reconsider his decision to cut Matt off?"

"Well I think that Paul really expected that when he gave Matt an ultimatum, Matt would just drop all of this nonsense about being gay. He expected Matt to do anything he said in order to keep that job and not be disowned. When Paul sees that Matt is not about to do that but has instead moved on and gotten a job on his own, maybe Paul will wake up and see that he's about to lose his son for good."

"You know, Diane, I'm planning to make a really big celebratory dinner for Matt next week, in honor of his new job. I'd love to be able to give Matt his gift that night, and if you could talk Mr. Porter into coming with you, we could surprise him."

She smiled at me sweetly. "I think Matt is really lucky, ya know. You're such a sweetie."

Her compliment was embarrassing me, but I'd noticed she really hadn't answered my question. I'd extended the invitation, nonetheless. I wondered, though. If she and Mr. Porter did show up to our dinner party, how would Matt react? I guess it would all depend upon what Mr. Porter had to say.

At the photo studio, Blake was as hyper as I'd ever seen him. His red hair seemed like a flame as he bobbed his head excitedly while talking to us. He just was so funny that he made the perfect photographer. His subjects couldn't help but laugh at him, or at least smile. He had me cracking up, and he was also really good with Petey Pup. Obviously he'd photographed animals quite a bit, because he seemed to know just what to do to get the canine to pose the way he wanted.

Blake confessed to me when I first arrived that he didn't know whether I'd show up or not. He'd been very concerned about the way I had been so panicked earlier in the week when he'd seen me outside of the mall. I apologized profusely and assured him everything was fine. I pressed him to give me a work schedule so that I could begin working off my debt to him. He said I could start the very next day—Saturday morning.

After the photo session, Diane and I headed over to the cake decorating store. We had Petey Pup kenneled in the back of the car. It was really cool to see how excited she got when we were inside the store. Apparently cake decorating had been a hobby of hers, but it had been years since she'd done a cake.

"Hey! I have a great idea," I gushed. Suddenly I, too, was excited. "Why don't you come with me back to my apartment and help me finish Alex's cake? I can make us lunch, and it'll give you a chance to see our place."

"But what about Matt?" she asked, frowning slightly.

"His job this afternoon is to keep Alex out of the house until five o'clock. He won't be home, I promise. Drew might end up being there though. I'm not sure exactly when he's supposed to get home. He had to teach a class this morning and then do a bunch of last-minute stuff before graduation tonight."

She thought for a minute, glancing around at the piping bags, fondant, and cake pans. Finally she sighed and shrugged her shoulders simultaneously. "Why not!" she exclaimed, smiling broadly.

"Oh, we're gonna have so much fun!" Before I knew it, I was hugging her.

The frosting sheet I'd ordered of Alex's picture turned out absolutely perfect. His dark features showed up so clearly, and the picture itself was, well, sizzling hot. Alex is definitely a good lookin guy, and if I didn't have my own Master that I loved with all my heart, Alex would definitely be one I'd be interested in.

"So this is Drew's … um … boyfriend?" Diane asked.

I laughed. "Yep," I lowered my voice so as not to embarrass Diane in front of the sales clerk. "He's a hottie, isn't he?"

"Oh my god, I'll say."

On the way over to our apartment, Diane and I talked non-stop about hot guys. She admitted to me that she was deeply in love with Brad Pitt, and I confessed that I had a crush on Orlando Bloom. Somehow our conversation shifted to television and we began talking about the sitcom Will and Grace. We both thought Karen was absolutely hysterical, and without her there wouldn't really be much of a show at all. I told her even though I was gay, neither one of the gay central characters on the show were my favorite.

That comment reminded Diane of a gay friend she'd had in college. For the longest time she harbored a secret crush on him, and had hoped that one day he'd see the light and turn straight. She thought maybe if he met the right woman—

"No offense, Diane, but it really doesn't work that way. If I were older and straight I'd definitely have the hots for you. You're really attractive, but since I'm gay, there's nothing you could do to make me interested in ... well, ya know."

"Petey, you're adorable," she laughed. "Things are just a lot different now. Back then not as many gay people were out of the closet. We didn't have TV shows like Will and Grace, and people didn't know."

"People thought they had the power to turn gay people straight?" I laughed.

"Well, yeah, and actually a lot of people still think that way. A lot of churches teach that you can be cured of homosexuality."

I shook my head and made a face. "I don't wanna be cured! Even if I could change, I'd never want to. That'd mean I'd have to give up Matt."

"You really love him, huh?"

"With all my heart," I felt myself becoming overwhelmed with emotion. My eyes brimmed with tears, and Diane reached over and grasped my hand, squeezing gently.

"Well, I can see why he fell for you."

"Stop it! You're making me cry."

We both laughed as she released my hand in order to steer into our parking lot. I pointed out our building and she pulled into an empty space near the door.

The apartment was empty when we got there, and I quickly made my way to the answering machine to see if Matt had left me any messages. It was flashing so I depressed the button. Diane was a few feet behind me, just looking around and politely waiting for me. What I heard on the machine sent a terrifying chill down my spine.

"Hope you enjoyed the little present on the driver's side of your sports car, *Master!*" I knew immediately whose sarcastic voice it was. "I just wanted to leave you a little something to help you remember me by. I'll probably be going away to prison pretty soon, thanks to you. Then who're ya gonna have come over to your office and suck your cock when your little faggot boyfriend's not around? I just wanted to say, *fuck you* Matt Porter! I dominated that little wimpy bitch just like you told me to do, and what is the thanks I get? Incarceration? Prison? A fucking rap sheet? Go to hell, motherfucker, you and your dogboy both!"

I stood there staring at the machine in a state of shock and disbelief, covering my mouth with both hands in a gesture of horror. Diane was at my side, her arm around my shoulder. "Petey," she said, "who was that? Was that—?"

"Ryan," I whispered.

"He's the one who ..."

I nodded. "He's the one who assaulted me."

"Call the police!" she demanded.

"Oh my god, no!" I cried. "We can't!"

"Petey, that person is deranged. You have to call the police right now."

"Listen to me!" I cried, "Matt doesn't know about the car."

"You've gotta tell him, Petey. You've got to tell him for your own safety. For *his* safety."

I shook my head frantically. "He can't hurt Matt. Matt would kill him."

"Come here, let's sit down," she said. "You're so upset right now."

"Please Mrs. Porter, I beg you, don't call the police! Don't tell anyone about this. Let me handle it."

"Petey! I can't promise you something like that. If you won't report this, then I will. Matt's my son, and that ... lunatic ... God knows what he's capable of."

"Then just wait. Just till tomorrow. Please! Tonight after the party I'll tell Matt everything. I promise I will. I want him to hear it from me. I'll tell him about the car and about ... well ... becoming your friend. The picture. Everything."

"Petey, you're shaking," she said. "Are you all right?"

I nodded frantically. "Yeah, yeah I'm fine. Please let's try not to think about this now. We gotta get this cake done!" I jumped up and headed for the kitchen. She was right behind me.

"Okay, listen to me, Petey. Stop!" I turned to look at her, my eyes now spilling over with a steady flow of tears. "I'm gonna let you handle this, like you asked. I promise. Okay?"

"Thank you," I whispered and nodded.

"But I'm calling you tomorrow morning. If you haven't told Matt everything, I'm taking matters in my own hands. Understand?"

Again I nodded. "Yes, ma'am," I said meekly. "I'll tell him. I promise."

She walked over to me and took me in her arms. "It's only because I care about you. I don't want you getting hurt again, and I definitely don't want that crazy psycho doing anything to try to hurt Matt, either."

"I know," I said as I clung to her. "I don't want that either."

"Okay, where's that cake?"

Although the ominous threat of Ryan seemed to loom over my head the rest of the afternoon, Diane and I were able to have a lot of fun with the cake. Soon we were engrossed in the project and I'd nearly forgotten about the horrible answering machine message. I had thought I was all but done with the cake except for the photo sheet, but once Diane started working with me, I realized there were so many little extras that she knew how to do. She was absolutely great at making flowers, and soon she was teaching me some things I didn't know.

By the time we were done, it was a masterpiece.

"We've absolutely *got* to do a wedding cake together someday!" I insisted.

"Oh that'd be so fun," she agreed.

"I've always wanted to do one, but I haven't had a chance yet."

"Oh I've done my share, honey. They're a lot of work, but it's worth it in the end. They're like a work of art."

"I wish I could keep Petey Pup here for awhile ... overnight," I said.

"You can anytime," Diane said.

"But not tonight. We have the party, and plus I have to wait until after I talk to Matt ... about everything." Petey was scampering around the apartment. I'd gone and gotten him from the car. I walked over to the cupboard and retrieved a bowl. Filling it with tap water, I placed it on the kitchen floor, and Petey eagerly lapped it up.

"Wow, he must've been thirsty," Diane laughed.

"I am, too, come to think of it. Would you like an iced tea?" I asked.

"Oh honey, thank you, but I really should get going."

"I thought you were gonna stay for lunch."

"Let's do lunch sometime together, but it's already after two, and I really should get back home. Are you gonna be all right, though?"

"Oh sure," I said. "Drew should be home soon, I think. He's got to get everything ready for tonight. Graduation is at seven."

"You don't really sound okay, Petey. Maybe I should stay till Drew gets here after all."

"Oh don't be silly! Really I'm fine, and ya know, now that you mention it, I have a ton of stuff to do myself. I've gotta get Matt's suit ready for tonight, his shoes polished, his shirt ironed ... and mine too! I don't even know what I was thinking. It's already so late!"

She stared at me suspiciously and gave me a wry smile. "Oh all right. If I don't hear from you by ten tomorrow morning, I'm calling here. If nobody answers, I'm calling the police."

"Oh no, please don't worry. I'll call you, Ma'am, I promise. I'll call you by nine, okay?"

"Deal," she said. "Gimme a hug." As we embraced I realized where Matt had gotten all of his goodness. Perhaps the dominant side of him was genetically inherited from his dad, but there was no denying he'd gotten a lot of qualities from his mother as well. It truly was a privilege to now have her in my life.

"Thanks for everything," I said. "I really mean it."

"You mean everything you say, Petey," she stated matter-of-factly. "You're a very sincere person. And there is no need to thank me. I consider you both to be my boys. You know what, since you're talking to Matt tonight about everything, I'm gonna talk to Paul!" She sounded very resolute in her declaration.

I pulled back from her and smiled as I looked her in the eye.

"I'm not about to let his stubbornness keep me from my own son, not for one minute longer!"

"Good for you, Diane!" I said. "Matt would be proud of you."

"Well I'm proud of me," she said. "I'm proud of me!"

We both laughed. "I'll get Petey's leash and walk him out for you."

6

I figured out how to get the answering machine to stop
blinking without completely deleting the message. I knew that after
I told Matt everything, he was gonna want to hear it. If he decided
to contact the police, I knew they, too, would need it.

It did not really surprise me that Ryan would go psycho like
that, because I'd already seen his rage firsthand. He seemed to be
the type of guy who got really angry about things and then just
suddenly snapped. I bet he had harbored a lot of bitterness within
himself over this whole ordeal, and then, as it festered within him,
eventually it got to the point where he reflexively lashed out. I
sincerely hoped that was all it was. I couldn't really see him trying
to physically hurt Matt. That would literally be suicide. He might
decide to come after me again, though, but I knew that Matt would
protect me.

The thing that bothered me the most about his message,
though, was the comment he'd made about giving Matt blowjobs in
his office. What office was he referring to? The one at his dad's
gym, perhaps? Could there possibly be any truth to this statement,
or was it yet another of his deranged fantasies? Ryan was so
consumed with jealousy and resentment that it was altogether
possible that his twisted mind would turn fantasy into reality.
Maybe he had wanted to serve Matt so badly that he actually
started to imagine it had really happened.

If there did happen to be some truth to this comment, and I
found out that Matt had engaged in some form of sex with Ryan, I
wondered what this would mean for us. We had just come through

79

a really rough patch, and we'd managed to weather the storm. Matt seemed to have no interest at all in being with anyone else besides me. Not even chicks. To find out now that the very same person who had raped me was secretly servicing my Master sexually—that would be devastating.

I really couldn't allow myself to start worrying about all of that yet. I had enough stress to deal with already. How was I going to tactfully tell Matt that I'd gone to his mother behind his back? How was I gonna tell him I'd hidden the fact that his car was vandalized? How was I going to make him understand that I was just trying to handle everything myself and make him proud of me?

It was so stupid of me, really. I should have called Matt immediately when I saw what had been done to his car. Now the evidence was gone. I should have told him about my day from hell. Of course he'd have understood how everything could go wrong for me. I'd come practically face-to-face with Ryan! Matt wouldn't have punished me for anything, and he certainly would have been no less proud of me.

Somehow I had to just completely come clean with him. I had to bare my soul, so to speak. He might be upset with me, but I also felt that he would understand my motives. If there was anyone on the planet who truly understood my heart, it was Matt. I simply had to now do what I should have done all along. I had to trust him.

Everything was ready for our Masters when they arrived at 5:30. Drew had gotten home around three that afternoon, and he was exactly as I'd expected. Nervous! But true to character, he conducted himself in a calm and classy manner, and everything seemed to come together magically. Both Drew and I were showered and dressed already when Matt and Alex got home, so we just patiently waited for them in the living room. Drew was prattling on and on about how proud he was of Alex and how he couldn't wait to see him in his new suit, when Matt finally stepped into the room.

Immediately I was on my feet, in awe of the perfect specimen before me. "Sir," I gasped, "You look amazing!"

"You like it?" he said.

"No, Sir ... I love it!"

Matt raised his eyebrows slightly and stepped toward me. "You look pretty handsome yourself, pup," he said. Then he kissed me.

"Hey, why's there a bowl of water over there on the kitchen floor?" Matt asked, pointing toward the spot where I'd been giving Petey a drink.

"Um ..."

Alex stepped into the room before I could respond. "Hey!" Matt said. "Nice duds!"

Drew was practically in tears when he saw Alex in the suit he'd just bought. "Sir," Drew said, "I don't even know what to say ..."

While they were fawning over each other, I discreetly made my way to the kitchen and got rid of the water bowl. I checked on the cake while I was there and decided that Diane and I had really outdone ourselves. I then went into the bathroom and checked my appearance once more in the mirror. When I got back to the living room, Matt seemed to have forgotten about the water bowl, and we all readied ourselves to leave.

If you have ever attended a college graduation, you know that there is only one word which can adequately describe the ceremony: Boring! The only excitement at all was finally hearing Alex's name being called and seeing him receive his degree.

After the graduation ceremony, Matt and I drove back to the apartment and I began setting out the hors d'oeuvres. "Do you like the cake, Sir?" I asked.

"Pup, that cake is awesome! I had no idea you were that talented."

"Thank you, Sir," I said.

"Ya know, my mom used to decorate cakes. She was really good at it too, just like you."

"Really?" I said. "That's so cool."

"Yeah, I bet you'd have really liked her."

"Sir, no offense, but when you talk about her like that, it seems almost like she's … um … gone."

"Pup, I know you lost your mom and dad. It must be hard for you to understand how I can be … well, how would you say it?"

"Estranged?"

"Yeah. It must be hard for you to see this, but it really wasn't my choice. My dad is the one who disowned me."

"Maybe he'll come to his senses, Sir."

Matt shook his head. "You don't know my dad. He's very stubborn."

"And dominant, I bet," I smiled at him.

"There's a difference between being dominant and being an asshole," Matt replied.

"Oh really?" I said teasingly. "I hadn't noticed."

"You think I won't get out the spatula again? I don't care if guests are coming over or not."

For a second I was worried, thinking maybe he really interpreted my joke as serious, but then he smiled.

"Yes, there really is a difference. Maybe it just took me a little while to figure that out."

I wondered if it also had taken him awhile to figure out that it was not cool to get blowjobs in his office from other sub boys like Ryan. Then immediately I felt guilty for even allowing myself to question him this way. I wasn't going to allow thoughts of Ryan to ruin our evening, though. I'd have time to discuss it all with Matt after the reception.

There were only a handful of guests. Alex's parents and a few of his relatives were there. Drew's sister had also come. It was rather relaxed and informal, and there really were not even any graduation gifts. The gift exchange had occurred previously at the surprise party.

It was after the others had left that Matt and I presented Alex with our presents. I had picked out a titanium bracelet, which Alex seemed to love. When Matt told me to go to the hall closet and retrieve the big package from the bottom shelf, I was a bit surprised. I had known nothing about it.

When I opened the closet door, I realized that the package was nearly as tall as I was, and that all the shelves had been removed from the closet. Whatever it was, it was sitting flat on the ground. I wrapped my arms around it and tried to pull it out. It would not budge.

"Sir!" I yelled.

"Hurry up, pup!" Matt ordered, and I then dropped down to a squatting position and tried to pick it up from the bottom. It felt like it was made of lead. I could not even get it to move a centimeter.

"Sir!" I yelled back to him. "I can't get it!"

"I said hurry!" he demanded. Oh shit! What was I gonna do?

"It's too heavy for me, Sir," I said, "I can't even budge it."

"Come on, don't be a wimp," Matt yelled back at me. "We're waiting!"

Finally I walked back to end of the hallway and stood there facing my audience of three. I had my hands on my hips and stared over at them exasperatedly. "Sir, how can you expect me to move that enormous thing? It's bigger than me!"

Matt then cracked up laughing. "Come here!" he said, and I rushed over to him. "I'm teasing you. It weighs a hundred fifty pounds."

I gasped. "Geez Sir! I only weight 120!"

"You only weigh 110, and that's if you're soaking wet." He kissed me. "You wait here and I'll get it.

Matt returned a few seconds later carrying the bulky package. It was wrapped rather haphazardly in gold and white gift wrap. It looked almost like paper designed for a wedding gift. I imagined that Matt had attempted to wrap it himself, for it looked like something he might have done. With a thud, he deposited the enormous gift in the center of the living room floor.

"There ya go, bud," he said to Alex. "Open it."

We all started laughing.

"Dude, you shouldn't have!" Alex said sarcastically. "What is it, a blowup doll?"

"Yeah right ... that weighs 150 pounds!"

Alex stepped over to it and eyed it suspiciously. He walked around to the other side and continued his inspection. "Open it, for chrissakes!" Matt demanded.

Finally Alex did just that, reaching down and unceremoniously ripping off the gaudy paper. Then he just stood there and stared, suddenly realizing what it was. It was a life-size punching bag, one of those called the "Body Opponent". I think he was a bit startled, because it was actually quite an expensive gift. I'd seen them online and knew they were close to three hundred dollars.

"Dude! This is awesome!" he exclaimed.

"So you don't need to go punchin on my pup any more," Matt teased him.

At first it seemed Alex was taken aback, probably wondering how seriously Matt meant that comment, but when he saw Matt smiling, he relaxed and we all laughed.

"I've actually wanted one of these things. It's so cool. I gotta try it out!" He then assumed a combative stance, which looked rather amusing since he was still wearing his suit, and took a series of swings directly at the Body Opponent's face. *Boing-Boing-Boing-Boing-Boing!* The punching bag bobbed back and forth as he pelted it. Drew and I were both laughing as we watched our Sirs being boys.

I was a bit startled when I suddenly realized the doorbell was ringing. The other three were unfazed by it, though, and didn't even seem to notice. I got up, still chuckling as I glanced over to watch Alex once again spar with his defenseless and lifeless opponent. I turned and placed my hand on the door handle without bothering to look through the peephole, and then I pulled the door open.

My smile quickly faded and turned to an expression of shock and horror as I saw who was standing before me. It was none other than Ryan, and he was pointing a gun directly in my face.

7

The only sound in the room was the whir of the punching bag
as it bobbed back and forth until coming to a stop. I stood there
with my mouth agape, frozen in fear and unable to move. Never
before had I stared down the barrel of a gun, and it was a feeling so
surreal that it literally paralyzed me.

"Ryan!" Matt shouted, as I heard him from behind me.
Instinctively I raised both hands in the air, as you would see during
a hold-up in a movie "Put down the gun ... please."

"Shut up, motherfucker!" Ryan screamed. His voice was high-
pitched to the point of hysteria, and this made the whole situation
all the worse. He truly looked and sounded like a madman. I knew
that no one in the room but me knew about his phone message.
Nobody but me knew about what he'd done to Matt's car. Nobody
but me knew of the accusations Ryan had leveled at Matt about the
office blowjobs and the orders for him to sadistically dominate me.

"Ryan," I said nervously, trying to be calm. "I heard your
message, but Matt knows nothing about it."

"Shut up, faggot!" he screamed at me. "Shut your fuckin mouth
or I'll blow your goddamn head right off. Right here in front of your
Master!"

"No! Ryan please ... put the gun down," Matt pleaded. "Please,
we'll do anything you say."

"Damn right you will!" he said, stepping in the doorway and
kicking it closed behind him. "Faggot, you and your friends get over
there." With the gun he motioned to the sofa. "Matt, stay right the
fuck where you are."

85

I turned to look at my Master. I was terrified, mostly for him. Although Matt would surely be focused upon my safety, it was his well being I feared the most. I knew that Ryan had threatened him. I knew that Ryan blamed Matt for everything.

"Now!" Ryan screamed, and quickly Alex grabbed Drew and pulled him over to the couch, positioning his sub behind himself protectively.

"Petey, now!" Matt said. "Do as he says."

"Sir!" I cried, wanting to warn him.

"You heard me, now!" Matt repeated.

The tears were streaming down my face and my heart was beating so rapidly it seemed I could almost feel the beats within my head. I wanted so desperately to turn to Ryan and beg him not to hurt my Master. I wanted to drop to my knees and plead for him to spare my Matt. I couldn't do it, though. I couldn't say a word.

Ryan stood there pointing the gun directly at Matt as he slowly stepped closer. "Eric broke up with me today," Ryan said calmly. Then he laughed. His laughter was very cold and hollow-sounding. Demented. "He found out what I'd done to your car."

I was now beside the sofa, between where Matt was standing and where Alex and Drew were huddled together. Matt looked at Ryan with a somewhat confused expression on his face. Of course he knew nothing about the car.

"That was when I left you the message," Ryan went on.

Matt was holding his hands in the air, his palms outstretched on either side of his body. A crucifixion. "Ryan," he said in a very soothing tone, "I'm sorry, but I don't know what you're talking about."

"When I keyed your fucking car, asshole!" Ryan screamed. "At the mall! You didn't notice I'd keyed your precious car?"

"Of course I noticed," Matt replied evenly. "I had no idea it was you."

"So you didn't hear my message?"

"I got your message, Ryan. I got it loud and clear. Please put the gun down now so we can talk about this rationally."

"Rationally? Fucking rationally!" Ryan laughed again. "Did you tell your little bitch there how you were using me? Did you tell him how I'd sucked your cock right there in your office at the gym?" Ryan glared at me hatefully, then quickly returned his gaze to my Master.

"Petey knows what a slut I've been in the past. He knows I'm no longer interested in being with anyone but him."

"Oh that's fucking convenient! That's real fuckin rich, coming from the king of all whores! I guess he likes it when you treat him like a bag of shit. I guess he likes it when you treat him like he's subhuman. When you treat him the way you've treated *me!*" His voice cracked as he said the last sentence and the tears began to stream down his cheeks.

"Oh god!" he cried, "I loved you so fucking much!"

"Ryan, I'm sorry," Matt said. "Please believe me. I know how badly I treated you. I know how rotten I was to Petey ... to Tracy ... all of you. You have every right to be hurt. You have every right to be angry."

"Hurt? Angry? You stole my life from me! You stole my freedom! I'm fucking going to jail now!"

"Ryan, listen to me," Matt's voice was still calm. "You don't know that. You don't know what the outcome will be. You may not even have to do jail time."

"You're a fuckin liar!" he screamed, shaking the gun violently and inching his way even closer to Matt. "If you had your way, you'd lock me up and throw away the goddamned key."

"Please let us help you," Matt said. "Please don't do anything here you're going to regret."

This time he threw his head back as he laughed, louder and more evilly than before. "You actually think I'd regret toasting your ass right here? I'll blow your fuckin brains out right now. Right here in front of your little family, and I swear to god I'll never for one single second regret it!

"When you called me that day, asking me to spend the day with your 'pup,' you told me the whole scene was a way to discipline him. You made it so clear. You wanted it to be his punishment!"

"I wanted you to dominate him, not *rape* him!" Matt was starting to lose his cool, and I was terrified of the potential consequences.

It was as if Ryan didn't even hear what Matt had just said, though, and he continued, "You led me to believe you would fuck me ... make love to me."

"Ryan, I never said that! I would *never* say that, and I'd never do that!"

"Liar!" he screamed. "Shut up! Lies, lies, lies! Shut the fuck up!"

He was now sobbing as he held the gun with both hands, trying to steady his aim.

"All you've ever done is lie to me. You made me believe you might someday love me. You always hinted at it. You always led me on!"

Matt looked down at the floor, hanging his head. "Yes, Ryan ... I did lead you on," he confessed.

"How can you be so cruel? How can you hurt people the way you do?"

"Please Ryan, please let me make it up to you. Please ..."

I stood there watching my Master being humbled, and could do nothing to stop it. All I could do was pray that we all made it out of this horrible nightmare alive. I placed my hands over my face and cried, trembling involuntarily.

"Ryan, put the gun down," Matt repeated. "Please put the gun down now before someone gets hurt."

"Someone *is* gonna get hurt! Someone is gonna pay!" Ryan yelled at Matt. "You think you can go on your whole life using people the way you do, and never have to pay for it?"

"I already have paid a very dear price," Matt said. "I lost the trust of the only person I ever loved, and I lost my own baby." It was all coming out now. Matt was admitting to the abortion for the first time. "I lost my parents and my family. I got what I deserved ..."

"But you didn't lose your freedom! You still have him! You still have your dogboy."

"God knows why ..." Matt said. "God only fucking knows why I still have my pup."

"Your *pup!*" Ryan sneered. "You make me sick!" The look in his eyes was that of a madman, and I knew he was seconds away from going right over the edge. He was about to pull the trigger!

Without warning, I felt a powerful force shoving me downwards, knocking me to the floor. It was Drew as he lunged himself forward. He was hurling himself directly at Ryan, attempting to overpower him. It almost seemed to be in slow motion, as I screamed and craned my neck to look up at my best friend as he reached for the gun.

The sound was deafening—a single, explosive peal that ripped straight through my soul. Drew had been shot.

8

Drew was gone. They'd taken him away, but none of the rest of us were allowed to leave.

"I'm not waiting here!" Alex screamed. "My partner is in the fucking emergency room, and you want me to stay here to answer your questions. I need to be with him." He was talking to Detective Murray.

"Alex," he said calmly, "I'm so sorry. Listen to me. Calm down, because you're not gonna do Drew any good in your current state. I don't need you to answer any questions now, but I want you to wait and let an officer drive you over to the hospital."

"I'm not waiting!" he said again. "If I'm finally free to go, I'm outta here."

"Please Alex!" Matt urged him. "Please don't take off right now the way you are. Please let someone drive you."

Alex turned and glared at Matt. "Don't tell me what to do. Don't ever fuckin tell me what to do again!" He was pointing his finger threateningly at Matt.

"I'll drive you, Sir," a female officer offered. She'd been standing behind Detective Murray.

"Thank you, Tina," Rick said. "Alex, we'll contact you later to get your statement. Go be with Drew."

Alex nodded. "Let's go ... please."

Matt was standing beside me, pulling me against him. The strength of his grip was so intensely fierce that it almost smothered me. I wrapped my arm around his back and placed my other hand on his chest. I was still trembling and intermittently weeping.

Judging by Alex's response to Matt, I feared that Alex somehow blamed him for what had happened to Drew. It was easy enough to see how he could have this perception. Alex did not know that I was actually the one to blame. I could have prevented the whole incident had I just been honest with Matt about everything.

I remembered how I'd talked Matt out of calling the police after I'd seen Ryan earlier in the week. Even though I suspected that Ryan was the culprit who'd vandalized Matt's car, I never mentioned it. Even after I had listened to that horrible message that Ryan had left on the machine, I still did not immediately tell my Master.

I hadn't told Matt about all that had happened that day I was at the mall simply because I wanted him to be proud of me. I hadn't told him about the car because I didn't want him to think I'd betrayed him by contacting his mother behind his back. I had delayed telling him about the answering machine message because I wanted nothing to interfere with the party, and I felt I would have a better chance of making him understand my motives once we were finally alone in the privacy of our room.

But those motives now did not count for shit. Drew may be dead, and if so, what good were my intentions?

When the gun went off, Drew was directly in front of Ryan. The bullet went straight through Drew's chest. He was lunging at Ryan when it happened, and as his body slammed into Ryan, they both toppled to the ground and the gun flew from Ryan's hand. Immediately Matt and Alex were on top of them. Alex had Drew in his arms, and Matt had Ryan pinned.

Ryan, who only seconds before had been wailing like a banshee, was now utterly silent. He did not struggle against Matt, but merely lay there in a catatonic state. Silent tears streamed down his cheeks, but he didn't utter a word.

Drew was still conscious, and as Alex held him in his arms he repeatedly declared his love for his Master. I rushed over to them, reaching for my best friend, but Matt sternly interrupted me. "Petey, call 9-1-1!" he demanded.

I was hysterical on the phone, screaming for them to send help immediately. "My friend's been shot!" I cried. It was so maddening because it seemed all they wanted to do was ask a bunch of questions. I wanted to scream at them to shut the fuck up and just send help.

What broke my heart more than anything was hearing Drew gasp, trying to breathe. He cried out, "Is Petey okay?" Oh my god, how could he be thinking of me at a time like that? My Drew! My beautiful Drew!

There had never been anyone in my life who was as close to me as Drew. He knew me inside and out. He gave me support, advice, guidance, reassurance, and unconditional love. In many ways he'd been a mentor, teaching me to be patient and trust the leadership of my Master. He was extremely loyal and dedicated both to his Master and to all those he loved. Even when Matt had punched Alex, Drew did not show any disrespect toward Matt or me.

I remembered our late night pig-out sessions when I was depressed or confused. He always told me that junk food was the cure for all that ailed me ... that or a big fat cock up my ass. He said it would set the world aright once again. He was so correct on both counts.

He helped me accept things about my Master that I did not understand, explaining that it was not my role to question. He knew it was something that most of the world would never understand. Most people would have considered me extremely pathetic or naïve, or possibly even lacking in confidence to allow Matt a license to be with whomever he chose, whenever he chose. Drew reminded me that it was okay if other people did not understand. I had to make choices for myself based upon my own needs, and he realized that my nature as a sub yearned for a controlling presence like Matt within my life.

I wondered if Drew ever suspected that things would change the way they had. All I had ever dreamed of was that my Master would love me half as much as I loved him, and now here we were at a point where Matt was publicly declaring his love for me and apologizing for his infidelity.

It had been Drew who'd initially sensed Ryan's instability. Drew had never liked or trusted Ryan, and it was all he could do to hold himself back from literally throttling Ryan. Drew had known all along that Ryan told lies. He'd sensed that Ryan had selfish and misguided motives. Drew seemed to be an even keener judge of character than either of our Masters.

There had been four of us in that room facing the barrel of a loaded gun, but only Drew had had the courage to step forward and take action. Only Drew had risked his life to save my Master. In this valiant act of self-sacrifice, he may have literally given his life. He'd been shot in the chest, and none of us knew whether or not he'd even survive.

While we huddled together talking to the police detective, Ryan was escorted out in handcuffs. Matt surprised me by what he then said to Detective Murray. "He doesn't belong in jail. He seriously needs help."

"Well, that'll be for the courts to decide, I'm afraid," Rick responded.

Although I fully agreed with Matt's assessment, it truly shocked me to hear him say it. Matt had been ready to rip Ryan limb from limb only a few weeks prior when Ryan had raped me. This time Ryan had done something even worse. He'd shown up at our home and held a gun on us, then shot another member of our family, possibly killing him. It was not at a time like this that I would have expected to hear words of compassion coming from my Master's mouth.

But all four of us had seen something in Ryan that had not previously been apparent. To me it seemed that the puzzle was finally coming together. I imagined Ryan as being a very bruised and wounded soul. He had suffered a lot of hurt in his life, perhaps. He'd learned how to take care of himself by exploiting other people and manipulating them.

The fact that Ryan was sub only complicated things for him. By nature he needed control and guidance. He needed domination, yet his deceitfulness and selfishness simply repelled Masters. He was a very attractive guy, and I was sure that many Doms would love to do a scene with him, but he just wasn't relationship material.

Then he met Matt, and he realized the exact same thing that I had. Matt was everything he'd hoped for in a Master. Matt became his ideal. He fantasized about having a Master like Matt. He allowed himself to imagine actually being owned by Matt.

In the beginning Matt was cordial with Ryan. I'm not really even sure what Matt's motives were. Maybe at that time Matt did envision the possibility of fucking Ryan. Maybe he was only using Ryan to teach me a lesson about jealousy. Maybe he genuinely was concerned for Ryan's well being. Regardless of what it was, though, Matt's friendliness toward Ryan only fueled the flames of his desire for Matt. He fantasized about him all the more.

The night of the party, when we went back to Ryan's motel room with him, it was obvious that Ryan had hoped for intimacy with Matt. He wanted this so badly that he was even willing to tolerate my presence. I could see how badly it must have hurt Ryan when Matt completely rejected him. Ryan must have felt so jilted.

At some point, though, Ryan did get his wish. He did have the opportunity to sexually serve my Master. Matt's attitude about their encounter was probably identical to what he felt about the liaisons he'd had with women. Ryan was just a hole for him to use. It was just sex and nothing more. Ryan may have come to him begging to serve, and if Matt was horny at the time, he probably availed himself of the opportunity to get his rocks off.

After that, Matt again used Ryan, but this time it was an attempt to train me with a lesson in humility. He instructed Ryan to dominate me for a few hours, and his reward would be a hot four-way with Eric and myself. But it was just too much for him. The more time he spent with me, the more it irritated and frustrated him that Matt repeatedly rejected him while instead choosing me. His frustration turned to rage and he lashed out at me.

It was after this that everything began to come apart at the seams for Ryan. He was arrested and jailed. He was most likely facing a prison sentence. He then had absolutely no possibility of winning Matt's affection. He was furious and bitter, and he lashed out once again, this time vandalizing Matt's car. This desperate act was the last straw for Ryan's Master Eric, and it was when Eric finally dumped Ryan that he realized he'd lost absolutely everything.

Who knows where Ryan had gotten the gun? Who knows whether or not he'd seriously thought through his plan? Perhaps he just thought that at that point he had nothing more to lose. In his mind, all of his problems were due to Matt. His obsession with Matt was what cost him all he'd held dear. How could we ever really know what was going through his head at that point? Maybe he simply thought that if he couldn't have Matt himself, then nobody could. Maybe he felt that since Matt had hurt him so badly, Matt deserved to be hurt as well.

Ryan's actions that night were not those of a sane person. They were those of one who was desperate and lonely. While there was no denying that he was angry and bitter, above all he was just scared out of his mind.

It made no sense for me to feel any compassion for him whatsoever. He had just shot my dearest friend on earth. He had raped and beaten me. He had had sex with my Master. There was nothing about him worth forgiving. Yet oddly I did feel pity on him.

"Can we please go?" I cried. "I have to see Drew!"

"I'm sorry Petey," detective Murray said compassionately. "Why don't we go sit down for a minute so I can get your statements? I promise I'll be as brief as possible, and then we'll get you both over to the hospital."

"Can I call Drew's sister?" I pleaded.

"Yes, of course. Go ahead and make the call while I talk to Matt for a minute."

"Petey, Alex has probably already called her," Matt said. "Or if not, I'm sure he will."

"I hope so, because someone needs to be with him, too. I'm gonna call her, though, just in case. Is that okay, Sir?"

Matt placed his hand against my cheek and then leaned in to kiss my forehead. "Of course it is, pup." He then stared for a moment into my eyes. His own were brimming with tears. "God, I hope Drew is all right."

"I do too, Sir," I said softly. "I can't believe this has happened."

After calling Shari, I rejoined Matt and Rick in the living room, again curling up in the protective arms of my Master. All afternoon long I had dreaded having the inevitable conversation with him about the answering machine message and the damage to his car. I feared his reaction when I told him about contacting his mom and allowing her to help me with the dry cleaning dilemma. I'd been terrified of disappointing him. I was afraid he would be angry or even worse, hurt, that I had not trusted him enough to tell him the truth all along.

I wasn't afraid now, though. In fact, it all seemed so silly. It seemed ludicrous that I had jeopardized our safety just to save face with him. It seemed asinine that I'd been so concerned about myself.

I sat there then and told them both everything. I told the detective how it was Drew who had suggested I talk to Matt's mom. I told him how Drew thought it would be so cool for me to get a professional photo of myself and Petey Pup for Matt, and how we'd gone to her house the previous week to meet Diane. I told him about my day from hell, how I had screwed up and dropped the tie and then gotten lost in the mall. I told him about the horrendous scratch on the side of Matt's car and the fiasco at the dry cleaners. And I told him about the cake, how Diane had helped me with it, and of course about the awful message we'd discovered on the answering machine.

They asked me if I still had the message, and I got up and played it for them. When I was done, Matt again took me in his arms. "I'm so sorry," he said quietly, perhaps referring to Ryan's reference to his infidelity.

"Is this true?" Rick asked Matt. "Had you been having an affair with Ryan?"

Matt looked down at the carpeting in front of us and shook his head. "I never had an affair with him. One time I let him perform oral sex on me."

Hearing him say it like that—in such a sterile, dispassionate way—made it even worse. Was this what I did every morning to my Master—the man I loved with all my heart? Did I just "perform oral sex" on him? I felt myself again becoming overwhelmed with emotion.

"I'm sorry, Petey," Matt repeated.

It was so very odd to hear him offer such apologies. It was so out of character, coming from my Master. The entire time I'd known Matt, I had been aware of the rules. I knew it was his decision if he elected to have sex with other people. It never was something I particularly liked. In fact, I hated it. I knew it wasn't fair. It hurt me, to be honest. Yet I had allowed myself to accept it. It was something I *had* to accept, really. He was the Master, after all.

There had actually been times when I had felt turned on by the knowledge that my Master was being serviced by others. Seeing Alex that day when he'd knelt right here in this living room to "perform oral sex"... it was so hot. Having a three-way with Drew had been amazing. But in these instances, Matt had included me. There was nothing deceptive, at least not as far as his relationship with me was concerned.

It was different with Ryan though. Matt and Ryan had done the deed without me knowing a single thing about it. When Ryan had attacked me and raped me, it was after he'd sucked Matt's cock. Matt never told me. Even during the time we were separated, Matt had kept this secret.

"Did anyone else know about this sexual encounter you'd had with Connors?" the detective asked.

Matt nodded. "Yes, Drew knew about it."

His statement was a blow to my gut, and instantly I pulled away from him.

"What?" I said.

"Drew walked in on us. It was at my office at the gym. Drew was meeting me there to plan Alex's surprise party and Ryan showed up."

"What happened?" asked Rick.

"We stopped, and I made Ryan leave. He was pissed, but I didn't really care."

"So he probably felt rejected once again," Rick surmised.

"Probably," Matt concurred. "I thought of it as just sex. Ryan already had a boyfriend at that point. I already had Petey. It was nothing ... just a quick blowjob."

"Kinda like what I give you every morning when you wake up?" I asked. My voice was barely a whisper.

"No, pup. *Nothing* like that. I swear." Tears were streaming down my face. "I'm sorry," he repeated as he placed his hand on my arm. I jerked it from him and looked away.

"It doesn't matter," I said. "There isn't time for this now. All that matters is Drew. Sir, we need to get to the hospital. Please!" I looked pleadingly at the detective, who was sitting across from us.

"I just have to ask you about what happened here tonight," he said. "When Ryan showed up with the gun, did he state what his intentions were?"

"He said he was going to make me pay," Matt said. "He said he was gonna blow my fucking brains out in front of my little family."

The detective nodded his head slightly as he stared Matt right in the eye. "And he almost did."

"I know," Matt said soberly.

"Was the blowjob worth it?" he asked. *Wow*, I thought, *that remark was below the belt.*

"No," Matt responded quietly. "No, it was definitely not."

"Sir, he was crazy," I said. "It was like the day he attacked me. Like something had snapped in his brain. He was out of his mind with rage."

"Yet he was sane enough to plot Matt's demise," Rick said. "His actions clearly were premeditated."

"He didn't shoot Drew on purpose," I said. "The gun went off as Drew was tackling him."

"But if Drew hadn't done that, Matt might be dead right now."

"Drew might be dead right now!" I screamed. "Can we go?!"

The detective sighed. "Just one more thing," he said calmly. "If Drew was standing on the other side of Alex, right in front of where you're sitting now, how did he get past both you and Alex to lunge at Ryan?"

"He just bolted, Sir. He moved really fast, and it happened in like a split second. He pushed me down and rushed Ryan, all in an instant."

"Like sacking a quarterback?" Rick asked. I stared at him, confused.

"Yes, exactly," Matt responded.

"I hope he's all right," the detective said. "I'm sure there will be more questions, and I'll need to bring you in sometime within the next 24 hours to sign official statements, but for now you can go to the hospital."

"Thank you!" I said exasperatedly. "Matt, please let's go." I stood up.

"Petey ..." Matt said.

"Can we just go? I don't wanna talk about who else you're fucking. I just wanna be with Drew." Then I turned and headed for the door.

Matt's cellphone rang while we were on the way to the hospital. He answered it on speaker, "Alex, are you all right? Do you know anything yet?"

"Dude, he's okay! I mean not okay, but he's gonna make it. The bullet didn't hit any vitals, but there was a lot of bleeding. They had to do surgery right away. He's out already."

"Thank god!" Matt said. I held my hands over my mouth and sobbed, a cry of utter relief.

"Hey, I'm sorry about what I said ..."

"Man, don't fuckin worry about that shit. You were right anyway. That wasn't the time for me to be tellin ya what to do."

"I know you were only trying to help."

"Are you with Drew now?"

"They won't let me in yet. He's in recovery."

"We're almost there. You in the emergency waiting room?"

"Yeah, and Shari's here, and my parents."

"We'll be there in ten. We're so relieved ..." Matt said.

"Well it's not over yet, not by a long shot. But at least the surgery went good."

"See ya in few ... thanks for callin."

"Bye."

As Matt clicked off the phone, he reached over and grabbed hold of my hand. "Are you okay, pup?" he asked.

"Sir," I started crying. "I'm so glad he's okay!"

"Babe, why you cryin? It's okay now."

"I don't know," I sobbed. "I was just so scared! I was so afraid of losing him."

Matt squeezed my hand. "I love you so much," he whispered.

I thought about how I'd spoken so disrespectfully to him moments earlier when we were still at the apartment. I thought about how I'd snapped at my Master for the first time ever. I knew I should apologize to him for what I'd said, but I couldn't bring myself to do it. What I'd said was true. I really didn't want to hear any more about who else Matt had been fucking. Frankly, it just hurt too damned badly.

"I love you too, Sir," I replied.

"Even after all of this?" he asked, staring straight ahead as he pulled into the hospital parking entrance.

"Sir, how could I ever stop loving you? After all we've been through, how could you even think otherwise?"

"You do know that what happened with Ryan ... that was before he did what he did to you. You know that, don't you?"

I nodded. "Sir, I just wonder why you never told me. You could have told me when we were broke up. In fact, if you had, you might have actually been successful when you were trying to make me hate you."

He pulled into a parking place and sat there silently for a moment, absorbing the impact of what I'd said.

"Petey," he said, still not turning to look at me, "so much changed. In the beginning I wanted to fuck anyone I felt like. You knew this. You knew the rules, and you accepted it."

"But I didn't like it, Sir. I never liked it. I hated it. I hated worrying that you were gonna find someone you liked better than me. I hated waiting and wondering if you'd come back to me. I hated sharing you!"

"Then why did you?" he asked.

"Those were the rules. You are Master. I am sub. We both know how it works."

"Can we make new rules?" he asked.

"You, my Master, are asking me permission?" I asked, shaking my head.

"I'm making new rules," he rephrased his question into a statement.

"Yes, Sir," I said, somewhat sarcastically. "Please, Sir, tell me what they are."

He then turned and looked me directly in the eye. His own blue eyes were moist with tears. "Rule one," he said, "no more secrets."

"Yes, Sir!" I cried. "Please Sir, what is the next rule, Sir?"

He grabbed both of my hands in his own. "Rule two," his voice was beginning to crack, "no more sex with others ... unless we are both present."

"Yes, Sir!" the tears were now streaming down my cheeks. "Are there any other new rules, Sir?"

He nodded. "Rule three: if pup is hurting, afraid, worried, or angry ... he will tell his Master. Immediately."

"Sir, yes, Sir!" I said, lowering my voice to a whisper.

"And finally," he leaned in as if to kiss me, "thank you for trying to patch things up with me and my mom."

I stopped him as he attempted to kiss me, pressing my hands firmly against his chest. "But Sir, that's not a rule."

"Rule four," he said. "Pup doesn't resist his Master when Master is trying to kiss him."

He then enveloped me in his embrace and kissed me more passionately than I could ever remember. Rule four was by far my favorite.

9

"Petey, wake up." I heard the soothing voice of my Master as he gently shook me. I'd fallen asleep in a chair at the hospital waiting room. "Drew's awake. He's asking for you."

My eyes shot open and I immediately jumped to my feet. "Where? Where is he?" I asked.

Matt grabbed and held firmly to my wrist. "Calm down," he laughed. "Wake up a minute first."

I shook my head. "No ... I'm all right. Where is he? Take me to him, please."

"Okay." Matt smiled at me. "Come on."

"Sir, have you seen him?"

"Nah, been right here with you the whole time. Shari just came out to get you, and I told her I'd bring you. It's room 249."

"What time is it, Sir?"

"Bout seven in the morning."

The last thing I remembered before falling asleep was that Alex and Shari were finally allowed into Drew's room to see him. The hospital only allowed two visitors in the surgical ICU, and they were supposed to be immediate family only.

"I didn't think they'd let us see him at all," I said as we walked down the corridor together.

"Since he's asking for you, I guess they'll make an exception."

"But you're goin in to see him too, right?"

Matt shook his head. "He wants to see you alone. I'll wait outside."

I stopped walking.

"Come on, pup," he urged. "It's okay. I know how much you and Drew love each other. I'll see him when he gets out of ICU."

"I wonder if he's in a lot of pain," I said.

"Nah. He's got the good stuff, I'm sure. They're probably pumpin him full of morphine."

"Like when I ..." I remembered the last time we were here. It was when Ryan assaulted me—fractured my ribs and punctured one of my lungs.

"When you were here for your broken ribs," Matt finished my sentence for me.

"Yes, Sir. They had me on painkillers too."

Matt stopped at the end of the corridor and opened the big door that led into ICU. "I'll be right here in this waiting room." He pointed to the tiny enclave that was next to where we were standing. "It's room 249. Go on, you'll be fine."

"Yes, Sir," I said. I wanted to kiss him, but instead I reached down and squeezed his hand affectionately. "Thanks."

As I made my way into the ICU unit, it seemed so eerily quiet. The only sound was the blips and beeps of the monitors and equipment hooked up to the patients. I didn't hear any conversations or television sounds. The silence made it seem very somber and ominous.

I had to walk down a hallway and turn to my left, following the ascending room numbers until I got to 249. Cautiously I stepped inside, and there he was, lying flat on his back in the hospital bed. My precious Drew, with every imaginable cord, cable, catheter, and IV hooked up to his body. He appeared to be sleeping, his eyes closed peacefully.

I inched my way into the room, approaching the foot of his bed, and he opened his eyes. "Hey," he said. "Where have ya been?"

"Oh Drew!" I cried. "I've been right here. I was in the waiting room."

He reached out to me. "Come here," he said.

Quickly I stepped over to him and took his hand, squeezing it gently in my own. "I'm so sorry!" I said. "I'm so sorry about everything."

Drew laughed. "I should've known you'd find a way to blame yourself for everything. Why are you sorry?"

"Oh Drew, I could have stopped him. He left a message on our phone, but I didn't say anything."

Drew shook his head. "How would you know he'd be *that* psycho? It's not your fault. I'd have probably done the same thing ..."

"I was afraid it would spoil the party if I told Matt. I was planning to tell him last night, as soon as we were alone."

"Petey, are you okay?" How could Drew be worried about my well being at a time like this, right after he'd been shot and had emergency surgery?

I nodded. "I'm okay, especially now. Now that I see you and know you're gonna be okay ..."

Drew looked so very tired. His face was pale and gaunt, and his eyes looked extremely weary. I reached up and gently brushed my fingertips through his soft blond hair. In spite of his present condition, he still was so beautiful. I was trying not to become emotional, but I couldn't help myself. The tears streamed down my cheeks as I looked into the face of my dear angel.

"Funny, ain't it?" he said. "A few weeks ago it was you lyin in the hospital bed and me frantically worryin about ya. Now it's your turn to worry."

"Paybacks are a bitch," I laughed through my tears. I leaned in and gently kissed him on the forehead, hesitated, and then kissed him softly on the lips. "Drew, you're such an angel," I said.

He looked into my eyes and gave me a weak yet sincere smile. "I love you, Petey Pup."

"I love you too."

His eyes fluttered and as he began to talk, and I noticed his speech was labored. He just seemed so exhausted. "I need to talk to you," he said.

"Drew, I think you should rest first. We'll have much more time later, when you're better."

He shook his head slightly. "I feel so bad. I should have told you about seeing Matt with Ryan."

It truly amazed me that he would think about me and my feelings in the midst of his own life-threatening ordeal. "Drew, please don't even worry about that—"

"I should have told you so that you didn't have to find out the way you did."

"Drew, telling me about it then would have just hurt me." I immediately remembered my own secret which I'd kept from Drew for so long. "How can you tell someone you love so much something that is gonna devastate them?"

"I think best friends shouldn't have those kinds of secrets," he continued. "Best friends are honest with each other."

"Best friends do whatever they have to in order to protect each other," I said. "If I'd have known about what Ryan did with Matt, I probably would have lost Matt forever. I wasn't ready to hear that, and you saw how Matt was ..."

"I felt so bad for him," Drew said. "I really believe he loves you with his whole heart."

"I do too, and I love him the same way."

"So can you forgive him? It's always been so hard for you to accept ..." Drew pulled his legs up slightly and wrapped his arms around his torso as he stifled a cough. He winced painfully, and I stepped in closer, wishing there was something I could do. "Oh god that hurts!" he cried, and I nearly cried just looking at him.

"Baby," I said to him softy, "please let's just wait. We can talk ..."

"I'm okay," he said. "It's just a fuckin bitch when I cough." He hesitated a few seconds longer and then seemed to relax. "I know it was so hard for you when Matt was seeing that girl."

"Tracy," I said.

"Yeah, her." He rolled his eyes. "And I knew it would be even worse for you to find out about Ryan."

"But Drew," I said, "I already worked that out. I knew I had to accept the rules. I knew I had to deal with it. Matt is my Master, and it's his decision if he wants to be with someone else."

Drew smiled. "It sucks, doesn't it?"

"Well, those are the old rules," I smiled at him. "Matt made a new set of rules last night."

"Oh really?"

"No more secrets. No more sex with other people ... unless we are both involved. No more pretending everything's all right when it's not."

"Matt made those rules?" Drew asked. "Wow."

"I guess he could always change them later if he wanted to, but I believe that he wants it this way long term."

Drew nodded. "He does. He definitely does."

"He's just so romantic with me now ..."

"Do you like it?" he asked.

"Oh my god, of course I do. Wouldn't you?"

"Oh yeah, definitely. I love when Alex is that way. But ..."

I looked at Drew, perplexed, "But what?"

"Well the romance is beautiful, and as a pup I know how much you need that. You need more than just that, though."

"Oh he does give me more than just that. He still is very dominant. You should have seen how kinky he was the other morning."

"Well that's cool. I'm glad to hear it. I was starting to get worried."

"You mean because of how he was that day with the pillow fight? Drew, honest he was just so stressed ..."

"Nah. I just mean in general. It seems to me he's sort of gun shy." He paused for a second and smiled. "No pun intended."

I laughed. "Yeah, I think we all are gonna be gun shy for awhile now."

"Don't make me laugh, Petey. It hurts too much." He smiled up at me affectionately. "After all that happened to you, he may be a overly protective of you. He may be a little bit hesitant to dominate you the way he really wants to ... or the way you really need him to."

"I guess that would make sense. He does seem to be a lot less strict with me. I just thought it was because I was being so much better of a sub." I laughed, making sure he understood my remark was sarcastic.

"Petey, you *are* a good sub. You're an awesome sub. But let me explain something to you, okay?" I nodded. "This is just my opinion.

"Ya know how it was when you first met Matt, before you even knew what a sub was?"

"Sure, I remember."

"Remember how he helped you see who you really were? He showed you what it was that you truly needed."

"Exactly," I agreed. "He seemed to know me better than I knew myself."

"Well I think maybe the roles are starting to reverse. I think he may be starting to forget your true natures. He's so worried about protecting you, that he's forgetting how much you need his control and domination."

"But his protectiveness is a form of domination, isn't it?"

He nodded. "It is, but ..."

"Drew, I know what you mean. It's obvious that Matt has changed. I always thought that if he really did change and wasn't so arrogant, I might not be as attracted to him. I was drawn to him in the beginning because of the way he was. His confidence and assertiveness ...

"But now I think that as I've seen him change, I actually love him even more."

"We all change," Drew admitted. "And many of the changes you've seen in your Master have simply been due to the fact that he's matured. All of this drama and bullshit you two have gone through has actually helped him."

"So honey, what's the problem then? Why should I worry about him changing if I like the changes and if it's all just a part of becoming more mature?"

"Hopefully there *is* no problem," Drew said. "But if you do notice that he's starting to forget he's your Master, then you might wanna do something about it."

I looked at my best friend skeptically. Maybe the morphine was affecting his brain. "Drew, what could *I* do about it?"

"Well, when he helped you see who you really were as a sub, he didn't really change who you were. You were a sub all along; you just didn't realize it."

"True," I agreed.

"You will always be sub, and he will always be Dom. It's your nature. But just as he had to awaken the sub within you before you were able to realize your true identity, you, too, might have to reawaken the Dom in him."

He was starting to confuse me. "Drew, I don't have that kind of power."

He smiled at me and looked me in the eye. "Petey Pup, yes you do!"

"He's probably gonna have to have another surgery later. The bullet went straight through his shoulder," Alex explained in the hospital cafeteria. "It's just a miracle, ya know. He would be dead right now if ..."

"But he's not," Matt said. "He's gonna be fine."

"That detective is supposed to be coming around today to talk to me. I don't know what to tell him."

"What a ya mean?" Matt asked.

"Well, Drew really surprised me. He actually feels sorry for that motherfucker Ryan."

Matt just stared at Alex for a moment without responding. "Yeah, that is kinda surprising."

"I hope he rots in jail!" Alex said. "He almost killed Drew."

"And Matt," I added. "His goal actually was to kill Matt."

"That kid's messed up," Matt said. "I think we all see that now."

"And he raped Petey!" Alex lowered his voice and looked over at me as he spoke. "Sorry, Petey," he said, looking around to see if anyone had overheard.

"The things he's done are horrible, Sir," I said, "but I think Drew probably finally understood why he was so crazy. When we saw him like that last night, it all sort of made sense."

"Well ya know, it's not my decision what they do with Ryan. And I really don't give a fuck whether he rots in jail or goes to a nuthouse so long as they keep him away from my boy."

"I know what ya mean," Matt said. "I'll kill him if he ever comes near Petey again."

Alex took a swig of orange juice, draining the glass. "Petey, go get another juice," he said.

"Yes, Sir," I pushed back my chair to get up.

"I'll get it, Petey," Matt said. "I wanna get something for myself anyway." I looked at him, puzzled.

"Yes, Sir," I said and leaned back in my chair. "I can get it for you, Sir ... if you want."

"Nah, relax. You want somethin pup?"

"No thank you," I smiled at him. "Just you."

He ruffled my hair affectionately before heading over to the vending tables. When he was gone, I looked over at Alex. "Sir, I wonder why Matt wouldn't let me wait on him."

He shrugged. "Probably doesn't know what he wants exactly. Needs to check it out."

"Oh, okay ..." I said.

While Drew remained in ICU, we were only allowed to see him for a few minutes each hour. Matt told me he wanted me to go home to get some sleep, but I didn't want to leave the hospital. "Sir, what if Drew asks for me again?"

"Then Alex or Shari can call, and I'll bring you right over." I frowned. "Don't worry, we'll come back later. I promise."

"I have to call Blake, Sir." I'm supposed to work for him today at the mall."

"We can stop over there, and I'll just pay him for the picture. You don't need to work for him."

"But it was a deal, Sir. And if you pay for it then it won't be a gift from me ..."

"You are gift to me already. Don't need anything else."

"Sir!" I whined. "Please let me do it. It's a way for me to do something nice for you without having to spend any money ..."

"You already have your other job, and you have your responsibilities at home. That's enough."

"I don't have to do it right now. I'm sure Blake will understand that I have to reschedule ..."

"Dammit Petey! Stop arguing with me. You heard what I said."

I gulped as I stared up at him, then immediately looked down. "Yes, Sir, I'm sorry."

I guessed maybe Drew was wrong about Matt forgetting he was Dom. There was no question from his tone with me that he was still in charge.

It was already 10:30 when we got back to the apartment. Alex refused to leave the hospital as long as Drew was still in ICU, but the prognosis was that he'd be in a regular ward by the end of the day. Matt assured Alex that we'd stay with Drew so he could come home to sleep once Drew got placed in a regular hospital room.

The answering machine was flashing when we walked in, and immediately I felt a wave of panic rush over me. Then I remembered where Ryan was—safely in custody. Matt walked over and depressed the button to play back the message.

"Matt, this is your mom. I'm not sure if you know this by now, but I've been talking to your ... um ... partner. Petey. I hope I'm not getting him in trouble by telling you this. He was supposed to tell you himself last night and then call me this morning ...

"Anyway, your father wants to talk to you. We'd like to have you and Petey over for dinner one evening this week. Call me back to confirm ... please. I love you honey. Bye."

"Darn it!" I said. "I completely forgot I was supposed to call her."

"You wanna go to dinner at my folks house?" he asked me as he turned around.

"Of course, Sir. You know I will go anywhere with you."

"Not what I asked," he said.

"Yes, Sir," I replied, acknowledging his correction. "I would be honored to go with you. I'd like it very much."

"Come 'ere," he said. "Ya know I ought to beat your ass for calling my mom behind my back."

"Yes, Sir," I said, looking down at my Master's feet.

"But that wouldn't be much of a punishment now, would it?"

I grinned as I continued to look down, maintaining my submissive posture. "No, Sir, I guess not. I'll go get the spatula again if you'd like, Sir."

He grabbed me by the shoulders and pulled me into his embrace. "I know exactly what you need," he said, "and it ain't the spatula."

"Oh really?" I said. "You seem to always know just what I need, Sir."

"You need to be tied up and tickle-tortured ... for hours."

I pulled back and looked up at him fearfully. "I do?" I asked innocently. I remembered the last time he did that to me, and it was indeed torture.

"Or ..." he seemed to be thinking, "maybe I need to try out those nipple clamps on ya."

"Nipple clamps?" I said. He spun me around so my back was against his chest.

"Yeah," he whispered in my ear. "Nipple clamps." He then reached up with both hands and found my nubs, tweaking them playfully. As he squeezed them between his fingers, I squirmed just a little. It was when he twisted them both at the same time that I first realized how sensitive they were.

"Ouch!" I cried.

He laughed. "Ouch? Wait'll you feel the actual clamps."

"Is that what you're gonna do to me, Sir? As a punishment?"

He whispered in my ear again. "Whenever you're ready to endure a little pain for your Master."

I thought about it for a second. "I'm ready, Sir."

He wrapped his arms around me and squeezed. I felt his hard-on pressing against my back. "Soon," he said. "When everything's back to normal.

"Right now I gotta call my mom back. You gotta get in the shower and then get some sleep."

"I don't want sleep," I confessed. "I want nipple clamps."

He laughed. "Get in the shower, boy," he ordered. "And don't use all the hot water. I'll be there in a minute."

"Yes, Sir!" I said and headed for the bathroom.

I immediately hurried to the bathroom but deliberately dallied once in there. I wanted to make sure I wasn't done with my shower before Matt was ready to join me. I was just stepping under the spray of warm water when I heard the door behind me. Then I felt his naked body against my own, his strong arms enveloping me. I felt the tickly scratchiness of his whiskers against my sensitive neck as he kissed me from behind.

"Tuesday," he whispered, "we're goin to my parents' for dinner."

"I'm so happy, Sir," I said, turning toward him with a bar of soap in hand, ready to lather his chest. I became distracted, though, when his lips met mine. He took the soap from my hand and lathered me instead.

I stood there, relaxed, as he gently rubbed the soap bar across my smooth, naked body. Beginning at my shoulders and using small circular movements, he slid the slippery bar back and forth, inching his way downward.

"Sir ..." I whispered. "Will you let me clean you?" I knew the routine, for we'd done it dozens of times before. It was my job to clean my Master's body and to worship every inch of it while in the process.

"Shh ..." he said, and continued. "Just relax, pup." I closed my eyes, and he guided me into his embrace, pulling my body next to his. My back was against his chest, in my favorite, sheltered position. I loved feeling my Master's arms surround me. With the soap bar still in his hand he rubbed the sides of my torso, my hips, my obliques. I felt his fingertips brush against the tight round globes of my butt, carefully parting them in order to clean me. He made no attempt to enter, though, and soon those fingers made their way to the other side of me, and I felt them dance teasingly across my hardness.

I moaned and squirmed as he playfully and rapidly moved his fingers back and forth under my ball sac. "Sir!" I cried. "Oh please ... you really are tickle-torturing me!"

His response was merely a moan. He sounded hungry, almost as if he were growling. I heard the bar of soap fall to the floor, and then with his arms around me, he used one hand to cup my balls; the other he wrapped around my hard-on. He fisted my shaft, which was now throbbing wickedly in response to his touch.

"Sir!" I cried. "I need you inside me."

He pressed his face against my cheek and softly whispered in my ear. "No ... not this time."

I was confused, wondering if he was simply playing with me, starting a scene where I was expected to beg, but what he did next told me otherwise. Matt slid himself down to a crouching position as he spun me around to face him. Within an instant it was I inside of him as his mouth enveloped my throbbing cock.

"Ohhh ..." I moaned breathily. "Oh Sir!" I steadied myself by grabbing my Master's shoulders. Feeling weak in the knees, I almost thought I'd crumple in a heap onto the wet tile beneath my feet. "Please, Sir!" I gasped. "Please ... no."

He backed off momentarily, but merely to shush me. "Shh," he said. "Let your Master please you ... just enjoy."

Tears began to flow down my face, though I doubt he noticed. I was already very wet, and my Master was very busy at the moment. It was only the third time that I'd ever felt a mouth around my cock, and this time it was the most heavenly experience of my life. "Oh god!" I screamed. "Oh Matt!"

My weak knees finally gave out when I erupted, and my entire body trembled involuntarily. My Master was there to embrace me, steadying me against his own hard body. I then clung to him while he lathered himself, and we proceeded to shampoo our hair. He didn't allow me to serve him, though. "Not this time ... later," he whispered.

Matt then toweled me dry and carried me, still naked, to the bedroom. We spooned with each other as I dozed contentedly into a state of restful sleep in my Master's arms.

10

It was late that afternoon when I woke up, and I was confused about the time. I looked over at the clock on the bedside stand and saw it was 4:15. At first I wondered if that was AM or PM, but realized it was daylight. I was alone, but I smelled something in the kitchen. Could Matt actually be cooking?

Crawling out of bed, I slipped into a T-shirt and some shorts. My hair was a catastrophe, since I had fallen asleep while it was still wet. One glance at myself in the full-length closet mirror made me shudder. "Oh boy," I mumbled to myself.

I turned when I heard my Master's voice. "Morning, beautiful," he said.

I laughed in spite of myself, and then took in the sight of him. He truly was the epitome of beauty, and immediately I moved into his waiting arms. "How do you feel?" he asked.

"I feel like a bed-head," I complained.

"No, you look like bed-head cause you just rolled out of bed, but you're still beautiful.

"Mmm," I said as I inhaled his clean scent. "Sir, have you been cooking?"

He laughed. "Nah, you wouldn't wanna eat if I'd been cooking. You hungry? I got us a pizza."

"Famished," I admitted, "but don't you need me to do something for you first?"

"Let's eat first," he smiled down at me. "You can 'do something' for me afterwards. We'll call it dessert."

"Yum!" I giggled. "Let me pee first, please ... then I'll be right there."

Matt didn't wait for me to get done in the bathroom before he started eating. When I got out to the dining room, he was already on his second piece. With his mouth still full, he began to speak, "I called that portrait studio. We're gonna be passing out those flyers next Friday. You don't work at the bookstore that day, do you?"

I looked at him, astonished. "Sir, what did you just say?" I asked.

"Sorry," he said, pointing at his over-stuffed mouth. Apparently he thought I hadn't understood him cause he was chewing and talking at the same time. He quickly swallowed and then repeated himself. "I said, do you work Friday? I scheduled a time that day for us to pass out flyers at the mall."

My mouth dropped open. "Sir ... why?"

"You said you wanted to do it, didn't ya? You said a deal's a deal."

"Sir, I said that *I* wanted to do it. By myself, not with you."

"I see how ya are," he laughed. "Too bad, you're stuck with me." He took another bite.

Finding myself all-the-more confused and irritated, I just stood there with my hands on my hips, staring at him. He grinned at me. "Cute when you do that ..."

"Sir!" I complained. "The portrait is my gift to you. If you work for it, then how is it a gift?"

"You said you didn't want me payin for it. I don't want you at that mall working by yourself, not after what happened to you last time. We're doin it together."

"But Sir, *you* can't be working at the mall like that, passing out flyers!"

"I think I'm capable of passing out flyers to a bunch of mall rats. It doesn't exactly take a rocket scientist to learn that kinda job."

"I didn't mean you weren't capable of doing the job. It's just so ..."

"Beneath me?" he laughed.

"Well ..." I sighed. "I just can't picture you doin something like that."

"We'll have fun," he assured me. "We'll make a contest out of it. If you can sign up more customers than me, I won't paddle your ass."

"That's supposed to be an incentive?" I laughed. "I forfeit right now."

"Good point." He smiled. "Eat some pizza and quit tryin to start arguments with your Master."

"Can I kiss you first?" I asked.

"Real quick ..." I rushed over and gave him a peck on his tomatoey lips.

"You taste like pepperoni," I teased.

"You taste like pup."

"Can I please just skip right to dessert, Sir?"

"Sit down and eat," he scolded.

"Yes, Sir," I slid into the chair next to him and grinned as I grabbed a big slice and stuffed some in my smiling mouth.

Alex looked like the wrath of God when we walked into the hospital room. "Dude, you need to get some sleep," Matt told him.

"Fuck, I'm beat," he admitted. Nodding at Drew, he said, "He's a lot better." I looked over at my angel, sleeping there peacefully. "They say he'll be out in a few days."

"Has he complained about wanting a cigarette yet, Sir?" I asked.

Alex nodded and gave me a half-hearted grin. He really did look exhausted. "Yeah, he was whining bout that."

"That's a good sign ... I think."

"Maybe I should just make him quit. Now would be a good time."

Matt shrugged. "Long as he doesn't think of it as a punishment. What he did for us was pretty damned courageous. He's a hero, ya know."

As I watched Alex stare at his sleeping beauty on the bed in front of us, I thought for a second that he might start crying. "Yeah, you're right. He's my hero."

Drew's eyes fluttered a little and slowly opened. "I heard that, Sir," he said. Alex walked over and placed his hand gently against Drew's forehead. "It's true," he whispered. You're my little hero."

Drew smiled up at him, tears in his own eyes. Alex leaned in and gently kissed him.

"Get a room!" Matt teased.

"Fuck you, man," Alex retorted. "Now you know what we have to put up with. You mackin all over Petey all the time."

Matt laughed. "Seriously, dude, go home and get some sleep. Petey and I will stay with Drew. We can stay all night if we need to. We already slept."

"Shari's supposed to be coming back too."

"You guys, I'm okay. Nothin's gonna happen to me here in the hospital. You don't have to stay with me every minute."

"I'm not leaving you alone," I said.

"That's right," Alex said. "So you just shut your mouth, mister." Drew smiled affectionately at his Master.

"Sir," I said, "how's Alex getting home?"

Matt looked at me, an expression of realization on his face. "That's right, Alex doesn't have his car. I'll drive him. You can stay here with Drew."

"Yes, Sir," I agreed.

"Come on, Alex," Matt said. "You stink and need a shower. And ya need some sleep."

Alex rolled his eyes. "Ya know, I don't even give a fuck what I smell like. You're right, I'm dead." Matt put his arm around his best friend.

"Let's go."

"Go home, Sir," Drew said. "You do look really tired."

"I love you, Drew," he said.

"I love you too, Sir," Drew whispered. They kissed once more before Alex and Matt left.

"I'm so glad you're out of ICU," I said to my friend.

"And I got a private room, too ... thank God."

"Does your chest hurt?" I asked as I stepped closer to the bed.

"Oh, only when I think about it. Thanks for reminding me," he laughed.

"Sorry!" I said, laughing myself.

"Nah, it's okay. If I try to lift my arm, it hurts like a mother."

I didn't want to tell him Alex said he'd need another surgery. I pulled a chair up beside the bed and sat down. "You need anything, Drew? Some water?"

"I need a smoke," he said. Oh brother! I knew he was gonna say that.

"You know, I heard they have these patches you can wear for when you are trying to quit smoking. They take away the craving ..."

"They don't work for shit!" Drew said. "I've tried them."

"I'm sorry," I said. "I can't get you cigarettes, but maybe something else? Candy or something maybe. Something to stick in your mouth?"

"All I wanna stick in my mouth just walked out that door," he said.

"No kidding!" I agreed. "For me, too. Actually I just got done doing that before we came."

"You just blew Matt? Man, I wish I was out of this hospital ... after the things Alex said to me, I would give anything to blow him right now."

"Oh my god, Drew, you're not gonna believe what Matt did last night ... or actually I mean this morning. It was before we went to bed."

"What?" Drew asked.

"He gave me head in the shower!"

"Are you serious? Wow!"

"Does Alex do that?" I asked. "Does he suck you?"

Drew nodded. "He has before. Not usually. He jacks me off most of the time, if he wants to make me cum."

"I was thinking about what you told me—that whole reawakening thing."

"You think Matt's getting too soft?"

I shook my head. "I don't know. Not really. He's still strict, but he did something else that really blew my mind."

"Tell me," Drew said, shifting slightly to see me better.

"Do you need a pillow or something behind you ... so you can sit up more?"

"Can you find that remote thingy? I just wanna raise up the head of this bed."

"Here it is," I said. It happened to be sitting on the bed right in front of me. I depressed the button and adjusted the hospital bed.

"That's better. Tell me what he did."

"Okay, this morning, when you were still in ICU, we were down at the cafeteria. Alex told me to get him another orange juice, but Matt said no. He said he'd get it for him instead, and then Matt offered to get me one too."

"And ...?"

"And don't you think that's odd? Why would Matt want to wait on me like that, especially in public?"

"What did Alex say?" asked Drew.

"He just kinda blew it off, said Matt probably wanted to check out the selection himself."

"I kinda doubt that," Drew speculated. "I'm guessing that it is one of two possibilities."

"What?" I asked, leaning into him.

"One, he might be feeling a little bit guilty about Ryan, and so he's trying to make it up to you. Or two, he really is getting soft. I think it is a little weird that he'd do that."

"Maybe there's a third possibility," I said.

"What?" he asked.

"Maybe Matt is just a nice guy, and sometimes nice guys do nice things, even if they are Masters."

"But do you want that? Do you want him being a nice guy all the time?"

"I kinda liked it," I admitted. "Right after that he was strict again though. He said I couldn't work at the mall. When I tried arguing about it he scolded me."

"Well, the important question is, is this kinder and gentler Matt gonna start going soft in the bedroom … um… so to speak."

I thought about it for a second, then responded. "Well what he did this morning—when he blew me in the shower—you might think that was kinda soft of him, but actually he still was being dominant.

"And then just now when I blew him, he was aggressive like always."

"So what are you worried about then?"

I shrugged. "I don't know. It seems like I should be worried, but really I'm not. I like him even better, I think. I love him more every single day."

Drew raised his eyebrows. "Before ya know it, you two are gonna have an equal relationship. Just like Cam said."

I scowled at my best friend. "Drew, can you honestly look at Matt and me and say our relationship is equal? It will never be an equal relationship. He's always gonna be my Master."

"I was teasing," Drew said, "but it seems I might've struck a nerve, huh?"

"Don't you think it's normal, if two people love each other the way Matt and I do, that they would naturally become more affectionate with each other? Even though he's my Master, that doesn't mean that he has to be mean and aggressive all the time."

"What about when you need the control?" he said. He reached beside him to pick up a Styrofoam cup of water and sipped from its straw.

"He's still definitely in control. You know he bought nipple clamps for us to use?"

"Oh my god! I don't even wanna talk about those things."

"Why?" I said, suddenly worried.

"Petey, those things hurt like a bastard."

I grinned. "Really?"

"Really!" he said. "Maybe you're right. Maybe he's not going soft."

"Well he hasn't used them yet," I said.

"All I have to say is, it's a good thing you have a safe word now."

I smiled to myself as I thought about it. "Yeah ... although I doubt I'll ever use it. I trust him with all my heart."

"I know ya do, Petey Pup. I know you totally love him."

"Forever ..."

"You sure you wanna go to work tonight, pup?" Matt asked me Sunday afternoon. "It's been a rough weekend for you. Maybe you should call in and take the night off."

"Sir, are you ordering me to do that?" I asked.

He shook his head. "Nah. It's your call. Just wanna make sure you're okay; that's all."

"I'm okay, Sir," I said, "and I wanna work. Plus it wouldn't be fair to do that to Mr. Bartlett at the last minute."

"After school starts next semester, I don't want you working at all," he said.

I looked at him dejectedly. "But Sir, I love my job."

"Well, there'll be plenty of time between now and then to talk about it."

"You really do think of me as your housewife, Sir," I said, smiling broadly.

"My little housewife bitch," he clarified.

"Okay, I'm getting the spatula now, Sir." We both laughed.

"You're way too cute to be a housewife," he said. "House *boy* maybe."

We were sitting in the living room, Matt in the recliner and me on the floor between his legs. He ran his fingers affectionately through my hair, and I turned my head to look up at him.

"I'll make you dinner before I leave for work, Sir," I said. "Whatever you want."

"You say that as if you have a choice," he grinned.

"I choose to be your houseboy every day of my life, Sir."

"Good answer," he said.

"Well, what do you want Sir ... for dinner, I mean."

"Spaghetti," he said decidedly.

"Yes, Sir," I said, "spaghetti it is." I turned around and shifted to a kneeling position as I looked up at him. "I need to run over to the market real quick."

"Well, just make something else then. If you don't have stuff for spaghetti, no need to go out to the store."

"Sir, we live a block from the store. It's no big deal. I'll just ride my bike like I always do. Plus, I wanna give my Master what he wants for his supper."

"Okay ... sounds like a plan," he nodded. "You've convinced me. Then after we eat, I have a present for you before you leave for work."

"Sir!" I said excitedly, "you're teasing me."

"Go!" he said. "Hurry up 'cause I'm gettin hungry."

I placed my hands on each of his thighs and looked up at him. "I love you, Sir," I whispered, and then I leaned in to kiss the bulge between his legs.

"You better go *now*, or you'll be busy doin something besides making dinner. Then you *will* have to call in to work."

"I'm going!" I cried, quickly kissing his crotch one more time before getting up.

As I was at the grocery store, I thought about what Matt had said regarding my job. In a way I was glad that he didn't want me working and going to school at the same time. A lot of times it really did seem to be too much, and in truth I would much rather focus on serving Matt and tending to his needs than working at the bookstore. On the other hand, I really did like my job. I was lucky in that regard. I'd found a job doing something that really suited me.

I suspected that most gay guys would not be thrilled about giving up their jobs to focus all their attention on their partners. In fact, most probably would find it extremely emasculating, but in my case it seemed to be appropriate. Matt and I didn't really have what you'd call a typical relationship. He was my Master, after all. The dynamic reminded me of how it used to be in heterosexual marriages, back before the Sexual Revolution.

It used to be that the husband was the bread-winner. He went out and earned the money for the family while the wife stayed home and took care of everything domestic. She had his dinner waiting for him when he walked through the door each night. She laid out his slippers, did his laundry, ironed his clothes. She was the one who ran the errands and shopped for the groceries. She was the housewife.

The man, on the other hand, was responsible for providing for his wife and family. He also bore the burden or responsibility for making all the decisions. He was sort of like the king of the castle, and everyone in the family deferred to him and his judgment.

Was all of this really any different than what Matt and I had? He was the king of our castle. He made the decisions. He bore the responsibility. He provided for me and protected me. I, on the other hand, cooked and cleaned for him. I ironed his clothes and did his laundry. I looked to him for guidance and depended upon him to make wise decisions.

My sister thought this type of relationship was unfair and unequal. She considered it abusive. She and Carter lived together, and they made their decisions together. If he'd ever told her to quit her job, she'd have told him in no uncertain terms to go fuck himself. Kathie loved her independence, and she couldn't understand why I didn't feel the same way. She wanted me to be just like her in this regard, and because I wasn't, she assumed I must have low self esteem.

Repeatedly Kathie had told me that I just needed to love myself. What she didn't understand, though, was that by having a Master like Matt, for the first time in my life I felt safe. I felt proud. I liked my life better, and I liked myself more. Matt had helped me develop confidence. He'd taught me to stop being ashamed of who I was, and when he told me repeatedly every day of my life how much he loved me, it just reinforced within me the fact that I was loveable.

I really wasn't asking Kathie or Cameron—or anyone else, for that matter—to embrace my lifestyle. I wasn't asking for their approval or even their understanding. I simply wanted them to respect the fact that it was my choice. They did not need to analyze why I was the way I was. They didn't need to jump to the conclusion that I must really hate myself in order to let someone else boss me around.

I wanted Matt to give me direction; I wanted it more than anything. Nothing made me happier than to be given an opportunity to please him. Did this make me weak? Did it make me insecure and dependent? Perhaps. I'll admit that I am weaker than Matt. I'm weaker physically and emotionally both. I'm definitely insecure when I'm on my own. I never really felt like I was meant to be a loner. And I will shout from the highest mountaintop that I'm dependent upon Matt. I'd have it no other way.

So yes, I guess I was all of these things that they accused me of being. But the one thing I was not, was *pathetic*. I was not pathetic or worthless or stupid. Matt reminded me constantly that I was the opposite of these adjectives. I was his pup, and he loved me!

When Matt took that spatula and paddled my ass the way he'd done, calling me his little housewife, it really turned me on. It pleased me to know that he viewed our relationship similarly to how I saw it. He liked being the "Man of the House," and I liked being his "wife". I guess that would not be something that would turn on a lot of guys, particularly not guys my age, but it was perfect for me.

As I loaded my purchases onto the conveyer belt at the market, I smiled at the cashier and handed her a coupon for my spaghetti. She observed the items I'd laid out and guessed what I was having for dinner. "Oh, spaghetti sounds so good," she said.

"Yeah, well this isn't gonna be the best I've ever made," I admitted. "If I'd known I had to make spaghetti for supper, I'd have started the sauce hours ago."

"Don't you hate that?!" she said. "I guess they think all ya gotta do is just magically whip something up at the drop of a hat."

"Tell me about it," I laughed.

"So who's the lucky guy?" she asked.

"His name's Matt," I smiled.

"I'm Denise, by the way."

"I know," I said. "You're wearing a name tag."

She laughed. "And you are ...?"

"Petey. Nice to meet you Denise."

"I think Matt's a lucky guy," she said.

"Yeah, he is," I smiled broadly. "Very lucky."

On my way home from the market, I remembered that Matt had said he was going to give me a gift when I got home. I was a little excited, because I had absolutely no idea what it was. I loved those kinds of presents. Total surprise.

Not wanting to say anything about the gift or let my Master know I was anxious to receive it, I busied myself in the kitchen. "Sir," I shouted out to him, "do you know if Alex is gonna be here for dinner?"

"Fix him a plate, and he can eat when he gets home. Don't know how long he's gonna be at the hospital."

"Yes, Sir," I said.

It was four o'clock when I put dinner on the table. I didn't have to be at work until six. I was scheduled six till midnight. I wasn't even seated at the table when Matt began shoveling the food into his mouth. "Oh my god, Petey, I have no idea how you learned to cook like this."

I grinned at him. "Thank you, Sir. I like cooking for you. I love it, actually."

"But I swear I'm not gonna sit around getting fat. I can see how easy that would be with someone like you cooking for me."

"You're gonna be running a gym, Sir. I can't see you ever being out of shape."

"You, on the other hand, should eat more. Look at the size of that portion. A baby eats more than that."

"Sir! If I took more than that, I'd blow up!"

"Guess it's my job to make sure you get enough protein," he smiled evilly.

"Can I have some, Sir?"

"Before you leave for work, definitely."

"Sir, do you want me just to take my bike to work?"

"Don't be silly. It'll be dark when you get out."

"I'm used to it, Sir. I always rode my bike to work when I lived with Kathie."

"I'll drive ya and pick ya up."

"Yes, Sir."

We sat eating in silence for the next few minutes, and I watched my Master as we did so. I loved watching him. I loved every one of his mannerisms and gestures. He was so incredibly masculine. Sometimes it just felt like I should be pinching myself because surely this was a dream. How could a guy like that be my Master?

Without looking at me, Matt spoke. "Uhh ... what're ya lookin at, pup?"

"I don't know, Sir. What do ya mean?"

"I mean why you keep starin at me?"

"'Cause ... well, 'cause I love you," I whispered.

"You do, huh?" he said.

"Yes, Sir ... with all my heart."

"Well, since you're not gonna eat, go in the bedroom and strip. Hurry up!"

"Yes, Sir!" I said, quickly pushing my chair back and scrambling to my feet.

"Don't touch the package on the bed," he said.

"Yes, Sir," I responded as I scurried to the bedroom.

I was totally naked when Matt walked in about five minutes later. I just stood there in front of our closet, looking over at the bed. The package to which Matt had made reference was not big. It was a plastic bag, actually, and whatever was in it seemed to be rather tiny.

Matt stepped up to me, standing directly in front of me. He still was fully clothed. Instinctively I bowed my head, looking down at my Master's feet. He reached down with one of his hands and cupped my balls. "You're hard, boy," he said.

"Yes, Sir," I responded quietly. I felt my face reddening.

"Why you so hard already?"

"I don't know, Sir," I whispered.

"Speak up, bitch! I can't hear you!"

"I don't know why I'm so hard, Sir!" I shouted.

"Yes you do, boy," he said, squeezing my dick with his other hand.

"Because I'm excited, Sir," I admitted.

"I can see that," he said as he began to stroke me. But why?"

"'Cause I don't ... ahhh ..." I shivered a little as he slowly stroked my hard-on. I kept my hands at my sides, standing perfectly still like a soldier. "'Cause I don't know what you're gonna do to me!" My voice was now a high-pitched whimper.

Matt laughed. "But I do. I know exactly what I'm gonna do to you, boy," he taunted me. "Not sure you'll like it much, but I sure will."

I continued to look down, observing the way he was touching me.

"Go get the bag, boy. Take out what's inside, and put it on." He released his grip on my cock and balls, and I hurried over to the bed. As I opened the bag, I was surprised to find a pair of what looked to be navy blue bikini-style underwear. They felt odd, as I picked them up, though. The crotch was quite thick. I quickly slipped them on. They were very tight-fitting, and the thick panel inside the crotch pressed snuggly against my ball sac.

"Wear em with your cock pointing up, boy," he said. His command really wasn't necessary at this point, though, because I was still rock hard.

"Yes, Sir," I responded.

"Now bring me the other item," he said. I reached inside the bag and pulled out a small remote. It was like the kind that is on a key chain for unlocking a car door, only a little larger. I stepped over and held my hand out to my Master, continuing to look down at his feet so as to show my submission.

"Look at me," he said, sliding his finger under my chin and pressing upwards. "How do they feel?" he asked.

I gulped, feeling very intimidated. Matt was skilled at quickly bringing me into submission. I felt extremely small and vulnerable now in his presence. "Tight, Sir," I said. "They feel really tight."

"And now how do they feel?" he said as he stared me right in the eye.

Immediately a jolt of electricity passed through my groin, and as it did, my knees buckled. I dropped to the ground.

"Ahhh ... uhhh ... uhh ..."

"How do they feel now, boy?" he repeated.

"Oh Sir!" I gasped. "Please!"

"Do you remember our conversation, pup?" Matt asked, suddenly slipping out of his role. "Do you remember your safe word?"

"Yes, Sir!" I said. "I remember."

"How do they feel now, boy?!" he demanded.

"I wasn't expecting it, Sir!" I cried. "I'm sorry!"

"Answer me, bitch!"

"They don't feel very good, Sir! It hurts!" I whined.

Instantly I received another jolt.

"Ahhh!" I screamed as I fell to the floor in a fetal position.

"How does that feel?" he asked.

"Please, Sir!"

"Do you remember our conversation, boy?"

I was sobbing now. "I remember Sir!"

Instantly he delivered a third horrendous jolt of electricity. It was like someone was stabbing a fireplace poker into my nuts. "AAAAHHH ... Please, Sir! Please NO!"

"Say it!"

"Davenport!" I screamed.

He threw the remote onto the bed and instantly dropped to the ground, cradling me in his arms. I was sobbing. "Why?!" I screamed. "Why, Sir?"

"There is a reason why we have a safe word, pup. You have to use it when you need it."

"I'm sorry, Sir," I cried, trembling as I clung to him." He began to kiss my face and stroke my hair gently.

"Shh," he said. Matt continued to hold me for the next ten minutes while I cried, wiping away my tears with his fingers. "Are you okay, pup?" he finally said softly.

"Yes, Sir," I whimpered. "I'm sorry."

"Don't be sorry. Do you trust me?"

"Yes, Sir!"

"Go get the remote," he said.

I looked up at him fearfully.

"If you trust me, go get the remote."

I crawled over to the bed and retrieved the remote, turning toward him and looking in his eyes.

"You don't have to give it to me. I want you to hold onto it, okay?"

"Yes, Sir," I said.

"There are four buttons on there. See em?"

I nodded. "Yes, Sir."

"The blue button was the first one I pressed. Then the yellow, and the last was the red. The red one delivers the strongest voltage."

I nodded without saying anything.

"Press the green button," he instructed me.

I looked up at him fearfully. Was this another test? Should I say that word again? I shook my head as I stared at him.

"If you trust me," he said soothingly, "press the green button."

I started crying, tears streaming down my cheeks.

"Press the button, pup. Trust me," he said.

I closed my eyes and extended my arm. I squinted my eyes tightly together and winced, and then I finally did it. I pressed the green button. Instantly a soothing vibration began to tickle my cock and balls. I opened my eyes and smiled.

"How does that feel?" he asked.

"Good," I smiled.

"Release the button, and then quickly depress it twice," he said.

I did as instructed. The vibration resumed but now remained continuous. I started laughing. "It sort of tickles, Sir," I said.

"Come here," he said, and I quickly crawled over to where he was sitting on the floor. He took me onto his lap and held me, kissing me tenderly.

"Are you okay?" he asked.

"Sir, why? Why did you hurt me?"

"I wanted to see if you remembered our rules," he said.

"To tell you when I'm hurting?"

"Yes," he said.

"But I did tell you, Sir, and you shocked me again anyway."

"You said you were ready to endure a little pain for your Master."

"It just hurt so bad, Sir. I'm sorry!"

"Don't be sorry. You used the safe word. That's what you're supposed to do. Never feel like you've failed me by using it. Understand?"

"I think you were trying to make me use it."

"If I'd had to shock you fifty times, I'd have done it. You needed to use it," he said.

"I don't understand, Sir!" I cried.

"Before we can do any more, I have to know that you're willing to use the safe word. I knew this would hurt, but it wouldn't damage you. And I bet you won't hesitate to use the word again if you need to. Will you?"

"No, Sir," I said. I squirmed a little as the vibration continued to tickle me. "It's making me hard," I said, blushing.

"You like that?" he asked. He was laughing.

I nodded. "I like it a lot, Sir."

"On your belly, boy!" he ordered. Immediately I moved into position as he extended his legs and I slid between them. "Do you trust me to hold the remote, boy?" he asked.

I handed it to him without speaking.

"See this little button on the side?" he said. He pressed his finger against it, and the vibrations became a little stronger.

"Ohhhh!" I laughed. "Sir! It's gonna ... it's gonna make me cum!"

"Don't cum!" he warned me. "Don't you dare cum without permission."

I squirmed around on the floor, trying to control myself. He pressed the button back in the opposite direction, and the vibrations lessened. I laughed as I looked up at him.

"Roll over," he said, and I quickly rolled onto my back. He turned off the remote completely and reached down inside my electric underwear. He was adjusting the panel, sliding it upwards a bit, so that it was pressing right against my hard cock. He snapped the elastic back in place around my waist and then turned on the vibrator again.

"Ahhh," I laughed. "Oh my god!"

Quickly he adjusted it, turning it down. He laughed as I looked up at him. "I'm turning it off now, he said. If you're good, I'll turn it back on, but I don't want you cumming in your pants. Understand?"

"Yes, Sir!" I said.

"You're gonna be wearin these all night, and if you cum in em, you'll be wearin cum-soaked pants to work."

"I won't, Sir," I promised.

He pushed himself upwards, momentarily, in order to pull down his shorts. "Take em off," he ordered, and quickly I assisted him by pulling the shorts down his legs past his feet. Then I slid back onto my belly in between his outstretched legs.

"Get to work!" he commanded. Eagerly I wrapped my lips around his enormous, throbbing cock. He leaned back against the wall and relaxed as I bobbed on him hungrily.

I continued my attentive service for the next ten minutes, not even daring to look up, and then suddenly felt the vibrations against my hard prick. I started to suck harder. I formed as tight a suction as I could and forced myself to go down all the way, feeling his cock invade my throat mercilessly.

"Good boy," he said, and the vibration intensified.

I kept sucking.

Another five minutes went by when I finally heard what I'd been waiting for. His breathing started to become rapid. Then he moaned. His cock was throbbing in my mouth, and I was going for broke, sucking it fiercely. He must have flipped the vibrator switch to full power right as he grabbed my head and forced me all the way down on him. Then he erupted as I moaned and gulped simultaneously.

When he was done draining himself, he calmly turned off the remote and gently pulled me off of him. I looked up and smiled. "Good boy," he whispered, and then he kissed me.

11

I loved working at the bookstore with Jason, especially when it was a late night shift with just the two of us on duty. It was particularly enjoyable now that we had come out to each other. He seemed to have really lightened up around me, and we were quickly becoming rather close friends.

"Petey, you're so lucky to have a boyfriend like Matt," he said. He was at the cappuccino counter, wiping it down with a rag, and I was straightening the magazines. We hadn't had a customer in over an hour.

"I know," I smiled as I looked up at him. "I really love him."

"When will your friend be out of the hospital?"

"It was supposed to be this week, but now his boyfriend tells us they're gonna do another surgery."

"Oh man ... that sucks. I'm just glad that psycho didn't kill him. Can you believe I actually thought that dude was Matt?"

I laughed. "Better not say that to Matt."

"Why?" Jason laughed. "Would he punish me?"

"Or else maybe punch your lights out."

Jason rolled his eyes. "I was hoping for something a little more ... well ... kinky."

I gasped. "Jason! He's my boyfriend."

"He's your *Master*," he corrected me.

I stared at him for a moment, trying to assess his implication. "Are you saying you want a Master of your own?"

137

He shrugged. "I like guys like him ... like Matt. Don't worry, I'm not the type to hit on other guys' boyfriends. But I could see myself with someone like him."

"So you think you are a sub?" I asked.

He looked down and turned away from me, again shrugging his shoulders. He sighed. "I've seen some stuff ... on the Internet."

"What do you mean?" I asked.

"Shit like ... um ..."

"What?" I urged him.

"Well, like bondage and shit. Cock and ball torture, whipping, blindfolds ..."

I busted up laughing.

He turned around and smiled at me. "Is that the kinda shit you guys are into?"

I shook my head. "Not really ... well, not yet anyway. Matt keeps telling me he's gonna do some new stuff with me."

"Well, what have you done so far?" he asked.

"Jason, do you think we should talk about this here?" I felt my face reddening.

"Why not?" he said. "We're the only ones here."

"Well, when we first were together, he made me wear a chastity device. He totally controlled when I could cum ... or not."

"Oh dude, that's hot. But I bet it really sucked, too."

"You have no idea!" We both laughed.

"What else?"

"I don't know!" I said bashfully.

"Just tell me! Please ..."

"All right. Well Matt sometimes makes me worship his feet."

"Like when they're all nasty and rank and stinky?" he said, making a face.

I laughed. "Yeah, sometimes."

"Ewww ... but still it's kinda hot. It's just so humiliating."

I shook my head and smiled. "I don't think so. I like worshipping any part of him, especially his feet."

"You have a foot fetish then?" he asked.

"I guess you could say that. I just know I totally love his feet."

"Has he ever spanked you?" Jason asked.

"Yeah, many times. Sometimes for fun and sometimes for punishment. But ya know what? It's hot either way."

"Especially if it's a punishment!" Jason shouted. He was busting up laughing now. "How hard does he hit you?"

"Sometimes really hard, but honest, he is not mean. He kisses me afterwards."

"Well I don't think it's mean anyways. I think it's hot."

"Matt likes you, ya know," I said.

"Whaddya mean?" he asked, suddenly getting serious.

"He thinks you're cute."

"Too bad he's *your* boyfriend, dude," he said.

"I'm just sayin ... you said you wish you had a guy like Matt. Well, Matt thinks you're cute, so I'm sure other Dom guys like him would feel the same way."

"I totally know I want a Dom guy, or at least I know I wanna try it. I get so turned on by that stuff I watch. Plus I'm way more into straight guys than gay-acting dudes. And I think Matt is totally straight-acting."

"He's bi, actually," I said.

"Really? So he fucks chicks too?"

"Not any more. He used to—when we were first together."

Jason stepped around behind the counter and dispensed himself a fountain pop. "Want one?" he asked.

"Sure. Diet."

"I think that would be so gross, like if he had sex with a girl and then wanted you to ... well, suck him or something."

I made a face. "Thank god he never did that," I said, "... that I'm aware of."

"Oh trust me, you'd be aware of it!"

"Did you get all the displays re-stocked?" I asked.

"Dude, I told ya ... everything's done. Here, take your soda." He handed me my Diet Coke. Just as I reached out to take it from him, my entire groin area began to vibrate. My mouth dropped open and my eyes widened as I froze in place.

"Hey dude, you all right?" Jason asked.

I bit my lower lip and tried to act normal, suddenly feeling the vibrations intensify against my now-stiffening cock. "Um, sure. Thanks." I reached out and took the drink from him, immediately setting it down on the counter he'd just cleaned.

"Petey, don't set that there!" he snapped. "I just cleaned that!"

"Oh … uh, sorry," I said, just as I felt another wave of vibrations tingle my most sensitive body part.

"Jason," I gasped. "Um … I gotta go sit down," I said.

"You all right?" he asked.

I looked around nervously, knowing Matt must be close by. Was he inside the bookstore? If so, how could he have gotten in without us knowing? I quickly walked over and sat down in one of the booths on the other side of the cappuccino bar.

"You want me to call Matt for you, tell him to come pick you up? It'll be cool; we already got everything done."

I shook my head. "No … um, he's here already," I said.

Jason looked over at the door. "He is? Where?"

"I don't know …"

Jason laughed. "Man, you sure you're all right? I think you're losin it."

"He's here," I assured him. "I can feel him."

Suddenly the vibrations went to full strength, and I grabbed the sides of the table in front of me, squirming in my seat. "Ahhhh …" I moaned.

Jason stood there staring at me, and then he began to laugh. "You had me goin!" he cracked up. Then he started making sounds of his own, faking an orgasm for me. "Oh yeah! Ohhh! Ahhh! Ooooooh!"

I was breathing quickly, almost panting as I reached down to grope myself. "Sir!" I cried. "Sir, I'm gonna … oh god!"

Jason was really laughing hard now, nearly in hysterics. "Dude, you are *good*!" he exclaimed.

The way that the electrical panel was positioned in my underwear, it was pressing right against my now-rock-hard shaft. The vibrations were equivalent to being stroked off, and I already was horny when I got to work, having been denied the privilege of shooting when I'd sucked off my Master. I knew I wasn't gonna last long if the vibrations continued.

I looked around frantically, trying to see where Matt was at. "Please, Sir!" I screamed. "Wherever you are!"

Jason stood there staring at me, still smiling. At this point he seemed perplexed. He'd obviously thought I was messing around, but it must have been becoming apparent to him that I was actually on the verge of an orgasm.

"Petey, what is it?" he demanded. "Tell me!"

"Matt's making me wear a remote vibrator ... and he's got it turned on!"

"In your ass?" he cried.

"No! On my dick!"

"Oh fuck! That's so fuckin hot!" Again he began laughing. "Make him shoot it, Matt ... um ... Sir! Make Petey shoot in his fucking pants!" He looked around the bookstore, trying to see where Matt might be.

Just then Matt stepped out from behind one of the aisle displays, slowly moving closer. The vibrations had abated, and I sat there staring at my Master.

"You gonna cum without permission boy?" Matt asked.

"No Sir!" I cried ... "I mean, not on purpose."

"Whaddya mean, on purpose? When I tell you not to cum, you don't fuckin cum. No excuses!"

"Yes, Sir!"

He quickly depressed the button twice as he pointed the remote toward me. The vibrations immediately started again, and then he flipped the switch on the side of the remote, cranking it to full power!

Instinctively I reached down to grope myself again. "No!" he commanded. "Don't touch yourself!" I quickly placed both hands flat on the table.

"Please, Sir!" I cried. "I'm so close!"

"You cum in your pants boy, you're gonna be punished ..." he warned.

"I can't help it, Sir!" I felt myself right on the verge. I couldn't hold back; I was so damned close. "Ahhh ... Sir!" I screamed.

"You're gonna be punished," he repeated.

"Please let me cum! Please, Sir, I beg you!" I arched my back and made fists with both my hands, trying desperately to hold back.

"Don't cum!" he said, stepping closer to me.

"Ahh, ahhh, ahh!" I moaned.

Matt was grinning and staring at me intently. I couldn't take it any longer. I was gonna shoot. It was right there!

"I'm cumming!" I cried. "Oh, Sir!" My whole body trembled as I felt my hot cum fire out into the tight underwear. "Oh god! Oh, Sir!" Suddenly the vibrations stopped, and I was left with a big, embarrassing wet spot in my lap.

Jason stood there watching the entire scene, his mouth agape. "Oh fuck! That's hot." He grinned at Matt, then looked back at me. "Dude, you're gonna be punished so bad!" he said, laughing.

"And you're gonna do it ..." Matt said as he returned a smile to my coworker.

"I am?" Jason asked.

"You are, boy," Matt said. "You're gonna paddle my pup's ass."

"Yes, Sir!" he said enthusiastically.

"Petey, it's almost midnight. Get this place locked up," he said. "Jason, Petey's gonna call you and let you know when we're ready for his punishment."

"I'll be waiting, Sir," Jason said.

I then made my way quickly to the register, praying no other customers would happen to come in and notice my little accident. "Jason, can you lock the door?" I said.

"I told you to lock it," Matt said.

"But Sir ..."

"I told you to lock it!" he repeated. "Do it now!"

"Yes, Sir," I said. Grabbing the key from inside the register, I headed over to the door. Just as I reached the door I noticed someone approaching. It was one of our other coworkers, Carrie. Fuck!

"Hey," she said as she stepped through the door. "Can I get a soda before you close?" she looked down at me, obviously noticing the condition of my pants. She cocked her head slightly and stared at me. "Ya know, I think I'll just stop at McDonald's. You guys have a good night." She then turned and left while Jason and Matt laughed behind me. My face burned with embarrassment, but my dick was rock hard.

When I got up the next morning it felt odd to me that I didn't have to worry about classes any more. I was so relieved that there was finally one thing off my plate and that I could now concentrate on simply obeying and taking care of Matt. I also knew that Drew was going to need a lot of TLC when he got home. Alex had informed us that the doctor had decided to keep him in the hospital for a few days longer. They wanted to do the orthopedic surgery right away.

I remembered the conversation I'd had with Matt the night before as he drove me home from work, and I now was feeling quite excited about having Jason over. Initially when Matt mentioned that he'd noticed how cute Jason was, I couldn't help but feel jealous, but Matt's words to me in the car made me feel much more confident that he had no interest in trading me in for another model.

"You know you're my only pup, right?" he asked.

"Yes, Sir, I know," I said quietly. "But Sir, can I ask you a question please?"

"Shoot," he said.

"I know you don't want Jason to be your pup ... but do you want him for anything else?"

Matt grabbed my hand. "Pup, I don't want anyone but you. Ever," he said.

"Then why?" I whispered.

"Remember our new rules?" he asked. "I'm not gonna have sex with anyone unless we both are present." The rule was little consolation to me, though. Suddenly that same familiar feeling of anxiety washed over me, and it was reminiscent of how I used to get when Matt went out with Tracy.

"I remember, Sir," I said.

"Then what's wrong?"

"You're right, Sir. Jason *is* cute. Maybe even cuter than me."

Matt laughed. "Not!" he said. "There's no comparison. Trust me."

"Really?" I asked.

"Look, we can hold off on this. I wanted to bring Jason in on a scene with us 'cause I thought it'd be something we'd both enjoy. I thought it'd be hot, but if you're not ready ..."

"I'm sorry, Sir," I said. "I'm ready. Really I am."

"I wanna see him paddle my pup's cute little ass. Then I wanna see him suck my cute little pup's dick."

I laughed. "You do?"

"And then you both can suck mine."

"Let's go back and get him!" I exclaimed.

He laughed. "Nah ... it can wait. But you'll see; it'll be hot for all of us."

"You're right Sir. I'm sorry I'm such a brat."

"You're not a brat. You just love your Master."

"With all my heart."

I smiled to myself as I remembered our conversation. It was truly amazing to me the way Matt had changed after we'd been separated. He still was every bit as dominant and demanding as always, but now he seemed less selfish. Drew had noticed it, too, and it had sent up a red flag for him. He suggested I might wish to focus upon reawakening the Dom in Matt. Remind him that I needed his control.

As I thought of it though, I didn't really believe that Matt's dominance had changed at all. In some ways he was even more controlling than he'd been previously. He certainly was more protective of me. And now that we lived together, he had complete control of my day-to-day activities. He also could get sex-on-demand without having to track me down. I got to cook and clean for him every day, wait on him hand-and-foot. I didn't see how there was really any part of Matt's dominance that was dormant and in need of awakening.

When I thought about Drew's relationship with Alex, I didn't perceive Alex to be any stricter than Matt. He seemed to be just as protective and loving toward his boy as Matt was to me. Of course, they'd been together longer and they weren't quite as affectionate as Matt and I, yet I didn't see Alex as any more of a hard-ass than Matt.

The thing I wondered about Alex, though, was whether or not he'd still go out and fuck women. He and Matt used to like going out with chicks together, playing the part of straight guys. Matt had stopped doing this, but neither Drew nor Alex had ever mentioned anything about Alex's behavior changing in this regard. I wondered if this was the basis for Drew's concern. Perhaps when he saw that Matt had made this decision to be more monogamous, he was a bit jealous.

I decided that it was best if I simply did not talk about this whole aspect of our relationship with Drew any more. I didn't want to say or do anything to hurt him. I'd always sensed that Alex had looked up to Matt, especially after I'd witnessed the way Matt had dominated him. Maybe Matt's commitment to me would inspire Alex to follow suit. Maybe the reality that Alex nearly lost Drew would have an impact as well.

The hospital was a bit too far away for me to ride my bike, and I really didn't want to drive, so I decided to take the bus. Before I'd met Matt, I used to ride the bus all the time. In fact, it was at a bus stop that I officially met Matt. This was when he'd saved me from two bullies who were attacking me. No matter what happened between Matt and me, I would always recall Matt's heroism in that situation. He had taken me to the hospital that day, the same one I was headed for now.

I stopped at the gift shop on my way up to see Drew and picked him out a huge Teddy Bear. It cost me thirty five bucks, but I knew Drew would love it. I hadn't seen my best friend at all the day before, and I really missed him.

As soon as I walked into his room, though, I sensed something was terribly wrong. Drew sat there staring at me, looking almost as if he were about to cry. "Drew," I said, "what's wrong?"

I saw his bottom lip begin to tremble, and suddenly, instead of a 28-year-old college professor, Drew appeared to be a little boy. "I've gotta have an operation!" he cried.

"Oh honey, I know," I said sympathetically as I stepped up to his bedside. "But you already had one."

"I know, but I didn't really know what was happening then. I didn't have time to be scared."

"Drew, the scariest part is over. This is not even life-threatening. It's just a surgery to repair your shoulder. Please don't cry!"

"I can't help it!" he sobbed."I'm so scared ..."

I placed the bear at the foot of the bed and gently slid myself onto the mattress next to him. "We're all going to be here for you, baby," I said soothingly. Please don't be afraid. And Alex told us you have the best orthopedic surgeon in the state—possibly the country."

"I know," he whimpered, "but I can't help it. You know I then have to wear a brace for three months. I'll still be in the brace when school starts next semester. How am I gonna be any good to Alex that way? How can I even *serve* him?!"

"Baby, is that what you're worried about? Drew, Alex loves you so much! He understands that he almost lost you. We all do! He doesn't care that you have to be in a brace. He wants to take care of you."

"But what about when he wants to be taken care of? How can I even make love to him?"

"Drew, oh my god! I'm sure you and Alex can be creative. I'm sure you'll find ways to improvise."

"He'll probably just go out and find some other sub ... or some bitch!" he cried.

"Sweetie, you and Alex need to talk about this." I gently squeezed his hand. "I don't know for sure what Alex will do or not, but I honestly don't think he'd ever do something like that. I know he loves you."

"Petey, I'd understand if he did go have sex with someone else. God, it's like he's done that dozens of times before, and I know it's his right. I'm just afraid that with me being all messed up like this, I might lose him in the process! He might find someone else—someone who's not crippled and useless."

"You're not gonna be crippled! You're gonna be wearing a brace. You'll still be able to suck cock and get fucked. You'll still be able to get your ass spanked. You'll still be able to do almost everything.

"When I had my ribs broken, do you think it stopped me from making love to Matt? It was actually the opposite; we had the best sex ever. He was so gentle and romantic with me."

"I know, Petey, but sometimes Alex doesn't wanna be gentle and romantic. Sometimes he wants to fuck my brains out."

I laughed. "I'm sure you two will figure out a way to do it. I know you will. Honey, please talk to your Master. I know you have nothing to worry about. Let him assure you of this. Please."

"You're right, Petey. I'll talk to him." He smiled and then leaned over to kiss me on the lips. "Is that for me?" he asked, referring to the teddy bear.

I shook my head. "Nah, I got it for some other patient but just carried it in here for the hell of it. Of course he's for you!"

Drew laughed, holding out his arms. "Lemme see," he said. I handed him the big Teddy and he hugged it affectionately. "He's so cute! Thank you Petey. I love you so much."

I pulled a tissue from the dispenser on his bedside stand and gently dabbed the teardrops from his cheeks. My precious Drew. Oh, to think that we'd nearly lost him! I smiled at him affectionately as he squeezed the bear tightly against his chest, primarily using his one good arm.

"Now I have something to hug when I cough," he smiled.

"Let me tell ya something funny, okay?" I said.

"Please," he said, taking the tissue from me and wiping away the rest of his tears.

"Last night Matt gave me some electric underwear!"

"What?" He was grinning broadly. "I never heard of such a thing."

"They have a remote, which Matt has, of course. When he turns the remote on, they vibrate."

"Oh my god," he said. "Does it hurt?"

I shook my head. "No, not the vibrations, but there are also buttons on there for electric shocks. Those hurt like a mother!"

"He used em on you?" Drew's mouth dropped open in surprise.

"Drew, he made me cry. I had to use the safe word!"

"Oh man ... was he pissed?"

"No ... he wanted me to use it. He kept shocking me until I did."

"Aww ... Petey! That must've been awful."

"I guess I'm not all that much into the pain thing, to be honest," I laughed. "I know Matt likes it ... or wants to try more of it, anyway. I'm afraid I'm gonna be a big disappointment to him, though. I'm kinda scared, really."

"Well now, you're the one who needs to talk to your Master," Drew scolded. "You need to tell him you don't like it."

"How can I tell my Master I don't like something like that, though? I mean, isn't it supposed to be about his pleasure?"

"I thought you were excited about trying the nipple clamps," Drew said. "You're not even gonna believe how much they hurt."

I sighed and then looked away. "Well let me tell ya the rest, okay? After he made me use the safe word, then he turned on the vibrator while I sucked him. This was right before I had to leave for work. I was still wearin the underwear at work. Well, Matt showed up right before the end of my shift and turned on that vibrator!"

"No way!" Drew started laughing.

"He made me cum in my pants right in front of my friend Jason. Oh God, Drew, it was so humiliating!"

"What'd Jason do?" Drew leaned in excitedly as I told him the story.

"It seemed like he got off on it. He totally loved it, and then Matt told him he wanted him to come over and paddle me sometime ... as punishment, cause I came in my pants without permission."

"And ...?"

"And what?" I said, smiling at him devilishly.

"And so you guys are gonna do a three-way with Jason?"

I shrugged. "I dunno. Guess that's up to Matt. Jason is like heavy-duty interested in pain stuff, though. He wants to do shit with cock and ball torture, shocking, bondage ... all kinds of kinky stuff ..."

"Maybe there is the answer to your dilemma." Drew raised his eyebrows.

"Whaddya mean?" I asked.

"Well, maybe since Jason is more of a pain slut than you are, Matt can use him that way while you just watch."

I shook my head. "I don't think Matt would do that," I said.

"Why not?"

"I think he wants to do it to me. I know he does. Look how bad he shocked me last night!"

"But he made you cry, then afterwards he made you cum in your pants."

"Which I still have to be punished for!" I reminded him.

Drew laughed. "You don't seriously think that being paddled by Jason is a real punishment, do you? Matt's just setting up a hot scene."

"I know." I smiled excitedly. "'Cause he said after Jason spanks me, he then has to suck me."

"See? And then I bet Matt will spank him, and it will go from there. Petey, anyone who knows you realizes you're too sensitive to be a pain pig. You're just a sweetheart, and you need affection more than beatings. That's why you're Matt's pup. Sure, he's gonna paddle you, maybe even use the clamps on ya a few times, but anything heavy duty, he's not gonna do to you."

"I hate to admit it, Drew, but I hope you're right. I hope he doesn't do stuff to hurt me. I've never been one to cry a lot from physical pain. I mean, I'll admit, I cry over everything. But usually it's cause I'm hurting inside, not physically. I cried last night, though."

"Because it hurt you physically ... or emotionally?" Drew asked.

I hesitated for a moment, but my friend continued to stare at me, waiting for an answer. "Emotionally," I confessed. "I couldn't believe he'd do that to me. I couldn't believe he'd be so mean.

"But I think it'll be different next time. I'll be expecting it, and I'll understand that it's only part of a scene ..."

"Petey, I hope you're right, but I don't think you should feel bad if you never get into that stuff. Not all subs are into being physically abused. Some hate it, actually."

"What about you?" I asked.

His eyes widened just a bit as he smiled at me. "I guess I'm kinda in the middle. I like a little bit of pain but nothing severe. I've done some bondage scenes, been in a sling ... that sorta thing.

"I do know this, though. Matt is crazy about you. He's not about to hurt you. If you are not into pain, he won't force you to take it."

"But Drew, I can never tell Matt how I feel!" I said.

"Tell me how you feel about what, pup?" I heard Matt's voice behind me, and quickly turned to see my Master standing in the doorway.

Thankfully a nurse entered the room directly behind Matt, and this allowed me to stall in answering my Master's direct question. When Alex came in a few minutes later, the conversation veered off onto other topics. I was relieved to hear Alex bring up his concern about Drew being afraid of the surgery. Their conversation with each other became more intimate, and it was a signal to Matt and me that perhaps we should leave and give them time alone. I kissed my friend goodbye, and he again thanked me for Teddy; then I left with my Master.

"What is it that you are afraid to tell me, pup?" Matt said once we were in the car.

I looked down at my lap. "I'm sorry, Sir," I said. I couldn't help myself. I felt as if I had to apologize, as if I'd disappointed him.

"Why would you be sorry?" Matt said. I could hear the irritation in his voice. "Ya know, this is starting to get a little bit frustrating. What more do I have to do to convince you that I'm trustworthy?"

"That's why I'm sorry, Sir!" I cried. Again I was becoming emotional. "I know I should have trusted you. And really, Sir, I *do* trust you. With all my heart!"

"Then Petey, for god's sake, tell me what you're afraid of!"

"The pain!" I exclaimed. "I just don't think I can do it, Sir. I don't think I can endure that kind of ... *torture!*"

Matt grabbed my hand before responding. "Pup, look at me," he said calmly, and I turned to him, tears streaming down my face. "I already decided you couldn't do the pain, and I'm cool with that. I never really expected that."

"You didn't?" I asked.

"You used the safe word after three jolts," he laughed.

"But ..."

"Yes, I did want you to use it, pup. I kinda thought it would take more than three, though. Like I said, I was prepared to go fifty, but when I saw you curled up on the floor like a newborn baby sobbing, I really wanted it over with."

I felt my face reddening. "I'm a wuss!" I said. "A big baby!"

He smiled at me affectionately. "You're *my* wuss, and *my* baby, and you're perfect just the way you are."

"I want to do anything that pleases you, Sir," I said. "I swear."

"I know ya do, pup." He brushed his fingertips through my hair.

"Remember how scared I was when you first made me drink your ... um ... piss? But then after I did it, I wasn't scared any more. And I was afraid at first when you tied me up, but then I decided to trust you, and it ended up being really hot. I think I can trust you with the pain ... if it's what you really want, Sir."

"Pup, if I really want something *that* bad, it's gonna happen. I'll train you, and you'll learn to like it. But this isn't one of those things. Sometimes inflicting pain can really be a turn-on, but it's just not like that with you. I end up feeling sorry for you." He laughed in spite of himself.

"So I'm turning you into a softie now, Sir."

"Say that again, and you *will* feel some pain." He looked at me sternly. "I'll take you out right here and blister your ass."

"I'm sorry, Sir," I said. "I ... uh ... oh god ..." I sighed. "I didn't mean you were soft. I mean I love you just how you are, and I don't want you to change yourself in order to please me. If you did, then you really wouldn't be the Master. *I* would!"

"Look at us, Petey," he said. "Look at where we are now compared to last September when we first met. Haven't we both changed? Haven't we both changed a *lot*?"

I nodded. Indeed, we *had* both changed a lot. I now felt so much more confident in myself. I wasn't ashamed of who I was. I even at times allowed myself to question authority. Matt had become more loving and affectionate. He had become more responsible and far more mature, just in this short period of time. We each had grown a lot.

"If we are gonna be together for a long time ... which we *are* ... then we have to change. When I first met you I didn't want anyone to know I liked guys more than chicks. That's why I kept on fucking girls like Tracy. I deliberately looked for her type. The ones who didn't really want a relationship, they just wanted a good lookin guy to be their trophy. That gave me the freedom to fuck who I really wanted to fuck ... *guys*!

"Do you remember when you first admitted to me who you were? You said you were a fag and asked me if I was one. I flatly denied it. I'd still deny it, to be honest, if you used that label. But at this point, I have no problem telling anyone that I love you and plan to spend my life with you. I love you! I fuckin love the shit outta you!

"I'm your Master, just like I always was. That is never gonna change, but after everything that's happened I've decided that being an asshole is not necessarily the same thing as being a good

Master. I still get off on it sometimes, though," he grinned. "I still like makin my pup squirm."

"I like squirming for you, Sir." I continued to weep as I looked into his eyes. Now I was not crying due to sadness. I was crying because of the beauty of his words. He'd moved me to tears.

"Stop worryin about whether or not I've gotten too soft. I'm gonna dominate your little fag ass whenever the fuck I wanna. Understand?!"

"Yes, Sir!" I replied, in my nasally, wimpy voice.

"Good boy," he said. He then pulled me into his arms and kissed me.

"Should I wear a suit, Sir?" I asked, rather seriously.

"Fuck no!" Matt replied offhandedly. "Throw on a pair of jeans or something."

"Oh dear," I said, staring at myself in the full-length mirror. "I don't really have any good jeans. Plus I really think I should look presentable when meeting your father for the first time."

"He's not gonna give ya any shit. If he does ..."

"I didn't mean *that*, Sir. I know he won't. I just want to make a good impression."

"Go get me a soda from the fridge, and I'll pick out your clothes," he said authoritatively. "If not, we'll be here all fuckin day."

"Yes, Sir," I said, and quickly scurried to the kitchen.

Forty-five seconds later, when I returned with his bottle of Mountain Dew, a pair of khakis and a polo shirt were lying on the bed. I stared at them and then looked back at my Master. They were identical to the clothes he was wearing.

"Good choice, Sir," I smiled.

"Come 'ere," he said. "Wear your necklace instead of the collar," he said. "Don't wanna freak em out too bad on the first meeting." He laughed, apparently visualizing the possibilities.

"I was afraid your mom would be freaked when she saw me wearin my collar," I admitted. "She didn't say anything, though."

"You wore it in front of my mom?" He said, his voice indicating approval.

"For the picture, Sir. She was with me during the photo session."

"We need to stop and pick that up," Matt said. "Let's go tomorrow. Then we have to do our time on Saturday."

"Well *I* have to do *my* time on Saturday, Sir. You're doin it 'cause you want to."

"True," he said, as he clasped the necklace around my neck. "Get dressed," he said. "We gotta leave in ten minutes."

"Ten minutes!" I exclaimed. "I haven't even taken my shower, Sir."

"Then ya better fuckin hurry," he said. "I'll be in the living room."

It wasn't until thirty minutes later that we left the apartment. I was actually ready in ten minutes as ordered, but then Matt received a phone call from his new boss. While he was on the phone I got his shoes and knelt before him to slip them on. I then curled up between his legs and sat there, waiting patiently for him to finish his phone conversation.

"Ready?" he said as he flipped his phone closed. "What took ya so fuckin long?" I smiled up at him.

"Ready, Sir!" I said and scrambled to my feet.

It was Diane who greeted us when we arrived, and I was nearly moved to tears watching her embrace her son. Of course Matt showed no emotion other than the sincere smile that he gave his mother as she pulled back to look him in the eyes. She was crying herself.

"Thank you so much for coming," she said warmly, and then she turned to give me a hug. "Oh Petey, you look so cute ... dressed just like Matt!" She started laughing. "You two are absolutely adorable."

Matt rolled his eyes and laughed.

"Come on in," she said. "Have a seat in the dining room, and I'll get us some drinks. Dinner will be ready in about twenty minutes."

"I can help you in the kitchen if you'd like, Mrs. ... er, I mean Diane."

"Oh that'd be nice, Petey. Matt, your dad's in the living room. Why don't you go tell him dinner's about ready?"

"I'm on it," he said, and then winked at me.

It seemed odd to see my Master in this context. I'd never seen him in his role as son.

As we entered the kitchen together, Diane asked about Drew. She told me that she'd had a horrible feeling that something was going to happen, especially after hearing Ryan's message on our machine. "I really wish I'd have made you call the police right then."

"I'm so sorry, Diane. If I'd have told Matt everything from the beginning, maybe my best friend wouldn't be in the hospital right now. It was totally my fault. I even talked Matt out of calling the Police that day I saw Ryan at the mall."

"It is *not* your fault, honey. Don't even think that. It's that boy, Ryan. He's unstable, and you can't be responsible for the crazy things he does. He's also the one who put you in the hospital and nearly killed you.

"And there's another thing you should think of, too, Petey. If you had told Matt about the car being scratched and seeing Ryan like you did, he just might have tracked the kid down and gotten himself shot. It could've been Matt who ended up in the hospital ... or the morgue!"

I nodded. "Maybe you're right. I've seen Matt lose his temper before, and it's not pretty."

"What do ya want to drink, Sweetie?"

I smiled and shrugged.

"Ice tea? Soda pop? Coffee? ... How about a glass of white wine?"

"Ice tea, please."

She opened the refrigerator and removed the carafe. "Do you take sugar in your tea?"

"Oh, no thank you. I can help you, ma'am. What does everyone else want?"

I got Matt a bottle of Mountain Dew and poured it over ice. Mr. and Mrs. Porter were both also having iced tea, so we decided to simply take the pitcher to the dining room with us. As I stepped through the door and saw Matt and his father standing there in the archway together, I was so surprised that I nearly dropped the tray of drinks I was carrying.

I'd never seen a father and son who looked so remarkably alike. Sure, most sons do bear at least a slight resemblance to their fathers. Many favor their dads to a noticeable degree, but in this particular case, it was uncanny how much the two looked like each other. They each possessed the exact same facial features, although Mr. Porter had a few subtle lines around his eyes and jaw due to the fact he was four decades older than Matt. They were the same height and had very similar builds. Matt's dad was in great shape for a man in his sixties. Truthfully, he appeared to be no older than mid-to-late forties.

"And this must be Peter," he said.

"Petey," Matt corrected him. "Everyone calls him Petey."

His dad chuckled a bit. "Petey is the dog's name," he observed.

"I named that dog after Petey," Matt said, laughing himself.

"Nice to meet you, Sir," I said, nodding in his direction. My hands were full at the time, but I quickly set down the tray and stepped over to shake the man's hand.

"Have a seat," Mr. Porter motioned to the table. Diane handed each of us our drink as we sat down. I waited for Matt to sit first, and then I took a chair next to him. He was positioned between his father and me.

"About twenty minutes till dinner's ready," Diane told us.

"Whaddya do, Petey?" Mr. Porter abruptly asked me.

I looked up at him, astonished by the question. "Petey goes to school," Matt said. "He works part time at a bookstore." Matt's tone was lighthearted, obviously conveying that he'd thought it a ridiculous question.

"Well, what are ya in school for?" he said. "What will you eventually be doing?"

I looked at Matt, unsure of how I should answer, and then Diane spoke up. "Honey, he probably doesn't even know yet. He's goin to community college, just like Matt."

"I'm gonna be a writer, Sir."

Matt looked over at me, rather surprised.

"Novels? Textbooks? Poems? Whaddya like to write?" Mr. Porter asked.

"What is this, twenty questions?" Matt interrupted him. I could tell he was annoyed.

"I'm just tryin to get to know your friend."

"It's okay, Sir," I said. "I'm not sure if I wanna be a journalist, write novels, or what. I just know I've always enjoyed writing. I like to read too, which is why I got the job at the bookstore. I sometimes think about what it'd be like to see a book I've written in a bookstore."

"Are you good?" he asked.

I started to feel a tad embarrassed. "I dunno, Sir. Um ... my teachers always told me I had a talent for writing."

He nodded, raising his eyebrows and frowning slightly. "Then you should do it. You should write a novel. What would you write about if you did decide to do it?"

"I'm not sure, Sir. That's a good question."

"Well maybe you should just concentrate on getting through school first," Diane said.

"Oh yes ... yes, I definitely agree," I laughed nervously. "Someday I'll write a book, but for now I do enough writing just for my classes."

"I hear ya got offered a job," Mr. Porter said to Matt.

"I did," he responded.

"At our competitor's. And you took it?"

Matt stared his father right in the eye. "After I was no longer employed, I needed to find something."

"Fair enough," his dad said, taking a swig of his iced tea. "How much they payin ya?"

Diane and I looked at each other, and it looked as if she were about to speak, but Matt responded to his father's question. "They made me an offer impressive enough for me to accept; that oughta tell ya something."

"I don't want you working for them," his dad said matter-of-factly.

"Dad, it's not your decision. I already took the job."

"I'm prepared to re-offer you the new store," he said flatly. Again Diane and I exchanged a glance.

"Let's just cut to the chase, all right Dad?" Matt said, leaning in toward his father. "I had a job with you. I worked my ass off, and I did a damned good job. Learned the business inside-and-out. But then you fired me, not because of anything to do with my job performance. You fired me 'cause of who I love!"

"I fired you because you were in jail," his dad responded.

"On false charges! And you didn't fire me because of that anyway. You fired me because you thought I was a fag!"

"Matt!" Diane said. "Honey, please ..."

Mr. Porter held his hand up to silence her. "It's okay. Let him say what he needs to say."

"Dad, I can't believe you kicked me out of my home, fired me from my job, and basically disowned me ... all because you were embarrassed by the fact you have a gay son." This was the first time I'd ever heard Matt refer to himself as gay.

"Is that what you are?" Mr. Porter asked.

"That's what I am, Dad," Matt stated assertively. "And Petey is my partner, and I love him."

Mr. Porter pursed his lips and stared at Matt, then glanced over to me. "It just ... um ... well, it's a shock. You always had so many girlfriends ..."

"I don't have girlfriends anymore. I only had them to conceal who I really was. I have Petey now, and he's all I want." He reached down and grabbed hold of my hand.

"Matt," Mr. Porter began, and then he sighed. "Son, this is hard for me. I'll admit it. I never thought I'd have this kind of conversation with you. I never in my wildest dreams thought you'd prefer the company of ... of other guys over women."

"It's not just their company I prefer," Matt said. His words were like weapons, spears stabbing repeatedly into his father's chest.

"Okay ... you want me to say it? I'll say it right here in front of your ... friend."

"My *partner*," Matt corrected him, squeezing my hand possessively.

"Your partner," his father repeated. "I'll admit I was an ass. I was worried more about what other people would think. I was thinking it was just a phase or something. I still wonder that ..."

"It's not a phase, Dad. I've always known."

"Then honey," Matt's mom spoke, "why didn't you ever tell us?"

"Because I didn't have it all figured out myself yet. I never wanted to be the way I am. I never really felt there was anything wrong with me, but it's not like it was a choice I made. People don't choose who they're attracted to. I doubted you'd understand though. I expected your reaction would be ... well, exactly what it was. I knew you'd disown me."

Diane's eyes were moist with tears. Mr. Porter spoke again, "Son, I haven't disowned you. I never did. I didn't disown Amanda, either. She's never discussed this with us, but it's obvious to all of us who *she* is. She lives with another woman and has for years." He was referring to Matt's older sister. Right after Matt and I met, he'd told me that he had a gay sister whom he did not know very well. She lives in Los Angeles.

"You've always been my son and you always will be. I overreacted. Like I said, I was an ass."

I was crying now. Matt pulled my chair closer to his and put his arm around me.

"Matt, I wanna try to understand this. Really I do. It's a lot to deal with, seeing that everything you've ever dreamed of for your son suddenly was all just a fantasy."

"That's what dreams are, Dad. This is reality. But ya know what? I'm the same exact person I was before you knew I was gay. Well ... almost the same person. I've matured a lot since I met Petey. A *lot*."

"Yes, you have," Diane agreed. She was wiping her eyes with her napkin.

"Well, I hope you'll consider my offer ... to take the store. I need a good manager, and we're scheduled to go live next week."

"I'll talk it over with Petey, and then I'll get back to you by Thursday," he said. "Is it the same salary we had agreed to?"

"Excuse me," Diane interrupted. "I've got to go get dinner. Petey, do you wanna help me in the kitchen?"

I looked over at Matt. He nodded.

"Sure," I said. Matt kissed my forehead before I got up.

Diane turned to me when we were back in the kitchen. "I just thought they needed some time to discuss this together ... without an audience."

"Yes, ma'am. I agree."

When Diane and I returned fifteen minutes later with beef pot roast and all the fixins, Matt and his father were animatedly discussing the features of their new gym. Diane winked at me as we placed the food on the table and slid into our seats.

I was very impressed with the meal, and I had to admit I couldn't have done it better myself. It concerned me for a second, because I realized that as Matt's current full-time cook, I had big shoes to fill. He obviously was used to his mom's cooking.

"Mom, this is so good," he complimented her. "Petey's a great cook, too."

"And a cake decorator," she added.

"Thanks for helping him with that cake." He looked over at me and smiled. "Petey's very talented."

Our dinner conversation was far more relaxed from that point on, and the more I listened to Matt's father, the more I liked him.

He did seem to be extremely confident about his opinions, but I really had expected nothing less. I just kept thinking of him as being an older version of Matt. It sort of excited me to think about the possibility of growing older with Matt, and knowing that this was what I had to look forward to. Of course I didn't truly imagine that Matt would age exactly the same way his father had, but I had to suspect the years would treat them similarly. They looked so much alike, after all.

Mr. Porter didn't give orders to his wife the way that Matt did to me, but it was clear that he was the dominant force in that household. The way that Diane catered to him and deferred to his opinions and preferences led me to believe that there was a little bit of a Dom/sub dynamic in place. I doubted that she ever would crave the kind of domination and control that I did—that I *needed* from my Master—but I think on some level she would be able to at least understand my role in my relationship with her son.

I also liked the fact that Mr. and Mrs. Porter seemed to genuinely love each other, even after all their years together. Before I'd met them, I'd always feared that Matt's parents would be this stoic, ultra-conservative couple who could barely stand each other and who remained together merely for the sake of appearances. In Diane, though, I saw a loving and devoted wife. She sincerely wanted nothing more than to take care of her husband. When he'd struggled to come to terms with his son's identity, she had hurt badly herself.

After dinner, when we retired to the den to have dessert, we got to talking about Matt when he was younger. Diane pulled out a stack of photo albums and I excitedly leafed through the pages, admiring all the pictures of Matt at different ages. He was always a very attractive boy. Very cute as a child, tall for his age. There were lots of pictures of Matt in various sports uniforms. His photos were also proudly displayed above the fireplace and throughout the room. Intermingled with his photos were those of his sisters. Both of them were quite a bit older than he and already out of the house by the time he was growing up. Obviously his parents had been extremely proud of him, their only son.

I guess the fact that this family had so much money had always caused me to speculate about them. I'd assumed things about their lifestyle and their family dynamic that were not necessarily true. I always assumed Matt was extremely spoiled, and honestly he was. But what I was learning was that he was spoiled by two parents who genuinely adored him. They spoiled him and gave him all they had because they dearly loved him.

It really was no different from how my own parents had raised me. They had wanted me to succeed in life, and they would have given anything to ensure this happened. In Matt's case, his parents just happened to possess more material things that they could hand down to him.

All along I had realized that Matt had a sense of ethical integrity. He had always demanded that I be respectful of other people and strive to do the right thing. I understood now where that lofty set of morals had come from.

When we left the house at ten o'clock that evening, I was truly pleased that I'd met Matt's dad, and I loved Diane even more than I had previously. I thought of my own parents and wondered if they would have been as welcoming of Matt as Paul and Diane had been of me. If Kathie was any indication, probably not. I was sad, in a way, that I didn't have the opportunity to find out. I suspected that my mom would have really loved Matt's mom. I knew she would have. It was sort of like I'd gained another set of parents.

I felt more connected to Matt than I ever had before, and when we got home we made the most passionate love. "Sir," I whispered, "I'm glad you said I was your partner."

"You are my partner, pup," he said, kissing me. "But you better not think that means you don't do as I say."

"No, Sir," I said. "I'll do anything you say."

"Good. Now get some sleep ... and wake me up in the morning the usual way."

"Yes, Sir," I said, and smiled to myself as I curled up in his arms and dozed off.

12

We were on our way to the mall when I asked Matt about a comment he'd made to his father the night before. "Sir, when your dad offered you the job, why'd you tell him you needed to talk it over with me and then get back to him?"

"Wanted him to see that the big decisions in my life affected both of us—me and my pup. "

I laughed. "So you're saying I have to give you permission?"

Matt was driving, but momentarily looked over at me, throwing me a stern glare. "That's not what I'm sayin at all. I never said I needed to get your permission. Said I needed to talk it over with you."

"But Sir, you've never talked over any other decisions with me. I've never expected it. I trust you ..."

"You better trust me," he said. "What I really wanted to talk over with you isn't the job. I'll decide that on my own. I wanted to see how you felt about my parents. I don't wanna step back into their lives again if they make you uncomfortable—if they don't treat you right."

"You already know how much I love your mom, Sir."

"What about my dad?" he said.

"Your dad is like you, Sir." I smiled as he grimaced.

"You want your ass paddled?" he said seriously.

"Sir! He *is* like you! He's like a carbon copy of you, only older."

"My dad is *not* like me ... or I'm not like him. We're totally different from each other. My dad's a real prick sometimes. He was bein nice last night—on his best behavior."

"No offense, Sir ... but you can be mean sometimes too."

"Shut it, pup," he said. I sensed he now was starting to get pissed. "You don't know what you're talkin bout. My dad can be a jerk, and I really don't wanna be anything like that. He's done shit you don't even know about."

"I'm sorry, Sir. I just mean you look a lot alike. You sound alike and have the same mannerisms and everything. And I think he really wants to have a close relationship with you. That's all."

"He needs me for his business. He can't keep managers cause he's such an asshole to them, and he knows I'm a good one. Plus my mom was pressuring him. Believe me, she can be very persuasive."

"Will you please do me a favor, Sir? Please just give him a chance. Wait and see if he is really trying to be different now."

"I plan on it, and I don't need some faggot sub tellin me how to manage my relationship with my parents. I thought I told you to shut it!"

His sharp words cut me to the quick. I couldn't believe he'd be so dismissive of me.

"You *are* like him!" I snapped back. "You're every bit the jerk that you say he is!" I then turned from him and stared out the passenger window, feeling hot tears stream down my cheeks. We rode in silence until we reached the mall parking lot.

After parking, Matt killed the engine and we sat there momentarily, a weighty silence looming, until finally he spoke. "I'm not sure what's gotten into you, pup. I want you to spend some time thinking about the way you responded to me, and then we will talk about a punishment that's appropriate.

"As for me calling you 'faggot' ... I shouldn't have. I lost my temper. But if you'd 've shut your mouth when I told you, everything would've been cool."

I guess that was the closest Matt could come to an apology. I continued to stare out my window, wondering exactly what kind of "punishment" I'd be subjected to. Another day with Ryan? I thought about reminding him of that—the last time he punished me—but I was feeling too defeated to even be argumentative at that point.

"Dammit Petey! Say something or I'm startin this car and taking us home. Fuck the picture!"

"You hurt my feelings!" I cried.

"You deserve to have more than your damn feelings hurt. You're being impudent! I oughta drag you out a this fuckin car right here and paddle your bare ass!"

"I didn't mean to be, Sir! I'm sorry!"

"You act like because I love you that I've suddenly stopped being your Master. That's bullshit! Where the fuck do you get off backtalkin me like that? Since when did it become okay for you to argue with your Master?"

I felt my face reddening. "I just misunderstood, Sir. I thought ..."

"You thought that because I told my parents we were partners that now all of a sudden we are equal. Well we're not! I still make the decisions here, and you still obey me. If you have a problem with that arrangement, then maybe you need to find a boyfriend like Cam."

I turned and stared at him in disbelief. How had our conversation suddenly gotten so far off track? How had he concluded that I thought of him as my equal, and why would he suddenly go all ballistic on me? "Sir," I said, "I shouldn't have back-talked you. I should have shut up when you told me to. I'm sorry. I don't want a boyfriend like Cam ... or like anyone ... I want you, my Master!"

"I really hope you don't see me as being like my dad, Petey. That really pissed me off when you said that."

"I meant it as a compliment, Sir! I *like* your dad!"

"Do you really think I'm mean? Do you think I'm a bully?"

"Do I have permission to speak freely, Sir? I don't want to say the wrong ..."

"I asked the question. Of course you are free to answer it."

I looked at him exasperatedly. "You're not angry with me right now for being impudent and back-talking you, Sir. You're angry because you hate being compared to your father. You're angry because I said you can be mean, too, sometimes ... and then right after I said that, you got pissed off and called me a faggot."

"But you *were* being impudent, pup. You'd 've never talked to me like that before ..."

"Before we had our new rules," I said. "Before you told me to tell you how I felt."

"I told you to tell me if you were scared or if I was hurting you ..."

"And I just told you, Sir ... you hurt my feelings."

"So that's your answer? I asked if you thought I was mean ... and your answer is yes?"

"I'm head-over-heels in love with you, Sir. No! I don't think you're mean. I think you're the kindest, most loving and caring Master in the world. You're strict, but I want you to be. I want you to have complete control over me!

"But you'd told me that we needed to talk this over—this situation with your job and your parents. I was telling you how I saw it. I was answering your questions. I did not mean for it to sound like back-talk. I stepped out of line, Sir. You're right; I deserve to be punished." I looked down at my lap, hanging my head shamefully.

"I haven't punished you since ... well since you know ..."

"Sir, we have to put that in the past. I need my Master's guidance. I need you to punish me and to give me discipline when I do wrong. I *need* you, Sir!"

"And you weren't punished for lying to me about the car ... and for not telling me about the answering machine message ... and for going to my mom behind my back."

"Yes, Sir," I said.

He sat there for a moment and then began to laugh. I slowly looked up at him, unsure of how to interpret his emotion. "It's funny," he finally said. "I've been trying so damned hard to teach you to have some backbone, to show a little self confidence. Now you're doing that, and well ... I guess it sort of surprises me. It sort of ..."

"Scares you?" I asked.

"Not in the sense that it makes me afraid. It concerns me. I wonder if I'm shaping you into a stronger, more independent person, and in the process may ultimately lose you."

"Oh my god, Sir! No!" I immediately started crying again. Goddammit! Why'd I always have to cry over everything? "Sir ... please."

"But I guess it's only normal that you'd change. I guess we have to accept the fact that we both are going to grow and change. And as you do start to gain more confidence, it may just take a little more effort on my part to keep you in line. Right?"

"I'll be better, Sir! I promise. I won't talk back to you anymore. I'll shut my mouth when you tell me to. You'll never lose me, Sir! Please forgive me, Sir. I beg you!" I wished we were not in the car right then, for I wanted nothing more than to drop to my knees before my Master and beg him for forgiveness.

"Pup," he said. "You're right. I am like my dad. I am a hot-head. I lose my temper and then I'm mean to the people I value the most. He's done that shit to me my whole life, and now I'm doing it to you. I don't forgive you, because there's nothing to forgive."

"But I do need to be punished, Sir. I already knew how wrong I was. I knew I should have told you everything, and I know that I should not argue with you."

"Petey Pup, you do a very good job of punishing yourself. You've blamed yourself for what happened to Drew. You spend hours fretting and worrying over everything. I'm not sure I really need to punish you ... not very often anyway."

"You're gonna punish me for the other night ... for coming in my pants without permission, Sir."

He laughed. "Yeah, damn right I am. But pup, that's sex-play punishment. That's part of the scene; it's not real punishment."

"It sure feels real when the paddle hits my butt," I said, and he smiled at me affectionately.

"Why don't you write me an essay?" he said. "In fact, that's an order. I want you to write me an essay explaining the importance of protocol. Include in it what you consider appropriate for a sub to say to his Master. That's your punishment."

"When we get home, Sir?"

"Yes. As soon as we get home, before you do your other chores, you'll sit at the computer and do it. No chatting with friends, no Internet searches. You'll just sit there and write the essay until you're done. Got it?"

"Yes, Sir!" I said, smiling at him.

"And then when you're done, you'll bring it to me and kneel at my feet while I read it, and then you'll suck your Master's cock."

This was starting not to sound like much of a punishment after all, but I tried to remain contrite in my demeanor.

"What do you think of *that* punishment, boy?"

"It's very strict, Sir," I said in mock seriousness.

He laughed. "Let's go see your picture," he said. But first he wrapped his arm around me and pulled me close to him. "You're a good boy," he said, and then he kissed me.

Seeing my Master's face when he viewed the proofs from my photo shoot instantly swept away all of the anxiety I felt over our heated discussion in the car. His eyes lit up as he perused the photos, examining each one carefully. "All right," he said decisively, "we'll take these three." He handed them back to Blake separately from the others.

"Three, Sir?" I said. "We're only paying for one ..."

"We'll pay the difference in cash," Matt said, pulling out his wallet. "But ya still have to keep your word and do your time as promised ... and I'll be helping you."

"I can't believe you want three of them, Sir," I said.

"Excellent choice!" Blake said. "Really these three are my favorites, too. Do you want them each in 8 x 10's or are you interested in purchasing a package, Sir?"

"Lemme see your price sheet," Matt said.

"Yes, Sir, of course." He reached under the counter and retrieved a photocopied hand out.

When I realized that Matt was spending over two hundred dollars on professional pictures of me, I didn't really feel like my original idea had been much of a gift to him. My contribution was only a mere eighty bucks, and now Matt was actually going to be working to pay for half of that.

"Sir, I feel bad that you're paying so much," I said as we walked back to the car.

"Don't feel bad, pup," he said. "I'm spending the money on myself. I'm buyin the pics 'cause I like em."

"I wish I could pay for them, Sir."

"Oh, you'll pay," he assured me. "You'll pay bigtime."

"Promise?" I said.

"Promise!"

I couldn't wait.

When we got home, I immediately went into our room and sat down at the computer to complete my assignment. Drew was scheduled for surgery the next morning, so I wanted to get all of my chores done at home in order to be with him at the hospital. I knew he was going to be scared, and I was willing to stay with him all night if necessary, providing Matt allowed it.

As I sat at my computer, I contemplated the interaction I'd had with my Master earlier when we were at the mall. I thought about what I had done wrong and why it had resulted in the heated discussion that had ensued. I thought about how I had disappointed my Master, and I vowed from that point on to be aware of the proper protocol that must be followed when conversing with my Superior. The essay I composed read as follows:

When I first met my Master nine months ago, I was afraid to talk to him. Simply being in his presence intimidated me. I was so acutely aware of the fact that he was superior to me, that I would have never dreamed of saying anything to him that was disrespectful. As our relationship progressed and he took ownership of me, I learned about specific rules that I was required to follow.

The first rule relates to the manner in which I address my Master. It is almost never appropriate for me to directly address him by his first name. There are a few exceptions to this rule, but these are rare. Times when we are in public situations where avoidance of his first name would be obvious and draw unwanted attention is an example of such an exception. I would not refer to him as "Sir" while we are at certain social functions or in the company of certain family members.

The majority of the time, however, I am not only required to address him as "Master" or "Sir," but I also consider this to be an extraordinary honor. If he were to suddenly instruct me to stop using these titles of address, I would certainly be devastated. I glean a significant amount of comfort and satisfaction in having a Sir, and I'm proud to acknowledge his ownership of me by using this title of respect.

The second rule of communication is that when my Master offers me instruction, it is not appropriate to question his judgment. The dynamic that exists between my Master and me is akin to that of a parent and a child, and it is perhaps due to this comparison that I've previously had a tendency to offer objections in the form of subtle arguments. On occasion these challenges have been overt and not so subtle at all.

My Master's expectation when issuing a directive is that it be received respectfully and unquestionably. He should never have to wonder if his instructions will be challenged. It is not my responsibility or privilege to make determinations as to the wisdom or appropriateness of my Master's decisions. It is my job merely to obey. In truth, the burden that my Master bears in being the decision-maker is one that is very weighty. Although it can certainly be regarded as both a right and privilege, it also is a huge responsibility.

The third rule relates to the tone with which my Master chooses to address me. If he is speaking to me in a lighthearted manner, it signals me that it is acceptable to be less formal in my responses to him. If I detect annoyance in his voice, or if I become aware that I'm being reprimanded or reproached, then my duty as his sub is to immediately respond to him submissively. Typically, in non D/s relationships, the opposite of this occurs. When a person is being criticized, they naturally begin to think of ways to defend themselves. As a sub, though, my Master's criticism is precious to me. It teaches me how to serve him better, and my obligation to him is to receive his scolding gratefully and then immediately take the steps necessary to correct my unacceptable behavior.

Being an obedient and faithful sub is not something that is achieved overnight. Our conditioning is such that we generally believe that inequality is the equivalent of unfairness. We regard criticism as a negative, and we automatically attempt to find rationalizations and justifications for our behaviors rather than acknowledging that we may be wrong. These characteristics unfortunately do exist even in subs, but a devoted sub will strive to root them out and eventually get to the point where he becomes an extension of his Master's will.

Does this make me nothing more than a robot? Does it mean I am just a puppet controlled by my Master? My opinion is that it would depend upon the Master, and in my particular case, I do not feel this way. My Master encourages my individuality and tries to foster within me a sense of pride for my uniqueness. He encourages me to pursue my talents and to always find the goodness within myself.

The fact that he controls my behavior does not take away from my individuality. Nor does it stifle my freedom. I have chosen to offer myself as his sub. I willingly have handed over the decision-making privileges to him, and this is something that gives me peace and satisfaction. It is not something that makes me feel less of a person. My Master has told me that I can walk away from this set of rules any time. I can retake the responsibility for my own life decisions, but to do that would mean I'd have to also take back all of the anxiety and uncertainty that go along with this responsibility.

I was born with a certain nature. My role in life is not to dominate others or to be in control. This does not make me feel any less significant as an individual. In my Master's eyes, it makes me special, and to me this is an incredible honor. I would not change who I am even if I were able to do so, and I'm thankful every single moment that I have found my perfect Master.

My goal is to continue to strive to obey the rules of protocol and to become an even more devoted sub to my Master. I suspect that as we mature together, the situations in which he chooses to address me less formally will actually increase, but even if not, I am very content to obey him submissively and to express myself in the appropriate manner.

I love my Master with all my heart, and it's my hope that my explanation of how I see the protocol is acceptable and pleasing to him.

I was shirtless and wearing my collar when I approached my Master with my assigned essay. He was reclining in an easy chair in the living room, the same one in which I'd watched him receive oral service from Alex a few weeks previously. Because he was watching sports on television, I did not wish to interrupt him, so I merely knelt at his feet, placing the printed text on the armrest beside him.

Feeling overwhelmed with desire to worship my Master, I bowed my head, lowering myself even further toward his feet. The words I had written for and about him had poured from my heart, and it was at this moment that I was overcome with the emotion that these expressions evoked. Silently I wept as I pressed my lips worshipfully against the tops of his feet.

I heard him above me, reaching for the document I'd laid at his disposal. I knew the writing assignment had been given to me as a form of punishment, but it had also served as a means of helping me to refocus.

Ever since the day that Matt had snapped at Drew during our pillow fight, I had harbored so many fears about my Master. I had worried that his gentleness and compassion toward me were indications that he was losing his desire to dominate me. I had listened to the advice of my dearest a friend—a friend who had so often steered me in the right direction with his wise mentoring; yet, this time these words may have come from a state of innocent misunderstanding.

My Master had not changed, not in the sense that Drew had assumed. Originally he had rescued me, and he always would remain my hero. Originally he had overwhelmed me with his strength and self confidence, and he always would be my idol. Originally he had taught me who I was and had helped me to love myself because of this identity; and he always would be my trainer and mentor.

Yes, the dynamic of our relationship had shifted in a certain sense. We now lived with each other and shared most of our time together. Our communication no longer needed to constantly remain so formal. In addition to Master and sub, we now were becoming the best of friends.

It was not my Master who had changed. It was not his Dom heart that needed to be reawakened. It was my heart ... I was the one who'd needed the reminder.

As I lay at my Master's feet, unable to even look up at him, I trembled. It was identical to the trembling I'd experienced the very first day we had met. Matt had asked me if I was cold, even though it was seventy-five degrees and sunny. I trembled now at his feet as I did that day because I was in awe of this man. This Master. My Master!

Matt sat quietly, not seeming to notice my presence, and when I heard him place the papers on the stand beside him, I had no desire to rise from my position of servitude. He made no indication to me that I needed to do so. He knew what I needed. He knew what I craved. For the next hour I lay there, kissing his feet reverently, until finally I rose slightly, but only to turn around and curl myself between his legs. Feeling him around me reminded me of how sheltered I was, and as he reached down to gently brush his fingers through my hair, I knew he approved of my essay. I knew he approved of my worship. And I knew he approved of my submissive heart.

"I love you, pup," he whispered.

"I love you too, Master," I said, my words barely a whisper.

13

It was late that afternoon when Alex came home, and he was obviously shaken. I was in the kitchen making a pasta salad. "Where's Matt?" he said to me.

"He's out on the deck, Sir," I said, "having a beer."

Without a word Alex headed toward the patio door, but Matt entered before he made it across the room. "Dude, what's up?" Matt said.

"Matt, will you let Petey go with me to the hospital … please?"

"Sure," Matt said. "He was gonna go up there in a few minutes anyway. What's wrong?"

"I need him to go now!" Alex said, his voice noticeably shaky. "It's Drew. I can't get him to stop crying."

"Is he alone?" I said, suddenly terrified for my friend.

"His sister's waiting there with him till we get back."

"Poor Drew!" I cried. "Sir, why's he crying? He's scared?"

"It's like this whole thing has just overwhelmed him. He realizes how close he came to dying, and now it's like he thinks if he has this surgery he really will die this time."

"Sir, can I go?" I cried. "Oh, my poor Drew!"

"Of course you can go," Matt said. "You think Petey will be able to calm him down?"

"I'm willin to try anything, man. He keeps crying and begging me to check him out of the hospital. No matter what I say, I can't get him to chill. He's just absolutely freaked."

"He's terrified, Sir. It's like maybe … what do they call that? Post traumatic stress? He probably keeps remembering what happened when he was shot."

"He does! He says the whole thing keeps playing over in his mind like a movie. I think he needs some help … like a doctor or something, a counselor."

"Well we need to get him the help he needs," Matt said. "Did you talk to his doctor at the hospital—his physician?"

"Not yet."

"Take Petey with you, and while he's with Drew, track down his doctor. Tell the nurses you demand to talk to him."

"His doctor is a chick," Alex said.

"Well *her* then, but he can't go into surgery like that. And Petey, just listen to him and let him cry if he needs to. Don't discourage him from talking about anything he wants—or needs to talk about. Understand?"

I nodded. "Yes, Sir."

"I'm getting dressed now, Sir," I said.

"Go ahead, and hurry up." I rushed into the bedroom and threw on a shirt. When I came back to the living room only seconds later, Alex was already headed out the front door.

"Petey!" Matt hollered. I had almost left without saying goodbye.

"I'm sorry, Sir!" I said as I turned to face him.

"Come here, pup," he said. I rushed over to him and he reached up and unsnapped my collar. "Get your necklace real quick before you go."

"Yes, Sir!" I said. "I almost forgot." He leaned in and kissed me quickly.

I feared the worst, but when I walked into the hospital room Drew was not crying, at least not at the moment. His sister Shari was with him, and I think he was putting up a brave front for her sake. She apologized, explaining that she really had to leave, and I hugged and thanked her for all she'd done. She had been very supportive of her brother throughout the ordeal.

Alex had also excused himself because he needed to go to the nurses' station to find out about contacting Drew's doctor. I sat on the bed next to my best friend and simply held his hand. "Drew, are you all right?" I asked.

Slowly he shook his head, and it broke my heart to see big crocodile tears welling in his eyes. Silently they streamed down his cheeks.

"I won't leave you," I assured him. "I'm gonna be right here with you every single second until you have the operation. Then I'm gonna be waiting for you when you wake up. So is Alex, and so is Matt."

"I just have a very bad feeling about it, Petey. You know, I should have died the other night. That bullet could have gone straight through my heart."

"But honey, it didn't! Thank god it didn't! Drew, you saved us. You saved all the rest of us by what you did. You're a hero."

"I keep remembering it all," he said hoarsely. "I remember how weak I felt and all the blood. It was everywhere. I was soaked with my own blood."

"And Alex was holding you ..."

"Holding me, knowing I was about to die."

"Holding you and trying to keep you from *not* dying!"

"Oh, Petey! Why can't I get this out of my head? I still see that horrible, terrified look on Ryan's face. I still see his pain. I still hear the gun going off. Ya know, that whole incident was like in slow motion, and now it just keeps running through my memory like an instant replay."

"Why do you think that is, Drew? Do you know?"

"Because I was so afraid ... I've never been more afraid, especially when they took me away from Alex. I thought I was gonna die alone!"

"And now they have to take you away from him again ... for the surgery."

"Yes!" he sobbed. "And it might be the last thing I ever see. I might never make love to him again. I might never feel him holding me in his arms!"

"It's okay, babe ... it's okay." I wanted more than anything to shush him, to try to quiet his emotion, but I remembered what Matt had told me. *Let him feel whatever he needs to feel.*

"I know how scared you were," I said. "I would've been terrified if they took me from Matt like that. Especially after being shot. But you do know why they had to do it, right?"

He nodded. "I know why, Petey. They did it to save my life ..."

"Yes ... and now they are going to take you away for just a little bit to fix you so that you can heal."

"Even though I know all this in my head, I can't stop myself from *feeling* this way!" he confessed. "I want to, but I can't. I've never been emotional like you, Petey, but it's like I can't stop crying. Even when I'm not actually crying, I feel like I am ... or like I'm about to."

"Well I want you to know that you can always cry when you're with me," I said. "If you feel like crying for any reason—even for no reason—even if you just feel like it and don't know why, you can cry ..."

"I'm a crybaby, and here that's what you always thought you were."

"We're both big blubber-pusses!" I laughed.

"I know!" He laughed and cried at the same time. "Poor Alex. Ya know, I begged him to take me out of the hospital. I told him if he really loved me, he wouldn't make me go through this."

"Drew, Alex knows you're scared. He doesn't blame you for saying that. He also knows you're aware of how much he loves you ..."

"I really do know he loves me, Petey! I'm so rotten to put him through that. Of course he can't take me out of the hospital, not when I've gotta have surgery."

"Well, listen to me, Drew ... please. It doesn't matter. Nobody—especially not Alex—cares that you said that. Everybody understands. We all know you are scared, and we know why. We are scared too—not that you're gonna die or anything. We're scared that we can't figure out what to do to help you not feel so alone and afraid.

"But we're gonna be here. There will not be one single second when you'll be alone. We are gonna be right with you until you fall asleep for your operation. Then we're gonna be here when you wake up. It will only seem like seconds to you and it'll be over. I had tonsil surgery once, and I didn't remember any of it. I dozed off and the next thing I knew I was awake and it was over."

He nodded and wiped his eyes with the back of his hand. "Will they let you stay with me overnight?" he asked.

I nodded. "Or else they'll have to drag me the fuck out of here! I'm not leaving!"

Drew smiled at me. "You got a cigarette?" he asked.

I shook my head. "I wish I did." I smiled at him. Although I'd always hated the fact he smoked, I'd have given him one now if I could. I'd have given him anything.

"In all honesty, I haven't really even been craving a smoke. I don't know why. I think about it sometimes, but I guess I've been too obsessed with everything else to worry about it."

"Just think what it'll be like when you get home. You'll be able to boss me around and make me wait on you hand and foot."

"Like my personal slave ..."

"Bet you never thought you'd have one of those," I grinned.

"And a cute one too! I hope Matt doesn't make you do all my work too. That'd be so unfair ..."

"Drew, we're like family. Of course it's not unfair. I already plan to do your work ... I just did Alex's laundry for him last night."

"I hope you folded it right. He's very fussy."

"Ohh ... me, too, but he didn't say anything. You can teach me when you get home, okay?"

"Well I'm gonna do as much as I can, and after I'm better I'll make it up to you. Promise."

"Yeah," I said, "cause you know what they say about paybacks."

Alex entered the room behind me. "They're a bitch," he said.

"Oh Sir," I said, "Drew was worried that I didn't fold your clothes right."

"You didn't," he said, "but it's cool. Don't sweat it."

"Please just tell me, Sir, so I can learn to do it the right way."

"Okay, deal," he said. He looked at Drew affectionately. "I just talked to your doctor. She said we can stay with you tonight. I asked about postponing the surgery and she didn't advise it. She said she'd prescribe you a sedative to help you rest, and that they'd bring us a couple cots so we can sleep right here with you in your room."

"She did?" he said. "Oh, Sir! Thank you."

"She thinks what you're going through is normal, and she said you might need to see another doctor about it, but not to worry. And I have a surprise for you too ..."

Drew grinned up at his Master. "You do?"

Slowly he reached into his shirt pocket and pulled out a single cigarette. Drew's eyes lit up. "She even said we could take you outside for a little bit."

"Oh my god! Let's go," he said, throwing back the covers.

"Hold on!" Alex cautioned him while laughing. "You gotta wait till I get a wheelchair. Actually, Petey, go down to the nurses' station and get one."

"Yes, Sir!" I said and smiled at Drew as I jumped up.

Matt had his arm around me in the surgical waiting room when the doctor entered. Drew's surgeon was a tall African American man named Doctor Wyatt. "Tompkins family?" he said, and the three of us stood up.

"The surgery went fine. Took a little longer than we expected, but everything seems to be just as we'd expect it to be. Drew's in recovery now, and you'll be able to see him in about a half hour or so. Do you have any questions?"

I sighed with relief and pressed myself tight against Matt's body. I was so happy to hear the good news, I nearly started to cry again.

A few minutes later I was standing by Drew's bedside when he awakened.

"Petey," he whispered. "Water!" I reached over for the sponge that I had used to swab his mouth. He sucked on it thirstily. "Ahhh ... so thirsty," he said. "Is it over?"

I smiled down at him. "It's over and you're fine! Alex and Matt are here, too."

"I love you," he said. "All of you." And then he dozed off.

14

The day after Drew's surgery, Matt informed me that he'd made a decision about his father's job offer. He had decided to accept the offer, albeit conditionally. He was going to tell his father that he wanted the new store, the one he'd originally been slated to manage. He also was going to ask his father to allow us to move into the cabin.

When Matt first told me this, I was extremely concerned for multiple reasons. First of all, the cabin was at least a half-hour drive from the city, and I truly hated driving. Secondly, Drew was going to be getting out of the hospital within the next few days, and I had already promised him that I would be around to take care of him. Thirdly, I would miss Alex and Drew terribly!

"I thought you'd be excited, pup," Matt said to me when he observed the crestfallen look on my face.

"I am, Sir," I lied. "I'm excited about the job, and I'm very happy we're going to have our own place."

"But you don't want to leave Drew?" he asked.

I looked down at the ground in front of me. "No Sir. He needs me right now. I promised him I'd take care of him until he's better."

"Well I'm hoping they go with us," Matt said. His remark was delivered rather offhandedly, and it took me by surprise.

"Sir, did you just say they could move with us? Alex and Drew?"

"Sure, if it's what Alex wants, but maybe he'd rather have his privacy back."

I was starting to get excited. "The cabin is much bigger than here, Sir. They would have more privacy than they do now."

"But if we were to move out of here, they'd have their own apartment to themselves."

I frowned as I thought about it. Of course Alex would decide to keep his apartment. He was too independent. He'd allowed Matt and me to move in with them due to our circumstances, but I doubted that he'd want it to be the other way around.

"Of course, it'd save them a bunch of money. There'd be no rent to pay."

"But they'd have to drive, Sir."

"Well Drew would, when school starts again and he's back to work. Alex is gonna be working from home."

"Sir, what about me? I hate driving ... it makes me so nervous."

"You'll get used to it, pup. And you do just fine when you drive. In fact you're a really good driver, just a little too slow."

"Do you think your father will agree to your conditions, Sir?"

"He's planning on giving me that cabin anyway. Just askin for it a little early is all."

"I'm glad we might be living there, Sir." I smiled as a thought suddenly occurred to me.

"Oh yeah? Why's that?"

I reached up with both hands and ran my fingers across my collar. "It's where I was when you gave me this, Sir."

"That it is," he smiled. "And then I tickled you till you pissed yourself and then spanked your ass ..."

"And made love to me in the shower. And then we ..."

"Okay! Yes, I remember. I remember it all, pup."

"You don't want me to talk about it, Sir," I said dejectedly.

"You're gonna end up gettin me hard, and I'll be late for tennis." Matt was meeting a high school friend to play tennis. He was supposed to be leaving any minute.

"I bet if you get really horny you'll end up kickin ass on the tennis court, Sir."

"Or I'll be so distracted I'll get creamed."

I laughed. "You're supposed to be the one doing the creaming, Sir. You're supposed to cream me."

"Enough!" he said, laughing as he leaned in to me kiss me goodbye. "Get all your chores done before you leave for work," he said. "And make sure Alex knows that you're fixing him his lunch."

"I will, Sir," I said. "I love you!"

"Love ya, too," he said, and then he left.

Alex was still in bed at the time that Matt left, but Matt wanted me to make sure I fixed his best bud a nice lunch. We hadn't gotten home from the hospital until quite late the night before, and Drew's sister suggested that Alex get some much-needed rest. She promised to go to the hospital in the morning while Alex slept in.

I didn't have to be at work until later that afternoon, so Matt had given me a list of responsibilities he wanted me to accomplish. They all were pretty basic cleaning jobs that I'd have done on my own, even without my Master's instructions. It was nice to feel as if I was specifically serving him, though, while in the process of performing what would otherwise be extremely mundane tasks.

I began by cleaning the windows in the living room, and then I dusted. I didn't want to run the vacuum while Alex was sleeping so I decided to wait until he got up. I then went in and thoroughly cleaned the bathroom while intermittently tending to the laundry. Finally, at about eleven o'clock, I started the preparation of Alex's lunch. A half hour later, when I was finished making him an over-stacked Reuben sandwich and homemade French fries, I decided that I'd better go see if he was awake. I really didn't want to disturb him, but I didn't want his food to go cold either.

Carefully I tiptoed down the hallway, listening for movement in his room. If I could hear him sleeping—or snoring—I'd just wrap the sandwich and reheat it when he awakened. I could always eat the fries myself and make him some fresh. I was relieved, though, when I did hear him moving around in his room. As I approached his door, I could actually hear his voice. He was talking to someone. I surmised that he must be on the phone.

The door to his room was slightly ajar, perhaps because he'd gotten up to use the restroom and not closed it all the way. I was about to knock on it when I heard him say something that took me by surprise. "Yeah boy, you want this big cock up your tight little ass, don't ya? Beg for it boy! Beg like the bitch you are … oh yeah … unnngghhh!"

My mouth dropped open in astonishment. Who was in there with him, I wondered. Poor Drew, if he only knew! Carefully I inched my way closer to the door, pressing my face up against the crack in order to try seeing inside. I could still hear Alex moaning, but I couldn't hear anyone else.

As my eyes adjusted, I began to be able to focus on the bed. Alex was sprawled out on it, completely naked, and he actually *was* on the phone. He had the phone in one hand and his fat cock in the other, stroking it wickedly.

"Beg for it, boy! Tell your Master how much you want it! Even with your arm in that sling, I'm still gonna fuck that ass of yours!"

Oh my god! Alex was having phone sex with Drew! Oh I was so excited! It was so sweet! I wanted so badly to crouch down there on the ground and continue peeking through the door, but it just didn't feel right to me. I felt like they deserved their privacy. I felt that to secretly sit there and watch my best friend's Master beat off would somehow be a betrayal. On the other hand, it might make for a really interesting conversation later with Drew.

I decided to take the high road, though, and quietly inched away from the door and back into the living room. I got out the vacuum and began to clean the carpets. Just as I was finishing up ten minutes later, I heard the bathroom door close right as I turned off the vacuum. Alex stumbled down the hall, wearing only a pair of long-legged lounge pants. He yawned and smiled at me.

"Morning, Sir," I said innocently. "I hope I didn't wake you with the vacuum."

"Nah, I was already up," he said. *You certainly were,* I thought. I just smiled in response.

"I made you some lunch, Sir. It's in the kitchen."

"Cool," he said. "Thanks."

"My pleasure, Sir. Are you going to be going up to see Drew?"

"In a few minutes. Gotta wake up first."

"I can make you some coffee if you'd like," I offered.

"Nah, thanks anyways." He walked over to the refrigerator and pulled out a bottle of Mountain Dew, uncapping it and taking a big swig.

As I stood there watching him, I thought about what Matt had said to me. I really hoped that Alex decided to accept Matt's offer to be our housemates. I was gonna really miss both of them if he did not.

As I clocked in to start my shift at work that afternoon, Mr. Bartlett was on his way out. Again it would be just Jason and I running the store. I got myself acclimated to my surroundings and counted my cash drawer while Jason continued to ring customers at the other register.

A few minutes later when we finally were alone, he smiled at me. "Guess what?" he said.

"What?" I replied, anticipating a juicy piece of gossip or something of that nature.

"I've got a surprise for you, but I've gotta run out to my car to get it."

"Why didn't you just bring it in with you when you started work?" I asked.

"Didn't want Bartlett to see. Watch the counter and I'll be right back."

A couple minutes later Jason returned with a long slender package. It was a white box, and it looked close in size to one that might contain chocolates. Surely that wasn't the case, though, for he wouldn't have reason to conceal such a thing from Mr. Bartlett.

He handed it to me. "Open it," he urged me.

I set the box down on the counter in front of me, looking around to make sure no customers were nearby. Carefully I removed the lid and gasped just a little when I saw what was inside. It was a mahogany paddle, the type you'd see hanging in a frat house. "Oh my god!" I said. "You're not gonna ..."

"Use that fucker on your ass?" he finished for me. "Hell, yeah!"

"Jason, it even has air holes in it. This thing's gonna hurt like a mother!"

"You know it, dude!" He busted up laughing. I didn't really know what to do, but I felt my face start to redden.

Finally I spoke again. "When?" I asked quietly.

"I'm just waiting to hear from Matt."

"He's picking me up tonight," I said teasingly.

"Are you wearin your special undies?" he asked.

This time I was the one to laugh. "No!" I yelled. "Be quiet in case someone hears us!"

He rolled his eyes. "As if they can't already tell you're a fag."

I scowled at him. "Maybe, but that doesn't mean they need to know I wear shocking underwear ... or like getting my butt spanked."

"Oh, so you admit you like it, huh?"

"No! I said it *doesn't* mean they ... oh, whatever, you know what I mean!"

Working with Jason that night was a riot. He was always a lot of fun to work with, but tonight especially he was in a really good mood. The thing that I liked about him so much was that he was genuinely a really good coworker who knew his job well. He always participated in the completion of the shift duties without grumbling, and he seemed to never stop being positive. He was just one of those cheerful, pleasant people. It was a little bit shocking to discover that there was a side of him that was really into gay kink. Outwardly he appeared so conservative.

As usual, we had all of our cleaning and stocking assignments completed prior to the close of our shift, and when it was time to lock up, we were ready to go. It was dark outside so I couldn't see by looking through the window whether Matt was waiting for me yet or not. I stepped up to the front door, stepped out and quickly looked around. It was then that I heard the store phone ringing. "I'll get it," Jason called to me from the back room. I turned and saw him pick up the phone at the front counter.

"Book World, this is Jason," he said. I clicked the door lock and then turned to him. He was smiling as he listened to the caller on the other end of the line. "Yes, Sir," he said. "Yes, Sir, I do ... Yes, Sir, I will ... Thank you, Sir." Then he hung up.

"Your Master will be here in five minutes," he said, "to pick *us* up!"

"No way!" I screamed.

He started laughing and pointing at me, extending both arms and aiming his index fingers at me tauntingly. "You're gonna be hurtin for certain, dude. Fuck yeah!"

I felt myself starting to get a little bit excited, partially because the paddling really did turn me on, but also because I remembered what Matt had told me. I knew Matt was not planning to limit our scene with Jason to just a fun little spank fest. He definitely had envisioned a full-on three-way session. I wondered if I should warn Jason or just wait and see what happened. I decided it was not my job to do so ... that was something I'd best leave in the hands of my Master.

We were both standing outside in front of the building when Matt pulled up a few minutes later. "Back seat, pup," he instructed me. He was driving the sports car, and being the littlest, it was by far easiest for me to squeeze into the back.

"Lemme see it," he said to Jason as he settled himself into the passenger seat. Jason handed Matt the box containing the paddle. With the car dome light still on, Matt opened the lid and examined the contents of the box. "Nice!" he smiled. He removed the paddle from the box and held it in his hand. It seemed so big, especially in the confined space of the small car.

"Whaddya think, Petey Pup?" he asked me.

I tried with difficulty to maintain the soberest of expressions on my face. "I guess it's what I deserve, Sir," I said contritely.

"You *guess*?" he said. "Well I guess Jason's gonna have to convince you ... so you know for sure."

"Yes, Sir," I said. My heart raced excitedly as we drove back to our apartment. Matt explained to us that we'd have the apartment to ourselves. Alex had decided to go out for the evening. Apparently there was a strip show down at one of the gay clubs, and he decided to go hang out with some of his friends. Matt had encouraged it, saying he deserved a little fun after the exhausting week he'd had.

We all were a bit exhausted emotionally because of what had happened to Drew. I was thankful that my best friend would be getting out of the hospital the next morning, and I was glad I had the entire day free to help get him settled back into his home. At the moment, though, I wasn't thinking too much about Drew. I was thinking more about my backside and what was in store for it. I squirmed nervously in my seat as we got closer to home.

Once inside the apartment, Matt instructed Jason to take off his shirt, and he told me to strip down to my underwear. He then had Jason help him move the furniture, pushing the sofa back to clear a bigger section of the living room. Without having to be told, I already had changed into my collar, and I stood nervously in the corner of the room awaiting further instruction. Matt placed a kitchen chair in the center of the living room and then he stood to the side of it.

"Get over here, boy," Matt commanded, pointing to the floor in front of him. Nervously I scurried over to stand momentarily in front of my Master and drop gracefully to my knees. "Bring me the paddle," Matt instructed Jason, and he quickly handed it over.

Matt took the paddle in his hand and examined it, smiling evilly. Slowly he rubbed its smooth surface with his other hand. "Tools," he said dramatically. "Tools to help us learn." He then looked down at me. "Are you ready to learn a lesson, pup?"

I nodded and then quickly looked down at my Master's Nikes. "Yes, Sir!" I responded.

"I have lots of other tools," he said. He was speaking slowly, as if contemplating. "But I think we'll save em ... this will be enough for now." He waited a couple moments before continuing, and I just knelt there submissively at his feet.

"Jason!" he yelled suddenly. "Get over here now!" Quickly Jason stepped over to stand in front of my Master. "I'm entrusting you to use this tool wisely to assist me in disciplining my slave boy. Are you prepared to do so?"

"Yes, Sir!" Jason responded enthusiastically. Matt held out the paddle for him to take. Matt then stepped aside and took a seat in his favorite recliner. "Make him kiss it," he said to Jason. "Make him show his gratitude for the tool that is about to teach him."

Jason was now standing in front of me, wearing only his khakis and socks. His smooth, slender body excited me, and I wanted nothing more than to stare up at him and take in the sight of his bare torso. I remained in my submissive position, though, with my head bowed. Jason held the paddle with both hands, one hand below the handle and the other under the opposite end. He pushed it in front of my face, balancing it there in his hands. "Kiss it!" he commanded, "and thank me for the discipline I'm about to deliver!"

"Thank you, Sir!" I cried, and then reverently leaned forward to kiss the smooth surface of the paddle.

"Do you know why you need this discipline, boy?" Jason asked me.

"Because I disobeyed my Master," I stated meekly.

"What?!" he screamed. "I can't fucking hear you!"

"Because I disobeyed, Sir!" I shouted. "I disobeyed my Master."

"That's better, bitch boy," he said.

"And just how many swats from this paddle do you deserve, boy?" he asked.

I truly did not know what to say. Quickly I glanced at my Master, but he just sat there saying nothing. He pointed to Jason, indicating he had deferred his authority to my Alpha boy Master. "I don't know, Sir," I said to Jason, "as many swats as you want."

"Okay," he laughed. "A thousand!" I glanced up at him in disbelief, almost laughing. "Something funny, faggot?" he sneered.

"No Sir," I said, instantly sobering my expression. "A thousand seems too much, Sir."

"How many, then? Answer me!"

"Ten?" I suggested shyly, grimacing just a bit as I did so for fear he'd disapprove of my suggestion.

Of course he did disapprove. "You can't be serious!" he yelled, leaning over me and slapping the palm of his hand with the paddle. He was starting to remind me of a very strict drill sergeant. "Fucking try again, boy!" he commanded.

"Fifteen, Sir?" I asked.

Jason stepped away from me momentarily and moved toward my Master. "Sir, can you believe this slime bucket? Can you fuckin even believe this shit I'm hearing from him?!"

I wanted so badly to look up at my Master. I wanted to see if he was smiling, if he was as rock hard as I was. If he did find it amusing, though, the tone of his voice did not betray him. In dead seriousness he delivered his command. "Fifty!" he said. "If he won't give you an acceptable number, then I'll fuckin choose."

"Please, Sir!" I cried. "Please let me try again, oh please! I beg you, Sir!"

"How many, slut?" Matt demanded.

"Twenty-five, Sir!" I bellowed. "I beg you for twenty-five swats, Sir!"

"Assume the position, boy!" Jason ordered, and quickly I scurried to my feet and leaned over the back of the chair. "Hands on the back of the chair, boy, ass out!"

I did as he said, spreading my legs wide and stepping back far enough so that when I bent over, my butt was in the air as ordered.

"I'm gonna let you keep your under panties on, boy ... for now!"

"Thank you, Sir!" I replied as I stared down at the ground beneath me. Jason then assumed his position as well, placing himself slightly behind me to my left. Matt was seated opposite us, where he got a full view of both of us.

"Are you ready for your punishment to commence, slave boy?" Jason asked calmly.

"Yes, Sir!" I replied.

"Then beg for it!" he demanded.

"Please Sir!" I cried, "Please commence with my punishment."

"Please what?" he said.

"Please give me my first swat, Sir!"

"Very good, boy. I want you to beg for every single one of them. Understand?"

"Yes, Sir!"

"And I want you to thank me for them afterwards!"

"Yes, Sir!"

Thwack!! He delivered the first blow. I bit down on my bottom lip, not because I was trying to avoid crying out in pain, but merely to keep from laughing. His swat was not hard at all.

"One!" I cried. "Thank you, Sir!"

"And ...?"

"May I please have my next swat, Sir?"

Thwack! The second one was a little harder.

"Two!" I shouted. "Thank you, Sir! May I please have another?"

Thwack! "Three! Thank you, Sir! May I please have another?"

The paddling continued, each blow increasing gradually in both speed and severity. By the time we were up to number ten, the blows were stinging fiercely, and it felt as if my ass was on fire. At this point I actually was biting on my lip from the pain.

"Eleven!" I cried and then gasped. I paused momentarily. "Thank you, Sir! May I please have another?"

Jason laughed. "I'm not sure you mean that, boy," he said.

"May I please have another, Sir!" I screamed as loud as I could.

"Take off your underwear!" he demanded.

I removed my hands from the back of the chair and forced myself upright. I already felt very stiff, and every bit of movement reminded me of the burning sensation I felt radiating from my butt cheeks down to my upper thighs. I slid my fingers into the waistband of my underwear and very gingerly slid them downwards over my flaming-red buttocks. My rock-hard cock popped out as I did so, standing at full attention.

"Now assume your position, and beg for it like you mean it, boy!" he said.

"May I please have another, Sir!" I screamed as I again leaned against the chair.

Thwack! This time the sound of the paddle was wicked as it smacked against my bare ass. "Aaaahhh!" I cried out involuntarily and winced from the pain. "Twelve!" I shouted. "Thank you, Sir!" I couldn't bring myself to beg him for another just yet.

He waited a couple seconds. "And?"

"Sir!" I cried.

"Should we start over at the beginning?"

"No, Sir! Please! Please may I have another?"

Thwack! "Thirteen! Oooohh. Ohh god! Oh, Sir!" I cried.

I didn't think I could go on. It hurt so bad! I knew I couldn't stop though. I knew I couldn't disappoint my Master. "Thank you, Sir! Please may I have another?"

Thwack! I screamed in agony this time, and hot tears flooded my eyes. "AAAAAAHHH! ..." I couldn't even bring myself to speak my scripted response.

It got very quiet in the room for a moment and then I took a deep breath and whispered. "Fourteen. Thank you, Sir! May I please—"

"Enough!" Matt said. He was standing beside me gently wrapping his strong arm around my chest and pulling me upright. I looked up into his eyes apologetically as the tears continued to stream down my cheeks.

"Have you learned your lesson, boy?" he demanded sternly.

"Yes, Sir!" I said, trying desperately to sound convincing.

He reached down to wrap his fist around my softening cock. Immediately it sprung back to life, and then he kissed me.

"Are you okay?" Jason asked. I nodded and smiled at him. "I ... um ... I didn't know how hard to ..."

"He's fine," Matt assured him. "Petey, go kneel in front of my chair, and don't touch yourself!"

"Yes, Sir," I said and did as he'd instructed.

"Strip!" Matt commanded Jason. My friend just stared at Matt for a moment, but then he complied. "Twenty-five?" Matt asked. "That was the number, right?"

"Yes, Sir," Jason said.

"And how many did you give Petey so far?"

"Fourteen, Sir," Jason answered.

"So we start at fifteen," Matt stated authoritatively. "Assume the position!"

As I was kneeling there my ass was completely ablaze. It felt very tender, as if sunburned, so I had to ease my butt cheeks down against my heels very carefully. My cock was throbbing and jutted out proudly in front of me, begging for attention. I knew, however, that I was forbidden from touching it.

Seeing Jason standing there in the very same position that I'd assumed for paddling was a delicious sight. Only seconds before, he had been the disciplinarian, and it had been with delight that he'd administered my punishment. Now, however, the tables had turned, and he was in the submissive position. I almost felt guilty for enjoying it so much, but when I noticed the throbbing bulge in Jason's underwear, I didn't feel quite so bad. Obviously he was as turned on as I was.

What was equally thrilling was seeing my Master in his position of authority. After Jason had taken his position at the chair, Matt pressed down against his back to force him into a horizontal position. Then Matt placed the paddle on the small of Jason's back, using it as a table while he stepped back and stripped off his own shirt. It was wickedly hot to see my Master standing there baring his masculine torso for me to see. I continued to kneel there and stare at him wide-eyed, hoping the striptease would continue.

Matt did not go further than to remove his shirt, though—not yet. Instead he reached over and picked up the paddle. "Are you man enough to take the remainder of Petey's punishment for him, bitch boy?" he asked.

"Yes, Sir!" Jason responded.

"If you can take it, then I guess little Petey here will be in your debt, wouldn't you say?"

"Yes, Sir! Yes, he will be ..."

"Well, if you're ready, you know what to say ..."

"Please, Sir! May I have my first swat?"

Matt looked over at me and smiled. "Uh ... well, I guess so, if you really want it." He stood there for a moment, not yet even raising the paddle into position.

"Please, Sir!" Jason begged.

Matt then assumed a stance beside Jason like a batter stepping up to the plate. Smoothly he raised the paddle in the air, winding up in preparation for his delivery. Then with one quick whoosh he swung the paddle down, and it made that delightfully distinct thwacking sound against Jason's underwear. Jason grunted and his body lunged forward just a bit.

"Fifteen!" he cried. "Thank you, Sir! May I please have another?"

Thwack! "Sixteen! Thank you, Sir! May I please have another?"

Thwack! "Seventeen! Thank you, Sir! May I please have another?"

Rapidly Matt continued delivering his relentless blows and did so until he was up to number twenty-two. I watched Jason's face as Matt paddled him. With each blow, he grimaced and bit down on his lip. He moaned a little but never cried out. I did notice the white-knuckled grip he maintained on the chair in front of him, though.

Matt stopped the paddling at number twenty-two, leaving only three swats undelivered. "Now take off your underwear!" he commanded.

Jason did not hesitate to obey, and when he did, I saw his cock for the first time. It was long and slender, just like Jason. His endowment was impressive but didn't possess the girth of my Master's. It could not have been any harder than it was, and I knew by Jason's arousal that he was not suffering too badly from his ass-paddling.

"Whaddya think of that bright red ass, pup?" he asked me. "That's what yours looks like right now, too."

"It's very red, Sir," I said as I stared up at my Master. "And very smooth ..."

"Should I make it a little redder?" he asked.

I thought for a second before answering. If I said no, I feared I'd be back in the line of fire. On the other hand, Matt had shown mercy on me only moments before, and maybe he was testing me to see if I would do the same.

"If he wants it, Sir," I said, feeling I'd come up with the perfect compromise.

Matt started laughing. "Think you're smart, huh, pup?"

I looked up at him innocently and smiled. "No, Sir," I said sincerely.

"What if I told ya you had to suck his dick for taking your punishment? After all, you just admitted you owed him a favor."

Matt had never had me suck anyone but him before. I'd never even been allowed to suck Alex. I was shocked by his suggestion, and frankly I didn't know how I was expected to respond.

"Huh?" he said, "Answer me, pup!"

"Sir, I don't think I'd like it."

"It seems like he turns you on though ... look how hard you are."

"I'm hard because of you, Sir! I only wanna suck you!"

"What if I wanna see my pup suckin someone else?"

"Then I obey you, Sir ... but you asked me what I wanted, not what I would do."

"Good answer, pup," he said. "And I *don't* want you to suck anyone but me. We'll work out some other way for you to repay Jason. Right now, though, his ass needs three more swats. You ready, boy?"

"Yes, Sir!" Jason cried. "May I please have another?"

Matt delivered the three remaining blows, and in the process Jason remained true to form. He did not shed a tear, did not cry out the way I had, and showed no signs of severe suffering. In fact, I think Matt could have gone on to deliver a couple dozen more swats and Jason would have remained unfazed. When Matt was finished he tossed the paddle to the floor and stood behind Jason, slowly rubbing his hands across the boy's smooth, reddened ass cheeks.

Finally Matt delivered a series of quick swats with his bare hand, and the sound of flesh on flesh was extremely exciting. I imagined him hauling Jason over his knee and spanking him like he would a little boy. When Matt saw me smiling he turned to me and said, "You like that, pup?"

I nodded. "Yes, Sir."

At this point Matt reached down and unbuckled his khakis. He then unzipped them and pulled them completely off. Next he removed his boxers. All the while Jason remained in his submissive position.

Matt's cock throbbed as he stared at the humbled sub who stood bent over before him. It was as if he were deciding which side he wanted to use. I smiled up at him as he stepped over to the chair and straddled it. "Open!" he said, and Jason obeyed.

I then watched jealously as he took my Master deep into his throat. Matt fucked his face hard, just like he usually did to me, and Jason expertly devoured the entirety of him. After Matt came, he made Jason kneel and jack off in front of him. I remained in my original kneeling position, only allowed to watch.

"Are you ready to go home, boy?" he asked Jason.

My friend looked up at Matt and smiled. "Yes, Sir, if you want. Are you asking me to leave?"

"I'm not asking you to leave, boy. I'm giving you an option. If you wanna stay here and watch me fuck my pup, you're welcome to do so ... or I can take you home first."

"I wanna watch," he said eagerly.

A wave of relief swept over me, for I was beginning to think my Master was going to conclude the scene without even using me. I thought it might have been part of my punishment. When he picked me up off the ground, though, and carried me over to the kitchen table, I knew I'd been wrong. He laid me on my back and then proceeded to mercilessly fuck me like a wild man. He literally fucked the cum right out of me, and I screamed gratefully as I shot my load all over myself at the same exact time my Master came inside me.

Afterwards Matt kissed me and told me to clean everything up while he drove Jason home. I was in bed, though not yet asleep, when Matt got back. After jumping in the shower he crawled in bed next to me. "How's your butt, Petey Pup?" he whispered.

"Wonderful," I said, and then turned to kiss my Master good night.

15

It was ten o'clock the following morning, and I was sitting on the living room sofa watching television when Alex stumbled out of his bedroom and grabbed the remote from coffee table. He pointed it at the TV quickly and pressed the power button, shutting it off. "Jesus Christ!" he said, "I'm tryin to fuckin sleep!" He then tossed the remote onto the couch beside me and headed back down the hall into his bedroom. I felt my face redden with embarrassment as he did so. I hadn't even realized it had been playing at high volume. Plus I had thought Alex would be getting up soon anyway, for I knew that Drew was going to be coming home today.

I decided to start making some breakfast. Once Alex did decide to get up, I thought a hot breakfast might put him in a better mood. Matt also was still asleep. We had been up late the night before, because our paddling session with Jason had lasted into the wee hours of the morning. I pulled out all of the ingredients I would need to make three omelets and placed them on the counter; then I commenced fixing breakfast.

About five minutes later Matt called for me from the bathroom. "Petey, get your ass in here!" he demanded. Quickly I turned down the burner on the stove and rushed to the bathroom. "Did you piss on this fuckin seat?" he demanded, pointing to the toilet.

I shook my head, "No Sir," I answered.

"Well clean it the fuck up!" he said. I stared at the toilet lid a moment in disbelief. Three guys were living in this household at the moment, and a fourth had visited the night before. Any one of us could have been responsible for the careless pissing, yet somehow I was to blame.

"Yes, Sir," I said. I knelt down to retrieve a spray bottle of cleaner and a sponge, which were kept in the vanity cabinet. Then I slid over, still kneeling, and thoroughly cleaned the toilet seat.

When I was finished I rushed back to the kitchen, only to discover that smoke was rolling up from the burner. My omelet was burning, and I realized that in my haste I'd actually turned the burner on high rather than low. Grabbing a kitchen towel, I quickly wrapped it around the handle and removed the pan from the heat. As I was doing so, I heard the phone ringing.

I dropped the hot pan into the kitchen sink, carefully turned *off* the burner this time, and headed for the phone. "Hello?" I said.

"Petey, where the hell is Alex?" It was Drew.

"Hi Drew!" I said excitedly. "I can't wait for you to come home."

"Petey, will you answer my damn question?" he said. Then he repeated himself, "Where the fuck is Alex? He was supposed to be here by now to pick me up!"

"Oh ... um, well, he's still in bed. I don't think he realizes that he was supposed to be there so early. Why don't you hang up and call him back on his cell?"

"I tried calling his cell first, dummy! He doesn't answer. Just go get him, would ya?"

"Okay Drew, I'm really sorry. Just hold on a second, okay? I'll get him."

I then rushed down the hall to Alex's room and rapped on the door. "Alex ...? Sir?" He did not answer so I knocked a little harder. "Alex, I'm sorry to bother you but ..."

The door flung open and Alex stood in front of me. "What the *fuck* do you want?" he screamed. "I already told ya I'm trying to sleep!"

"I ... uhh ... Sir." I just stared at him and then thrust the phone out for him to take.

"Petey!" I heard Matt behind me, standing in the bathroom doorway. "Didn't you get me any shaving cream when you were at the store?"

I turned to see him standing there with a towel around his waist. "No, Sir. I didn't know you needed ..."

"Goddammit!" he said exasperatedly. "It's your job to make sure I don't run out of shit like that. Alex, do you have any ..." Alex had already turned and closed the door, taking the cordless phone handset with him. "Petey, run down to the store and get me some shaving cream. Now! And hurry the fuck up!"

It took me nearly a half hour to get through the checkout line at the store because they only had one register open and an old lady with a huge cart was in front of me. As I stood there in line I looked up at Denise the cashier and saw her give me an apologetic smile.

When it finally was my turn at the checkout stand, she asked me how my day was and I just stared at her. As I tried to speak, I felt a lump in my throat and then suddenly I just blurted out, "It really sucks!" Then I started crying.

"Aww," she said, and immediately stepped away from her work station and made her way around the counter. She wrapped her arms around me and hugged me.

"Oh my god, I'm so sorry!" I cried.

"Oh sweetie, what's wrong?"

"I'm just having a bad morning! Everything's going wrong ..."

"Well, look what you're buying," she said lightheartedly. "I'm sure you can think of something fun to do with that shaving cream."

I smiled at her. "If only ..." I said.

"Is it what's-his-name? Matt, I think. Right?"

"Yes, his name's Matt, and yes it's him ... partly."

"Well, as wonderful as they are, at times they can be real assholes, too," she said. "And if he's being mean to you, you just let me know and I'll come over and kick his ass for you!"

I laughed. "Okay," I said. "I'm really sorry!"

"Don't be sorry, sweetie," she said, hugging me one more time. "Let me ring this up for you, okay?"

When I got back home a few minutes later, Matt and Alex were both in the kitchen. The burnt frying pan was soaking in the sink basin, and a separate large frying pan with scrambled eggs was on stove. I looked closely at Matt and saw he'd already shaved. He must've borrowed shaving cream from Alex after all.

"Come 'ere" he said to me, and held out his arms. "Sorry I snapped at you, pup."

"Yeah, Petey, me too," Alex said.

Matt hugged me and pulled me against his chest, and I wrapped my arms around him tightly. "I didn't even notice," I said. "What's for breakfast?"

Come to find out, Alex was not supposed to pick Drew up from the hospital until after twelve. Drew was just overly-anxious to be released. Had Alex actually gone up to the hospital early in the morning, he'd have still had to wait for the doctor to come around and sign the release paperwork.

When Alex and Drew did finally arrive at the apartment around 1:30 that afternoon, I rushed outside to greet them. Poor Drew was wearing the awkward brace that completely restricted the mobility of his shoulder. He also had his arm in a sling. As he maneuvered his way out of the passenger seat, I reached down and slid my hand under his good arm to help him stand up.

"Thanks, Petey!" he smiled at me. "I'm sorry I called you a dummy ..."

I laughed and leaned in to kiss him on the cheek. "Don't be silly," I said. "I didn't understand you, so I guess I was being a dummy."

He looked me in the eye and then leaned in to gently kiss my lips. "I love you," he whispered.

"I love you too," I said as I brushed my fingertips against his soft blond hair. "You've already been smoking, haven't you?"I accused.

"I had one in the hospital parking lot," he said. "I asked Alex to stop the car before we were even out of the lot."

I shook my head and smiled at him. "I already asked Matt, and he said it's no problem for you to use his recliner. I have your lunch ready for you and you can sit in the living room in the big chair and relax. I'll bring it to you and serve it to you on one of those little tables. Then I'll get you anything you need. *Anything!* And I'm here all day so you don't have to worry ..."

"Petey, slow down!" Drew laughed. "Thank you. Thank you for everything."

"Sorry," I said. I took a deep breath and looked him in the eyes. I knew I was about to start crying again. "I'm so glad you're home, Drew! I missed you so much!"

All four of us were home together that evening, and Drew insisted upon eating with the rest of us at the dinner table. "Honey, I can bring it to you," I offered. "We'll all understand."

"I'm not a complete invalid," Drew laughed. "I can sit at the dinner table just as easily as in this chair, and it's no problem for me to walk around. It's my arm that's injured, Petey Pup, not my legs."

"I just don't want you to over-do it," I said. "You just had two major surgeries."

He laughed. "I'm sure I won't overtax myself from the twenty-foot walk from the recliner to the dining room table," he said.

"Don't argue with me," I said defensively. "For once in my life I can actually kick your butt if I want to."

"Good point," he said, grinning broadly.

"Let me help you up," I said.

"No, hon ... I got it," he said, as he slid himself out of the chair. "What did you make for dinner?"

"Your favorite," I said. "Tacos! Are you okay? I'm gonna go tell Matt and Alex it's ready." They were out on the deck having their cigars.

"Sure, go ahead."

After telling our Sirs that dinner was ready, I turned and headed back toward the kitchen. Suddenly I stopped as I noticed

Drew standing over in the corner of the living room. He was staring at the punching bag that Matt had given Alex on his graduation night. Drew was frozen there in place, just staring like a zombie, and I could see that he was trembling.

"Alex!" I yelled.

Alex rushed inside and went over to where Drew was standing. I approached him from the other side and looked into my best friend's tear-filled eyes. His lip was quivering as he pointed at the Body Opponent in front of him. None of us had noticed, but there was a bullet hole right in the center of its chest.

"Oh my god," I whispered.

"Get it the fuck outta here," Alex said to Matt. "I'm sorry, man, but he can't ..."

"Dude, I'm on it," said Matt. "Petey, help Drew to the table." Alex and I gently guided Drew away from the living room and into the dining room area while Matt moved the punching bag out onto the deck.

"I'm so sorry I didn't notice that," I said to Alex.

"Don't worry bout it, Petey. None of us did."

"Drew, are you okay?" I said.

He nodded and looked over to me, then he shook his head slightly. "Yeah, I'm fine. Sorry."

"You ready for some tacos?" I said.

"Oh man, am I ever. I'm so fuckin sick of that hospital food!"

"*La comida es muy rica!*" Alex said, as he shoveled half a taco in his mouth at once.

I laughed. "What does that mean, Sir?"

"The food's good," Drew translated for me.

"Tell him thank you," I said.

"*Muchas gracias*, Senor," Drew said, and we all laughed.

Alex looked over at Drew and winked, gulping down the food and then speaking to his boy one more time in Spanish. "*Te quiero chuparle a mi verga luego, chico!*"

"*En verdad Señor! En verdad!*"

"What are you guys sayin?" I demanded.

"Alex can't help himself. Your authentic Mexican cuisine makes him want to speak his native tongue," Drew said.

"Is that what he said?" I asked.

Matt spoke up finally. "He said he wants his boy to suck his cock, and Drew said, 'definitely!'"

"Dude, I didn't know you spoke Spanish, too," Alex said.

"I don't, but I know some phrases."

"Apparently the important ones, Sir," I said.

"My cousin has a restaurant in Sarasota," Alex said. "I'll take you guys there sometime for some authentic food."

"When they all get to talking in Spanish, I can't even understand them," Drew confessed. "I took four years of Spanish in high school, but I've forgotten so much."

"So you've been to the restaurant?" I asked.

"Yeah, lots of times," Drew said. "Alex is right. It's so good, and when I go in there with him they just keep bringing out shitloads of food for us."

"Do they know about you and Drew?" Matt asked.

Alex nodded and shoved another bite of taco in his mouth. He grinned and quickly swallowed before answering. "Yeah, they're cool. My *primo* ... or cousin ... he's gay too."

"He's the one who owns the restaurant," Drew explained.

"My older sister's gay, too," Matt said. "The whole time I was growin up, though, nobody ever talked about it. It was kinda like she didn't exist or something."

"How'd it go at your parents' the other night?" Alex asked.

"Well, actually I just talked to my dad again today. He offered me my job back, and I accepted."

"You did, Sir?" I asked, realizing the implications of the statement. Apparently his father had agreed to Matt's conditions.

"Well, I'm glad we're all here, cause I need to talk to all three of you about this. I accepted my father's offer on one condition. I asked him to give me the cabin."

"You guys are moving into the cabin?" Drew said, suddenly crestfallen.

Matt shook his head and looked directly at me. "Nah, he said no."

"But you still took the job offer, Sir?" I asked.

"He made a counter offer," Matt said. "He wants to buy us a new house."

"He does?! Oh Matt!" I jumped up excitedly and ran around the table to hug him.

"I'm so happy for ya, man," Alex said. He and Drew were both smiling. "But god ... we're gonna miss ya."

"I insisted on a house big enough for four," Matt said. "You guys will have your own living quarters, complete privacy when you want it ... that is, if you're interested."

Drew looked at his Master excitedly. "Oh, Sir!" he exclaimed, and I didn't really know which Sir he was addressing.

"Wow!" Alex said. "I don't even know what to say."

"*Dios mio!*"exclaimed Drew.

Alex laughed. "Yes! Fuck yeah, we're interested. A house! Our own living quarters ... fuck! I've been dreading the day when you guys would decide to move out."

I was now standing beside my Master, cradled in his arm. "Sir, it makes me so happy to hear you say that," I said to Alex. "We love you guys so much ..."

"We're a family now," Matt said. "A fierce foursome!"

"Oh my god, that sounds so gay!" exclaimed Drew.

I busted up laughing and then leaned in to kiss my Master on the lips.

"Petey and I have gotta go tomorrow to pass out flyers at the mall. Afterwards I'm meeting with a real estate agent. I'll arrange a time with her for us to go look at houses. If they don't have anything listed that fits our needs, then my dad's hiring a contractor."

"This just blows my mind," Alex said. "Your dad really came through for you."

"Well, I have a feeling I'm gonna be working my ass off," he said. "He also just acquired four more stores. I'm sure I won't be running this store for long. I think he wants to promote me to a regional manager position eventually."

"He wants you to run the whole company, Sir," I said. "He even said so."

"Yeah ... eventually. I want a house with a full basement, though. That is a mandatory requirement."

"Aren't all requirements mandatory, Sir?" Drew asked.

Matt laughed, "Yeah, I guess so. I've got a mandatory requirement for you, Drew. Get yourself healed up, and let my pup take care of you."

"Yes, Sir!" he said. "I like that requirement."

The mood for the rest of the evening was upbeat, and we were all enjoying each others' company so much that Matt got out a game of Scattergories. We were gonna play cards instead, but we decided it would be too difficult for Drew to manage one-handed. Alex had gone to the market and gotten a couple bottles of celebratory champagne and a case of beer. Drew wasn't supposed to be drinking while on his pain killers, but Alex assured him that one glass wouldn't hurt. Matt let me have two glasses, which were enough to make me feel quite tipsy.

I fell asleep in the living room that evening in my Master's lap. We had finally ended up renting a horror movie. When I awakened the following morning I was comfortably tucked in my bed, cradled in Matt's arm, having no memory of how I'd gotten there.

16

It was Sunday morning, and Drew and I were sitting out on the deck. He had the newspaper laid out on the deck table so that he could leaf through the pages with one hand.

"Drew," I said, "I've never had such a great time as I did yesterday with Matt. He was such a riot."

"I just can't picture Matt doing something like that. Passing out flyers."

"He was funny. When this one dude started giving me shit, Matt came to my rescue. He totally humiliated the guy."

"What'd he say to him?" Drew said, looking up from the paper with sudden interest.

"He asked him where he got his hair piece!" I busted up laughing.

"He didn't?!" Drew laughed.

"Then Matt was like, 'Better go back to Men's Hairclub and tell em they got your wig on crooked.' It's not like the guy could even say anything back to Matt or he would've kicked his ass."

"What started it? I mean, what'd this guy say to you to begin with?"

"He called me a fag."

"I'm surprised Matt didn't beat his ass anyway."

"That dude was such a loser anyway. He really did have an ugly toupee."

We sat there together for the next hour, Drew leafing through the paper and I reading a novel. I felt so content with my life at this point. I hadn't even known Matt for a full year yet, but it felt as if we had been born to be together. It was like I never really existed until I met him.

"You want me to help you take a shower?" I asked Drew finally.

"Nah. I think I'll just skip bathing until I'm out of this thing," he said jokingly.

"I guess maybe I don't want ya to move into the new house with us after all," I said.

He laughed. "Yeah, I do need a shower. Not sure how we're gonna do it though."

"We can wrap a plastic bag around your brace and sling. I'll help ya. Don't worry."

"Ya know this whole thing sucks. I can't even wear my sneakers cause I can't tie em one-handed."

"Drew, you moron! That's what I'm here for. If you need your shoes tied, I can do it."

"It's just a pain in the ass."

"Hon, you're gonna start getting used to doing things one-handed. By the time they take that brace off you won't even remember what it's like to have two hands."

"You were right about the sex," Drew said. "Alex is totally cool with improvising."

"Why? What'd you guys do?" I asked.

Drew started smiling really broadly as he leaned toward me to share. "At first he was mocking me. Ya know, laughing at me and saying how convenient it was for him cause now he didn't have to tie both of my hands, only one."

"Ha! That totally sounds like something he'd say," I smiled.

"So then he makes me kneel down by the end of the bed with my good arm closest to the bedrail. Then he uses one of my neckties to bind me to the end of the bed. So I'm kneeling there like totally helpless."

"This is hot," I said.

"Then he stands like three feet in front of me and tells me to come get his cock. He's got it out and is holding it in his hand. He's totally like taunting me with it. It was so wicked! I was so turned on by him, and I wanted it so bad. I tried getting close enough to him but he was just barely out of reach."

"And then he made you beg?"

"Oh my god! I had to beg for like ten minutes. He kept stroking himself and laughing at me, calling me all kinds of names and shit."

"And then finally he did make you suck him?"

"Yeah, and ya know what was so cool?"

"What?" I asked with anticipation.

"I actually came before he did, and I wasn't even able to touch myself. I just got so excited!"

"I did that with Matt before," I admitted. "Just a few days ago, actually ... in the kitchen."

Drew laughed. "He let me suck for a long time too, but he kept pulling out before he got close enough to climax. Then finally he untied my hand and picked me up. It was just so romantic the way he carried me to the bed."

"I love that!" I said. I was starting to get emotional.

"Yeah, me too. He was just so gentle and loving, and then he made love to me while I was lying on my back."

"Did you cum a second time?" I asked.

"Yes! And it was almost at the exact second that he came. And he was Frenching me at the time!"

"Oh wow, that's so romantic, Drew. I love it when the kinky stuff turns into romantic stuff."

"Yeah ..." Drew sighed.

"Petey!" I heard my Master calling for me from inside. Quickly I jumped up and rushed to the bedroom. "All right, I start my job tomorrow, and I need to look sharp," he said to me. "I'm gonna wear a suit, but I don't want to be over-dressed either. I want it to be an outfit with a jacket that I can take off."

I nodded to him. "This one, Sir," I suggested, pulling one of his blazers from the closet. "You can wear it with khakis, and it'll be sort of dress-casual."

"You think?" he asked. "Or do you think this one's better?"

It seemed odd to have my Master asking me for wardrobe advice. From the beginning it had always been he who made those decisions for both of us. "Please, Sir, you decide. I like both of them."

"Hmm," he said. "Yeah, I think you were right to begin with. I'll go with this one. Now I want you to get everything ready for me. Press my shirt, have my shoes shined and by the door. I just want a light breakfast ... like maybe a bagel or something."

"Yes, Sir," I said. I remembered when Matt and I first were together he'd never let me make him breakfast. He said he usually didn't eat in the morning. So much about him had changed, and I loved reflecting upon the details.

I liked the way his protectiveness of me seemed to now stem from the love he had for me rather than just from his sense of ownership. In the beginning it was like he loved me in the same sense that he loved his car. I was his property and so of course he valued me. That, however, was different from the way he loved me now.

And yes, he still was my Master and he still gave me direct orders—plenty of them every day—but it just seemed so much more natural now. He no longer gave me orders as a means of flexing his authoritative muscle. Instead it was more like the way a parent instructs a child. They love that child wholeheartedly, but they know it's their job to lay down rules and offer guidance.

Even our sex had changed. He still completely dominated me, and there was no doubt that he loved doing all sorts of kinky stuff, but during or after almost every kinky scene, he would show me tenderness and affection. He knew I craved his domination, yet he also remembered I was a pup. I needed that love. I needed that constant reassurance.

It thrilled me to know that Matt relied on me to tend to his domestic needs. I loved ironing his shirts, folding his laundry, and even cleaning up after him. He even had me give him pedicures when he needed them.

When he called me into our bedroom that morning to give me my instructions, nothing seemed out of place to me. It all just seemed so right—so perfect. I wanted nothing more than to spend my entire life in this state of domestic bliss.

But then once again, we heard from Ryan.

It was actually Tuesday, the day after Matt started his job managing his father's gym, when we got the call from Ryan's attorney. The lawyer asked if the four of us would be able to meet with him, and of course Matt immediately said no. He gave the attorney the phone number of his brother-in-law who was also a lawyer. Matt told him not to contact us again directly, but to direct all of his communication to our attorney.

The very next day, Matt's sister Karen called from Phoenix. Karen said her husband Brandon had received a call from this other lawyer, and Matt discussed with her the entire situation. She said their mom had told her about the drama and the shooting, and she couldn't believe that the attorney of the assailant was calling for a meeting with the victims. She also said that it would be difficult for Brandon to represent us—in that he was in Phoenix and we were in Tampa—but Matt said he didn't think he should have to pay for an attorney since we were the victims. He had just used his brother-in-law's name to get Ryan's lawyer off our backs. He asked his sister if Brandon could just send him a letter or something stating we were not interested in speaking with Ryan or his attorney.

Two days later, Matt's brother-in-law called him, urging him to reconsider a meeting. He said that the assailant, Ryan Connors, had submitted himself to psychiatric testing and the results had indicated unequivocally that he was a very messed up kid. He had also seen the police report that quoted Matt as saying that he didn't feel Ryan needed to spend any more time in jail. Brandon felt it might be in his best interest to actually hire an attorney after all, simply because he was concerned that Ryan was going to end up getting off scot free, and that Matt would then again be in danger. He offered Matt a referral to a female colleague of his who happened to be located in the Tampa area.

After a lengthy discussion with Alex, Matt called a family meeting. Our Masters explained the situation to Drew and me, and we agreed with Matt and Alex that we should at least talk to the attorney. Her name was Maureen Bowman, and when we met her for the first time, I immediately liked her. She sort of reminded me of that famous lawyer who had defended the Menendez brothers a few years back. She had frizzy hair and was extremely feisty.

The four of us met with Maureen in a conference room at the attorney's office complex. After we got the formal introductions out of the way, Maureen cut right to the chase and told us her opinion of the situation.

"I can understand why you'd want nothing to do with this kid again. My god, he sexually assaulted one of you, shot another one of you, and threatened to kill a third. It certainly appears, at least upon first glance, that he's a menace to society ..." She sighed before continuing.

"But we do have some problems here, the first of them being that this guy is nuts. I don't mean he's crazy in the sense that he's delusional or schizophrenic or anything like that, but it could certainly be argued that he suffered diminished capacity.

"He was not of sound mind when he came over to your house that evening. For one thing, he'd just gotten out of jail for a crime of which he has not yet been convicted, and shortly thereafter his significant other abruptly ended their relationship.

"Then he obviously had developed an obsession with Matthew. The fact that the two of you did at one point engage in sexual activity together does not particularly help either.

"Now add to all this the fact that Matthew told the police detective that he felt sorry for the kid and that Mr. Connors did not belong in jail ..."

"That's not exactly what I said," Matt clarified.

"But you did say something to that effect?"

Matt nodded. "I honestly don't think he belongs in jail."

"How can you say that?" Alex argued. "He tried to kill you, and he almost killed Drew! Plus he raped Petey!"

"I know exactly what you're sayin, Alex. I wanted to kill him myself after he did what he did to Petey, but after seeing him that night, I agree with what the lawyer is saying. He was not right. He was totally crazy."

"And that's an excuse? He just gets off because he was nuts? Most serial killers are nuts too, but that doesn't give em a get-outta-jail-free card!"

"You're right, Mr. Juarez, it doesn't," Maureen said. "It's my job to help make sure this doesn't happen ... if this is what you want, that is. Actually, it is the prosecuting attorney's job, but I'm representing you simply to make sure that you as victims do not get used as pawns by either side. We want to see justice served, but we also don't want to push for a stiff sentence if you are opposed to that."

"Well, Petey and Drew are the real victims here," Matt said. "How do they feel about it?"

The attorney turned to Drew. "Do you think this punk should go to jail?" she asked.

Drew sat there for a moment, looking first at his Master and then over at me. It appeared he was thinking, and then he spoke. "No, I don't want him to go to jail."

"Drew!" Alex said. "He *shot* you! He almost took you away from me forever!"

"Sir," Drew said, "I think that Ryan's been a very lonely person all of his life. All he ever wanted was for someone to love him. When he met Matt he mistook Matt's friendliness for this love he was seeking. Then when it became clear that Matt really wasn't interested in him, he was devastated. He just sort of snapped."

"But all of us have to deal with rejection," Alex argued. "I've been dumped before, myself, and it hurt like hell, but I didn't go find a gun and starting shooting people."

"No sane person *would*," Drew responded. "I'm not saying I want Ryan to ever be in our lives again. I'll never be his friend, and for the longest time I hated his guts. I hated the shit he did to Petey. I'll never forgive him for that! But I just think he needs a psych ward more than a jail."

"And if the courts agree with you," Maureen said, "within a few months he could be back on the street. If he is placed in a mental health facility, all he will need to do is convince them he is sane enough to return to society; then, after they sign the papers, he's free."

"That's bullshit!" Alex said.

"Can't the judge force him to remain in one of these institutions for a set period of time?" Matt asked.

"Sure," she said, "but they rarely do. Petey, what do you think?" she said as she looked over at me.

I suddenly felt as if I were under a microscope and all eyes were staring at me. "I ... um ..." Matt placed his hand on top of mine and gently squeezed. "I want to forgive him," I said. "I love you, Drew, for saying you could never forgive him for what he did to me ... but I honestly wish I *could* forgive him. I don't like hating people that way, especially people who are sick, and I think that's what he is."

"But he almost killed Drew!" Alex repeated.

"He almost killed Petey, too," Matt said. "He kicked in little Petey's ribcage and it punctured one of his lungs!"

"I know it!" Alex said. "So why the hell are we talking about forgiving him? I don't think that life in prison would be too strong of a punishment! Let him rot there for all I care."

"Alex," Maureen said, now addressing him by first name, "I completely understand your feelings, and I think that if I were in your position I'd feel exactly the same way. However, Peter and Andrew are the victims here."

"We all were victimized!" Alex exclaimed.

"Yes, you were. I'm sorry. Legally speaking, however, Peter and Andrew were the ones physically harmed."

"So when someone barges into your home and sticks a loaded gun in your face ... and then shoots the person you love with all your heart—shoots him right in front of your eyes—you don't think that is victimization?"

"Sir, I *do* think it is. I *know* it is, but from a legal standpoint I know that the crimes for which Mr. Connors was charged have two victims: Peter Drinkell and Andrew Tompkins. They both are saying that they want to forgive their assailant."

"I can't believe this shit!" Alex said.

"I'm sorry," she repeated. "Would anyone like coffee or bottled water or something?" We all declined.

"Okay, well let's just take a couple days before we do anything. I will notify Connors' attorney that we will be in touch with him. Take the next forty-eight hours and think it over. Talk it through. Andrew and Alex—you two especially. We do not have to decide anything here now, and you definitely do not have to meet with Connors or his attorney."

"What happens if we do meet with them?" Matt asked.

"Well, I believe they're going to want you to talk to Ryan himself. My guess is that he is going to apologize to you and ask for your forgiveness."

"But even if we do forgive him, how does that change anything?" Alex asked. "The prosecutor is still going to try getting him convicted."

"I'm sure they're going for a plea bargain," she said. "If they can get the victims on their side, then it will be easier for them to argue for leniency from the prosecutor. If they get your testimony, they may even be able to get a judge to let him off with no jail time at all."

"No matter what happens," Matt said, "I don't ever want him around Petey or Drew again."

"This whole thing is just really messed up," Alex said. "Why don't we just ignore his damned attorney? Why should we help Ryan after everything he's done?"

"Sir," I said, "because we're better. We're better than that. If *we* don't help him, nobody else will. He'll just get worse, and then more people will get hurt."

"Not if he's in prison!"

"People get hurt in prison too," I said. "No disrespect intended, Sir."

"Well like I said, you don't have to decide anything now. Think it over. I just want to say one more thing ... off the record. You guys are amazing; you really are." She pointed to Drew and me. "I never would have expected it … the victims themselves being the ones who want to forgive."

"Petey's amazing in many ways," Matt said, "and so is Drew."

17

I really did hate driving, but I had no choice. Drew certainly couldn't drive with his shoulder in that brace and his arm in the sling, and I certainly wasn't going to make Drew ride the bus with me. I had already called ahead, and so I knew exactly what time we had to be there. Visitors were only welcome on certain days of the week at specific times.

It seemed that Drew and I were beginning to make a habit of paying unsolicited visits to people our Masters may not have wanted us to see. Somebody told me once it was better to just do something you were uncertain of and beg forgiveness later than to ask permission first and simply be denied. And we both knew that neither Matt nor Alex would grant us permission to visit an inmate of the county jail, let alone one who had previously nearly killed us.

"Are you ready?" I asked my best friend as I pulled into the handicapped parking space. Drew pulled the red "Temporary" handicapped permit from the glove compartment and dangled it from the rearview mirror.

He gave me a serious look. "Yeah," he said, and then reached over to open his door using his only moveable upper appendage.

I'd never visited someone in jail before and had no idea what to expect. I'd seen a lot of television shows depicting such visits, though, and so I anticipated a monitored visit wherein we would be separated from the inmate by bullet-proof glass. We'd probably have to talk to him using one of those phones on a cord, similar to the house phone my parents used to have when I was a baby.

I expected that Ryan would be wearing a bright orange or yellow jumpsuit with the word PRISONER boldly emblazoned across his chest. His ankles would be shackled, and two guards would escort him to the tiny little cell which was completely empty except for that corded phone.

The reality was much more mundane and ordinary than my speculation. We did have to endure a security check upon entry. We were required to empty our pockets and turn them inside out. Then we had to walk through a metal detector and wait in a very sterile, unadorned room with a whole bunch of other visitors. There was a window in this room, and on the other side of the window sat a receptionist. It reminded me of being at the dentist office waiting room. Periodically this receptionist—who was actually a jail police officer—would announce that a prisoner was ready to see his visitor.

Drew and I sat together in the back corner of the room. Both of us were somber, not really in the mood for chitchat. After about fifteen minutes we heard the guard announce, "Visitors for Ryan Connor." We scurried to our feet and headed for the door where a guard was waiting to escort us into the "visitors' lounge."

The visitors' lounge was actually like a cafeteria. It had tables set up in the same manner you would see in a high school dining hall. The tables were completely empty and clean, and neither visitors nor inmates were allowed to bring anything into the room with them. Even pens and pencils were disallowed. Three guards were present, each maintaining a post at the perimeter of the room.

I noticed Ryan immediately when we stepped into the room. He was sitting at one of the corner tables, alone, waiting for his visitors. A look of astonishment crossed his face when he saw us enter; apparently he had not been told who was visiting him. Ryan was not in a jumpsuit as I'd imagined, but instead was wearing a pair of jeans and a light blue denim shirt. Actually all of the inmates were dressed this way. Apparently this was their uniform.

I took a deep breath and looked over at my best friend. Drew nodded, and we headed over to Ryan's table.

"Ryan," I said, nodding to him.

"I can't believe you came ..." Ryan said quietly. He looked at Drew very seriously. "Did I do that to you?" He was staring at the brace.

"Yeah," Drew said, and then we sat down across from the inmate.

"Um ... I'm sorry," he whispered.

"Do you know why we're here?" I asked him.

He shook his head. "Maybe ... well ... maybe to tell me what you think of me? To tell me to go fuck myself."

"Maybe," I said.

"We're here because your lawyer said you wanted to talk to us," Drew said.

"Really? I wonder why he'd say that? ... I mean, I do—I do want to talk to you, but I never asked him to call you."

"He wants us to testify on your behalf," I said. "He wants to try using our testimony to help you get a plea bargain."

He shook his head. "No, you don't have to do that ... I mean, well, you already know you don't. But I don't expect that. I'd never ask that of you ..." There were tears in his eyes.

"Ryan—" Drew whispered.

"Drew, I was so scared! I was so afraid I'd killed you!" he sobbed.

"You almost did," Drew said without emotion.

Ryan was covering his face with both hands, and I was unsure if this was out of embarrassment for showing emotion or out of shame for what he'd done. Probably both.

"Look at me, Ryan," Drew asked, "Please."

Ryan removed his trembling hands from his face but not completely. He continued to hold them up, resting his fingertips against his chin.

"I know you didn't come to the apartment to shoot me," Drew said. "I know that part was an accident."

"I didn't plan on shooting anyone. Not even Matt! I ... I don't know. Maybe I did plan to shoot him. I *wanted* to. Or I at least wanted to scare him. I really don't think I even knew what I wanted."

"You were confused and angry, and you were hurting ... and you were afraid," I said. Ryan nodded, tears streaming down his cheeks. "If you only planned to scare Matt, why was the gun loaded?" I asked.

He shook his head. "I don't know! I swear to god, I don't even honestly remember loading it. I don't remember much about that whole afternoon ..."

"Do you remember shooting me?" Drew asked.

"Yes ... the one thing I wish I could forget! I keep seeing it over and over. It's like—"

"A movie playing in your head," Drew said.

"Yes!"

"Why did you have sex with Matt?" I asked.

"Petey, it's not like that, I swear. I didn't really even have sex with him ... I mean he never, ya know, fucked me."

"You had oral sex," I said.

"I begged him to let me blow him. I followed him to his office at the gym—that one at the mall where we had Alex's graduation party."

"I know where it happened," I said.

"At first he told me to leave, but I ... I don't know, Petey. I'm sorry!"

"Tell me!" I demanded. "Tell me what happened. You owe me that much."

He looked me in the eye and nodded. "I told him I'd do anything if he'd let me serve him. I begged him ... I begged him and I meant it. It wasn't just a scene ..."

I knew the feeling he was describing.

"So he ordered me to my knees and then walked up to me and let me suck him. It was only for a couple minutes, and he didn't even ... um ... he didn't even cum or anything. Then he told me to go. He was mad, I think."

"At himself," Drew said. "He was furious with himself."

"I thought you two had an open relationship," Ryan said.

"Then why'd ya hide it from me?" I asked. "If it was an open relationship, he'd have had no reason not to tell me, and neither would you."

"Nothing really happened, Petey. I sucked him for ... god! ... it couldn't have been more than a minute or two. He wasn't even fully hard."

I looked at Drew and he nodded.

"And then even after that, Matt trusted you. He asked you to dominate me as a punishment ..."

"And he told me not to hit you. He told me not to beat you or injure you in any way. In fact he gave me his cell number and said if I thought you were starting to freak or something I was to call him."

"But you did beat me. You kicked the fuck outta me and put me in the hospital. And you ... *raped me*!!"

At the sound of these words he hung his head and wept. Placing his arms in front of himself on the table, he buried his face in them. "I'm so sorry!" he cried. "I swore I never would ... not after he did it to me so many times!"

Drew and I looked at each other silently.

"Ryan," Drew said. "Ryan, please ..."

"Who did it to you?" I asked. "Who are you talking about?"

"My ..." He raised his head slightly to look up at me, and all I could see in those eyes was pure agony. "... stepdad."

"I'm so sorry," I whispered. "Your stepfather raped you? How often?"

"Dozens of times ... more than I can count."

"How old were you, Ryan?" Drew asked.

Ryan sat there staring straight ahead. After a few seconds he responded. "Nine. That was the first time. He did it until I was fifteen."

"Until you were big enough to fight back?" I asked.

"I guess so. After awhile I stopped resisting. It only made it worse when I fought him."

"Is that why you're gay?" I asked.

"I don't know," he said. "Maybe, but I don't think so ... I mean, I think I always knew I was gay. I think maybe he did, too, and he did this as my punishment."

"Oh Ryan!" I choked as I spoke his name. "I'm so sorry!" Now I was crying. I wanted so desperately to grab hold of his hand. I wanted to take him in my arms and comfort him, but I knew I was forbidden to touch him.

"I don't want you to testify for me; honest I don't. I would never ask that, not now. Not after what I've done."

"All we can do is tell the truth, Ryan," Drew said. "We can tell what happened, and the things you said, and I'm not sure that will even help you."

"Why should you help me anyway?" he asked. "Look at me! Look at what I am ... I'm an attempted murderer and a rapist! I'm a liar and a thief! I don't want your help—I don't deserve it ..."

"What *do* you want from us then?" I asked.

He again looked at me, staring me right in the face. "Someday I hope you can forgive me," he said. "That's what I want."

"I wouldn't be here if I hadn't forgiven you," I said quietly. "But I have to tell you, it's hard for me to forget. Forgiving is a lot easier than forgetting. I saw you in the mall right after you got out of jail, and it scared me. It totally freaked me out. I'm not sure I'll ever trust you again. I'm not sure I'll ever want you in my life."

"I don't blame you," he said.

"And Drew—he's been so traumatized by what you did to him that he has nightmares. He has flashbacks that he sees constantly, and he's terrified of being alone."

"I wish I could take it back," Ryan said. "I wish I could undo the awful things I've done."

"You can't," Drew said. "You can't go back; you can only go forward."

"Drew, are you gonna be all right?" he asked sincerely. "Is the damage to your ... um, is it your shoulder? ... Is the damage permanent?"

"They don't think it's permanent," Drew said. "The bullet fractured my clavicle bone, and they had to reconstruct it. I gotta wear this thing for a couple more months."

"That bullet could've gone straight through his heart," I said. "Or any other vital organ."

"I know," he said. "I hope someday you can forgive me, Drew."

"It's like Petey said, I already forgive you. My forgiveness doesn't change what happened though. We still have to deal with the after-effects."

"Is there some way I can help you?" he asked. "I know I'm in jail and everything ... I don't know what I could do ..."

"You need to get some help for yourself," Drew said, "so you don't freak out and do this to someone else someday. You're never gonna be any better until you deal with your past."

"I never told anyone about this before. I don't even know why I told you."

"You need to," I said. "You definitely need to tell someone now. You need to tell your lawyer, for one thing."

"Ryan, do you have any family close by?" Drew asked.

"My mom," Ryan said. "She's only been to see me once, though."

"Is she the one who hired your lawyer?" I asked. "Or is he court-appointed?"

"She didn't hire him," he said. "He's not court-appointed either. I'm not sure who hired him. I think it was Eric, but he hasn't even been to see me either. He dumped me that day ..."

"We know," I said. "Maybe he felt guilty and so he's covering the lawyer."

"I don't know why he should feel guilty," Ryan said. "I'm surprised he put up with me as long as he did.

"My mom always spoiled me so much. She was always buying me things, and I could get just about anything I wanted. I think she knew what was going on and it was her way of making up for it. Sometimes I even played her; I used her guilt to manipulate her."

"What did she say to you when she visited?" I asked.

He looked away and again tears began to well in his eyes. "She said she was through. She washed her hands of me."

"Well maybe she did hire the lawyer after all," I suggested. "I can't imagine a parent not trying to help their kid when he's in jail."

"Whoever it was, my lawyer isn't sayin. I asked and he wouldn't tell me."

"It's probably her, then," I surmised. "She probably still feels guilty."

"They're motioning for me," he said. "I'm gonna have to go."

"We'll talk to your lawyer," Drew said. "We'll do what we can."

"I'm so sorry about everything," Ryan said as he stood up. "I gotta go, but thanks for coming. Thanks ..."

"Bye Ryan," I said. "We'll come back again."

"Bye, and thanks." A guard came and escorted him out of the room.

Drew and I looked at each other, speechless. I'm not sure our visit really resolved anything. I felt more conflicted now than ever.

"I went to the jail today, Sir," I said to Matt when we were alone in our room.

"You *what*?!" He turned to look at me. "Petey!"

"Drew went with me, Sir. We had to talk to him."

I could practically see the steam rising around him from his seething anger. "Petey, what is wrong with you? Why would you do something like that without talking to me?"

"Would you have let me, if I had?" I asked.

"Absolutely not!" he said.

"I was afraid you'd say that, Sir, which is why I didn't ask."

"You need to have your ass beat! And I don't mean sex-play either! Petey, that is bullshit! Haven't you learned your lesson yet? You can't be doing shit like this behind my back ..."

"Sir, I'm sorry! Please don't be mad."

"I *am* mad!" he screamed. "Ryan raped you, and then he shot Drew! And you went to the jail to visit him?"

"Sir, you told me ..."

"I told you he needed help. I told you we'd try to help him if we could, but I also told you that I didn't want him anywhere near you!"

"Sir ... please!" I dropped to my knees in front of him. "Please don't be angry. I had to do it."

"That's not gonna work, Petey," he said. "Go get a blanket from the closet. You're sleeping on the floor tonight."

"Yes, Sir," I said as I bowed my head submissively.

"Hurry up. Obey your Master."

"Yes, Sir." I quickly got to my feet and went out to the hall closet to find a blanket. When I returned, Matt was already in bed.

"On the floor over there," he pointed. Then he tossed a pillow in the general direction he had indicated. "No crying, no back talk, I don't wanna hear a fuckin sound outta ya! Now!"

I obeyed my Master and hurriedly curled up in the corner. Well, I tried to obey him, but after he turned out the light I cried silently into my pillow. I wished he'd have spanked me like he threatened. That would have been a much easier punishment. I'd known my Master was going to be upset with me, but I had done what I had to do. I also knew that I had to tell him I'd done it, though. I truly did not want to keep secrets from Matt.

I was sure Matt would punish me when I told him the truth, but I was really hoping it would just be another essay, or even a paddling. I never expected isolation. I lay there on the floor and thought about how I'd disappointed him. By not talking to him first, I'd basically demonstrated the exact opposite behavior of what I'd written about in my essay.

Hopefully he would be calm enough by morning to hear my full explanation. Hopefully he'd let me tell him about what Ryan had said.

After a half hour I still was not asleep, and I couldn't stop crying. I didn't even hear him as he approached me, but when he slid his arms under me to scoop me up, I quickly embraced him and let out a tiny sob as I did so.

"I'm sorry, Sir," I cried.

"Shh ..." he said. Then he carried me to bed where I curled up in his arms and finally fell asleep.

Early the next morning, before we even got out of bed, Matt talked to me about my visit with Ryan. At first he was stern and told me he should have made me sleep on the floor all night like he'd originally ordered, but then he softened a little and asked me about the visit. I told him everything, including the fact that Ryan confided he'd been the victim of long term sexual abuse.

Matt made me promise not to pay Ryan any more visits unless he accompanied me. I was glad he didn't out-and-out forbid me to contact him again. The more I remembered Ryan's words to us and the more I recalled the hurt I saw when I looked into his eyes, the less I hated him.

In fact, at this point, I don't think I hated him at all anymore. I felt pity, and I no longer was afraid of him. I doubted that he and I would ever be friends even if he did get out of jail. I just didn't think I'd be able to forget what he'd done to me. It was true what Drew had said about forgiving being different than forgetting.

After my discussion with Matt, he pushed me down toward his morning hard-on, and I eagerly serviced him. Then I made him some coffee and a light breakfast while he showered and got ready for work. He scratched out a list of instructions for me on a notepad—chores he wanted me to do that day—then he gulped down his breakfast and headed out.

Drew and Alex were up and around a few minutes after Matt left, and I made them breakfast as well. Alex was quiet, and it seemed to me he must be brooding. Perhaps Drew had told him about our visit with Ryan as well. Alex didn't say anything about it, though. He left about an hour later. Another company had hired him to install some software for them.

"I had to sleep on the floor last night," I told Drew after Alex was gone.

"I'm sorry Petey," he said. "So I guess you told him, huh?"

"Yeah, but he didn't make me stay on the floor for long. He came and carried me back to bed after only a few minutes."

"He did? Wow, that's a surprise."

"It was nice, actually. I love when he picks me up like that."

"Alex was pissed too," Drew confessed. "He yelled at me a few minutes and then when we did go to bed, he just turned away from me. He didn't kiss me or anything."

"And he's still mad?"

"It seems that way ..."

"Did you tell him everything Ryan said?"

"Oh yeah. He doesn't care though. He said that's no excuse, and ya know, he's actually right. Lots of people are victims of abuse, and they don't go out hurting other people."

"Well it seems that Ryan really wants to change," I said.

"But don't all criminals say they want to change when they're in jail?"

I nodded. "Good point. I don't know, though. I kinda do believe him."

"I want to," Drew admitted. "He has to prove himself, though."

"The question is, will he ever get the chance to do that? He won't be able to prove anything while locked up in prison."

"Well, we did our part. We talked to him and then we told our Masters. I think it's now up to them to decide. I'm not gonna do anything else to upset Alex. If you decide you want to help Ryan, you'll have to do it on your own, unless Alex tells me otherwise."

I smiled at my best friend. "That's a good decision, Drew. I totally understand, and I even promised Matt pretty much the same thing. I'm not sure there's anything else we can do for him now anyway. If Matt agrees to take me to Ryan's lawyer, I'll go, but otherwise I'm done."

Just then my cellphone rang. I rushed over to the counter to pick it up and saw it was Matt calling. "Hello, Sir," I said.

"Petey," he said. "Go in the bedroom and get my checkbook from out of the desk drawer. I need you to bring it to me."

"Yes, Sir," I said. "Should I borrow Drew's car?"

"Unless you want to walk five miles ... yes of course borrow his car. He won't care."

"Yes, Sir. I'll get it and bring it to you right away."

"Okay, good. Hurry, but be careful."

"I will, Sir. See you in a few minutes."

"Bye." He disconnected.

I told Drew what I was doing, and he said it was no problem to use his car. He declined going with me, saying he wanted to do some stuff online. I told him I'd help him take a shower when I got back.

I rushed into the bedroom and located the checkbook, then threw on a pair of sneakers, grabbed the keys, and headed out. It didn't take me more than ten minutes to get to the mall where Matt's gym was located. I found a parking space not too far from the entrance and pulled in. I then reached over to grab the checkbook, but as I did so I accidentally knocked it off the seat. It fell open onto the floor, so I leaned over to pick it up and saw a carbon copy of one the checks he'd written. It had been a check for two thousand dollars to "Richard Nelson and Associates."

I'd heard the name before, but I wasn't exactly sure where. I scooped up the checkbook and made sure everything was tucked neatly in place. Then I got out of the car and headed toward the mall entrance. About halfway to the door, I realized who Richard Nelson was. He was the lawyer who'd called our house. He was Ryan's attorney, and Matt had paid him.

I came to a complete stop, stunned and confused. If Matt had been the one to hire Ryan's attorney, then why had he initially declined the request that we meet with him? Why had he gone through this charade of calling his sister and hiring yet another attorney to represent our interests? It all seemed crazy to me, and I didn't see why he would not have trusted me enough to explain what he was doing.

I considered the situation for a moment and then resumed my trek into the mall. If there was one thing I'd learned during the time I'd been with Matt, it was that I could trust him. I recalled how I had doubted him the day he planned the surprise party for

Alex. I'd thought he was stealing away with Drew, taking him to the cabin for a sexual rendezvous, but in reality the two had been throwing a huge party. I remembered how he'd broken up with me and it had torn my heart to shreds, but then learned he had done it as a means of protecting me. When Matt and I attended the party while we were on spring break and Matt informed me we were leaving with Ryan, I'd assumed that Matt wanted to have sex with him, but then learned he actually wanted Ryan to serve me as a reward.

Literally every time I doubted Matt I later learned that my fears were baseless. He did sometimes keep things from me, but it always was for a good reason. I decided I wasn't going to second-guess him this time. I was going to trust my Master and allow him to tell me what he felt I needed to know when he felt I needed to know it.

As I walked into the gym, everything seemed different. The last time I'd been there it had not been open yet. It seemed like an entirely new place now that they were up and running. Seeing all the customers using the equipment and interacting with one another really brought the place to life.

It took me only seconds to spot Matt. He was behind the sales counter leaning over the computer monitor and talking to one of the employees who was with him. It was a young female, probably no more than twenty-two or twenty-three years old. She looked over at him as he spoke. It seemed he was explaining something to her, and she was staring sweetly at his face with wide-eyed interest. Her shoulder-length medium-brown hair was silky, and as she tilted her head from side to side, it seemed to flow almost like what you'd see in a shampoo commercial. I guessed that she must be a trainer, because what I could see of her indicated that she had a perfect physique. She was wearing a tight sports bra, and it was fully packed.

Matt turned to respond to her and smiled. They both laughed at whatever had been said. For a second I hesitated, uncertain if I should interrupt. Then I remembered that Matt was expecting me, and he'd told me to hurry, so I took a deep breath and pushed back my trepidation. Swallowing hard, I willed myself to continue forward. As I approached the counter, I saw the young lady place her hand softly on Matt's bicep. It was at this point that Matt looked up and saw me.

"Hey," he said, holding out his hand to take the checkbook, "thanks for bringing that right down, Petey." I reached out and handed over the billfold, smiling meekly at my Master.

Then Matt turned to the girl beside him. "Kelli, I'd like you to meet my partner, Petey."

She smiled warmly at me. "Oh, wow!" she said. "What a pleasure to meet you! I've been telling Matt since we opened that he needs to bring you in for us to meet. Oh my god, aren't you just adorable?"

I felt my face reddening as I smiled back at her. "Thanks," I said.

Matt then stepped around the counter and wrapped his arm around me. "And he's all mine," he bragged. "So hands off!"

She laughed. "Petey, I gotta tell ya something, though. You're a lucky guy."

I beamed at her and said proudly, "I know!"

Matt leaned in and kissed me quickly on the forehead. "Petey, do you remember where my office is?"

"Yes ... um, yes, I remember."

He winked at me. "Go wait for me. Give me ten minutes."

"Okay," I said, and I hurried across the room, glancing back at him a couple times as I did, and then heading down the hallway to his office.

As I waited in the office I remembered the last time I was there, and how Matt had held me on his lap in his big leather office chair, right after Alex had punched me. I recalled how he had danced with me in the gym while wearing his tuxedo and then made love to me on the weight bench. I smiled and wondered if he had something kinky like that planned for today.

A few moments later my thoughts were interrupted when he opened the door and walked in. "Come here," he said, and held his arms out to me. He pulled me into himself and this time kissed me on the lips. "I didn't really ask you to come down here because of the checkbook," he confessed.

"Really, Sir?"

"I've just been thinking ... about last night and then this morning, and I need to talk to you. I didn't wanna wait till tonight. Let's sit down ..." He motioned toward a chair. I looked at him seriously and then moved to the chair and took a seat, staring intently at him all the while. Matt moved over to his desk, leaning against it, and sort of half-sat on the edge of it.

"I was really pissed at you last night."

"I know Sir," I said. "I'm sorry ..."

"Quiet. Let me finish ... please." He took a deep breath and then smiled at me. "I was pissed that you went to the jail yesterday without telling me, but I think you might have gotten the wrong idea. I think that when I yelled at you, it might have come across as if I was really disappointed in you."

I looked up at him quizzically. "You were disappointed, Sir, and I don't really blame you."

"Petey, my number one concern is your safety. You already know how I feel about this."

"But Sir," I said, "did you really think Ryan could do anything to me at the jail?"

"No, not physically. I didn't think he'd attack you or anything, but I also remembered how upset you were the day you saw him at the mall. I'm worried about your emotional state as well."

"It was just a shock to see him that day, Sir. It took me by surprise because I wasn't expecting it. Then I started remembering what he'd done to me, and I just sort of panicked."

"Right, and I didn't want that to happen to you again. If you felt like you were ready to see Ryan again, I think it would have been better if I'd gone with you, then if you did start to freak out, I'd be right there ... to help you."

"I just thought you'd say no, Sir."

"And when I do say no, what does that mean?"

"No," I said. "It means 'no,' Sir."

"Exactly. So basically you didn't ask me because you didn't think you'd like my answer. That is why I was disappointed. You should have asked and then accepted my answer, whether you liked it or not."

"Yes, Sir," I said.

"Well then last night I gave you your punishment. I told you that you had to sleep on the floor, but then after I got in bed I worried about you. I worried that you might really be traumatized by seeing Ryan, and I thought the punishment I'd assigned you might not be appropriate."

"It was the worst punishment I've ever had, Sir," I admitted.

"Good," he said, and looked at me seriously. "Punishments are not supposed to be a picnic. And it's not a picnic for me either ... I don't like not having my pup in bed with me."

"Thank you, Sir," I said as I looked into his eyes.

"But a punishment is a punishment, and when I give you one, it's my job to make sure you complete it. I didn't want to do that last night. I had to make sure you were okay ..." He sighed before continuing. "You have to sleep on the floor tonight, the whole night. Even though I don't like it and even though I know it's really hard for you, you have to do it. Understand?"

"Yes, Sir," I said as I bowed my head and looked down at the floor.

"Okay ... good. Now I have to tell you something else. Look at me." I looked back up at him and reestablished eye contact. "I hired an attorney for Ryan."

"Mr. Nelson?" I asked.

"Yes. I hired him because I knew Ryan needed help, and there was no one to give it to him. If he'd gotten stuck with a court-appointed lawyer, he'd end up going to prison for years."

"Then why did you say no to him when he called and asked for a meeting with us, Sir? And why'd you tell him to contact your brother-in-law?"

"All I did was pay the retainer fee on Ryan's behalf. I'd met this lawyer when I was in jail. He's the one my dad hired for me. I told him at the time I hired him that I wanted him to do whatever he could for Ryan but to leave us out of it. For one thing, I didn't want Alex to think I was betraying him by hiring a lawyer to defend the person who'd shot Drew. Secondly, Ryan raped you, and I was concerned about what you'd think.

"So when he called me, at first I told him no way. I told him we had already established these boundaries in the beginning, and that he was to keep us out of it. He kept calling me though, urging me to reconsider. Finally I got pissed and told him to stop calling. He returned the check to me, and told me he'd decided to represent Ryan pro bono."

"Why'd he do that, Sir?"

"He really believes Ryan's sincere. He thinks it would be a really bad mistake to send him away to jail, and it seems he's really passionate about it. When he called the house that day when you were there ... when you first learned about it ... this was already after he'd returned the check. That's when I got really pissed and told him that from now on he had to talk to my attorney, and then I called Karen."

"Sir, I don't understand. Since Mr. Nelson returned the check to you, why'd you decide to even tell me about it? You really haven't hired him at all."

"Because every time I try to hide something important from you, it backfires. I didn't want you to find out about this from anyone but me. After our confrontation last night and then our discussion this morning, I couldn't stop thinking about all of it. I knew I had to tell you everything, and I had to do it right away. I didn't even want to wait till I got home tonight. That's why I called you down here."

"Thank you, Sir," I said. "I already knew you hired him, though."

He raised his eyebrows as he looked at me. "Oh?"

"Well I knew about twenty minutes ago, Sir. I knew when your checkbook fell open in the car and I saw the check receipt."

"Well, that's what I didn't want to happen. I didn't want you to find some evidence like that and start doubting me."

"When I first saw it, Sir, I did doubt you ... but only for about ten seconds. I thought about it, and I decided that I needed to trust you. I wasn't going to even ask you about it. I planned to just wait for you to tell me when you thought I needed to know."

Matt stepped toward me and squatted down so that he was at eye level with me. "Petey, I do love you. You know this, right?"

"Of course," I whispered. I suddenly felt overwhelmed with emotion.

"And it's gonna be hell tonight when you don't get to sleep with me ..."

"I know!" I whined.

"Now gimme a kiss," he said. I slid forward in the chair and wrapped my arms around his neck.

"Oh, Master!" I cried, "I love you so much" I pulled back slightly and kissed him passionately. He grabbed hold of both sides of my face as he found his way into my mouth with his tongue, and I moaned excitedly.

"Fuck, I wanna make love to you so bad right now," he said.

"You're the boss," I reminded him.

"I know ... but it's too risky. "I can't usually go for more than two minutes without being interrupted around here. We'll come back down here again some night after closing ... and use the weight lifting equipment again. I promise."

I smiled sweetly at him. "I can't wait."

I did sleep on the floor that night, and although it was difficult, I didn't cry into my pillow. It helped quite a bit to know that my separation from Matt was just as hard for him as it was for me. He woke me very early the next morning by crawling beside me on the floor and wrapping his arm around me, and then we made love right there on the bedroom carpet.

18

Kathie and Carter sat across the table from Matt and me, and my sister lovingly reached over to take my hand. "Petey, are you sure you're all right with this?"

I smiled at her and nodded. "Yeah, I'm more than all right. I'm really glad that he's getting the help he needs. I never really wanted to see him go to prison."

We were sitting together in a booth at Matt's favorite Italian restaurant, and the four of us had just returned from Ryan's sentencing hearing. Alex and Drew had attended as well, but they had plans to go to Alex's parents' for dinner that night.

"That was quite the letter you wrote," Carter said, referring to the one I'd submitted to the judge, asking for leniency in his sentencing of Ryan. "I just hope you're right about him. I hope he's really changed the way you think he has."

"Well I think this lawyer of his has made a big difference in his life," Matt said.

"What do ya mean?" Kathie asked.

Matt raised his eyebrows slightly and then looked over at me. "Well it seems their relationship has become a little more than just attorney and client," Matt said.

"Richard Nelson is Ryan's boyfriend," I whispered.

"Do you mean 'boyfriend' boyfriend?" Kathie asked, "or is it more like ... um ... like yours and Matt's relationship?"

"Yeah," I said and laughed.

"Well, which one?" she reached across the table and playfully punched me.

239

"Yeah, I think Richard's more like his Master," I said. "It's kinda like me and Matt."

"Richard is exactly what Ryan needed," Matt said. "They both seem really happy." Just as he said this I looked toward the entrance of the restaurant and noticed Richard and Ryan standing by the podium, waiting to be seated.

"They're here," I said, surprised. "Speak of the devil." I made eye contact with Ryan as I spoke, and I reached my hand up and waved to him. He waved back and then turned to his Master to whisper something in his ear. He then turned and headed over toward our table.

"Hi," he said, as he approached us. "What a coincidence."

"Hey Ryan," Matt said. "Haven't seen you in awhile." Ryan laughed.

"Hopefully I never have to see you under those circumstances again, Sir," he said. "I don't mean to interrupt your dinner, but I just wanted to say thanks again for everything. Without your testimonies, I probably would be on my way to prison right now."

"We don't think you belong there," Matt said. "I'm glad it worked out."

Suddenly Richard was behind Ryan, and he affectionately placed his hand on his boy's shoulder. He nodded to Matt. "We are, too," he said.

"Richard and Ryan, do you know Petey's sister Kathie and her fiancé, Carter?"

"Nice to meet you," Richard said, extending his hand to shake Carter's.

"Kathie and I have met," Ryan said.

"Well, we don't want to disturb your dinner," Richard said, "but I do want to tell you how grateful I am for the kindness you showed to Ryan. We don't expect you to forget all you've been through, but I hope that Ryan will have a chance to rectify some of the hurt that his actions have caused you. I hope someday you will be able to see his heart the way I do."

"We hope you find happiness, Ryan," Matt said, "and we just want to move on and put all this in the past."

"I've found happiness, Sir. Thank you. I did such terrible things, and I really don't even know why I did them, but I don't think—actually, I *know* I won't ever do anything like that again. I have Richard now, and he's everything I ever dreamed of ..."

I looked up at the couple, and was a little surprised by what I saw. Richard was not the type of partner I'd have imagined for Ryan. He was much older, almost old enough to be Ryan's dad—at least in his late thirties or early forties. He was in pretty good shape and rather attractive, but he did have a receding hairline. It seemed strange to me that Richard identified as a Master because he was so mild-mannered. He was very professional and businesslike.

On the other hand, I suspected that a man like Richard was exactly what Ryan needed. He needed guidance and constant instruction. He needed someone who loved him, and it certainly seemed he'd found this in Richard. Of course I'd only ever witnessed Richard within the context of a professional setting. I really had no idea what he was like on a personal level.

"Thank you, Petey," Ryan said, and it appeared for a moment that Ryan might be on the verge of crying. "I owe you my life ... I really and truly do."

I turned around in my chair and looked up into his tear-filled eyes, and then I stood up. We embraced each other without another word, and as I held him, I felt him tremble as silent sobs wracked his torso.

When we separated from each other, he again looked into my eyes and smiled. Now I, too, was crying. "I can't believe I hurt you," he whispered.

"I can't believe I hated you," I responded softly.

Ryan stood there for a few seconds and it seemed the silence enveloped us, making me feel as if we were frozen in time. Then quickly he looked away. "I guess our table is ready," he said, wiping his face with the back of his hand. Matt reached out and handed him a table napkin.

"Thanks," he said. "I guess we should get going." Richard again placed a hand on his boy's shoulder.

"Keep in touch, and thanks again," Richard said.

After they'd gone I looked over at my sister and saw she too had been crying. "Petey," she said, "I don't even know what to say. Mom and Dad—they'd be so proud of the man you've become."

"Stop it," I said. "You're gonna make me cry again."

She laughed through her tears. "Right!" she said. "This is supposed to be a celebration. Your ordeal with Ryan is over. You're moving into your new house next week. Matt's doing great in his new job ... and Carter and I ..." she reached over and grabbed his hand. "We have some exciting news of our own."

Matt and I looked at each other, and I wondered if he was thinking what I was thinking. "Okay ..." he said. "Don't keep us in suspense."

"We're expecting," Carter said, beaming proudly. He wrapped his arm around my sister's shoulder and pulled her against him.

"Oh Kathie!" I cried, clapping my hands over my mouth. "I'm gonna be an uncle?"

"Yes!"

I jumped up and ran around the table excitedly, hugging her while we once again started crying. Matt was laughing at me, soaking up my exuberance. "Congratulations, man," he said to Carter and reached out to shake his hand. After hugging Kathie, I moved on to Carter and embraced him as well.

"What do you want?" I asked him. "Boy or girl?"

Carter beamed proudly, shaking his head. "Ya know I don't even care. I just want a healthy and happy baby."

"Kathie!" I said excitedly, a brilliant idea occurring to me. "I can throw you a baby shower!"

Matt gave me a funny look.

"Why not?" I said. "In our new house!"

Matt laughed. "Why not?" he repeated.

My eyes filled with tears as I looked at my sister once again. "I just thought ..." I said. "I just thought of how happy Mom would be right now."

"I'm sure she *is* happy," Kathie said. "I can feel her with us now. I know she's just as thrilled as we are."

"Well, I'd order us a round of drinks to celebrate," Matt said, "but in your condition, I don't think you should be drinking." He looked at Kathie and winked.

"I'd love a virgin daiquiri," she said.

"Coming right up," he said, motioning for the waiter.

Often when people see someone like Ryan Connors, they're amazed that this sort of guy seems to always end up getting away with things. If you'd have spoken to me about this very topic a few months ago, undoubtedly I'd have agreed with such a statement. After Ryan assaulted me and tried to kill my Master, he almost fatally injured Drew, my dearest friend on earth. At this point I wanted nothing more than for Ryan to just go away. I would have been thrilled to know he was going to rot in jail for years, possibly his entire lifetime.

With the knowledge I now have, I see the whole thing from a much different perspective. Not only do I understand that Ryan himself was a victim of abuse—horrible, relentless, long-term abuse—I also see that he was trapped in a situation where he had nowhere to get help. His stepfather was molesting him, and his mother was doing everything she could to buy Ryan's silence. Even without her bribery (or perhaps it wasn't even intended as such but rather was out-and-out "guilt money"), I doubt Ryan would have been able to speak the truth about what had happened to him.

Ryan spent all of those years harboring the bitterness, regret, depression, and pain that such abuse causes. He desperately wanted to find someone who really loved him. Someone who would love him for who he was, rather than someone who simply wanted to use him.

Then Ryan fell in love with Matt. I don't believe it was the same sort of love that I feel for my Master, but to Ryan it was the most significant feeling he'd ever known. Matt seemed to be the perfect guy. He possessed all of the physical characteristics that Ryan found attractive, and he also was incredibly kind. He was polite and courteous to Ryan, and this was not treatment Ryan was used to. He began to imagine that Matt really wanted to be his Master. He allowed himself to think that Matt could love him in the same way that he felt he loved Matt.

Of course, none of that happened. Matt never fell in love with Ryan. He never had any such attraction to him at all, and this was a cruel and crushing blow to the boy. He was devastated, and finally he threw himself at Matt in a last-ditch attempt to win Matt over. When Matt rejected him, it was more than he could take.

Then Eric came into the picture, and Ryan thought perhaps he could have with him what he had hoped to find with Matt. But Eric was not equipped to handle a sub like Ryan. He was so new himself that he didn't begin to comprehend the depth of Ryan's problems. He had no clue how to guide him or help him.

After everything was over, and Ryan was in jail, we learned all the sordid details. We learned of Ryan's past, his abuse and heartbreak. We learned about how he had obsessed over Matt and how that obsession caused him to hate me because I was merely an obstacle that was blocking Ryan's pathway to happiness.

After Drew and I met with Ryan at the jailhouse, I was able to sort all of this out in my mind. I made a decision to try to help Ryan. It felt to me as if he truly was remorseful for his actions. I really believed he wanted to get help for himself, and when I talked it over with Drew, I learned that he felt the same way.

We did end up meeting with Ryan and his attorney, and this time our Masters were present. Alex was still angry and skeptical, but he did come to the meeting, mainly out of love for his Drew. That meeting was nearly as gut wrenching as was the previous encounter that Drew and I had had with Ryan at the jail. It was then that Alex finally began to see Ryan the way we other three viewed him, and finally, with Alex's blessing, we gave our statements.

It was as a family that the four of us decided that we would help him. Each of us wrote letters that were submitted to the judge and prosecutor. Michele, the prosecuting attorney, then met with us and asked pointedly what we were gunning for. We told her we had no desire to place Ryan in prison; we just wanted him to get help.

Finally a plea bargain was offered to him. Originally he'd been charged with sexual assault, assault with a deadly weapon, attempted murder, and possession of a concealed weapon. The plea agreement reduced the charges simply to two counts of assault.

Ryan pled guilty to these reduced charges and was given two years of probation, alcohol and drug counseling, mandatory drug testing, mandatory therapy, anger management training, and community service. Although it may sound like he was getting off easy for the crimes he'd committed, he actually had to endure quite a list of punishments. He also ended up paying enormous fines, court costs, jail fees, etc.

My only concern was that if Ryan did not actually get the help he needed, one day it all would happen again, and he'd victimize someone else. In truth, though, it seemed as if Richard was exactly what Ryan needed. He seemed to be everything that Ryan had been looking for, and they fit well together. It was so obvious how taken Richard was by his boy. Richard acted pretty self confident, similar to the qualities I'd witnessed in Matt and Alex, and as a Master, I imagined he would be rather strict. Yet on the other hand, he acted proud to be with Ryan.

Wasn't this the key? Wasn't this the answer that Ryan had always been seeking? Richard was someone who truly wanted to be with him. He wanted other people to see them as a couple. How wonderful it must have felt to Ryan to finally be able to love and to be loved in return, without shame.

"Sir, I really feel good about this—the way things turned out for Ryan. Don't you?" We were lying in bed together watching late-night television.

"Yep. I'm proud of you, pup. I'm proud that you were able to forgive him, and I love you for being the loving, kind-hearted person you are."

"But ... I don't know, Sir. Sometimes it seems you don't really want me to be kindhearted."

"I don't want you to be a doormat. There's a difference," he said.

"Well I like being your doormat, Sir," I smiled and turned to look up at him. My head was leaning against his shoulder, and his arm was wrapped around me.

"That's different," he laughed. "You'll be what I tell you to be ... including my doormat."

"Yes, Sir," I said. "Can I suck you?"

He smirked as he stared down at me. "Where'd that come from?" he asked.

"Right here," I said, pointing to my chest. "It came from my heart."

"Oh really? Or did it come from here?" With the arm he had wrapped around me, he quickly reached over and squeezed my dick. I laughed.

"There too," I said.

"Kiss me first. Then I'll decide if you can blow me." I turned completely around to face him and crawled up on top of his hard body. I loved when he allowed me to do this. I loved the feel of his firm torso beneath me, and it thrilled me to know I could so carelessly rest the entire weight of my body atop his without it even being slightly uncomfortable to him.

His arms wound around me, and he gently squeezed my buttocks. "Mmm," he said, and I leaned in to kiss him. The kiss at first seemed to be like any other—like the thousands of kisses I'd given him before, but feeling him beneath me like that really excited me. As I became more aroused, the intensity of my passion for him increased, and I hungrily drilled my tongue deep into his mouth.

He responded in kind, and we began gasping for air, tilting our heads from side-to-side and frantically clutching each other's face. He ran his fingers through my hair, then he slid them down my shoulders, across my back, and finally again down to my buttocks. I felt the hardness of his arousal beneath me, and I wanted it inside of me.

Finally I pulled my face free from his and looked into his deep blue eyes. "Sir," I gasped, "have you decided?"

"Suck it!" he whispered, and instantly I slid down his body. His boxers were off within seconds and my mouth was around his throbbing hard-on. I loved everything about this experience—the smell, the taste, the feel of it in my mouth. I had memorized every square millimeter of my Master's cock. My mouth knew it. My throat craved it. My tongue delighted in it. Matt's cock was my favorite snack. It was the greatest reward he could give me, and it was with this degree of appreciation and respect that I then bowed my head to worship him.

My Master's moans of pleasure were like music to my ears as I slid up and down on his shaft. The more he responded to the attention I was giving him, the more I wanted to please. Yes, I truly loved when he held my head in his hands and took control, face-fucking me forcefully; but it was so beautiful when he simply would lie back and allow me to worship. It was both beautiful and exciting. Purely erotic. My own rigid hard-on pressed against the mattress beneath me as I lay there on my belly bobbing hungrily on my Master's rock-hard cock.

He must have been quite excited himself, for he did not take nearly as long as usual to achieve orgasm. Within a matter of ten minutes he was at his point-of-no-return. As I felt the cum load firing into his shaft, I knew he was ready to blast, and I eagerly slid all the way down to the base of his cock, devouring him entirely. He arched his back and thrust his pelvis upward as he drained himself into me, and I remained happily in place until I finally felt his body relax beneath me.

Like a kid with an ice cream cone, I continued to lick him and savor his taste. "Good to the last drop," I whispered, right as I pulled my mouth off of him.

"Fuck!" he sighed. "Fuckin nice, Petey Pup." Then he laughed. "I don't think I need to expend the effort to face-fuck you anymore. I can just order you to do it yourself."

I looked up at him and grinned. "But Sir, it's so much fun when *you* do it."

He laughed harder this time. "Come 'ere, pup," he said, and I crawled up into his arms. "I love you," he said, and then we kissed again.

"How is it possible to have so much stuff in one little apartment?" I asked Drew as I looked around at the stack of boxes that surrounded us.

Drew laughed. "I guess we just accumulate shit ... without even realizing it. But ya know, when we get everything moved into the new place—it's just so huge that it'll seem like we have hardly anything. It'll look bare."

"Well ya know what that means?" I grinned with excitement. "Shopping!"

Drew was practically jumping up and down at the thought. "And we'll have some money to spend too. With what we're gonna be saving on rent ..." he rubbed his hands together excitedly. "What should we buy first?"

Drew's brace and sling had just been removed the day before, and I think that he was availing himself of every opportunity to use his hands together. He was like a blind person who'd suddenly been awarded 20/20 vision.

"A new bed?" I suggested.

"Well, yeah, we've got to get some cool furniture, but we also need to think about decorating. Art work. Wall hangings. Curtains!"

"Oh my god, Drew, you sound like some old queen or something!"

"I am *not* old!" he retorted. "I'm just so damned glad I didn't go back to work this semester. That would've just sucked."

"How do you like the online classes?" I asked. Drew had told me right after we met that when Alex graduated he would be going back to school to finish his post-graduate work, provided that Alex ended up landing a good job. Alex had done quite well over the summer, securing several large contracts with software companies. Being that Drew was still incapacitated with his brace, it seemed like the perfect opportunity for him to take a sabbatical from work and finish his degree program.

"Honestly, Petey," he said, "they're boring as hell, but it's a lot better than having to go back on campus."

"Matt's only taking one class right now," I said, "and I still worry that might be too much. He just works so many hours and stuff ... I wonder if he even needs to get a degree. He already knows he's gonna own the business."

"Well don't worry, Petey. Matt knows his limits. If it's too much for him, he'll decide on his own."

"I know," I sighed. "But he won't even let me work now that school's started. Thank god he let me have Mr. Bartlett put me on the schedule for two days a month. At least that way I'm technically still employed."

"Do you like your classes?"

"I wish ... I don't know ... I just sort of wish I'd have stayed at the community college for another year. I don't like the great big campus at the university, and in my one class, there are like a hundred and fifty students."

"I hate those lecture classes," he agreed.

"Hey, guess what's coming up?" I said. We had moved into the kitchen and I was pulling a bottle of water from the fridge.

"What?" Drew said. "Hey, can I have one?" I handed him a bottle and closed the door.

"Our anniversary."

"Yours and Matt's?" he asked. I nodded.

"September 14th... next Tuesday."

"That's the day those two punks beat you up?"

"That's the day my hero saved me! That's when Matt took me to the hospital ... and now it's a year later, and the rest is history."

"It's really a romantic story," Drew said. "It's like something you'd see in a movie ... or a book."

I laughed. "Yeah, could you imagine our story being in a book? What if it had our sex life in it?" We busted up laughing. "It'd be hard-core porn!"

"So, what are you planning ... anything?"

"I'm not sure exactly, but I want it to be special. I don't wanna say anything to Matt about it, though ... cause I wanna see if he remembers."

"Petey ..." Drew was using his cautionary voice. "Don't set yourself up for disappointment like that. Guys like Matt and Alex are not all sentimental and mushy like us fags. He might not even think about it ... but that wouldn't mean he loves you any less."

"Oh I know, but I bet you anything he does remember. I mean, how could he forget?"

"Maybe you'd better drop him a hint or a reminder or something. Just in case."

"Well, if he doesn't remember, that's okay too. Then it will be all that much more special when I do something nice for him."

"You already do *everything* for him now, Petey." Drew laughed. "You cook for him, clean for him, do his laundry, ironing, errands, shoe-shining. What more is there you could possibly do?"

"Maybe I'll just get him something nice. Like maybe a watch with an inscription or something ... with the date of our anniversary."

"Aren't you still forbidden to spend money on him?" Drew gave me that look again.

"Well don't you think our *anniversary* would be an exception?"

"Who cares what I think. What will *Matt* think?"

"I guess there's only one way to find out," I said, smiling broadly at my best friend.

Matt had found us the perfect house, and when the four of us went to look at it for the first time, we all were extremely excited. It was a duplex, but Matt contracted a builder to make modifications that afforded us some shared living space. The entire main floor would be communal space, and it included a kitchen, family room, bathroom, and exercise room. The full-sized basement was also accessible from both units of the duplex.

Our private living quarters were upstairs. Each couple had a private kitchen, bathroom, living room, and bedroom as well as a separate phone line. The house came with one garage, but Matt had a second built on the opposite side of the home so that Alex and Drew would have their own. There was a large swimming pool, patio, and deck in the spacious backyard.

It really was almost too-good-to-be-true, and I couldn't believe that Matt's father was paying for it all. According to Matt, though, the new gym was a huge success already. They had so many memberships that they were literally turning customers away or referring them to other gyms. It seemed that Matt's dad was making a wise investment by agreeing to Matt's hiring contingency.

The move itself was not nearly as bad as I'd feared. Drew and I had packed everything, and then a team of movers had come that Saturday morning and hauled it all away. A few hours later, our entire household was set up in the new home. The four of us went out to dinner that evening to celebrate, and afterwards we headed over to the bar.

Certainly Matt had no problem gaining entry, in spite of the fact he was underage, but when it came to me, this was usually a challenge. We generally avoided the situation, and I wasn't really that disappointed by this fact. I remembered how jealous I'd felt the night Matt and I had first met Ryan. I didn't particularly like that feeling, and going to a bar was almost like sending out an open invitation for someone to hit on my Master.

On our first night in the new home, though, we all were pretty giddy and excited, and going to the bar seemed like the perfect way to celebrate. We weren't there but ten minutes when Matt stripped his shirt off and dragged me to the dance floor. Seeing his bare, chiseled chest as he effortlessly danced beneath the strobe lights was wicked hot. He kept grabbing me and kissing me, groping my ass obscenely while doing so. Since it wasn't a leather bar, I wasn't wearing my collar, but there definitely was no question who owned me.

It was only three days until our anniversary, and as the big day grew closer, I became more and more excited. I wondered if I should plan a big meal for him—something special that he liked—or if I should assume that he'd be taking us out for dinner. I wanted to ask him, but there was no way I could do so without reminding him of the date's significance.

When Monday arrived, I decided I was just going to have to figure out a way to ask him casually, so as not to be suggestive about Tuesday's significance. "Any idea what you want for dinner tomorrow night, Sir?" I asked.

"I have no idea, pup," he laughed. "Why're you worried about that now? Shouldn't you be thinking about breakfast and lunch first?"

"Oh, I just wondered, Sir," I said. "I have to go to the store in the morning, so I figured I could get whatever you want."

"Surprise me," he said. He was sitting at the computer reading an online newspaper, and I didn't want to press him any further. He tended to get testy when I interrupted his concentration while he was using the computer.

Well, Matt loved pasta, I thought. His favorite cuisine was Italian, so I guessed that would be the wisest choice for our dinner. It seemed that Drew must have been right about Matt forgetting. Of course he wouldn't remember something sentimental like that. I would just make him a really nice dinner, and then I'd slip the watch underneath his pillow. That way he'd find it that evening at the end of the day. I didn't want to make too big of a deal out of it, but I did want him to be aware of how thankful I was to have been his pup for an entire year.

The evening ended up being rather relaxing. I had dinner on the table when Matt got home. Afterwards he retired to the living room while I cleaned up the table and kitchen, and then I joined him, kneeling at his feet like I did every night. Sometimes he wanted oral servicing. Sometimes he wanted foot worship. Sometimes he wanted to fuck me like a wild animal, and sometimes he just wanted to sit and watch television. I knelt there and awaited his instructions.

"Sit," he very calmly stated, and so I turned around and settled in between his legs. We watched a couple TV shows together, during which he occasionally reached down to stroke my hair affectionately.

At about nine-thirty Matt informed me that we were going to bed. I found that extremely strange, because we had never gone to sleep that early. Usually we were up until at least eleven or twelve, even on nights when he had to work early the next morning. He said he'd had a tough day at work and was tired. I secretly hoped this was code-speak for "let's fuck," and so without question got ready for bed, brushing my teeth, stripping down to my briefs and crawling beside my Master beneath the covers.

When I rolled over to kiss him, I was disappointed to see that he was already sound asleep. He apparently didn't even feel the watch box that was nestled beneath his pillow. Gingerly I slid my hand under the side of the pillow and discovered it had slid over when he'd lain down, forcing it out to the edge. I gently pulled it out from under the pillow and placed it on my nightstand. Then I turned my light off and tried to fall asleep myself.

As I lay there, I couldn't help but feel sad that Matt had not remembered. I realized that he wasn't the type to get mushy all the time. He wasn't sentimental and sensitive the way I was. That's why he was Master and I was pup. I was softer and weaker and far more emotional than he. I should have been able to simply accept this fact. Cripes, we'd been together for a year now, and I still could not just realize he was wired differently than me.

In spite of my good intentions of being strong and logical and stoic, my emotions overcame me, and I rolled away from my Master, lest he wake and hear me crying. Silently I wept, feeling a sense of utter disappointment. I felt so let down. It had been such a long day, waiting for him—planning our special night in our new home on our first anniversary. Now here it was, not even 10 PM, and my Master was asleep, and he hadn't even remembered what today was.

I reached up to my nightstand and retrieved the watch. I decided it best for me to simply hide it in the drawer. I would hate for him to find it tomorrow and feel bad about the situation. I doubted that he would actually feel guilt for forgetting, but he might worry about me getting overly upset.

Finally I settled back in against my pillow and cried myself to sleep. It would be better in the morning, I told myself. A new day where I could focus upon the future. I wanted to be thankful for all I had, not sad about some stupid anniversary. That was the last thought I remembered until I was suddenly awakened six hours later.

My Master had his arms around me and was whispering in my ear. "Pup, you need to trust me. Don't be afraid … you have a blindfold on."

I tried to open my eyes but could only see darkness. I tried reaching up to feel my face, but he grabbed my wrists and gently pushed them down to my sides. "No," he said, "keep it on. Trust me."

"Yes, Sir," I whispered. I wondered for a moment if this really was happening or if I was merely having a dream.

"I'm going to put some clothes on you now, and I need your cooperation," he said. "Sit up." He slid his arm behind my back and pulled me into an upright position where I remained until he'd pulled a shirt over my head.

"Sir," I said, laughing just a little. "Can't I get dressed first and then put on the blindfold?"

"Obey your Master," he said.

"Yes, Sir." Matt then had me stand while he put my pants on. That was followed by my socks and shoes. Then suddenly I felt his strong arms under me, picking me up. He began to walk, carrying me across the room. He carried me down the steps, then out the door of our home. I knew we were in the garage, and then he opened the car door and told me to duck my head. He slid me into the passenger seat.

"Keep the blindfold on, or you'll be punished," he warned me.

"Yes, Sir," I said.

This all was so weird, and I had no idea what was going on. Why was Matt doing this? Was it part of some kinky scene? Was he going to take me to some strange place to do something crazy? I trusted him too much to fear him, but I really was perplexed.

He got in the driver's side and started the car. We backed out, and after only a couple seconds, I was lost. Without the visual, I had no idea which direction we were headed. I lay back, resting my head against the seat, and yawned.

"Pup's tired," Matt said affectionately. "It's still the middle of the night."

"I thought it was, Sir. Can you tell me where we're going? Please, Sir."

"Shh," he said. "I told you to trust me, so stop asking questions."

"Yes, Sir," I said, once again yawning widely. Maybe it was a dream. Maybe I should just let myself fall back asleep and when I awoke in the morning I'd realize it never really happened.

After about ten minutes, the car slowed, and I knew Matt was pulling to a stop. "Don't move," he said, "and don't take off the mask."

I smiled and tried to look in the general direction of his voice. "Yes, Sir," I said. This was starting to excite me a little.

A few seconds later my door opened, and I felt Matt's hand grabbing my own. "Step out of the car, pup," he said. "I'm not gonna carry you this time."

I obeyed, but he guided me. He instructed me to be careful because there was a curb, and he told me exactly when to step up. It felt like we were walking on pavement as he wrapped his arm around my shoulder and led me about thirty or forty feet from the car.

"You need to kneel," he instructed me, "but we are on pavement, so there is a cushion for you to use." I felt him suddenly press the small pillow against my chest, and I grabbed hold of it. I lowered myself to the pavement carefully, placing the cushion under my knees. Then I remained there obediently, waiting for further instructions.

"It's going to be bright when I take off the mask," he said. "Don't be frightened. Just give your eyes a moment to adjust." I felt his fingers against the side of my head as he gently pulled against the face mask. I surmised it was the type of mask that women frequently use for sleeping.

"Open," he said, and I did so.

Matt was correct. It was very bright. In fact, it seemed almost like floodlights. At first all I could do was blink, and I really couldn't make out where I was or what was going on. A few seconds later, though, it began to come into focus. I saw my Master standing in front of me, and he looked damned nice. He was wearing a tuxedo.

I looked down to see what I was wearing—definitely not dress clothes. It was an outfit I was familiar with, though—it was the exact same set of clothes I'd been wearing the day I met Matt one year earlier. Quickly I looked around

Standing in a circle around us were several people I knew and loved. Alex and Drew were there, smiling down at me affectionately. My sister Kathie and Carter were there as well. Then I saw Jason. To the right of him were Richard and Ryan. Then I saw my friend, the detective, Rick Murray. "Sir," I whispered, "what's going on?"

"Do you know where you are?" he asked.

At first I shook my head and started to answer no, but then I looked around. Yes! Yes I did know where we were. I knew exactly! We were at the bus stop downtown. We were right downtown in the center of the city at the bus stop near the apartment where I used to live with Kathie. This was the exact location where—

"This is where I met you, pup," he whispered.

I placed my hands quickly over my mouth to stifle a gasp. "Oh, Sir!" I exclaimed. "You did remember!"

Tears began to stream down my face as he smiled down at me affectionately.

"Happy anniversary, pup," he said. He then turned to Alex, who was standing beside him, and held out his hand. Alex handed him my collar. "I've already collared you once," he said, "but I want to do it again now where we first met, and I want everyone to see. You are mine. My pup." I held my head upright in spite of my urge to bow it respectfully, allowing him to gently snap the collar in place around my neck.

"Petey Pup," he said, "will you be my pup forever?"

"Yes, Sir!" I cried, suddenly overcome with the strongest wave of emotion I think I'd ever experienced. "Oh thank you, Sir!"

"Thank *you*," he said. "Thank you for making my life complete. Thank you for giving me your submission. Thank you for sharing your purity and innocence with me—for sharing yourself with me every day. Thank you for allowing me to own you.

"Petey Pup, look up at your Master. Look up at me with pride as you kneel here in front of all those who mean so much to us." I stared lovingly up into his eyes.

"Petey," he said, as he reached into his pocket. "Will you truly be mine for the rest of your life?" He pulled out a shiny golden ring, just a solid band with one square, masculine-shaped stone. "Will you marry me?"

I gasped as I stared up at him in disbelief. My mouth was open, but I couldn't speak as the tears streamed down my cheeks.

I heard my best friend beside me. Drew gently urged in his high-pitched weepy voice. "Answer him, Petey!"

I quickly nodded. "Yes! Yes, Sir!"

Matt dropped to his knees in front of me and slid the ring on my finger. I felt his arms around me as his lips pressed against mine. This *must* be a dream! This must be the best dream I've ever had. I heard the applause and laughter around us as I closed my eyes and passionately kissed my Master/fiancé.

19

After Matt's proposal, our entire gang was escorted by
Detective Murray and a couple of his squad cars over to an all-night
diner. Matt had arranged with the detective to have the entire
street blocked off for the proposal, and the only time of day that he
could make this happen was the middle of the night. I was very
impressed by the fact that all these people hauled themselves out of
bed in order to be Matt's witnesses.

"Sir," I said to him while we rode in the backseat of the police
car, "I've never been inside of one of these ..."

Matt laughed. "Unfortunately, I have."

"I know! But isn't it so much better this time?"

"It's perfect this time," he said as he pulled me onto his lap. He
held his wrist up to show me he was wearing his new watch.
"Thanks for the anniversary gift." Then he gently kissed me.

"You found it!" I said.

"I found it under the pillow," he told me. "Took it out of the
box before you crawled in bed."

I started giggling. "So I have the empty case in my
nightstand?"

"Yep," he said, smiling lovingly at me.

"Well, let's see what time it is," I said. He held up the watch
and I saw it was almost five in the morning. "Oh man, I can't
believe all these people came at this time of night ... to see you
propose to me. I can't believe it!"

259

"Everybody loves you, Petey. They'd come no matter when it was, and I kinda like it this way—stealing away with you in the dead of night."

"You tricked me, Sir! You made me think you forgot our anniversary. I was so sad."

He grinned at me and kissed me again. "You gonna help me decide on a wedding date?" he asked.

"I thought the Master made all the decisions," I whispered into his ear. "I want you to decide … please."

"No pup, some things do require your input. We're gonna be legally married … I think that's something that will require your consent."

"*Legally* married?" I asked.

He nodded. "First we'll fly to someplace where same-gender marriage is legal, and we'll get it done. Then we'll fly back home for a ceremony here with our families and friends."

"So it's gonna be a big wedding?" I asked excitedly.

"Big or small as you want it, pup," he said.

"Sir, I never thought I'd get to have a big wedding! Never in a million years! I wonder what Kathie's gonna say …"

"She's happy for us," he said.

"I don't think she's ever seen me wearing my collar, Sir," I said. "But I want to wear it during the wedding …"

"You *have* to wear it during the wedding, pup. That's non-negotiable."

"For *everyone* to see!" I beamed. "I want Drew to help me plan it all. I want your mom to make our cake! I want Blake to be our photographer! Are we having a reception? With a band?!"

He was laughing again. "We'll have plenty of time to decide everything, pup. We're here now … let's go eat."

The restaurant seated the ten of us together at one big, long table. Matt was sitting on the very end, and I sat right beside him. Drew was on the other side of me, sitting next to his Master. "I'm getting pancakes!" I said excitedly to my best friend. "With lots of syrup … to celebrate!"

"Better be careful," he warned. "Don't wanna get fat before your wedding."

Several people laughed, including my sister who was sitting across from us. "I think you'd be cute if you did get a little bit pudgy," she said. "You're so damned skinny."

I made a face at her. "Oh man, I bet my hair's a freakin nightmare!" I suddenly realized Matt had dragged me out of bed.

"Your hair's fine, Petey Pup," Drew said, affectionately reaching up to smooth it down on my head. "I bet this was exactly how you looked the day Matt met you."

"Yeah, but I had glasses on back then." I was currently wearing contacts. Matt had gotten me the extended-wear type that I could sleep in. He'd promised that I could get laser surgery someday. "And when Matt started talking to me that day, I was so nervous I couldn't even say anything! I just started shaking."

"You were cute," Matt remembered. "You were trembling like you were freezing cold or something."

"I always had a crush on Matt," I confessed to everyone. "Back when we were in school I used to really like him, but he didn't even know I existed."

"Things were different then," Matt said. "I was different."

"It wasn't all that long ago," Kathie said. "It seems like you've changed a lot just in the last few months."

"Maybe," he admitted, "but I'm still me. Petey's still Petey. I wonder if we really have changed all that much, or if it's just that everyone else is starting to see who we really are."

"I don't know either," Kathie said honestly. "After Petey was in the hospital, I didn't want him to have anything to do with you. I was so devastated when he moved in with you because I was afraid of what you'd do to him. I don't feel that way now. It's hard to believe that my feelings have changed so much in just a few months."

"How do you feel now?" I asked her.

"I'm positive that he loves you. I don't understand all of it, but I know you're happy. Petey, you made your choice, and I have to respect that ... whether I fully understand it or not."

"What's there not to understand about love?" Rick asked. "How is it any different than the love you have for Carter here?"

"I guess there really isn't any difference. Love is love. But just think about it ... a relationship like mine and Carter's would have been misunderstood and forbidden just a few decades ago. Interracial marriage remained illegal in a lot of states until fairly recently."

"So would you say that the problems you had with accepting Matt and Petey as a couple stemmed from the fact that it was a gay relationship, or because of the fact that Petey calls Matt, 'Master'?" the detective asked. I looked around the table to gauge the reaction of the others, and I realized there wasn't anyone there I would have hesitated to be honest with about my relationship with Matt.

Kathie turned to look at Rick as she answered. "I never had a problem with Petey being gay. I think I knew it before he did. I had a problem with Matt being Petey's boss. It felt to me like Matt was manipulating and controlling him for his own purposes. I thought Matt got his jollies out of bullying someone weaker than him."

"So what is it that changed your opinion?" Matt asked.

"Seeing Petey," she said. "Seeing how happy he is. Seeing how all of the fears and concerns I'd had about Petey seemed to improve after he was with you. He was always so timid, and he seemed to always have such a low opinion of himself. Now he has more confidence. He has a little backbone. He's matured a lot."

"Thanks," I said as I smiled at my sister.

"I still don't know why you need to have someone decide things for you. I don't know why you seem to want to have your life dominated. I don't know why you ... um ... why you wear that collar.

"But I do know you love Matt. I do know he makes you happy, and he tries his damndest to keep you safe. He loves you, too ... it's obvious."

"Kathie," I said, "the thing I think you and Cam had a problem understanding about me is that I'm in a relationship that seems one-sided, but it's really not. In fact, there is nothing about it that is lopsided.

"Matt does make our decisions. He does give me orders. He does get to kick back and let me wait on him hand-and-foot. But it's not free! When you look at us, that is *all* you see, but there's so much more that you don't bother to even think about.

"Matt has a responsibility for me, and this is something that you probably will never have with Carter ... no offense. Carter is not responsible for making every decision, so he doesn't always have to worry about whether he's been right or wrong. Matt does! If Matt decides wrong, then I get hurt. Matt also has to protect me. He has to reassure me constantly. He has to be strong when I am weak. He has to be all of these things for me!

"All I have to do is obey. I don't think that's bullying. I'm the one who has the easier role."

"Amen!" said Drew. "Oh Petey, I couldn't have described it any better. We are not sub because we hate ourselves or because we have low self esteem. We're sub because it's part of our identity, and having a Master—like Matt or Alex or Richard—this completes us."

"Like Carter completes me," Kathie nodded. "Yeah, I see your point. I kind of understand it. I think of it like Mom and Dad's relationship. Dad was the breadwinner, and Mom was the housewife. He pretty much made most of the major decisions, and she pretty much obeyed him—as much as I hate to admit it."

Matt finally decided to speak. "Bottom line is that you're Petey's sister, and he loves you very much. We're not asking or expecting you to understand or approve of every aspect of our relationship, but we do want you in our lives. We want you to understand and accept us for who we are, but even if you can't do that yet, we still want you to remain a major part of Petey's life—and mine. You're family, and Petey needs you."

"Well I hope it can be more than that," she said. "I hope it can be more than me just tolerating you in order to keep contact with my brother. I've always prided myself as being so liberal, but I had some issues here. I think I had a problem with who you are because of who *I* am."

"And who are you?" he asked.

"I'm a damned independent woman! I don't need a man telling me what to do and making my decisions for me. I don't need him protecting me, because I can take care of myself. I don't need domination!"

"You need equality," Matt said.

"I fucking *demand* equality!"

"But can you understand that Petey needs something much different? Can you see how before I came along, Petey relied heavily upon you to be that dominant force in his life? He's always needed a leader. It's the way he's wired ..."

"Yes. Yes, I can understand that, and ya know, I think this was part of the problem. I always was his protector. I was the one who offered him those reassurances he needed. You came along, and suddenly I wasn't really needed any more."

"Oh Kathie!" I said. "Nobody—not even Matt—is gonna ever replace you. You'll always be my big sis, and I'll always need you."

She reached across the table and grabbed my hand. "I know, Petey. I love you so much, and I'm just glad you've found the happiness you deserve."

"Is anyone else here starving?" Alex piped up.

A few of us laughed, and Matt motioned for the waitress. "All on one bill," he instructed when she came over to take our orders.

Matt took most of that day off work. He did go into the office briefly just to check on things, and while he was doing this, he told me to rest. I tried to tell him that I was far too excited to sleep, but he told me to do it anyway. As usual, he was right, and not more than two minutes after my head hit the pillow, I was sound asleep.

It was a tickling sensation that awakened me about three hours later. I opened my eyes and saw my Master staring up at me. He was holding my erection in his hand, gently stroking it, and with his other hand he was tickling my balls.

"It tickles," I moaned.

"You don't like it?"

I laughed. "No Sir ... I *love* it ... but it still tickles!" I squirmed in spite of myself as he continued.

"Do you like this?" he asked, just before taking my throbbing cock into his warm mouth.

I moaned loudly as I frantically clutched the bed sheets. "Oh, Sir!" I cried.

He pulled off of me and laughed. "Now you know what I feel every single morning when I wake up to you blowing me."

"No wonder you love me, Sir," I teased.

"Yeah ... and you're better at it than me. I never sucked anyone besides you, pup."

I smiled at him. "Not even before? I mean when you were a teenager?"

"I'm still a teenager," he corrected me with a grin.

"Just barely, Sir."

He took me in his mouth again, this time sliding up and down a bit and making it last longer than his first taste.

"Sir!" I cried excitedly. "I think you're becoming an expert!"

"You need to shave," he said.

I realized he was correct. It was part of my responsibility to my Master to keep myself completely smooth and clean-shaven at all times, but I was starting to sprout some pubic hair and had procrastinated when it came to shaving myself. "I'm sorry, Sir," I said.

"I don't think I should have to remind you," he said. "I thought we got beyond that ... a long time ago."

"I'm sorry, Sir," I said again.

"When you get up, you need to go shave first thing. Understand?"

"Yes, Sir," I said. He took me in his mouth once again. "Aaahhh!" I moaned, taken by surprise. This time he didn't stop, and as I felt the wetness and warmth of his mouth around me, I closed my eyes and prayed he never would. Within the matter of a few short minutes, though, it was over. I wasn't used to being on the receiving end of oral copulation, and it only took a short while for me to achieve orgasm.

He pulled off of me before I shot my load, though, and wrapped his big fist around my cock head. He made me fire into his hand, and then he had me lick it clean. "Pup always swallows his Master's cum," he explained. "You belong to me, and so your cum is mine, too."

"Thank you, Sir," I whispered. He had rolled me over face-down on the mattress and was lying on top of me with his arm around me. This was how he'd fed me my own cum. Then he proceeded to kiss my neck affectionately.

"Did you like that?" he whispered.

"Sir! Oh ..." I was trembling just a little, as I typically did after my climax. I loved feeling the warmth of his body completely surrounding and sheltering me. "Oh Sir, I loved it."

"I wanna be inside you, pup," he growled into my ear.

"Oh god, Sir! Oh please!" My entire body was so sensitive, and as he slid his hand across my smooth chest and found my nipples, I squealed delightedly. Even though I had just cum, I was rock hard again. While he tweaked my nub with his right hand, he clutched my fist with his left, obviously aware of the ring I was wearing—the one he'd just given me.

"You're mine!" he said seductively. "You're all mine ... forever!"

"You own me, Sir," I whispered.

"Say it louder," he commanded.

"You own me, Sir!" I shouted.

"Fuck yeah! I own every little piece of you." He twisted the nipple that he held between his thumb and forefinger, and I squirmed beneath him. "I own this tight little ass, too," he said as he slid his hand down my torso and then playfully smacked my bare ass cheek.

"Use it, Sir!" I begged. "Oh please, use my ass. It's yours!"

His finger was suddenly probing my pucker, and I frantically reached over to the nightstand, groping for the lube. After slicking up my hole, he slid himself into me and then again wrapped his arms around me.

"You're my Master," I whispered, "and now you're gonna be my husband."

"Mmm," he said as he nibbled playfully on my ear. "Are you gonna be my wife?" he asked.

"Am I?" I asked.

"My little man-wife?"

"Your house-husband," I laughed. I felt him slowly begin to hump me, sliding gracefully back and forth inside of me.

"My *little* house-husband," he clarified.

"Oh Sir!" Feeling him inside me made my own dick throb. "And you're my *big* Man-husband."

He laughed. "Master and slave. Owner and pup. Husband and man-wife."

"I'll be anything for you, Sir." He began to thrust into me, all the while clutching my body tightly against his chest.

"My housewife bitch!" He ground his cock deep into me as he said it.

I reached up and grasped the strong arms around me, moaning unintelligibly.

"Can you handle it? Do you want it every day for the rest of your life?"

"Yes!" I cried.

"Say it!" he ordered.

"I want it, Sir! I want to be yours forever!"

"Oh yeah! Fuck yeah!" He now was rapidly humping my ass while squeezing me tightly against his chest. "I'm gonna fill you up! I'm gonna shoot my fuckin load!"

"Oh god!" I cried. "Oh Sir!"

He thrust his pelvis forward, pressing his groin forcefully against my ass checks. As he held me tightly in place, I felt him tremble slightly as the orgasm washed over him. "Aaaahhh!" he moaned, and then it turned into more of a growl.

"I love you, Sir!" I cried.

"Oh god, I love you!" he echoed. "I love you Petey Pup, and you're mine forever."

He remained inside me for a good twenty minutes afterwards, cuddling affectionately, stroking, whispering in my ear. When he finally released me, I turned and kissed him before getting up to go to the bathroom, where I shaved myself—as-ordered—and took a shower. I then went out to the kitchen and made supper, thinking all-the-while how much I looked forward to getting used to this.

The four of us spent a quiet evening at home and watched movies on the big screen in our shared living room. I made us all popcorn and curled up on the floor beneath my Master's legs while Drew and Alex sat snuggling together on a loveseat opposite us.

By the time we were halfway through the movie, I'd removed a throw pillow from the sofa and sprawled out on the carpeting, lying on my belly. A few minutes later, Drew joined me, sliding beside me as he rested his elbows on his own pillow. I inched my way closer to him, simply because I loved him so much and enjoyed the physical contact. He slid his arm under my own and laced his fingers into mine, holding my hand affectionately. He then looked down to admire my ring.

"I'm so happy for you, Petey Pup," he whispered, and then he leaned in to kiss me on the cheek. I smiled back at him and gently pressed my lips against his, kissing him tenderly

"Give 'im a real kiss." I heard my Master's voice behind me. I turned to glance back at Matt, who was staring at us intently, and once more leaned in to kiss my friend. This time I opened my mouth slightly and pressed harder against him. He responded by tilting his head to the side, opening his own mouth as our lips met, and sliding his tongue into me.

We smiled at each other sweetly as we separated, and I again turned to look at my Master.

"Take your shirts off." This time it was the voice of Alex that we heard, and when my own Master nodded his assent we immediately began to comply with the instruction we'd received. Drew and I both slid upright in a kneeling position, facing each other, and I reached down to grab his shirt tail. He lifted his arms and allowed me to pull the shirt smoothly over his head. I then removed my own.

"Touch him," Matt said to me, and I reached out and placed my fingers against sweet Drew's chest. He was so smooth and soft, and I loved the tightness of his physique. His slender frame and narrow shoulders seemed so delicate to me, especially in contrast to those of my Master, to whom I was most accustomed.

Drew responded by gently running his fingertips down the length of my arm. We leaned in toward each other and once again kissed. This time Drew grabbed my head and held my cheeks in his palms as we French kissed each other in front of our Masters.

I loved my Drew so very much, and it was not difficult for me to express my affection for him, even in front of our audience of two. Soon he had his arms around me, cupping my ass with both palms, and I was grinding my pelvis forward, pressing against my best friend's hard-on. I already had my fingers inside the waistband of his shorts when I heard Alex give the order for us to strip off our pants.

I pulled down Drew's shorts, removing his underwear at the same time, and my heart beat excitedly when his throbbing erection popped up to enthusiastically greet me. Quickly I rolled onto my back and thrust my hips upwards, allowing Drew to strip off my pants. We now were completely naked except for our white ankle socks.

"Stroke him, Drew," my Master ordered my playmate. Drew looked at me first and grinned, then he took me into his hand and began to slide up and down on my rigid shaft. I spread my legs wide as I lay there on the floor in front of the three onlookers and allowed myself to be pleasured. Closing my eyes, I grinned as Drew's gentle touch sent shivers throughout my body. "It feels so good," I whispered.

"Take him in your mouth," Alex told Drew. Instantly my eyes shot open and I looked to my Master for approval. He was grinning as he stared down at us. I saw him nod approvingly, and I also noticed he'd cupped his hand around the bulge in his own pants. I smiled up at him as I felt the moistness of Drew's lips against my erection. This was the second time in one day I'd experienced this feeling.

Matt had been correct when he'd stated that we subs are better at sucking cock, and Drew's mouth proved the point. He slid around me like silk encasing my hardness. All the way down, in one slippery movement, he engulfed me, and I threw my head back, laughing out loud with ecstatic pleasure.

"Fuckin hot," I heard Alex say.

"Slide down, Drew," Matt said. "Lie down next to him." Apparently Drew knew exactly what Matt was talking about, and quickly slid himself into a sixty-nine position with me, all the while keeping my cock in his warm, wet mouth. I opened my eyes and saw his throbbing erection right in front of my face. Slowly I inhaled, taking in his clean yet slightly musky scent.

I reached up and grabbed hold of my friend's hips, awaiting my Master's orders, and when I heard the words I'd been waiting for, quickly obeyed. "Suck him, Petey," Matt said. For only the second time in my life I took a cock in my mouth that was not my Master's. The first time it had been Drew as well.

As it slid into me, I began to suck hungrily, forcing myself to take it all as smoothly and deeply as he'd taken mine. Hearing his moan excited me, and I felt his reaction with my own cock as he sucked me even harder in response. As we continued, it was an amazing feeling, almost as if I were sucking myself. The more attentive I became to my sweet Drew's pleasure, the more eagerly he serviced me.

Drew's moaning got louder as we continued, and I felt myself hedging toward orgasm. I wanted desperately to cry out a warning that I was close, yet I didn't want to take him out of my mouth. My concern vanished, though, when I heard my Master say, "Shoot it, pup! Shoot your fuckin load right down his throat!"

I moaned loudly and released, forcing myself to continue sucking on Drew's now-throbbing erection. Then I heard him moan as well, in spite of the load of my cum he was gulping down his throat. His cock pulsed in my mouth as he released, and I eagerly gulped down his warm seed. We both were gasping and trembling as we pulled away. Frantically we clutched at each other, our mouths meeting once again. Passionately we kissed, right in front of our Masters.

Alex was on his feet first, but I didn't even notice him stripping off his clothes. I was too overcome by the euphoria I'd experienced from my orgasm. Then I felt my Master's naked chest against my back, and quickly I pulled away from Drew to turn to Matt. He grabbed my head with both hands and kissed me. Apparently Alex did the same to Drew, and within seconds Drew and I were both on our hands and knees facing each other in a doggie-style position.

I looked up at Alex and Drew at the exact second that Matt rammed his cock deep into my tight ass. Alex was impaling his boy simultaneously. My friend and I both cried out excitedly as our Masters drilled themselves into us. Then Matt began to fuck me. It was with fierce abandon that he pummeled my ass with his hot, throbbing prick. I cried out uncontrollably as the pleasure-pain experience swept over me, causing me to go rigid-hard again beneath my Master. Matt grabbed hold of my hips and ferociously pounded my ass as we watched our two best friends in the exact same position in front of us.

Moments later it became clear that this was not going to be a long fuck session. Matt's moans of pleasure signaled me that he was about to nut. He slammed into me, balls-deep, and remained buried as he emptied himself into my hot, tight hole. I moaned in response and, looking up at my best friend's face directly in front of me, I heard his Master cry out as he ejaculated into his own hole.

The four of us crumpled to the floor, exhausted and thoroughly spent. I turned to roll over onto my Master, kissing him passionately. "I love you, Sir," I cried, as tears of exuberance streamed down my cheeks.

"I love you, too, pup," he gasped, and then he began to laugh. "Fuckin hot!" he said, and then I heard my Master's best friend respond in kind. They both were laughing hard as Drew and I turned to look at each other. Drew shrugged and smiled. I smiled back at him, and then once again turned to wrap my arms around my hot fuckin Master's beautiful chest.

I think I laughed just a little myself before I got up to get dressed and make us all more popcorn.

20

Diane and I were sitting out by the pool having a glass of iced tea. "Oh Petey, I'm just so excited to be planning another wedding!"

I looked at her and smiled. "And it's *mine!*" I jubilantly exclaimed. We both started laughing. "I never thought I'd have a wedding," I admitted.

"And I never thought I'd be planning one for my son and his *husband*," she laughed.

"Well we're just engaged right now. We're not husbands yet."

"Technicalities," she said, shaking her head. "But let's start with the basics, okay? Have you picked out a date yet?"

I nodded. "March 13th," I said. "My mom's birthday."

"Perfect!" she said. "You and Matt agree on this?"

I looked at her, somewhat stunned that she'd ask such a thing. "Oh yes. I wouldn't be telling other people the date if he hadn't approved ..."

"Of course." She nodded. "Well that's still several months away, which is good. Gives us time to plan everything. Where are you having the ceremony?"

Nervously I bit my lower lip, wondering if I should actually be talking to her about this or if I should wait for Matt. Then I remembered he'd told me to work with his mom on the wedding plans, and there really was no way to do so if I didn't tell her the details.

"Well, Matt was going to talk to you ..." I said.

"Why don't you talk to me right now? That's why we're here, right?" She placed her hand atop my own and sweetly smiled at me.

I nodded and took a deep breath. "Well, I ... um. *We* wondered if we could have it at the cabin ...?"

She lifted her hand to cover her mouth, which had flown open. "Oh Petey! That'd be just perfect! An outdoor wedding, and there is so much space there. Oh, this is gonna be just beautiful!"

I grinned at her in spite of the fact I was trying to remain very professional and mature about the whole thing. "So you'll let us do it?" I asked.

"Oh, of course! I mean, I'd just assumed it would be a church wedding ..."

"We don't really go to church," I confessed. "I used to when I was a kid, but ... I don't know. We're really not religious, and it just seemed hypocritical to both of us to have a big church wedding."

"And do you have someone selected to officiate? Have you chosen your attendants yet? What about a photographer, a caterer, ushers? Do you have a color theme? Are we having a band? A big reception?"

I grabbed hold of my head with both hands. "Oh man! There's just so much to decide!"

She laughed. "Oh, I'm sorry, honey," she said calmly. "Ya know what? I'm gonna hire you a wedding planner." She nodded decisively.

"A wedding planner?" I asked.

"Yes, someone who will take care of all these details. You won't have to worry about a thing."

"Really?" I asked. "Well, I do know I want Drew to be my best man."

"Oh yes, of course," she agreed. "Have you talked to him about it yet?"

I smiled. "Yes, that morning when Matt proposed. I asked Drew before we even left the restaurant."

"Good," she said. "Has Matt chosen a best man?"

"He hasn't told me yet, but I think it'll be Alex."

"Oh that'll be so nice."

"And I want Jason, too ... as a groomsman. But I have a question."

"Okay ... what?"

"Do my attendants all have to be guys?"

She cocked her head to the side as if thinking. "I don't see why they'd have to be. No."

"I want to ask this friend of mine ..."

"I think that'd be real nice. What about your sister?"

"I'm having her and Carter give me away."

She was teary-eyed for a second. "Oh she's gonna love that." I knew she was wondering if Matt would have her and Mr. Porter do the same on his behalf. I knew he planned to talk to her about it and decided I should wait and let him broach the topic on his own.

"Well Petey, let's do this. Let's make a list of all the things you know for sure you want. Then I'll contact a wedding planner and we'll have a meeting."

"I'm already so nervous," I confessed as I took a sip of my iced tea. "I'm afraid of standing up there in front of all those people."

"Well, do you want it to be a smaller wedding?" she asked.

I looked at her intently and thought for a moment before answering. "Well ... I guess the size of it doesn't matter so much to me. I'll be nervous no matter what. And honestly I'm so in love with Matt, I'd just as soon the whole world knows ..."

"I know you are, honey. I can see it in your eyes. You're crazy about him, but you know what? He's crazy about you too. I've never seen him so happy."

"I'm so glad he took the job from his dad. He really loves it."

"Paul says that store is doing so well. He can't believe how well Matt's doing there. He is very pleased with his decision to re-hire him."

"I just can't believe he bought us this house ... or, I mean, that he bought it for Matt."

"Well, Matt would have eventually inherited all that money anyway. His dad felt it worth it to give him the money early so he gets a good start."

"We want you to do our cake," I said suddenly.

"Oh honey, I don't know. It's been years since I've done a wedding cake, and I want yours to be just perfect."

"If you make it, it'll be perfect," I assured her.

"Oh, now I'm getting excited!" she said. "We actually can work on it together. I mean, you can give me your input how you want it. It's gonna be so neat. We'll have two grooms on it instead of a groom and a bride."

I smiled and giggled. "You better make sure they're not the same height. My replica should be shorter than Matt's."

"Oh definitely," she agreed. "Do you know what kind of tuxedos you'll be wearing?"

I shook my head. "No, Matt will decide that."

"Sweetie, I think you should have some input, too."

I shook my head again, more vehemently. "No, Matt's always decided what I wear. I wouldn't want it any other way for our wedding."

She squinted at me a little and sort of smiled, indicating she was perplexed. "Okay, well that's fine I guess. Then I'll talk to him about that."

"If he tells me to decide, then I will," I told her. "Otherwise I'll wear whatever he picks out. What I'm hoping for are matching tuxes."

"Really? Why's that?" she asked.

"Well, sometimes Matt used to dress us alike. He did that a lot when we first were together. It was a way to let everyone know I belonged to him. I just think it'd be cool to have that incorporated into our wedding."

"Why do you think he decided he wanted a wedding?" she asked. "It kind of took me by surprise. It seemed to me that he was more the type who resisted the trappings of conventional institutions such as marriage."

"Oh, no offense, but I really don't see Matt like that at all, Ma'am. I think at heart he has always been a bit of a traditionalist. He likes being the man of the house. He likes being in charge and protecting and caring for me. The fact that he wants to marry me sort of fits into that, ya know."

"So would you then consider yourself to be the 'woman' in the relationship?"

I laughed. "No, not really. That's so funny. I'd never say I was a girl, but I guess it's true that I'm more like the 'wife.'"

"Well, let me ask you this, Dear," she said, leaning into me and again holding my hand. "Are you positive that this is the kind of lifestyle you want long-term? Can you picture yourself ten or fifteen years from now still happy being so ... well, submissive, I guess ... to your husband?"

I looked away for a moment as I thought about her question, smiling to myself as I envisioned Matt and me in the future. It made me smile to picture him at his father's age. I could see myself still being hot for him. I could see myself still feeling lucky to call him my Owner and my Master ... and my husband. I smiled sincerely at her. "Yes!" I said confidently. "I can picture it very clearly, but I do have to say one thing about this subject, and I hope you don't take it the wrong way. I really do love and respect you, Diane, and I'd never want to hurt your feelings or upset you ..."

"Please, Dear, tell me what's on your mind. I'd never be offended."

"Well, when I met you and Mr. Porter I got the impression that you have always been a little bit submissive yourself. My guess is that over time your husband has mellowed a lot. I look at Matt now compared to a year ago when we first met, and he's changed immensely. I think both of us will continue to change, just like you and Mr. Porter. Matt will always be the dominant one, just like your husband, but the way it's gone so far, he seems to just love me more and more every day. And at this point it's less about him having control over me than it is about him loving, protecting, and caring for me. I think the glue that will hold us together is not his dominance; it's his—*our*—love."

"Nicely put," she said. "I can understand what you're saying, but ya know what? Mr. Porter has changed, yes. But so have I. I'm far more independent than I was twenty years ago. When we first got married, I used to be afraid of him at times. I got his permission for every little thing I did. Nowadays I do what I want, and he doesn't usually say too much."

"I can see where it might be possible for our relationship to evolve that way," I admitted. "I know that I do feel a lot more confident in myself now than I did a year ago before I knew Matt. It's ironic in a way, because his goal for me has always been that I become stronger and that I grow to be proud of who I am. I think it's natural that as I do start to accomplish these goals I'll feel more independent ... and maybe even less submissive. But I also recognize that I need him. He's the one who gives me this strength ..."

"But someday maybe you'll see that this confidence you're describing doesn't really come from him. It doesn't come from anywhere other than right there." She pointed at my chest. "Petey, you have every reason to love yourself and be proud, with or without my son."

I felt myself beginning to become emotional. "Thank you, Diane," I said, "but you also have to understand that it's not really just about whether or not I love myself. It's about who I am—how I'm wired. I wasn't born to be a loner. I've always been more comfortable in a role where I admired and followed the guidance of others who had the confidence I lacked. Matt's taught me that I can accept this about myself and love me for being *me*! Not only am I in love with Matt, but I also know he fulfills a need in me. I *need* to be submissive. It's who I am."

She grabbed hold of both my hands this time and looked me in the eye. "We all love you just the way you are, Petey. And it seems to me that you and Matt fulfill the needs of each other."

"We do," I agreed, tears now streaming down my cheeks. "Thank you for understanding."

She then leaned into me and we embraced. "I love you, Petey. I'm so lucky to have you in my family."

"No," I whimpered, "I'm the lucky one."

"Have you been down to the basement lately?" I asked Drew. We were relaxing by the pool in our bathing suits.

"No, why?" he said, tilting his head down and staring at me over the top of his sunglasses.

"There's some really interesting stuff down there," I laughed.

He sat up a bit. "Like what?" he asked.

I leaned toward him and whispered. "Like *bondage* stuff, I think."

"Oh my god!" he said excitedly. "Can we go look?"

"I don't think we should ... I mean, not without permission."

"Well, you must've already looked once. How do you know about it?"

"Drew, I had to sign for the deliveries, and then I saw some of it when they were bringing it in. Matt told me it would be coming and said I had to sign for it and have them put it in the basement ... but I was not to touch any of it."

"Well, did he forbid you from going to the basement and looking at it?"

"Not specifically," I admitted.

Drew was already out of his seat. "Let's go," he said. "I'm not forbidden to go into the basement either, so we're safe."

"Oh my god, Drew!" I said as I jumped up to follow him. "You better not be getting me in trouble!"

"Stop worryin so much, Petey Pup! Worst that can happen is that our Masters might actually use some of this shit on us. Now wouldn't that be a shame?"

"Good point," I laughed as I scurried to catch up to him.

Matt's dinner was not quite ready when he walked into the door that evening, so after giving him his typical welcome-home kiss, I suggested he relax in the living room while I brought him something to drink. Sixty seconds later I was kneeling at his feet removing his shoes while he sipped a cold beer.

"How soon before dinner's ready?" he asked as he flipped on the TV remote.

"About fifteen minutes, Sir," I said. I was now massaging his sole as he stretched his foot and wriggled his toes.

He set the beer on the stand beside him and reached down to undo his fly. "Good," he said. "Get up here and blow me."

I eagerly complied.

Twenty minutes later we were seated together at the dining room table. "Alex and Drew not joining us?" he asked.

"No, Sir," I said. "Drew has his online class tonight and Alex won't be home till later. He has a job clear over in Orlando."

"Take em some food when we're done, pup. I'm sure he'll be hungry when he gets home."

"Yes, Sir," I smiled at him affectionately. I loved how considerate he was of others. I'd already planned to take food to both Alex and Drew. I almost always did when they weren't able to join us for dinner. "Sir, I have to tell you something," I said rather sheepishly.

Matt must have sensed my trepidation by the way I looked down at my plate rather than making eye contact. "What'd ya do?" he asked, rather seriously.

"Drew and I ... well, Sir ... we looked at the *equipment* in the basement," I confessed.

Matt laughed. "What'd ya think?" He shoved a heaping forkful of lasagna in his mouth.

"It's a little scary, Sir," I admitted.

"Nah," he said. "It's fun."

"Fun?" This time I laughed.

"Did you see the sling?" he asked.

"I saw a picture of it on the box," I said. "It's not put together yet."

"Some assembly required," he laughed. "Yeah, Alex and I will get it set up, and then I'm gonna have yer ass in it by this weekend."

I giggled excitedly. "I was afraid you'd be mad that I looked at it, Sir."

"Said not to touch it. Never said you couldn't look."

"That's what Drew told me, Sir. But some of that other stuff ... that electrical stuff ... oh man. And all the whips and dildos and stuff."

He was now cracking up. "Gonna have Jason over again. Some of that stuff is not for the pup."

"Really?" I asked, suddenly feeling rather crestfallen.

He looked at me seriously and gently placed his hand under my chin. "Look at me," he said, tilting my head upwards. "You remember our rules, don't you?"

"Yes, Sir," I whispered.

"I'll never have Jason here—or anyone, unless you're a part of it."

I smiled at him. "I remember, Sir."

"Good, 'cause Jason's more into the pain stuff. You saw how much he liked getting his ass paddled."

"Oh that's right, Sir," I agreed.

"You'll always be my pup ... and soon my husband. But I can have a pain slut, too. Don't you agree?"

"Definitely, Sir. You know you don't need my permission."

"Not askin permission." He glared at me. "Watch your mouth, boy."

"Yes, Sir," I said as I again looked down at my plate.

"Was askin if you agreed with your Master. That's different than getting permission. But anyway, I'm glad you agree." His tone was again lighthearted.

"Sir, may I ask a question?"

"Shoot," he said.

"Well, last week, the day you proposed to me—" I smiled at him sweetly. "You let me suck Drew. He's the only one besides you that you've ever let me suck."

"Yeah?" he said, "and ...?"

"And I just wondered ... am I gonna have to do that a lot?"

He shook his head. "Pup only sucks his Master. I'll never have you service another Dom. Never, ever!"

"Then why Drew?" I asked.

"Drew is different," he said. "And we had the two of you play together in front of us mainly for our own entertainment. His Master was right there. The other time you sucked him was when Alex owed me a favor and let me use his boy in a three-way with my pup."

"Yes, Sir ... So if you owed someone a favor, you wouldn't make me suck them?"

"Not my style," he said. "I'd be too jealous. Don't wanna think of my pup with anyone but me. You're *mine*."

I smiled at him proudly. "Thank you, Sir," I said. "And I'm glad it was Drew. I'm glad you let me do it ..."

"I knew you'd like it," he said. "It's not always just about my pleasure. Masters always say that, I know. We like to say it's all about our pleasure and not the sub's, but really if you didn't enjoy it, you wouldn't be a sub to begin with."

"Sometimes it gives me pleasure just to please you, Sir ... even if it's something I don't like doing."

"Exactly," he said. "Like when you rim my asshole."

"Why do you think I don't like that, Sir?" I asked.

"'Cause you don't," he said. "I know my pup."

I felt myself blushing. He was correct. I did hate rimming, but I did it obediently when ordered. "I like doing anything that pleases you, Sir," I said.

"Good answer," he said. "Even if it's not a hundred percent truthful."

He grabbed hold of my hand and leaned in to kiss me. As he pulled away he looked down at my ring finger. "You like the ring?" he asked.

"I love it!" I said. "Your mom needs us to come over some night to go over the wedding plans. She's hired the wedding planner already."

He rolled his eyes. "Figures," he said. "I thought I told you to take care of it, pup."

"But Sir, some things I just can't decide on my own!" My voice was a bit whiney as I felt myself getting excited.

"Like what?" he asked.

"We have to pick out invitations, do a seating chart, choose our tuxedos, plan the menu, pick a band ..."

"You can decide those things," he said.

"I can't decide what our tuxedos will be, Sir! You always choose my clothes for me."

He nodded and smiled at me. "That's true," he agreed. "Okay, well, I'll call her. I'm not gonna get into all these fuckin details, though. Some of this shit you're just gonna have to decide between the two of you. If you don't know for sure, just use your best judgment. Then after you're done, give me a list and I'll tell you if I approve."

"Yes, Sir," I said.

"Oh my god, this is the best lasagna I ever tasted," he said.

"Really?"

"Really."

"Thank you, Sir!" I smiled as I took only my second bite of food. He was right, it was some damned good lasagna, if I do say so myself.

21

I'd never been in a cage before, and when my Master woke me
early Saturday morning and attached a leash to my collar, I had no
idea that this was precisely where I'd end up. He had special mitts
for me to wear that seemed similar to boxing gloves, and they laced
tightly around my forearms. Without the assistance of another
person, there would be absolutely no way I could remove them
while wearing them both at the same time. He then rolled me over
onto my stomach and carefully inserted a lubed butt plug in my
behind. The end that protruded from me resembled a pointy dog
tail.

Of course I was still naked at that hour of the morning. He
instructed me to assume my canine position at his feet and ordered
me to "heel." He then took me for a walk, first around our
apartment, and finally downstairs and out into the backyard. This
is where I was required to do my morning "business," lifting my leg
appropriately beside a bush that was in the yard. I felt my face
redden as I did so, and prayed secretly that no onlookers saw us.
Thankfully, we had a fenced yard.

My owner led me to the basement, and it was not without
effort that I made my way down the steps in my canine position.
Thankfully my Master had provided me with knee pads, which he'd
applied before I was even out of bed. I knew better than to try
speaking to him in my human voice at this point, and quickly
learned to express my feelings with yelps, whimpers, woofs, and
barks.

285

I certainly was fearful when I first eyed the cage to which he was leading me. I immediately felt as if I were being punished. My Master's words of assurance quickly calmed me, though: "Pups sometimes need to be kenneled ... it makes them feel secure." Of course I knew he was correct. I knew nothing could hurt me while my Master had me within his protection.

Obediently I crawled through the doorway of the kennel and turned to look up at my Master. "Good pup," he said encouragingly. "You be good while Master is gone. You have your food and water, and don't worry. I will be back soon."

Immediately I yelped, expressing my anxiety that my Master was about to leave me alone! It scared me, and I didn't understand. Why would he bring me down here to this cage and then inform me he was going away?

"Shh," he said. "Alex and Drew are upstairs, and I will give them the key to your cage if there is an emergency. If you become too frightened, just lean on the buzzer in the corner, but I don't want you to use that unless it is absolutely necessary. Do you understand, pup?"

I nodded my head vigorously and yelped.

The box to which my Master referred was like a doorbell, a small remote with a big red button. When I looked at it, I was reminded that my Master was always concerned for my safety, even while in the midst of an intense role-play scene such as this. Tears began to well in my eyes as I considered his love for me.

"Don't cry, pup," he soothed me. "I won't be gone long. Lie down like a good pup."

Obediently I curled into a fetal position in the corner and stared up at my Master with my big brown eyes. I wondered if I looked as sad to him as I felt in my heart. I truly didn't want him to leave.

Seconds later, he was gone.

My cage was in the corner of the basement, and as soon as my Master left I sat up to look around. The confines of the cage were small, and it forced me to remain on all fours, but I was able to see most of the room. On the opposite wall was a big clock, and I saw it was currently 8:17 AM. For the next four hours I remained in my cage with nothing to do. Occasionally I sat up to look around. I lapped at the water in my bowl from time-to-time. My Master had left me a big plastic bone, and I held it in my mouth, sucking on it as I thought of him—awaiting his return. It became a pacifier of sorts.

Eventually I fell asleep.

When I heard the upstairs door opening, I awakened and sat up. I looked over at the wall clock and saw it was ten minutes past twelve. The sound of my Masters footsteps excited me, and I immediately began to yelp loudly.

"How's my pup?" he said, in a childlike voice. "Did pup miss his Master? Aww ... pup's a good boy!" He walked briskly over to my cage where I was sitting up with my paws pressed eagerly against the wall. He reached in his pocket and retrieved an animal cracker. Inserting it through the cage, he held it there for me to take. My reward for being his good pup. Hungrily I snatched it from his hand, and he laughed.

My Master then turned to the boy who was beside him. Jason. "Strip!" he ordered, and then My Master walked away from my cage over to the side of the room.

I stared up at Jason and observed how he quickly and obediently began to peel off his clothes. His smooth and lithe body excited me, and I wagged my rear end happily, shaking my tail as I did so. I was anxious to see what my Master had in store for the boy ... and I wondered if my only role in the scene would be to simply watch.

Once Jason was completely naked, my Master stepped up to him. "Are you ready to begin, boy?" he asked authoritatively.

"Yes, Sir!" Jason answered.

"What is your safeword?" Matt asked him.

"Divinity, Sir!" Jason replied.

"Very good, boy," he said. "Hold out your arms." Jason immediately complied with the order, holding his hands out in front of him. "To the side, bitch," Matt elaborated.

Jason spread his arms out in a spread-eagled position, and Matt stepped over and attached a leather manacle to the boy's right wrist. He then moved to the left and did the same. Each of the bands had a large metal hoop to which my Master attached separate chains. As I looked up at the ceiling I observed that the chains were looped through two pulleys. Following them across the room with my eyes, I saw that they came down on the other side of the room and were attached to a wheel. Matt briskly stepped over to the wheel and slowly began to crank it, tightening the slack of the chains.

The slow and methodical manner in which my Master tightened the chains of his prisoner seemed almost medieval to me as I watched with anticipation. The boy's body was gradually being stretched as his arms lifted farther into the air. Eventually he was spread wide apart, completely exposed, and even had to stand on the tips of his toes because there was virtually no slack remaining in his restraints.

Jason's cock throbbed wickedly, as did mine.

My Master was dressed as he always was in casual preppy attire. He was wearing a pair of designer jeans that showed a little sag, and a tight-fitting polo shirt. He stepped over to the center of the room in front of his bound victim and slowly removed his shirt, tossing it aside carelessly. Then cockily, he groped himself.

I was nearly frantic, wagging my tail and pressing my paws anxiously against the cage. "You like that, huh, pup?" he said. "You like seein your Master tie up a helpless boy?"

I yelped my approval as my Master slowly unfastened the belt from his pants. He continued to stare directly at me, and then suddenly whipped the belt out the loops in one smooth movement. He then stepped over to the other side of Jason so that he was standing directly behind him, holding the belt in both hands. He folded it over and loudly snapped it together, then fisted both ends together in his right hand.

I stared at Jason, realizing that he must be aware of what was coming. He remained there in his bound position, completely motionless. His engorged cock protruded from his body, pulsating from his excitement.

Crack! My Master snapped the belt across the boy's ass. Jason barely flinched. *Crack! Crack! Crack!!* Three more times in rapid succession Matt whipped Jason's perfectly smooth globes. Finally it evoked a nearly inaudible moan from the victim.

"You need your discipline, boy!" Matt yelled. "Thank your Master when he gives you what you need!"

"Thank you, Sir!" Jason cried.

CRACK! CRACK! CRACK! CRACK! Matt continued to beat his ass.

"Aaaahhh!" Jason screamed. "Thank you, SIR!"

Matt tossed the belt behind him and stepped over in front of the helpless boy. "You need that discipline, don't you boy? Don't you, *faggot*?!"

"Yes, SIR, Thank you SIR!"

Matt reached down and cupped Jason's balls in his hand. I stared at his grip intently and watched as he started to squeeze. After a few seconds the boy was moaning. "You like that, don't ya boy? Ya like that *pain!*"

"Yes, SIR, Thank you, SIR!" he again cried.

"Then maybe you'll like this," Matt said as he stepped over to the countertop to pick up a small object. When he returned to his position in front of the boy, he was holding up a small metal clip. A nipple clamp!

"Bite down on this, bitch," Matt said, as he shoved something in Jason's mouth. It was a thick rubber rod of some sort. A dildo? Then without warning Matt quickly reached up and snapped the clamp on Jason's left nipple. The boy went nuts!

Writhing and thrashing ferociously, he pulled against his restraints and cried out in agony. "Aaahhhhh!" He was biting down fiercely on the rubber tube in his mouth.

Matt stood there emotionless and calmly watched as the boy squirmed in pure agony. *Fuck!* I thought. *I'm glad we didn't ever use the nipple clamps.*

As the wave of intense pain washed over the victim before finally abating, Matt groped himself once again. Then he reached down and slowly stroked Jason's cock. It continued to throb wickedly. "You like that pain, don't ya, slut?"

Jason moaned his assent and nodded, his mouth too full to enunciate intelligibly.

With his free hand Matt reached up and snapped on a second clamp, this time to Jason's left nipple, and an identical reaction was provoked from the victim. The chains above Jason's body shook violently as Jason pulled against them, his entire body trembling in agony. Matt stepped back a few paces and watched, an evil smirk on his beautiful face.

My Master then stepped over to my cage and opened it. "Out, Petey!" he ordered. "Assume human role!"

"Yes, Sir!" I responded, as I slid out of the cage and knelt before my Master. Matt reached down and effortlessly pulled the butt plug from my ass, tossing it aside. He left the mitts on my hands, however. I knew that when he addressed me by my human name, I no longer was to behave as his canine pup, and thus I was required to respond verbally to my Master when prompted.

"Over there," he said, pointing to an area a few feet to my right. Without getting up, I quickly scurried to the place my Master had indicated. There was a small plank sitting flat on the floor, and attached to it was a sizeable dildo, sticking straight up. The rubber cock was about eight to ten inches in length, though not incredibly thick in its girth. Attached to the plank were wires and an electrical cord. The cord appeared to be plugged into an outlet.

Matt had me kneel in front of the plank, facing the front of the room. He instructed me to bend over, and I again resumed my four-legged position with my ass sticking up. He picked up a bottle of gel and squirted some lube into my hole, then immediately shoved his finger inside. Slowly he worked his finger back and forth, loosening me. He then picked up the plank behind me and shoved the head of the dildo into my ass. He worked it in gradually at first, and then quickly thrust it downwards, impaling me. I cried out at the pain from the sudden invasion, but it quickly subsided.

Matt then pushed me backwards, so that I was in a kneeling position, sitting right atop the dildo. The plank rested against my heels, forcing the dildo to remain deep inside me. He then attached Lycra bands to my upper thighs and secured them to my ankles, making it impossible for me to pull myself upright off the dildo. Next he ordered me to hold out my hands in front of me, and I did as he instructed.

My Master stepped away from me momentarily, but then returned holding two leather wrist straps. They were similar to those he'd used with Jason, only smaller. He fastened one around each of my wrists, and then pulled my arms above my head. One at a time he attached them to ropes that were hanging from the wall behind me. He didn't bother to tighten the slack as he'd done with Jason, though.

Matt then squatted down in front of me. He was holding something in his hand that I could not see. "Pup, he said quietly, in a reassuring voice. "You're not gonna be able to use your safeword. I need to know you're not scared."

I smiled at him tearfully. Every time I saw this side of him, it moved me emotionally. "I'm not afraid, Sir ... thank you."

"All right, bitch," he said, "I won't hurt you," and then stuffed a ball gag into my mouth. He then cinched it tightly around my face, attaching it securely behind my head.

He was still squatting in front of me as he reached out to stroke my cock. The sensation of his grip around my shaft was exhilarating, and I squirmed with delight. He grinned as he played with me for a few moments, slowly and teasingly stroking me. Then he reached behind me to retrieve one of the wires that was attached to the plank. He pulled it beneath me, feeding it between my legs. The wire had an electrode attached to the end, and he very carefully positioned it against the underside of my throbbing cock. He then pulled out a piece of first-aid tape, which he wrapped around it, securing it to my hard-on.

Finally Matt stepped over to the counter to retrieve one more item. It was an adjustable bar of sorts, and he placed it on the ground between my knees. He pulled it to the length he desired, and then locked it in place. It slid neatly between my legs, preventing me from moving even slightly from my current position.

I had a dildo up my ass that was rammed deep inside of me, pressing mercilessly against my prostate. My wrists were bound with my arms stretched above my head. I was locked in a kneeling position that I could not even slightly alter for comfort. My mouth was gagged. And worst of all … I had an electric wire attached to my throbbing cock!

Matt stepped back to observe his handiwork. "Whaddya think, Jason?" he asked. "Think he looks comfortable?"

Of course Jason could not respond. He still had the rubber tube in his mouth. Instead he moaned affirmatively.

"Yeah, I think you're right. Can't really tell just yet." Matt then reached over to the counter and picked up a remote box. "How about now?" he asked, as he flipped a switch.

I felt the dildo begin to vibrate in my ass. I moaned and bit down on the ball gag, closing my eyes momentarily. Matt was laughing heartlessly. "Cool thing about this is that I can set it on a timer. I can make it go on and off at pre-programmed intervals. Wanna see how that works?" he asked. "Okay, let's set it for five seconds every minute." He adjusted some buttons and I felt the vibrations resume again. He was correct; they continued only for five seconds and then stopped. "Fifty-five seconds from now, they'll begin again. Now let's try the other one …"

Matt adjusted the knobs of another switch and I felt vibrations against my cock. I squirmed frantically, not from pain but from the pleasurable vibrations that the electrode delivered to my throbbing erection. This pleasure was short-lived, though, and stopped after only five seconds.

The way he had the remote programmed now, I was getting alternating vibrations up my ass and against my dick every thirty seconds. Each stimulation lasted only five seconds, not nearly enough time to bring about orgasm.

He placed the remote control down on the floor in front of me and walked back over to Jason. Very callously he reached up and pinched open each of the nipple clamps attached to the victim's chest and suddenly released them, causing them to snap rapidly back in place over the sensitive, already-throbbing nipple flesh. Jason was sent into another fit of agonizing pain.

As Jason writhed around and screamed into the rubber tube that effectively muffled his cries, Matt stepped back over to the counter opposite him. He picked up what appeared to be a whip of some sort—perhaps a riding crop. It had bushing protruding from the end, and Matt playfully snapped it in the air, demonstrating how agile he could be with his weapon.

Just as Matt stepped behind Jason and snapped the whip across his back, an electrical current passed through my dick and I began to moan, biting down on the hard rubber ball in my mouth. My cock was throbbing so hard, and I was so very close to orgasm ... the vibrations were almost enough to send me over the edge, and I cried out excitedly. Just before I reached that point-of-no-return, however, the current abruptly stopped. I screamed into my gag in frustration and violently pulled my arms against the restraints.

Matt continued to whip the slave boy in front of me.

A few seconds later a jolt of electricity throbbed deep within my ass. The dildo buried inside me pulsated against my prostate gland, once more causing my dick to throb. I moaned once again, squirming frantically in my restraints.

I couldn't count how many times Matt whipped the helpless sub who was strung up before him. I was far too busy dealing with my own dilemma. After what seemed an eternity, my Master finally tossed the whip aside and stepped back in front of his tethered victim. He reached in his pocket and removed a thin silver chain, which he deftly attached to the nipple clamps. The chain dangled all the way down, extending beyond Jason's throbbing cock.

Matt then attached another clamp to the bottom end of the chain, and without warning he snapped the clamp to the underside of Jason's ball-sac.

The boy again went berserk, kicking his legs frantically. As he did so, his arms were pulled tightly by the strong chains. He learned instantly that he must keep his feet on the ground, and he scrambled to resume his original position on his tiptoes. Matt stood there with his arms crossed, calmly observing the boy, and then walked over to the counter to retrieve another set of leather cuffs. He crouched down and wrapped them around the slave's ankles, snapping them securely in place. He then opened one of the cupboards and pulled out a thick wooden plank that had clamps attached to each end. He positioned the plank between Jason's ankles and snapped the clamps to the hooks on each of the leather cuffs, creating a spacer bar so that he no longer could move his legs at all.

My initial thought was that my Master was restricting the slave's movement in order to heighten the torture, but then I realized it was also for Jason's protection. If he were to reflexively thrash his legs and lose his footing, he could accidentally pull so hard against his arm restraints that he may dislocate his shoulder. After the spacer bar was in place, Matt picked up Jason's sneakers, which were on the floor in the corner. He slid each of them under the boy's heels, using them as wedges.

"Don't move your legs again, boy," he warned, "or I'll teach you what pain *really* is."

Jason moaned into his gag as tears streamed down his cheeks.

"You remember your safeword?" Matt asked him. The boy nodded. "Do you need to spit the gag out and use it?" He shook his head frantically.

Matt then grabbed firmly to the thin chain that was connecting the slave's nipples to his balls and pulled it taut. Jason bit down on the gag and grimaced as he did so. My Master continued to pull, staring the slave right in the face, until finally Jason cried out in pain. Matt reached down and stroked the boy's throbbing cock.

All the while this was occurring I continued in my own state of torture. No matter what I did, I could not bring myself to orgasm. No matter how frantically I pulled against my restraints, I could not free myself. All I could do was kneel there and continue to endure the continuous onslaught.

Finally Matt stepped over to the table and picked up a large dildo. It was metallic black, and as he held it up, the ceiling light reflected off it magnificently. Matt held it there in front of the boy, twirling it in his hand. "You ever take it up the ass, boy?" Matt teased him. Jason's eyes got real wide, and slowly he nodded. "You ever take something *this* big up the ass?" Matt whispered to him, pressing his face against the boy's cheek as he spoke into his ear.

Jason shook his head slightly and moaned.

"You're about to," Matt said calmly. "You're about to take the *whole* thing ..." My Master's voice was light and cheerful as he said it, almost as if he were delivering very good news. The dildo was huge, not only in terms of its length, but also its girth.

He then turned to look at me. "Aww, look at little Petey over there," he said sarcastically. "Looks like he's having a real good time. See how delightfully he's squirming around. He likes it! Hey Petey!" His laughter was cold and sadistic.

"I think we'll start with something a little smaller," Matt reasoned as he placed the enormous dildo back on the counter. He picked up a different one, much smaller. He stepped over behind Jason once again, and pressed the dildo against his tight hole. "To lube, or not to lube ..." he said, *"That* is the question." Again he laughed at his own joke and stepped back to the counter to set the dildo down and pick up a bottle of gel. "Even I'm not *that* cruel," he quipped as he turned to me and winked.

God he was sexy when he was being this cocky!

My Master then squeezed some of the lube onto his finger and quickly slid it into the boy's ass. Jason squirmed in his restraints and bit down hard onto the gag. I watched his face as he grimaced and then finally sighed. Matt was twisting his finger inside the boy, loosening him up. He then pulled out and re-inserted, this time using two fingers. "You like that, boy, don't ya?" Jason moaned into his gag and nodded frantically.

Matt continued probing the slave boy and then reached around with his free hand to stroke the boy's cock. He pressed his face against the slave's neck, whispering in his ear. Matt's body was pressed firmly against Jason's back as he fucked and stroked him simultaneously. "You're my little pain slut, aren't ya, boy?" he hissed. "You like it that way! You *need* it that way! Don't ya, boy? Huh?"

Jason moaned, and Matt released his cock and quickly jerked on the chain dangling in front of him. The slave once more writhed around, thrashing himself against my Master's body, which was enveloping him.

Matt then pulled his fingers out of the slave's ass and picked up the smaller dildo. He didn't bother with any theatrics this time, but instead stepped right back behind him and quickly shoved it all the way in to the hilt.

"Aaaahhh!" Jason screamed as Matt twisted the hard prong deeply into his ass.

Matt then laughed a little, in spite of himself. "You like it rough?" he asked. "You like taking those big hard cocks up your tight, smooth, little ass?" He then began pumping the dildo in and out. Faster and faster he fucked him, and as he did so he resumed stroking the boy's cock.

Jason was now moaning loudly, biting down hard on the rubber gag, and squirming wildly against his restraints. My Master's body was pressed firmly against the boy as he drilled the dildo in and out. "You gonna cum for your Master, boy?" he asked. "You gonna shoot that load out all over the floor?"

"Mmmmmm!" Jason moaned as his eyes squinted tightly shut.

"Do it for me, boy! Let me see you cum! Let me see you shoot that big load!"

Jason spit the gag out of his mouth and it flew across the floor. "Oh god! Oh fucking god!" he screamed.

"Shoot it!" Matt commanded as he pumped Jason's cock furiously.

"Oh Master! Oh god! Yessss!!" His cock erupted rope after glorious rope of pearly-white hot cum onto the cement floor beneath him. He was trembling, his entire body wracked by the sensation of his powerful orgasm, as Matt masterfully milked the load out of him.

"Fuck yeah," Matt whispered into his ear. "Fuckin hot!" Jason was laughing, crying, and trembling at the same time as Matt pulled the dildo from him and tossed it to the floor. "We'll save that big boy for later." He pointed to the other, gigantic dildo that remained on the counter. He wrapped his arm around the boy's waist and gently kissed his cheek.

"Good boy," he said. "You're my good little pain slut."

Matt stepped back over to me and quickly ripped the ball gag from my mouth. He undid his pants and released his throbbing hard-on. "Suck!" he commanded, and slid his cock forcefully down my throat.

Gripping my head with both hands, he violently began to fuck my face. As he did so, the vibrations in my ass and against my cock continued, and I remained there on my knees, bound helplessly. He drilled himself into me without mercy, repeatedly causing me to gag on his engorged cock. Within moments, though, he was ready to climax.

He thrust himself all the way in finally, holding my head in place as my nose pressed firmly against his pubes. Then he pumped his load! Deep down my throat he blasted the volcano, and all I could do was gulp.

I was gasping when he pulled out of me, and he gently cupped my head in both hands. "Only my pup takes the Master's load. Only my pup!"

He then turned around and picked up the remote from the floor behind him. Quickly he twisted the dials and the vibrations began simultaneously at both ends—my ass and my cock. I cried out. "Oh god! Oh please let me cum!"

"Shoot it!" he screamed, and instantly I erupted.

Matt was laughing as he watched me, and the broad smile on my face told him I felt exactly the same way. He reached up and unfastened my restraints, then dropped to his knees and kissed me.

"Good boy," he said. "Good boy!"

After he'd carefully removed the mitts, spacer bar, dildo plank, and electrode wires, he helped me stand up. I felt a little sore, but I knew it was worth it. The two of us then went over to our pain slut friend and helped him out of his restraints as well.

That was my initiation into the dungeon.

22

Our first Christmas together was amazing. Although Matt and I had originally met in the fall, we did not actually get together as a couple until another two months after that, and so didn't spend the Christmas holiday together that year. This was actually our first Christmas, and now we were in our new home, engaged to be married.

Matt allowed me to plan a big family gathering on Christmas Eve, and I invited all those who had grown close to us. I was especially excited to include my new friend Denise, who worked at the supermarket near our former apartment complex. Of course Alex and Drew were included along with Richard and Ryan. Kathie, who was now six months pregnant, was invited with her fiancé Carter. We also included Detective Murray and his boyfriend and, of course, Jason.

I wanted to invite Matt's parents, but we were instead planning to spend part of Christmas day at their home. He informed me he did not intend to invite them, and although I understood his reasoning, I'd hoped he would reconsider his decision.

In addition to our family Christmas gathering and the Christmas dinner we had at his parents', Matt also took me to his company's Christmas party, where I got to mingle with all of his employees and co-workers.

Of all the holiday festivities, though, our Christmas Eve gathering was the most meaningful to me. I remembered the party for my birthday that Matt had attended so many months prior, and how I had been so shy and nervous about people showering me with all their attention and gifts. It now seemed as if I were an entirely different person. I loved being surrounded by all these people whom I loved.

We did have a gift exchange that evening and afterwards gathered around the pool for a little late-night relaxation and socializing. It surprised me when I found myself conversing with Richard and Ryan, and I was pleased to see how well-mannered and amicable Ryan had become. We talked about our big wedding that was quickly approaching in another two-and-a-half months, and Ryan whispered in my ear that he and Richard had been talking about getting married themselves. He was simply waiting (and hoping) for the day when Richard popped the question.

Denise chatted with me at length about the grocery store where she worked. She said she really missed seeing me there all the time, but was so thrilled that we had managed to remain friends even after Matt and I had moved. We started talking about music and school, and it became apparent that we had a lot more in common than just the supermarket. I then popped the question to her, asking if she would be interested in being one of my attendants at the wedding. She shrieked with delight and quickly embraced me. "Oh my god! I'm gonna be in a gay wedding!" she shouted, and kept repeating it to anyone who would listen.

Kathie told me she was a bit concerned about the date I'd chosen for our wedding. She would be eight-and-a-half months pregnant at the time. I told her not to worry. Even if she did go into labor a little early, it was all good. We would be honored to have our nephew born on our anniversary date. She made a face at me and said that was not the point. She didn't want to miss the wedding! "Fine," I said, "We'll deliver the baby at the cabin in between the ceremony and the reception. You'll be back on your feet in time to dance with the grooms." She playfully slugged me and assured me that the baby was just gonna have to wait till after the wedding day to make his appearance. Yes! They already knew they were having a boy.

Rick and his partner Terry had been together for many years, and in a way they reminded me of Matt and me. Rick was tall and muscular while Terry was of diminutive stature and rather slender. I took Terry on a tour of our home and Denise tagged along. Everything was fine as they took in the sights of our now well-decorated living space until, of course, we came to the basement. "Do you use all this stuff?" Denise asked.

I smiled at her and winked. "Sometimes," I said. "Did I ever tell you about my tattoo?" I ended up showing both of them before we rejoined the others upstairs.

It felt so wonderful to be surrounded by a circle of people who lovingly accepted Matt and me for the gay, Dom/sub couple that we were. I knew that night beyond any shadow of a doubt that I'd made the right decision when I chose to remain with Matt rather than seeking the so-called "equal" relationship that Cameron had described to me. I knew that I had found true happiness, and that I had all of the approval I needed right here amongst the people I loved and cared about.

To be honest, even without this circle of friends, I had more than enough. I had the man of my dreams and we were living the life I'd always dreamed of. I did not need a life that passed the test of public opinion in order to be happy. Actually if I'd pursued that kind of lifestyle, as I'd been advised, I would likely be alone and miserable, and I wouldn't have my Matt.

I never expected that I would ever have a happy Christmas again after my parents died, but I have to say that this particular year proved me wrong. It was by far the best holiday season of my life, and as I looked around the poolside area to take in the sight of my Master and all the loved ones I held dear, I knew I'd found paradise.

"Merry Christmas, Everyone!" I shouted as I stood atop the patio table.

"Petey, what are you doing up there?" Matt asked. "How much eggnog did you have?"

"I didn't have any, Sir," I said. "I'm just so happy! I'm so happy to have all of you in my life, and I love you with all my heart ... every single one of you!"

The others looked up at me strangely, and then Denise broke out into a broad smile and began applauding. Matt stepped over and scooped me into his arms. "We love you too, pup," he said, and then he kissed me before gently setting me down on the tile.

"You're my life," I whispered, my arms still wrapped around his neck. "Merry Christmas, Sir."

"Merry Christmas, pup," he whispered, "and you're *my* life."

Two hundred people were gathered that Saturday morning, far more than we had originally planned to invite. They were seated in white, cushioned wooden folding chairs specifically chosen by Diane. The chairs were designed to match the two trellises that were positioned on either side of the audience. A pathway of red rose petals led from each trellis up along the perimeter of the seating area. They eventually connected beneath a scalloped gazebo, where Alex and Drew patiently and expectantly stood, dressed in crisp white tuxedos.

My tuxedo was charcoal grey and identical to that of my soon-to-be husband—my Master and best friend. I wore a single powder-blue carnation boutonniere, while Matt's was a deep burgundy rose. Around my neck was a specially-designed thin collar, much different than the bulky dog collar he had originally awarded me. It was light blue to match the carnation. The collar was studded with tiny diamonds that sparkled in the sunlight.

We wore matching haircuts and shoes. As I had hoped during the initial stages of our preparations, I was dressed as his miniature. It reminded me of the very first time we'd gone out together, when he had dressed us alike in matching shoes and he'd laughed at the way I fawned over the contrast between our shoe sizes. His were the daddy shoes and mine were the babies. His response had simply been, "Oh brother."

I smiled first at my extremely-pregnant sister who stood proudly beside me, her arm looped around my own. Then I turned to Carter, who was standing at my opposite side. "I love you," she whispered in my ear.

"I love you too," I said, gently reaching down to pat her belly—ever so delicately. "I love all three of you," I smiled.

As the music started, Denise looked back at us with a big grin on her face and gave us a quick thumbs-up. My heart began to race as she stepped forward. On the opposite side of the yard, Jason began to walk up the aisle at the exact same moment. I squeezed my sister's hand as we watched them make their way toward the gazebo. Finally they met in the middle and positioned themselves beside our two best men, Drew and Alex.

It suddenly became very quiet. Although it was merely a matter of seconds, it seemed an eternity. My heart was pounding, and I feared momentarily that I might just pass out. I held firmly to both Kathie and Carter as I heard the opening bars to our song. Instantly tears began to stream down my cheeks, and as Kathie looked over at me, she affectionately shook her head. "Baby, don't start crying yet," she whispered.

"I can't help it," I said, quickly reaching up to wipe my eyes and then grabbing hold of her again, even tighter.

As if in slow motion, we began to make our way up the rose petal aisle. Finally I saw him, his parents standing to each side of him. He was everything I'd envisioned he'd be. My hero. My Master, My Everything. I gasped as I looked him in the eye, and suddenly it was as if the world had vanished and we were alone together, locked in each other's loving gaze. "I love you, Sir," I mouthed to him.

"I love you, too."

We both ceased walking at our designated stopping-points. I kissed my sister on the cheek and affectionately squeezed Carter's arm. Matt embraced each of his parents. We then again turned toward each other and stepped forward.

Matt took my arm in his own as he looked down at me and smiled. We then stepped forward, entering the gazebo and finally stopping before the clergy who was officiating.

"Family, friends, and loved ones," she began, "we proudly gather here today to witness the union of two hearts. Matthew Christopher Porter and Peter Allen Drinkell have come together to declare their love for each other, and to begin a new life as wedded spouses—husbands.

"We are blessed to witness and share in their love, and it is due to this love that we are reminded that when two souls are united in this manner, we all are grateful for the benevolence of a loving God who has afforded us the capacity for such love.

"Who here gives this man, Matthew Christopher Porter, to become the wedded spouse of his partner?"

"We do," Mr. Porter's voice boomed proudly.

"And who here gives this man, Peter Allen Drinkell, to become the wedded spouse of his partner?"

"We do," Kathie responded. I turned and smiled at her affectionately.

Quickly I glanced at my best man, Drew, and saw that tears of joy were already streaming down his cheeks. I wanted desperately to embrace him right there, but instead I turned to face my legally wedded husband. We had been married in Canada the week prior.

"Matthew, what token do you present to your partner to signify your love, fidelity, and devotion from this day forward for the rest of your life?"

He turned to Alex, who handed him the ring. "This ring," he stated.

"Please state your vows," she instructed.

I had not yet heard my Master's vows to me, nor had he heard mine, and I began to tremble slightly as he looked down lovingly into my eyes.

"Petey," he began, "you've changed my life." He stepped closer to me and reached down to take my hand. "You've helped me to learn and accept who I am. You've helped me to grow and mature and become a better person. You've taught me what love is.

"I vow to you this day to always be your loving Master. I vow to do my absolute best to guide and protect you in all that you do. I vow to be your partner and friend, and to always strive to do everything within my power to meet your needs.

"I vow to be faithful to you, and to always keep my promises. I vow to try to always be fair and to take into consideration your desires and your sensitive heart when making my decisions.

"I vow to never deliberately hurt you.

"I vow to remain with you in sickness and health.

"I vow to love you with all of my heart, and to always place you at the center of my life. Petey Drinkell-Porter, if you will be my husband, you will be my life ... forever."

He then slid the ring on my finger.

I was so overcome by emotion upon hearing his beautiful words to me that I did not know if I could go on. Trembling, I looked up into his misty eyes and declared my love for him.

"I love you so much!"

Drew reached in his pocket and retrieved a tissue, quickly handing it to me. I wiped my eyes before the minister continued.

"Peter, what token do you present to your partner to signify your love, fidelity, devotion and obedience from this day forward for the rest of your life?"

Drew handed me the ring and exchanged it awkwardly for the tissue. I smiled at him as my trembling hand grasped the ring. I then once more looked up into my Master's eyes.

"Sir," I said, "I love you with my whole heart. When I first met you I thought I was in a dream. It didn't seem possible to me that someone as perfect as you could actually love someone like me." I paused momentarily.

"I don't feel that way anymore," I stated authoritatively. "You've taught me to love myself for who I am, and I know you're damned lucky to have me!" The entire crowd of two hundred guests immediately burst into laughter as my Master smiled down at me sweetly.

"Sir, we are so lucky to have each other," I continued. "It is true, I do depend upon you. It's true that I do seek your guidance, affection, security, protection, discipline, and training. I thank you for all you give me, and I pray it will always be this way.

"But it is not because I am inferior or weak or somehow less of a person that I submit to you. I submit to you because it is who I am and because I love you with all my heart. We were meant to be together! You were born to be my leader, my guide, my teacher. You were born to protect me and shelter me. You were born to be strength to me when I feel weak ... to remind me of my own inner strength!"

Tears were now streaming down both our faces as I dropped smoothly to my knees.

"Sir, I pledge to you my obedience now and forever. I promise to love, honor, and obey you for the rest of my life. I promise to devote myself to your care, tending to your needs in any imaginable way. In sickness and in health I will be there for you—serving you, obeying you, pleasing you, and most of all *loving* you!

"I love you, Sir, and am honored to call you my Master and my Husband. I promise you eternal devotion and signify this promise now with this ring."

I then slid the ring onto his finger and bowed my head.

Matt did not wait for the minister's permission, but reached down and swiftly pulled me up to my feet. He then embraced me and planted on me a powerful, passionate kiss as I swooned in his arms.

"You may now kiss your husbands," the minister said lightheartedly. Our guests were already on their feet applauding. "I now pronounce you married!" she declared.

I have never been kissed so many times in one day as I was the day I got married. Not only did Matt kiss me about a million times, but so did Drew, Kathie , Diane and so many others.

I did not have a bouquet to throw, but we each threw our boutonnieres. I had hoped that either Drew or Ryan would catch one of them, but instead they were both caught by cousins of Matt.

I met both of Matt's sisters for the first time that day, and immediately I fell in love with Amanda. Matt had referred to her as a "dyke" when he'd described her at the beginning of our relationship. I now understood why he used such a terminology. She was quite masculine—in fact, much more so than me.

The cake was absolutely spectacular. It had four tiers, and the miniature grooms were custom made to look exactly like Matt and me. Terry helped serve the cake, and he was also one of the ushers.

Blake was our photographer, and he gathered all of us immediately after the ceremony for a session of picture-taking that seemed endless. He didn't quite understand when we tried explaining to him that we did not want a picture of the two of us feeding each other cake. Instead I knelt and Matt fed me cake. Finally he just shrugged and took the pictures while Matt and I laughed at each other.

Most of the wedding party changed out of their tuxedos and dresses after pictures were taken, but Matt and I decided not to. We knew there would be pictures later while we danced. For awhile Matt did remove his jacket, though.

My best friend and I had an opportunity to go for a walk together that afternoon, sneaking away down one of the trails behind the cabin.

"Petey," he said, "when you and Matt said your vows ... that was the most beautiful thing I've ever heard."

"Well, it really does feel like a dream to me," I said as I wrapped my arm around Drew's waist. We walked over to the edge of the trail and sat on the embankment together. "Ya know, if five years ago I'd 've had to make a list of everything I wanted in life, I think that wish list would've been fulfilled today. How could I want anything more than this?"

"You will, though, Petey. You will always strive for more. You'll always try improving yourself; that's just how you are."

"Thanks Drew." I squeezed his hand. "I'm just sayin that having Matt, being married to him, and having all the wonderful people like you and Alex in my life ... those are the things that are most important to me.

"For awhile it felt like I had so many enemies. My sister didn't understand me. Ryan hated me, and there was Devin and Kyle, who beat the crap out of me. I felt so alone ..."

"And now look at you! Look at us!" There were tears in Drew's eyes as he draped his arm around my shoulder. "Remember the day we first met?" he asked. "We were sitting just like this on the steps of the student community center."

"And Alex made you proposition me!" I busted up laughing.

"Yes! He thought you were really cute. He could tell right away you were sub."

"Can't everyone? Isn't it tattooed on my forehead or something?"

"No hon, you're thinking of your ass."

"Oh that's right," I laughed.

Our laughter faded but Drew continued to look at my face. He was still smiling. "I was so impressed by what Matt said in his vows, Petey ... about how you'd changed him."

"Me too, but I really honestly don't wanna start cryin again."

"If you can't cry on your own wedding day, when *can* you cry?" he asked.

I shrugged. "Drew, when you told me that I might need to reawaken the Dom in Matt, you really had me worried."

"I think that might not have been the best advice I ever gave you. I think the Dom in Matt never went away. He is who he is."

"But even he admitted that he's changed ..."

"Yeah, we all change. But Petey, I think that sometimes we confuse what we consider to be 'hot' sexually with what we want for our lives. The Matt that you met a year and a half ago, he was hotter than fuck. We both loved how cocky and demanding he was. We loved how 'straight-acting' he was, the fact that he fucked chicks. It was like the fulfillment of this major fantasy of ours, to be with guys like that. Matt and Alex, they were the same way.

"But if Matt had remained exactly like that, you wouldn't be married today. Personally I think that the changes you've seen in Matt make him even hotter. He's still every bit as Dom as he ever was, but he's just so much more responsible. He doesn't fuck around on you. He has an awesome job where he works his ass off. It seems like he handles all these decisions so amazingly well ... almost like you'd expect to see from a man twice his age.

"Those are all characteristics that I find incredibly hot. I see them in Matt and Alex both. I guess when I said Matt needed to reawaken his Dominant side, I was thinking that he needed to start being an asshole again. I was wrong ... totally."

"But you were partially right, Drew," I said. "After our breakup he had a lot of guilt. He was afraid, too. He'd made some decisions that were not so great, and he did need to have his confidence reawakened."

"Maybe he needed to go through that to make him stronger. Maybe he really needed to question himself. In my opinion, it didn't make him any weaker. In fact, I think it strengthened him."

I nodded. "Even the way he is with sex now ... it's amazing! He can be so fuckin hot when he dominates me, yet he is also so loving and careful. He sometimes stops right in the middle of a scene to remind me I have a safe word. I can tell he wants to make it hot for both of us, but he also doesn't ever want to hurt me. Ya know, that touches my heart ..." I started to become choked up.

Drew smiled at me. "Everything touches your heart, Petey Pup," he teased. "But I agree. That's really sweet, just so long as it doesn't ruin the scene."

"Oh, it doesn't. Trust me."

I placed my hand on Drew's thigh. "Ya know, you're absolutely beautiful. You're the most beautiful, intelligent, and *wise* person I know. I'm so lucky to have you as my best friend."

"If we weren't both sub, I'd be so in love with you, Petey."

"Can't we be in love anyway? Why do we have to be lovers to be in love?"

"Good question, because that's how I feel. If Alex and Matt ever left us, I'd stay with you forever."

"Well, they're not going to!" I said.

"You know what I mean, Petey. I'm just saying I love you so deeply. It's different than I feel about Alex. I don't love you like a *husband* or boyfriend. It's more like you're my soul mate."

His words struck a chord in my heart. It was so true; this was exactly what he was to me—my soul mate. "Yes!" I said. "Not just best friends—*soul mates*!"

"And ya know what else?"

I shook my head.

"Since you and Matt got back together last spring, there has been a part of you that has reawakened. I think that ever since your parents died, you'd felt empty. You'd felt so lost and abandoned, and you were just terrified ..."

I was crying now, tears streaming down my cheeks. His words were so very true.

"You have confidence now. You have genuine happiness. Most of all, though ... you're not afraid! I bet this new Petey that we are just beginning to see now—I bet he's the Petey your mom and dad knew. I bet they'd be so proud of the fact that this Petey has reemerged. They'd be overjoyed by who you've become."

"Oh Drew!" I cried as I grabbed him in my arms. "Thank you for saying that," I sobbed.

"Well, I knew I could get you to cry if I tried hard enough."

I held onto him and squeezed him tightly against me. "We really are soul mates. We really are!"

Dancing with Matt under the stars was the most romantic moment of my life, in spite of the fact that several dozen people were standing around watching. After our dance, we each danced with countless numbers of other guests.

When Ryan stepped up to take me in his arms and dance with me, I truly was surprised. "You look so handsome," I said to him.

"Petey," he said to me tearfully, "you were right. Matt really is damned lucky."

"I think Richard's pretty lucky too," I said. He then leaned in and very softly kissed me on my lips.

"Thanks again for what you did for me. I will always love you for it."

"Stop it!" I laughed as I looked up at him. "I've already cried enough today."

"Me, too!" he whimpered, wiping the tears from his face. "Dance with me, Puppy Boy."

"Yes, Sir!" I said as I took him in my arms.

I checked with Kathie that evening before we left the reception. I wanted to make sure she was not about to go into labor as we were leaving for our honeymoon. She promised me there had been no signs of contractions, and so we promised we'd check in with her at least once a day while we were gone to see if we were soon going to be uncles.

We stayed that evening in a high class hotel in Tampa, and the next morning we boarded a flight to Hawaii. Our wedding night was beautiful, and although I had expected my Master to dominate me sexually in a manner more intense than ever before, it actually was just the opposite. He was so tender and romantic, and his lovemaking was attentive to my needs.

The next morning, however, before we left for the airport, I was pleased to see him back to his typical sexually dominant self. I blew him before he was even out of bed, and then he fucked me like a wild man. "Sir," I complained afterward, "I'm gonna be sitting on my butt for a long time on that plane!"

"Guess you'll have a lot of time to think about who owns your ass," he said and then kissed me.

"Yes, Sir!" I said. "Good point."

We were in Hawaii when we got the call that Kathie had gone into labor. We didn't get to see our new nephew until we got back home three days later. They named him after us, using our middle names: Christopher Allen.

After the wedding and honeymoon things began to settle back into normalcy. Apparently Alex had been inspired by the fact that Matt and I had taken the plunge, and he proposed to Drew. The two of them began talking about having a double wedding with Richard and Ryan. I begged them to consider allowing me to make their cake, and of course they agreed.

As I looked back upon all that had happened over the course of the previous years I was amazed at how all of our lives had evolved. I certainly had struggled through several personal conflicts during the earliest stages of my relationship with Matt. Initially I had agonized over his infidelity and inability to commit to me exclusively. I had struggled with my own feelings of insecurity and my identity as both a gay man and a sub. Matt had broken up with me after he'd placed me in a situation where I was seriously injured.

It was during this period that I learned that Matt's former girlfriend had gone through an abortion, a fact Matt had failed to mention to me. He did finally tell me all the details about what had happened, and we grew closer because of his honesty.

When my best friend Drew was shot, I learned that Matt had engaged in sexual activity with the very same person who had both raped me and shot Drew.

There had been so many hurdles, so many challenges, and yet we weathered every storm together. Every moment we were together made me love this man more, and when I got to the point where I knelt before him and slipped that ring on his finger, I knew that this relationship was the real thing. I was and am his "for keeps."

As I look forward now to a lifetime by the side of this man who is my Master and Husband, I know there are no obstacles we cannot face together. I know that Matt and Petey are in it for the long haul, and I plan to spend my life with him from this day forward and ... for happily ever after.

23

One Year Later

"What are ya doin, pup?" my Master asked me.

"I think I've decided what I want to write ... for my first novel, I mean." I was sitting at my desk in our family room, staring out the window. My laptop was open in front of me.

Matt stepped up behind me and leaned over. "What is it?" he asked.

"Sir, I'm just starting it ... Maybe we should wait, and you can read it when I'm done."

"Maybe you should stop telling your Master what to do," he scolded.

"Yes, Sir," I said.

"I just wanna read the first paragraph. What's it about?"

"Us," I said, as I turned to look up at him. I smiled and he leaned in to kiss me.

"About us, huh?" he asked. "Who'd wanna read a story about us?"

I shrugged my shoulders. "I dunno," I said. "Someone might want to."

He started to laugh. "Well it's cool. It'll be interesting anyway ... at least for us to read. Doubt if it'll be a *New York Times* Bestseller."

"Yeah, maybe not ..."

"Let me see," he said as he leaned forward and tilted the monitor back so that he could read these words:

> "Why are you shivering? It's seventy degrees." I looked up sheepishly at the tall jock standing beside me and shrugged my shoulders in answer to his question, then quickly looked back toward the ground at my feet, shivering again. "You sick?" he asked. I shook my head.
>
> I knew who he was. His name was Matt, and I'd admired him from afar for the past four years of high school.

THE BEGINNING